A PREGNANT YOUNG LADY IS MURDERED. A MEMBER OF THE FAMOUS DUPONT FAMILY ALLEGEDLY COMMITS SUICIDE. IS THERE A CONNECTION? WAS THERE A COVER-UP?

"Where were you Wednesday night?"Detective Drummond asked.

Father Milford laughed. "Why do I get the feeling that you suspect me of killing Miss Dugan?"

"Did you?" my partner, Detective Adelia Bern, said.

He smirked. "Don't be absurd. May I ask what evidence you have to make such an accusation?"

Drummond said, "We're not making any accusations. I'mquestioning everybody who knew Miss Dugan. She was killed by someone she knew, someone she trusted, and someone who was very angry at her."

"How can you be so sure?"

"The manner of death."

"Are you sure her killer is a male?"

"Odds are it's the father of her baby."

"Well, detectives, I've taken a vow of celibacy."

"Priests have been known to violate it."

"Well, sir, I assure you that I have not."

"And I have to take your word on that?"

"Yes, you do. Now, if you'll excuse me, there are people in need of my comfort. Is there anything else?"

"You didn't answer my question. Where were you Wednesday evening?"

"...brilliant and compelling mystery based on an actual crime...in which a young, working-class woman by the name of Katie Dugan is brutally murdered...the trail begins to lead to the DuPont family, which results in a fateful decision...This novel has it all: historical interest, social and political conflict, drama, romance...with the ever present specter of Edgar Allen Poe applauding in the shadows."—*Preston Holtry, author of the Arrius Trilogy and the Morgan Westphal mysteries*

"True crime enhances historical fiction in *The Katie Dugan Case* by William Francis. This well-written narrative combines with riveting dialogue as Detective Drummond and newly hired Detective Adelia Bern, the first female on the Wilmington police force, pursue suspects and leads in solving one of the most notorious crimes in history. Mr. Francis' meticulous research brings authenticity to his historical account, which makes *The Katie Dugan Case* a must read for all historical fiction lovers and true crime aficionados."—*Carmen Baca, author of El Hermano*

"*The Katie Dugan Case* brings you back in time to old-fashioned gumshoes and societal cover-ups. William Francis puts you right in the middle of a murder investigation of a young woman, a hush-hush pregnancy, and adds enough twists and turns to keep you reading well into the night."—*Susan Kotch, author of High Flier and Casey of Cranberry Cove*

"Detective Drummond shines as an elegant, no-nonsense gumshoe from the gilded age in *The Katie Dugan Case*. A case full of murder, intrigue, scandal, and political machinations, it will keep you on the edge of your seat."—*Kellie Butler, Author of The Laurelhurst Chronicles series.*

THE KATIE DUGAN CASE

William Francis

Moonshine Cove Publishing, LLC
Abbeville, South Carolina U.S.A.

FIRST MOONSHINE COVE EDITION
NOVEMBER 2017

This book is a work of fiction. Names, characters, places and incidents are products of the author's imagination or are used fictitiously. Any resemblance to actual events, locales or persons, living or dead, is entirely coincidental.

ISBN: 978-1-945181-25-2
Library of Congress PCN: 2017916989
Copyright © 2017 by William Francis

Front cover image public domain, cover and interior design by Moonshine Cove staff.

About The Author

William Francis, raised in Newark, Delaware, received a Masters of Arts in Writing Popular Fiction from Seton Hill University after he took the opportunity to spend ten yearsliving in various locations throughout the UnitedStates. When he returned home, his nomadic experiences inspired him to write. He reveals the great and unique history of Delaware in 4 books of vintage photographs he contracted through Arcadia Publishing: The *DuPont Highway, America's first divided highway; Along the Kirkwood Highway, Along the Christina River,* and *Newark Then & Now,* a retrospective of his home town. His first fiction, *A Life Told to None,* is set in Newark and includes many childhood experiences. The novel is a mystery without a murder, or more direct, why did a friend commit suicide? *The Umpire* is also set in Newark. It's a semi-autobiographical novel, the story of William's pursuit to become a professional baseball umpire. *Seacrest* is a novel set in Maryland just prior to the U. S. involvement in World War 1 and it reveals a little known fact, German saboteurs were in America. And *The Katie Dugan Case,* a historical fiction mystery novel set in Wilmington, Delaware in 1892 and loosely based on an actual unsolved murder and the suicide of Louis du Pont.

Whether William's books are fact or fiction, he hopes to entertain as well as inform and leave the reader with a satisfying experience.

Checkout his Facebook page: https://www.facebook.com/William-Francis-542158412788405/or find his books on Amazon.com

Acknowledgement

Writing historical fiction would be impossible without the work of historians who record past events and the libraries, archives and websites that store the information. The number of books and articles I consulted while researching *The Katie Dugan Case* are too numerous to mention, but I am indebted to all. I particularly want to mention the great work of the Delaware Historical Society and the Hagley Museum in Wilmington, and the Delaware Public Archives in Dover for their on-line collection titled: A Photographic View Of Delaware In The 1890s. I also wish to thank everyone who has supported me throughout the process to the final product.

THE KATIE
DUGAN CASE

CHAPTER 1
July 8, 1919

The murder of Miss Katie Dugan exploded upon the people of Wilmington, Delaware like one of the accidental blasts at the DuPont Gunpowder Mills. The first indication that her death would play a significant role in the most interesting case of my career came shortly after dawn on Thursday October 20, 1892 in a telephone call from my Chief of Police, Theodore Francis. On that fateful day I had been a widower for eight months and sleeping in the parlor of my home at 819 Jefferson Street. It was an ordinary house with squared corners and a flat roof, nothing like the newer Victorians going up on the block. My wife Jane and I moved into this home shortly after I helped preserve the Union.

Wearing a gray robe, I hurried to the front hall not knowing who'd be calling at this hour and quietly cussing them under my breath. I lifted the conical-shaped telephone receiver from its perch and put it to my ear. Chief Francis, normally a hard man who kept his emotions in check, said hello and then released a deep and mournful sigh that warned me something tragic was about to follow. "Are you coming back today?"

I spent the last sixty days with my son and his family in Chestertown, Maryland in the hope that it would renew my spirit. I thought it did. My two granddaughters, ages eight and six, were delightful, my son and his wife perfect hosts. Unfortunately, I returned to the same house Jane and I shared and everything that compelled me to flee the city in the first place again reared its ugly head. The silence was unbearable, and I kept imagining I saw Jane's ghost in every room. I worried I was losing my mind. Some people say that people living alone for an extended period of time went insane. I witnessed men locked in jail talk crazy. One habitual thief believed he had become a mole and tried to burrow his way out of his cell. He tore the flesh off his fingers scratching at the stone walls before he was removed to the former insane asylum at Third and Broom Streets.

"Yes," I said, sounding irritated, which was not my intention. I had to return to work. It would be the best thing for me. It was either that or jump off the Third Street Bridge. "I'm coming back. I'll wear my best pin-striped suit for the occasion."

"That's great, David," Chief Francis said. He sounded like he really needed me, but I could never be too certain with my boss. I was more of a tool in his collective tool shed. If I could help him get ahead politically, such as solving a news-worthy crime, I was his best friend. If something went awry and journalists or Mayor Willey criticized him, I was his scapegoat. "But I'm warning you it'll be one hell of a day. I need you to get out to Sycamore and DuPont, by the Bush estate. Two constables from the Tenth Ward are here in my office, and they've informed me that there's been a murder that's certain to get all the citizens riled up. The victim's a young woman around sixteen to eighteen years old. She was found about an hour ago and it's a terrible and bloody mess."

"Dear God. Only sixteen to eighteen? What could she have done to deserve such a fate?" Then I remembered some unfinished business. "Did you fire McDonald during my absence? If you didn't, I'm not working with him."

Chief hesitated before saying, "Not exactly."

"Not exactly?" I repeated, fearing what he meant by such a vague response. "I can hardly wait to hear this explanation. You know I don't get along with that drunk. I'd rather work alone."

Chief Francis released another sigh. "I'm aware of how you feel about him. I had to stop you from beating him to death, remember? McDonald's not fired. He's not here either. I'm sure he's sleeping off another stupor at the Ebbitt. I wish I could dismiss him, but you know he's a friend of the mayor. Instead, we had to hire someone."

"*Had* to hire someone? You mean another political appointee? How many friends does the mayor have?"

Chief Francis feigned a cough. He was a political appointee. "No, it's not exactly like that."

"Another not exactly?" I said, my temperature rising. "Maybe I should reconsider my decision to return to work. What the hell's going on down there?"

"Remember how the reformers were breathing down the mayor's neck to implement some progressive ideas into city government?"

I remembered it all too well. A number of organized groups were promoting social reforms throughout the United States to improve the plight of the poor, working class, women and children. The noisiest were advocates for ending child labor in factories in favor of mandatory public education, better treatment of immigrants, labor unions promoting a forty-hour work week with better pay and working conditions, women's suffrage, and banning alcohol because it was destroying the American family.

"Has Mr. Moran pushed through another of his initiatives?"

On the local level, a pug-nosed journalist with a bulldog attitude named Casey Moran used the power of his typewriter and his column in the *Every Evening* to clean up city government. He was successful in ending the "political police force" that had plagued Wilmington until last year. The Police Commission Law of 1891 ended the practice of each mayor hiring his own police, from chief on down to constable, who then held their jobs for the duration of the mayor's two year term. Chief Francis and McDonald were holdovers from this practice. Needless to say, most had viewed this patronage system as highly corrupt and it had made my job all the more difficult.

"Well," Chief said, "one of the reforms was hired four days ago. I'm surprised you didn't read about it in the papers."

"I haven't picked up a paper since I got back."

"Well, Mayor Willey hired a *lady* detective. It's just shocking, just shocking if you ask me, that a woman wants to do this line of work. However, they say she trained with the Pinkerton agency in Chicago."

I almost fell over, dumbfounded. In my twenty-three years with the Wilmington Police Department I never heard of anything so extreme. "They hired a *female* detective. I don't believe it. Where did they get the money for her salary? One of the mayor's favorite excuses for doing nothing is that the city has no funds, *budget cuts*, he yells." And city government was generally conservative on social issues. "Why would they take on the controversy of hiring a woman to the police force?"

"Trust me, David, I'm just as appalled and surprised as you are."

"Incredible, just like that, the mayor hires a lady detective without consulting us. But we don't need her. McDonald and I hardly have enough work to keep us busy. So what does this mean? Are you assigning her to work with me?"

Chief Francis took a long moment to answer, so I knew he was afraid to tell me. "Yes, you and *Detective* Bern are assigned to the case. It's the best thing for her anyway. She's done nothing except sit at her desk and read the *Morning Herald.* Don't hate me for this. The mayor wants me to put her to work. The reformers want it. I have no choice."

I closed my eyes and rubbed my forehead, anticipating a headache, yet gradually accepting my fate. If Mayor Willey wanted the lady detective put to work, probably because of the favorable publicity it would generate among the progressives, then it had to happen. Of course if she failed at the job, the conservatives would scream that they were right in saying women didn't belong on the police force. Like Chief Francis, I had no choice. "What's her name again, Bern?"

"Adelia Bern. She was born and raised in Illinois by Swedish parents. I'd really like to know her story, but that's all I know. She won't tell me anything. She's very private."

"All right." I said, not too pleased. "I hope this works out. There'll be enough reporters hounding me. When they see me actually working with her, they'll question my manhood and my ability to solve the case. They'll probably even hint at some romantic involvement. Which believe me, is the last thing on my mind."

"I know. More importantly, we have to find out if she can do the job. Test her. See if she faints when she sees the victim. If she fails to do her job, or gets in your way, I'm sure with enough ammunition we can get her dismissed, despite the mayor and the progressives."

I groaned. "I'm not going to wet nurse her. I'm going to work her as I would McDonald. You say she has training from Pinkerton? Then hopefully she'll be an asset. Maybe she can teach me a thing or two. Tell her to meet me at the Bush estate."

"Well," Chief said, sounding apprehensive. I anticipated another problem. "Since she's new to the city she doesn't know anything about it, doesn't know her way around. Can you educate her? Teach her what she'll need to know to survive here. So in that regard, can you come to the Hall and escort her?"

I yelled into the phone. "What?" Then I took a deep breath. "I need to get out to the Bush estate while the scene is still fresh."

Chief laughed. "David, you know damn well the coroner doesn't show up for work until after nine o'clock. You have time. Oh, one other thing, as a favor to me, please clear this up before Election Day."

It was October 20. Election Day was November 8. The voters, men over twenty-one years of age who owned property or paid at least ten-dollars a month in rent, could choose to keep Benjamin Harrison in the White House or return Grover Cleveland after a four year hiatus. That, however, was on the national scene. Chief Francis was more concerned with local elections. Mayor Stansbury Willey was in the middle of his two year term and not up for re-election. Each of the twelve wards had two representatives in City Council. My boss needed these men to get re-elected to keep the status quo, and to keep his job.

I hated when politics put pressure on my duties, but that was a sordid fact of life in my hometown, and I suspect in many others. Generally, these politicians were less educated and less refined than I

12

was and yet I had to answer to their every whim in order to stay employed. In Wilmington a politician or "statesman" was seen as a parasite, feeding on businessmen and citizens alike for his own social and financial gain. They were generally men who had failed at every respectable profession. The occupation attracted the unscrupulous. Yet *I* had to bow down to *them*.

"Don't worry, Chief," I said with little enthusiasm, "I'll do my best to meet the deadline."

I hung up the phone and got dressed. Before heading out, I grabbed my black frock coat because October mornings were generally cool and slow to warm. I checked my appearance in a full-length mirror and cringed. I was only 49 years old, yet I had enough gray hair for a man a decade older. My skin was pale. I had sad and mournful eyes, with thick bags underneath. My cheeks were flat, and I had severe wrinkles on my neck and forehead. In summary, I looked like a withered old corpse wearing his burial clothes.

CHAPTER 2

As I walked the seven blocks to Market Street and my second home at City Hall, I greeted citizens I recognized and considered Chief Francis' request that I bestow my knowledge about Wilmington upon my new partner. Yet how was that possible? What I knew about the city had been acquired over a lifetime of living in this town between the Brandywine and Christina Rivers. I could tell her historical facts such as the city had been founded by Swedish colonists, and that they had named the Christina River after their child queen, but how could she possibly appreciate all the intangibles that made me content to live here? Wilmington currently had a population around 60,000, but the city was expanding westward to accommodate an influx of Europeans, primarily German and Irish who came for its vast opportunities. The DuPont Gunpowder Mills employed mostly Irish labor; it produced the best black powder in the country and was world famous. Blumenthal's made the best Morocco leather. Railroad car manufacturers and shipbuilders dominated the banks of the Christina, the largest being Harlan and Hollingsworth. Streetcars were manufactured at Jackson and Sharp. The city was bustling with industry and definitely a boom town.

Of course it wasn't all good. Like other cities, Wilmington had its tenement districts and slums, patronage and corruption, but as severe as my melancholy had been I had no desire to leave. How could I convey my passion about this metropolis on a hill to a newcomer while tracking down a murderer? Playing tour guide didn't exactly mesh with chasing down a killer.

When I arrived at Market Street from Sixth, the bustling heart of Wilmington spread out before me. Market was lined on both sides by three-four-and-five-story brick buildings that housed retailers, service professionals, investment firms and banks. I waited to cross the street with other citizens next to a brownstone that housed the Security Trust and Safe Deposit Company, where I had an account.

"Read more about Lizzie Borden!" Joey the newsboy yelled from his usual place on the sidewalk in front of City Hall. He held up copies of the *Morning Herald*, one of five daily newspapers, but the only morning issue. Joey wore the same tattered gray jacket over a dirty-white shirt, black cotton sack pants, wool cap, fingerless gloves and black shoes. He was a rare urchin in that he could read and write and made an honest living. At twelve years old he had taken on the responsibility of caring for his younger sister and brother. His unemployed parents, confronted with the choice of starving as a family or leaving Wilmington and their children behind, chose to flee the city and start a new life elsewhere. Joey never shed a tear. He took on his new role with gut-wrenching courage and a determination to keep his siblings straight and honest.

I was familiar with the Lizzy Borden case. The 32-year-old woman of Fall River, Massachusetts allegedly murdered her father and stepmother with an axe on August 4th. When I initially read about the crime in the *Every Evening* I gave the article only a cursory glance. After all, the killings took place over 300 miles away and I was fully aware that women were capable of murder. Even in little Wilmington, I have investigated cases where wives had killed husbands or lovers, even their children. Yet the citizens of my hometown surprised me with how many of them crowded around Joey, eager to relinquish their penny to obtain the latest news about the axe-wielding Miss Borden. Now more than two months after the murders, I doubt these latest articles were anything more than hearsay, conjecture, or the journalist's imagination.

"Welcome back, Detective Drummond," Joey said after I muscled my way through the crowd. The boy's smile revealed a missing front tooth. His cap shaded a black eye. "I'm happy to see you, my friend."

"I'm happy to see you too, son," I said, overhearing the groans from citizens that I had cut in front of. "Have you been fighting again?"

"Got to fight to defend me spot from the micks," Joey said, using a derogatory nickname for poor Irish boys. Joey had prime real estate for his business and occasionally another newsboy, some as young as five years old, challenged him for it. "You know how it is."

"Did you win?"

Joey stuck his chest out. "I'm standing here, ain't I?"

I reached into a vest pocket for a penny and handed it to Joey. "Here you go, son."

"Oh no, sir," Joey said, shaking his head. "Molly already done buy a paper for you. She's all excited, said you'd be back today." He winked. "She's sweet on you, Detective Drummond. You know she is."

I knew Molly Delmar was "sweet" on me, and had been for some time, but I couldn't return her feelings. "Tend to your business, young man, and I'll tend to mine."

Joey laughed. "It's a deal, sir."

I entered City Hall, a Georgian building with a bell and clock tower that has hosted United States Presidents Thomas Jefferson, John Quincy Adams, Andrew Jackson and William Henry Harrison. In all sincerity, I doubt a single improvement had been made to the Hall since Jefferson. I smelled the decay and dampness the second I stepped into the dimly lit main hall, an aroma created by a mixture of dust, crumbling plaster and water damage. The floorboards sagged, and with each step I took, the wood sounded ready to break and send me crashing to the jail in the cellar.

"Welcome back," Municipal Court Policeman Joseph Hinder said. The blue uniformed officer stood guard at the double-doors to the Court Room. When I was eight years old, my father dragged me to the courtroom to view the dead body of Kentucky Senator Henry Clay, whose coffin was on a national tour. My father said Senator Clay was a great man. Lying in repose, he didn't look so great. "Did your time away refresh your body and soul?"

"It did indeed, sir," I said, trying my best to be cordial while lying. It wasn't easy. I fought a strong urge to return home and bolt the door. Would I ever shake this feeling? "It was the medicine I needed. I see that the city survived without me."

A couple of unsavory looking gentlemen wandered in from outside and sought admission to the courtroom. Each working day a city judge handed out justice starting at 9 a.m. to law-breakers that had been captured by police in the previous twenty-four hours. Oddly enough, court sessions were theatre for the poor. They couldn't afford a ticket at the Grand Opera House so they'd wander into the courtroom throughout the day filling the rows of benches to listen to other peoples' woes, sometimes taking naps at their seats.

Officer Hinder opened the door and let the men inside. "Be quiet once the judge enters." Then he turned to me. "Yes, the city survived just fine without you, but it's not the same."

"If you're referring to the female detective, I've already heard about it."

Officer Hinder frowned. "I don't understand why she wants to do this work. She's not plain. She don't have to fend for herself. I think any man in the city would be happy to take care of her."

I nodded, accepting the information. Chief didn't mention her physical appearance. "Maybe she doesn't want to be taken care of. You know how these suffragettes are."

The officer shrugged. "It's a sin, it is. Just a plain sin."

I excused myself and climbed the nearly hundred-year-old stairs to the second floor. I walked past the mayor's office and Council Chambers and approached the closed door to the office of the Chief of Police, Theodore Francis.

"Detective Drummond," Molly Delmar said from her desk chair. She stood and hurried to me. Her busty torso was covered by a white shirtwaist and her blue skirt scraped the floor. "Welcome back." She threw her arms wide and gave me a good and long squeeze. "It's so great to see you. The place just wasn't the same without you." She looked up with wet hazel eyes that could melt a man's heart, but for some reason had no effect on me. I couldn't understand why. Molly was a fine-looking widow woman, too young to be a widow, but working in Wilmington's factories and mills was dangerous. Barely a month went by without an accident claiming a man's life or leaving one maimed. Molly's husband suffered a horrible but quick death after he fell into a vat of molten iron at the Lobell Car Wheel Foundry. Some say he was drunk. Nevertheless, Molly was left to raise three children on a paltry income, and compelled to live with her sister and brother-in-law to avoid being destitute. "Did you get the rest you needed? How's your son and his family? Did you catch a lot of fish?"

"I caught my share. My son and his family are well. Johnny's oyster and crab business is doing well too. They just bought another boat and hired more men."

"That's great." Molly brushed the front of my frock coat with her hands, and then stepped back to scrutinize me from head to foot. I squirmed under her gaze, knowing I didn't look well. I usually loved the attention I got from women, although it had taken some time to get accustomed to it. I had been an awkward and shy boy, bony and uncoordinated. As I matured, however, I developed good muscle tone and sprouted to just over six feet tall. I attributed this change to laboring on the family farm and the three years spent in the Union Army. "You look good."

I didn't believe her, but thanked her. "How are you? And how's your family?"

Molly shrugged. "The same. My children are doing well and are in school, but my Joseph wants to quit and explore the world. I'm afraid one of these days he's just going to hop on a ship and leave me."

"Well," I said, remembering how my own son, at age six proclaimed that he was running away from home, "you can't hold onto them forever. Is the Chief alone? I already talked to him on the

17

telephone."

"He is." She leaned in and became sullen. "Earlier he was visited by two constables from the Tenth Ward. Something awful has happened. I don't know what it is, but I could tell by the look on their faces that it wasn't good."

"Well, I know what it is. A young lady's been murdered and I have a new partner. Where is *she*?"

Molly covered her mouth for a second. "Murder? Oh, how dreadful." Then she pointed toward the open door to the Detective's Office and whispered, "*She's* in there reading the paper I bought for *you*. So what did the Chief tell you about her?"

"Nothing much. Do you know anything about her?"

Molly shook her head. "No, she's been pretty secretive."

I nodded. "Well, excuse me."

I had to get a look at this anomaly because females were the delicate sex and men worked together to keep them from being exposed to crime and violence and the seedy realm of society. It was our sacred duty to protect them. Yet there were women advocacy groups inspired by Elizabeth Cady Stanton who wanted to break down all barriers, taking the good with the bad, in order to have greater participation at all levels of society. Primarily, women wanted a voice in politics, and to work outside the home in professions other than teacher, nurse, seamstress, secretary, midwife, or telephone operator. Yet why would any woman want to do police work? It was a physically demanding job that forced encounters with the worst examples of humanity, a job that could get a woman assaulted or killed. There had to be something mentally wrong with this lady.

I stepped over the threshold to the Detective's Office. Someone in a gray dress and a pair of high-button boots did indeed occupy a chair next to a new roll top desk, but her face was obscured behind the *Morning Herald*. The headline read: *GROVER CLEVELAND ATTEMPTS HISTORY*.

I feigned a cough to get the newcomer's attention. "So, do you think Cleveland has a chance of winning the Presidency again?"

The newspaper came down and the first thing that grabbed my attention was her sky-blue eyes.

CHAPTER 3

Detective Bern's eyes were somewhat feline in nature, but there was starkness behind them that signified a hard life. For that reason I guessed she was older than she appeared, maybe in her early forties. She kept her creamy-blonde hair pulled tight and pinned in a bun. The rest of her face resembled the common traits I had seen among the descendants of our Swedish colonists: a straight nose, high cheekbones, small mouth and rounded chin.

She smiled, revealing perfect white teeth. "*God morgon*, as my parents would say. Good morning."

Although she greeted me pleasantly, there was something about her that warned me to be careful, that I shouldn't treat her like other ladies. "Good morning."

"To answer your question," she said in a confident tone of voice, "since Mr. Cleveland doesn't favor women voting, I hope he's defeated."

"President Harrison isn't promoting voting rights for women either," I said, surprised to find myself engaged in a political discussion with a woman.

"Not yet," she said, placing the newspaper on her desk. "But President Harrison has shown a tendency to help the oppressed. He appointed Frederick Douglass as Minister to Haiti, did he not? He has tried to stop the Southern states from imposing voting restrictions on Negroes."

"Those are good points." I was impressed by her knowledge. I then used the opportunity to give her lesson number one in my attempt to educate her about Wilmington and the First State. "I don't know how familiar you are with Delaware, but our down-state residents, meaning anyone who lives south of Wilmington, are generally Democrats and still influenced by southern politics as they had been prior to the Civil War. Wilmington is Delaware's enclave for Republicans. So if Grover Cleveland wins the White House again, we're certain to hear all the fat jokes from four years ago." I whispered. "Honestly, they weren't that funny the first time."

Detective Bern shielded her mouth with a hand over a pleasant chuckle just as Molly stepped into the room and made introductions. "Detective David Drummond, I'd like to introduce Detective Adelia

Bern. She just moved here from Chicago."

"I understand you schooled with the Pinkerton Agency," I said.

Adelia stood. She was a few inches shorter than me, but with her hair up and two inch heels on her boots, she was actually shorter than she appeared. The lady bowed. "Detective Drummond, I'm pleased to make your acquaintance. Going forward, however, please do not mention the name of Pinkerton again."

"The pleasure is mine, Detective Bern, but why the animosity toward Pinkerton?"

"They have betrayed their noble aspirations to fight crime," Adelia said in an excited and superior tone, "and have instead become a force of hired thugs. At this very moment they continue to suppress striking workers at Homestead who just seek better wages and safer working conditions."

"I'm familiar." Steel kingpin Andrew Carnegie hired a small army of Pinkerton men to quell a labor strike that started in June at his mill in Homestead, Pennsylvania. The strikers shot and killed some Pinkerton men, prompting violence and death on both sides and turning the steel plant into a small fortress. Pennsylvania's governor had to call out the National Guard to keep the peace. Four months later, the stalemate continued. "Fortunately, labor unrest is rare in Wilmington. Is it because of Kate Warne that you've taken up this profession?"

Adelia's eyes widened and she grinned. "I'm impressed, Detective Drummond. You know your history."

Molly giggled. "Oh my yes, that's one thing you'll learn fast about Detective Drummond. He knows his history, and he helps out at the historical society."

Adelia nodded, but did not reply, so an awkward silence fell between the three of us. We looked at each other, all waiting and expecting someone else to speak. I had plenty of questions, especially in regards to Adelia's past and what had motivated her to pursue this type of work, but I wasn't certain how to approach the subject or phrase the questions because of protocol. I didn't wish to offend Detective Bern or make her uncomfortable.

"So," I said, just to make conversation, "do I have you to thank for the clean office?"

A woman detective and a third desk weren't the only changes to my second home. My roll top desk and wooden chair had been oiled to look brand new. On each side of the tall window that overlooked Market Street brown velvet curtains had been hung. They were separated, and the clean window glass let in sunlight that revealed swept floorboards. My spider roommates were gone, their webs ripped down from the corners. The hole in the baseboard used by visiting mice was sealed. A row of black file cabinets were no longer covered by a thick layer of dust, nor were the law books stored here because space in the building was limited. The books were available in case a lawyer or judge might need a reference. They never did.

Molly answered. "Chief actually spent money to get maids in here so that the place looked presentable for the public announcement of Detective Bern's hiring. All the reporters in the city were here, along with every dignitary from the twelve wards. Detective Bern was quite popular."

"But not always in a good way for a lot of people," Adelia said. "I had trouble finding a place to live because landlords refused to rent to me, claiming they don't rent to single women. I finally found lodgings on Fourth Street with a widow lady."

"Well," I said with a bow, "I welcome you to *my* city."

"*Your* city?" Adelia asked with a smile.

"Oh," Molly said, "he thinks it's his city. And after you spend some time with him and he tells you all about it, you'll be convinced that it *is* his city."

"Yes, Detective Bern," I said. "The Swedes may have founded the first settlement here. And William Shipley and Thomas Willing are credited with laying out the original streets, but as far as I'm concerned it's *my* city and I take great pride in it."

"I think that's admirable. Perhaps I will come to love it as much as you do."

"Well, judging by your response I assume Chief Francis hasn't informed you, but we'll be working together starting right now on a murder case."

Adelia's eyes widened. "Murder? When did it happen? This morning?"

"Yes, this morning. Chief telephoned me at home and assigned the case to you and me. So you better be ready for this. I'll do my best to educate you on our procedures and the people you need to know."

Adelia grinned and looked ready to cry, but suppressed the emotion. "Thank you, thank you very much. I can't tell you how bad the last few days have been for me. I've been treated like a leper. The Chief resents my hiring. I've only seen Detective McDonald once and he was flat-out rude to me. I asked a few constables if I could follow them on their duties. They laughed at me. I must say, Detective

Drummond, you're the first man in City Hall that's been polite to me."

"Well," Molly said with a friendly wink, "Detective Drummond is a rare man. He always said he prefers the company of women."

"Socially," Adelia said, "or just in the bedroom?"

Molly blushed. "Oh, my."

I too was surprised by Adelia's candor. Men and women never discussed in public anything related to the bedroom. They could think about carnal activity. They could even imagine it, but any conversation about it was practically forbidden. "I prefer the company of women in *all* aspects of life."

Adelia sounded skeptical. "Well, it's good of you to say so, Detective Drummond, but let's see if you really *live* it."

The quickest way to arouse my temper was to question my integrity, so I spoke with some malice in my voice. "I assume you're not married, no children."

Adelia was smug. "I *was* married. I have no intentions of ever making that mistake again. No children."

Molly sighed as if the devil had entered the room. "A *divorced* woman?"

Adelia put a hand up. "Please, spare me the lectures on the evils of divorce. Marriage is an evil. However, I'd appreciate discretion. If the wrong people found out that I'm divorced, especially my landlady, I might be forced to leave town."

She wasn't wrong. Society demanded proper decorum, especially from women. What was perceived was more important than reality. I knew several high-classed ladies on Delaware Avenue who had long ago stopped sharing their husband's bed. Yet they pretended to be happily married out of necessity. Men could be divorced, but a divorced lady was ostracized. Men could have mistresses, but society had a vocabulary of derogatory names for women with a lover. Fathers could abandon their children, but it was unthinkable for mothers to do so. Men could spend their lives single. Yet the public reacted to an older and unmarried woman as if something was mentally and physically wrong with her.

Adelia asked me, "Are you shocked?"

"No, Detective Bern," I replied. "No woman with your moxie would be subservient to any man."

"Moxie?" Adelia said with a perplexed expression on her face. "What is this word?"

"It comes from a patent medicine that's supposed to give people stronger nerves," I replied. "It's to help strengthen your courage, your toughness."

Adelia grinned. "I like this word, *moxie*."

"You're definitely different, Detective Bern, but I admire that. I think it's a good thing. Chief told me your parents are from Sweden."

"Correct, sir." Then she headed for the door. "But let's not waste any more time on personal discussions. I assume there's a crime scene we need to get to."

"You're correct." At least she was eager.

Molly hurried between us and presented me with an opened cigar box. "Don't forget to take some of these."

There had been a cigar box on top of my desk, but I expected it to be empty because of my absence and McDonald's tendency to steal. However, the box that Molly presented was full of six-inch Henry Clay's, my favorite. "Did you buy them yourself?"

She was coy. "Yes, I did. I thought you'd like it."

I removed a cigar and held it under my nostrils and inhaled, savoring the aroma of the Cuban tobacco. "Oh, I do. Thank you very much. But you didn't have to do it. I know they're not cheap."

"I wanted to," Molly said. She frowned at Adelia with an odd and almost jealous expression. "Please accept them as my gift."

I thanked Molly again and put three cigars in one of my vest pockets. I heard the Chief's door open. "Excuse me."

CHAPTER 4

My boss stood in the hallway. Chief Francis had a tall frame that was usually covered in a full suit, but he was currently without his jacket, revealing black suspenders against a white shirt. He had more brown hair on his cheeks and chin than on top of his head. Like most of his predecessors, Chief Francis did not have experience as a policeman. It wasn't required. What was necessary for the job was a submissive personality to play the political game of compromise, to swallow pride in order to keep the mayor and ward leaders happy. I could never do the job. Pride has caused me trouble in the past and I was certain it would cause me strife in the future.

"David," Chief said as Molly and Adelia joined me, "so good of you to come. I see you've met our new detective. Let me know if this woman becomes a hindrance to your investigation."

Adelia's face turned beet red and she couldn't refrain herself. "You bastard."

"What did you say?" Chief said. He looked ready to slap her. I was surprised my boss didn't fire her on the spot. However, as the mayor's political token and darling of the progressive elements in the city, Adelia had protection. She could afford to be rebellious, but for how long? "Face facts, dear lady, this is no place for a woman."

Adelia pointed at Molly. "What about her?"

Chief ignored the question. "I warn you, when women abandon their duties, children will run wild all over our country and we'll have a breakdown of society and total chaos."

"Chief," Molly said in a calm voice, "we already have children running wild."

That was true enough. Unlike Joey the newsboy, most abandoned children lived on the streets and earned money by less honorable means. For their own survival they formed into gangs, gave their band a nickname, and defended their portion of town with stones and fists. One of the roughest groups was the Church Street Rangers. They had no fear of cops, including me.

"David," Chief said, switching back to compassion, "you better get going. Use whatever manpower you need. *You* have my full confidence."

I looked at Adelia. She didn't release another outburst, but I saw

24

the fire in her eyes. I admired her restraint, and her willingness to stand up against what had to be a tidal wave of public disapproval. Would I have such courage if I were in her place? I had fought in battle, but I had been surrounded by thousands of men who supported me. Adelia fought her battle alone.

No more. At that moment, I picked up Adelia's flag and spoke to my boss with added emphasis. " *We* won't let you down."

Adelia and I returned to the Detective's Office. I pulled the lid up on my desktop. Papers and letters that had been there prior to my absence were still in their little wooden slots. One slot was stuffed with my calling cards. Our police department was too cheap for badges, so I handed out cards. They contained my home address and telephone number as well as the phone number and address of the Detective's Office. A new pile of invitations was next to my ink pen and blotter. Even though I was a lowly policeman, I had a good reputation, so mothers and fathers have been leaving their invites in the hope that I'd meet their daughter. My dear wife hadn't been in her grave a month when I had received the first one. I tore it up, as well as any more that had come in after that. Molly must've preserved these and left them for me, which surprised me given her feelings. Should I tear these up too?

I opened the desk's top drawer. Fortunately, the maids hadn't cleaned it out. I collected my notebook and pencil and handed them to Adelia. In the bottom drawer, I was relieved to find my shoulder holster, Remington revolver, box of cartridges and handcuffs. I normally kept my weapon at home, but Chief Francis confiscated it fearing that I might use the gun on myself.

"It makes sense to be prepared," I said, loading the pistol. I then removed my coat and jacket and put the holster on and slipped the gun into it. "Did you train in firearms?"

"I did. I own a derringer." She removed the small pistol from a pocket in her dress and showed it to me. The single-shot Colt .41 rimfire might only be deadly at close range, but it would certainly inflict damage. "A girl can never be too careful."

"Good," I replied, putting my outer garments back on. "This could get dangerous. Murderers don't hesitate to kill again if they feel threatened. Have you worked a murder case?"

"No, I was assigned to financial crimes, such as embezzlement, but don't let my lack of experience in homicide bother you. I had classroom training and I'm very willing to learn. I can draw on other experiences."

"Let's get going," I said, desperate to leave.

"Wait, Detective, does the police department own a camera?"

"A camera? You mean one of those photographic devices?"

"*Ja.* I mean, yes, it's helpful to take pictures of the crime scene rather than rely solely on notes and memory."

"Well, Detective Bern that may be true, but our poor department doesn't own a camera and I wouldn't know how to operate one."

What? Why did I admit my ignorance about cameras?

"Then I'll sketch the scene. And since we're working together, you don't have to be so formal. You can call me Adelia."

I feigned a smile. I wanted to be less formal with my partner, and the fact that she suggested it first was a positive sign for our working relationship. "Well, Adelia, I appreciate that. You can call me David. We better get going if we intend to beat the coroner and the reporters. We'll use the back door."

"Back door? Why?"

"Two reasons." I led her to the window and pointed across Market Street. "See that dilapidated two-story building, the one that looks ready to collapse and doesn't fit in with the newer brick structures?" She nodded. "We refer to it as the Rats' Nest. It's where reporters assigned to cover crime and politics in the city spend their time waiting for news. It has a bar. They play cards. They smoke. However, most of the time they peer out the window waiting for a cop or politician to come out the front door of City Hall so they can ambush him with questions and hopefully get a story. No doubt the constables who came to see the Chief this morning have already spilled the beans."

"Why would they do that?"

"Reporters pay for information," I replied, exiting the office. "Our police are so poorly paid you can almost forgive them."

"Understood," Adelia said, following me. We said goodbye to Molly and headed for the stairs. "What's the second reason for using the back door?"

"Can you ride a bicycle?" I said as we descended the creaking steps.

"A bicycle? I have."

"Well," I said as we reached the first floor and waved to Officer Hinder, "I'm known as the Biking Detective, and it's at least twenty blocks to DuPont and Sycamore. That's a long walk. I'm not fond of riding horses. I don't want to waste time hitching a rig. The trolley schedule is haphazard at best and doesn't reach all parts of the city. So if we want to get to the crime scene ahead of the coroner and reporters then a bicycle is the fastest means."

"Then let's ride bikes."

CHAPTER 5

After Adelia and I exited City Hall it occurred to me that we had started something historic, and something I hoped the citizens of Wilmington would embrace. My partner and I would be the first man and woman detective team in the city's existence. Until now, I never liked working with someone because partners slowed me down and seemed more interested in generating publicity and promotions for themselves. To do the job right, or more accurately, to do the job my way, I had to be a lone wolf. Then again, I might've felt differently had I worked with a capable partner. McDonald was a fool. Before him had been a string of political appointees more incompetent than the next. Adelia appeared to have the intelligence and determination to do an excellent job. However, the true test lay ahead. Could she tolerate seeing the victim, viewing the violent death, the blood and gore? Could she handle facing a crowd of onlookers and inquisitive journalists?

My Victor bicycle, manufactured by the Overman Wheel Company, was stored with a couple other bikes in a saltbox attached to our government-owned stable behind City Hall. The livery was easy to find, just follow the smell. It was a combination of mud, hay and manure from six horses. The animals were tended to by colored boys who were also responsible for caring for two coaches, a hansom and an open barouche. I brought my bicycle out into the sunshine. It had some rust on the frame, but its hard rubber tires were in good shape. I dusted off the seat with my hand and mounted the two-wheeler. Adelia selected a black Columbian. She mounted the seat and lifted her skirt to her calves to keep the dress from possibly getting tangled in the pedals. A portion of her stocking-covered legs was revealed above her boots. She caught me taking a peek.

"Mr. Shipley and Mr. Willing were Quakers from Philadelphia," I said, using the opportunity to further educate her on my hometown, "so they laid out Wilmington streets in the same grid pattern as that city. Named streets, such as Jefferson, Adams and Monroe travel north-south while numbered streets travel east-west. Some of the roads, like Market, are paved in brick, a few are cobblestone, but most are gravel and clay, and watch out that you don't get your tire caught in a trolley track."

Adelia nodded, and we set out for the Bush estate. Wilmington's population was spread out over ten square miles, so the streets were not crowded. Still, Adelia and I traveled at a safe speed, maneuvering around the occasional streetcar, pedestrian, horseback rider, horse-drawn carriage, coach, supply wagon or other cyclists. On Madison, we passed through a residential area of lower class single clapboard or brick homes that were occupied by hard-working citizens who lived within earshot of the Philadelphia, Wilmington and Baltimore Railroad. Two sets of tracks paralleled the Christina River through the southern and eastern portion of Wilmington and then headed north to parallel the Delaware.

"I worked this area," I said as Adelia rode next to me, "back in the days when I was a regular cop."

Adelia did not respond. She seemed more intent on observing the scenery and learning the streets and landmarks. She was also proving to be a strong and agile rider. By the time she and I reached Newport Pike, my leg muscles were feeling the effects of inactivity. The strain was made worse by the fact that Wilmington rose in elevation as we headed west.

A half-hour later, we closed in on Sycamore Street, which was nothing more than a dirt strip with no houses. This area was considered "out in the country" until recently. Roads for what would become southwest Wilmington were laid out and corner signs with the street names posted, but new home construction wasn't scheduled to begin for another year.

"Wilmington keeps expanding," I said, breathing hard and straining to pedal. "It's a boom town, Adelia, a boom town."

She and I rode around Delamore Park. After we circled the property and cleared its trees, I experienced a mixture of anticipation and apprehension because I saw the grim reality of the task before us. The expected crowd of curious onlookers had gathered in front of the Bush estate and in proximity to a barren persimmon tree. Most of the citizens were female, sporting their long dresses and coats and autumn hats. A few of them had even brought their children.

"That's the Dr. Lewis Bush estate," I said of the Victorian mansion. Behind it, dense woods had some leaves just starting to turn yellow, gold or red to provide a colorful background. "Dr. Bush was a prominent physician who led the way in improving sanitation conditions in the city. Sadly, the old gentleman passed away in March. We've had a few reports from citizens who swear the old man's ghost is still on the premises."

Adelia said, "I like ghost stories."

I spotted four saddled horses with blue blankets tied to a hitching post in front of the mansion. "The police are still here." I also looked for reporters. They were harder to find because they dressed like citizens. "I see Max Hinton from the *Daily Republican* and Joe Snead from the *Delaware Gazette*. No sign of Casey Moran or the coroner, but they'll be here."

Adelia and I dismounted our bicycles and made our way past the citizens to within view of the crime scene. The victim lay in the road near the persimmon tree. She was covered in burlap, a bad choice. The porous material absorbed the blood it had been meant to hide, and the sheet wasn't large enough to shield all the blood that had spilled from her body. The red liquid had flowed like a stream with the slant of the road until it formed a puddle. It always amazed me how much blood was stored in the human body. After three days of fighting at Gettysburg, the waters of Rock Creek actually flowed red. Of all the horrors of war, I remembered that bloody stream most of all.

Adelia looked at the victim. I expected her to faint and got ready to catch her.

CHAPTER 6

Whatever Adelia felt, she hid it well, showing no emotional reaction. She coldly pulled out the pencil and notebook from her dress pocket and started sketching with a steady hand. She glanced back and forth between the victim and her notebook with such a sense of calm that she might've been drawing a flower instead of a bloody murder scene.

"Since we don't have a camera," she said in a firm voice, "I can at least draw what I see. It might be useful later. There was a case where a sickly old gentleman was found dangling from a rope tied to a ceiling beam in his room. Everyone was convinced it was suicide, even the policeman and sketch artist. But later, the artist looked at his drawing and realized there weren't any tables or chairs at the man's feet. So how did he get up there? Turns out he was murdered."

"Did you learn sketching at Pinkerton? Oh, sorry, I mentioned the name."

"I did." Adelia's pencil continued to scratch out the image of a body covered in burlap.

I glanced over her shoulder. She was no Howard Pyle, but I understood how her drawing might be useful because memory, especially mine, was not always dependable.

Officer Matt Ormond approached. He wore the blue woolen pants and sack coats of the Wilmington City Police. The cop stood a few inches taller than me, and with the blue policeman's cap covering Matt's blonde hair, he looked even taller. He was one of the few high-ranking members of the Tenth Ward who managed to keep his job through all the patronage upheaval. Rumor was he had dirt on elected officials. So Matt ruled his neighborhood like a small tyrant, jealous and suspicious of intruders, but he and I had always managed to get along.

I introduced Detective Bern.

Matt scrutinized Adelia from head to foot, and then grimaced as if he smelled something bad. "As you can see," he said in a cordial tone, "it's rather gruesome, and apparently no witnesses."

"Do you suspect local gangs?" I asked, testing Matt's loyalty. Like most cops, he took money to protect gambling halls, opium dens and pleasure houses, so he might be reluctant to point a finger at anybody. "Any roving boys?"

Matt shook his head. "There's no way they'd do this to a young lady, nor would *I* tolerate it." He handed me a small green purse. "I found this on the ground near her."

The woolen purse had a tartan design and a small strap. I opened it and looked inside while my partner continued to sketch. I found three coins equaling 31 cents and a typewritten note. I read aloud. "Meet me Wednesday night at the same place and time."

"She obviously had a rendezvous," Matt said.

"So her killer lures her with a note, and yet leaves it behind?"

"That note shows it was premeditated," Adelia said, anxious to contribute her opinion.

"It seems like an odd place for a man and woman to meet," Matt said. "I think they'd rendezvous in a park. There's nothing romantic about meeting in front of a dead man's house. Do you want to hear my theory?"

"Go on," I said with a smile.

"I don't think the guy who wrote the note killed her. If he had, he'd take the note with him. Why leave it behind? I think she'd already met her lover, say in Delamore Park, left him and was followed by a jealous suitor, and *he* killed her in a fit of rage. A jealous suitor wouldn't know about the note, and this crime was obviously committed by somebody very angry."

"How do you know it's a *he* who killed her?" Adelia said. "It could be a jealous wife."

"Chances are it's a man," I said. "I like your theory, Officer Ormond, except that it doesn't explain why she's *here*. She was obviously killed here, not somewhere else and dumped here. So why leave Delamore Park and head in this direction instead of back to the city, back to where she can get a trolley or cab? There's no streetlamps. The Bush home has been locked up for months. Too bad the note's typewritten. Tracing the note to a specific typewriter would be near impossible."

"And that's the other thing," Matt said. "A typewritten note is hardly romantic. What lover in his right mind would use a typewriter? He'd write it in his own hand."

"Unless he needed to be discreet," Adelia said just as I was about to. "Adultery?"

"Probably," I said, "or it's someone with a recognizable name who shouldn't be seen with the young lady."

"Did you find any identification?" Adelia asked.

"No," Matt replied. "I only located her purse. But the man that found her knew her through her father."

"Oh," I said, pleased to have identification. "Who found her?"

Officer Ormond pulled a chubby little man in a moth-eaten suit out of the crowd and introduced him as William Carswell. Mr. Carswell held his bowler hat in front of him and shook visibly.

"You knew the young lady?" I said to Mr. Carswell and Adelia took notes.

"Yes, sir," the man said in a trembling voice. "Her name's Katie Dugan. Her father, James, owns a barbershop on Broom Street. I deliver coal to his business, get a haircut sometimes, and I saw her occasionally when she stopped in to visit."

"When did you find her?"

"Just around dawn. I walk this way to work."

"Where do you work?"

"Munster Coal." William pointed a shaking finger at a mountainous pile of coal next to a single-story brownstone two blocks north and adjacent to the Wilmington Gun Club.

"What else do you know about Miss Dugan? Was she married?"

"No, sir. She was popular, though."

"How do you know that?"

"Just from conversations with her father. I have two daughters myself, so we talked about our concerns while I unloaded coal."

"What was Mr. Dugan concerned about?"

"The usual stuff with daughters," William said, wetting his lips with his tongue. "When might she marry? Would she pick the right sort of man for a husband? Hopefully, no babies out of wedlock."

"Do you know if she had a lover?"

William appeared shocked by my question. "I can't say for certain, sir."

"Did Mr. Dugan ever express any other concerns?"

He thought for a moment. "No, sir. None that I can remember."

"Did he mention if she had any enemies? Any men she might've upset?"

"No, sir. We weren't *that* close. Most of our conversations was just idle talk to pass the time while I unloaded coal into his basement, or when I got a haircut."

"So Mr. Dugan never mentioned a beau?"

"Not to me, sir."

"Did he mention anyone he found untrustworthy, like an employee in his shop?"

William shook his head. "No, sir. Sorry, sir."

"Can you think of anything that might help me understand why someone would do this to her and why she'd be out here?"

He shook his head. "Sorry, sir. I don't know anything more. I was just on my way to work. I saw no one. I didn't hear a thing. I just found her like that. Poor child."

"Did you touch anything?"

"No, sir. I ran for a call box as soon as I saw her. And let me say that was quite a run. There ain't any around here."

I asked my partner, "Do you have any questions, Detective Bern?"

William grinned. "What? A *lady* detective? I thought you were his secretary or something, the way you're writing everything down."

"No," Adelia said. "If you had taken the time to read a newspaper you'd know I'm a detective with the city police."

William stared at Adelia with a mixture of awe and revulsion, the way people looked at a strange and rare creature on display at the zoo. Adelia was aware of the scrutiny. To combat it, she stared right back. William blinked, looked away and said nothing more.

I gave the man one of my calling cards. "If you think of anything, don't hesitate to contact me day or night."

William looked at the card. "I will, sir. I certainly will."

After Mr. Carswell left, I asked Matt, "Was the victim's dress up or down when you came upon the scene?"

It took the policeman a second to understand. "Oh, dress down, sir. I don't think she was molested."

I nodded and turned to my partner. "We're about to look at the body. Are you ready?"

"Yes," she said, indignant. "I'm no dandelion. I won't faint. Don't ask me that type of question again. Forget that I'm a woman. Say and act as you would around Officer Ormond, or any other man. You won't offend me or bother me in the least. I have to do this. I *want* to do this."

"All right," I said, trying not to be offended by her bluntness and appreciating her spirit. "I like your attitude. Come with me."

I removed a handkerchief from one of my vest pockets and stooped next to the bloody end of the burlap, resting the handkerchief across my thigh. I grabbed hold of the edge of the burlap and looked up at Adelia.

She gulped. "Go ahead. Do it."

I pulled back the material, revealing the victim's front from head to hips. Adelia sighed, nothing more. Some of the citizens moaned and gasped in horror, yet had no intention of averting their eyes or leaving.

It always amazed me how fascinated citizens were with ghastly scenes. They acted repulsed, but achieved a bizarre entertainment from it. I, on the other hand, kept my mind on the task at hand. It helped me cope with the grotesque spectacle in front of me, a ghastly destruction of the human body on a scale I hadn't seen since the war.

"The victim," I spoke clinically to Adelia, who continued to sketch and take notes, "is a young brunette said to be Katie Dugan. She's flat on her back, with her head tilted to one side, her left arm against her body, her right arm extended. She has a gaping wound across the base of her throat, obviously the cause of death. Her green dress is blood-soaked. Some of her black hair is resting in the blood that has spilled onto the street. No visible jewelry. There's only a hint of cosmetics on her cheeks and lips."

"A real shame," Matt said.

Adelia sighed. "You're so very calm."

"So are you," I said. "I'm not so calm on the inside." My stomach churned. Later, I'd wash my hands a dozen or more times to cleanse them of the blood that covered my fingers. I'd probably have nightmares about the victim's pale skin and blank eyes that stared at the sky, and the wound that almost severed her head from her shoulders. "But I… *we* have a job to do."

"Hey, Drummond!"

"Oh, no," I said with a disgusted sigh. "The Vulture."

"Who?" Adelia said.

"Casey Moran. I nicknamed him The Vulture because he can always be found circling tragedy."

"Oh, yes, I met him at my hiring, but didn't know he was called The Vulture."

"Drummond," Casey repeated my last name like a command. He never prefixed it with Mr. or Detective, but I had long ago given up being offended by the reporter's behavior. Casey's portly body tried to get past Officer Ormond, but the constable produced his foot-long truncheon and threatened to use it on Casey's skull if the journalist took another step. So Casey hollered over the policeman's shoulder. "What can you tell me? What's her name?"

"I'm not telling you anything before I notify her family," I said, inspecting the folds of her dress for anything of interest. "You know that."

"Oh, come on."

"Come on nothing. I'm not having her family find out what happened to her from a newspaper. You'll have to wait just like the other journalists that are circling around, who are kind enough to let me do my job before they bother me."

"I don't care about them. Who do you think did it?"

"When I know that you'll know."

"I don't believe that for a minute. You'll keep me in the dark because you don't like me."

"*Nobody* likes you." That got a laugh from the crowd. Then I whispered to my partner. "He knows he can trust me. He just likes to argue. It's a game to him, the give and take, releasing a verbal jab here and a poke there, until he gets a reaction. He's not happy until he gets people mad at him."

"*Ja,*" Adelia said. "I like him. He favors women's rights."

"Hello, Detective Bern," Casey said, showing her more respect. "It's nice to see you again. What can you tell me?"

"Nothing."

"Are you working this investigation with Drummond? That's quite a story, your first case. How about you, Drummond? Are you happy working with a woman? Are you teaching her everything you know or ignoring her? I hear the police department isn't too pleased to have her around."

I didn't respond. Instead, I moved Miss Dugan's head enough to visually inspect the deep wound that had split open her throat.

"There's only bone left to connect her head to her body," I said, and Adelia wrote. "All muscle, arteries and skin have been severed rather cleanly so it must've been something very sharp and thin."

"I assume she was standing," Adelia said, "when her throat was cut. So wouldn't she fall forward, especially if the killer came up behind her to cut her?"

"Not necessarily," I said, aware of the intelligence behind her question. "But it's possible the killer cut her and then gently laid her down on the street to bleed out."

"Oh, that was nice of him. So her killer should have a lot of blood on his clothes."

"Absolutely." I inspected Miss Dugan's cold forehead and cheeks and found no sign of bruising, just the usual blemishes from someone so young. I examined her blood-soaked hands and well-manicured fingernails. "No wounds on her hands. She never fought back, never had a chance, so he obviously surprised her, or he was someone she knew and trusted."

"From the looks of her dress," Adelia said, "and from her fingernails, her family must have some money."

"Yes," I said, "that's why we have to investigate."

"I don't understand."

I sighed and revealed a sad truth. "We rarely investigate anything that happens in the slums. On the other hand, we don't investigate anything that involves the rich and politically connected because they have enough influence to stop us. But since Miss Dugan is a young white woman from what I assume is a working class family, we'll investigate her killing because it may bring a reward or it can be used for political gain."

Adelia sighed. "It's the same in Chicago. I hoped it would be different in Wilmington."

"It's the same. I have to ask, why did you leave Chicago?"

"That is a long story, and this is not the time or place to talk about it."

"All right," I said, agreeing with her reasoning, "perhaps another time." I then noticed some petals in the blood on Miss Dugan's dress. "Write this down, please. Miss Dugan's body is cold and stiff, so she's been dead for a few hours." I picked up the petals and wiped the blood from them with my fingers to expose a white flower. I stared curiously. "I found some Baby's Breath on her dress."

"Really?" Adelia said, leaning in to look. "I'm surprised you know that. Were you schooled in botany?"

"No. My wife was quite the gardener and she'd be upset if I didn't recognize the flower."

Even though I grew up on a farm, I always hated working in the dirt each spring helping Jane plant her annual assortment of seeds that come summer would blossom into a spectacular array of colors. I appreciated the beauty that flowers brought to our property, but I believed if it couldn't be eaten, why invest the time and effort? Then throughout the summer, Jane had me pulling weeds, watering, and picking dying stalks. I wanted to be anywhere else except those gardens. Now I wished I had those moments back.

"Where would she get Baby's Breath? Is it a native plant?"

"It's grown locally," I replied, "but they were on her dress like somebody dropped them there, a sprinkling of petals."

"Like they do at funerals?"

"Damn. The killer slit her throat. He laid her down on the road to bleed out. Then before leaving, he dropped Baby's Breath on her dress as his goodbye. He must've really hated her."

"My name is a flower," Adelia said for the record. "Not a very pretty flower, though. Doesn't Baby's Breath mean pure and innocent?"

I nodded. "I believe it does."

"Do you think there's any significance?"

"There might be." I rolled up Miss Dugan's sleeves and found nothing unusual about her wrists and forearms. I stuck a hand in her pockets. They were empty. I unfastened a few of her mother-of-pearl buttons on her bodice. A couple ladies in the crowd protested that I shouldn't, for dignity sake and because I was a man. "There it is."

"There what is?" Adelia said.

"Some ladies," I said, pulling back the material, "especially those with an actual wardrobe, have their names embroidered on the inside of their clothes. This confirms her name."

"Didn't you believe Mr. Carswell?"

"Yes, but confirmation is always good."

Casey shouted, "Give me something to print, Drummond!"

I wiped my hands on the handkerchief. I then stepped back from Miss Dugan's body and saw something protruding about an inch from under her right shoulder. Using the handkerchief, I pulled the item loose and discovered an open and bloody straight razor.

"What did you find?" Casey yelled. "I'm coming to look."

Matt slapped the truncheon in his open hand, once again stopping Casey in his tracks.

I turned my back to everyone and showed the murder weapon to Adelia. "A straight razor is pretty common. However, this one has an ivory handle, which makes it more expensive." I wiped the blood from the razor and saw letters etched in the steel: WOSTENHOLM & SON I*XL SHEFFIELD. "Wostenholm is a well-known manufacturer of razor blades located in Sheffield, England. But I'm not familiar with I*XL."

"It looks like Roman numerals meaning one and forty. If only we could find out who touched the razor before you. Are you familiar with the new science of fingerprinting?"

I had already appeared ignorant to her in regards to cameras. I didn't want to show my ignorance again, so I lied. "I read something about it."

"Well," Adelia said, showing me the underside of her index finger, "science has determined that each person has their own unique set of lines on the tip of their fingers. Meaning that no two people have the same pattern, and when they touch something, they leave this pattern behind from the oil in their skin. I then read about a method to raise these fingerprints from objects using some sort of powder. It was a fascinating read, but I don't know of any police department that's actually using it and no court has yet accepted it as a form of evidence."

I looked at the lines on my own index finger and compared it to Adelia's. "So no two people have the same pattern. If it's true, then we could fingerprint everybody arrested and keep such a record for future crimes."

"Exactly. It could prove to be more valuable than the Bertillon system."

I once travelled to New York to learn about the Bertillon system. It was a means of criminal identification created by Frenchman Alphonse Bertillon. As a clerk in the Paris Police Department, Bertillon kept the files on all known lawbreakers. He recorded not only a criminal's height and weight, but measured their foot and hand size, nose and mouth and ears, a total of fourteen measurements. He discovered that the same two people having the exact measurements would be extremely rare and such information could prove valuable in criminal investigations.

"Come on, Drummond," Casey said. "What did you find?"

I cleaned off the razor the best I could, closed it, and dropped it in my pants pocket.

"Jack the Ripper slit throats," Casey said, more to the crowd than me. "There's two London detectives in New York right now investigating similar murders to those that happened in Whitechapel." Some mothers hugged their children. "They think the Ripper left England and is in the United States."

CHAPTER 7

The Ripper murders captivated the imagination of people and law enforcement on both sides of the Atlantic, including me. Five women were brutally murdered in the Whitechapel section of London four years ago, and then the killing just stopped. Did the Ripper die? Did the Ripper escape to another country? Had the Ripper been out for revenge against these five women, and once they were dead, achieved satisfaction? There were more questions than answers, and more fiction than fact thanks to wild stories created by unscrupulous newspapermen and dime novelists.

I put the burlap back over Miss Dugan and sighed, disgusted. "Don't be ridiculous. Why would you say such a thing?"

"Nobody knows where the Ripper is," Casey said. "So he *could be* in Wilmington."

"The Ripper is *not* in Wilmington. Everyone, don't listen to him."

"Why can't the Ripper be here?" Casey was full of excitement.

"You know why. You're just trying to scare these people to sell newspapers. Have you no scruples, sir?"

"Well, a couple women were recently slashed Ripper style in New York. That's why those London detectives are here. New York isn't that far by train. Why couldn't it be him?"

"For one thing," I said, tired of Casey's game, "the Ripper killed prostitutes. He mutilated their bodies, removed their organs. Neither is the case here."

I also wanted to state that the Ripper never lured his victims with a love note, but that would've revealed too much. My reply calmed the men and women. However, a few mothers had put their hands over their children's ears and shot me a scolding look for what I assumed was the mentioning of prostitutes. I should apologize, but the boys and girls shouldn't be here in the first place. If their mothers were irresponsible enough to bring them to a murder scene, then those mothers shouldn't be surprised by anything they saw or heard.

"Her throat was slashed," Casey said. "The Ripper killed the same way. Maybe he got scared off before he could do anything more to her."

I sighed, tired. "The Ripper is *not* in Wilmington."

"Then who killed her?"

"Like I said, when I know, you'll know."

"All right then, but don't go arresting some innocent person just to keep Chief Francis happy. I know he's worried about Election Day, and you don't want another Joe Garnet on your conscience."

"Joe Garnet?" Adelia whispered.

I shook my head and revealed a dark episode in the police department's history. "We had a couple policemen assigned to the tenement district along the Christina River who arrested men on made up charges as a way to make money. If the men paid, the charges were dropped. If they couldn't pay, they were arrested and jailed until someone did pay. Joe Garnet was falsely charged with burglary. When he refused to pay the bribe, he was bludgeoned to death. The incident set off street riots that exposed the entire scheme."

"There's corruption everywhere." Adelia sighed. "And it seems even more prevalent against the poor."

"Because they have no one to defend them. It's no wonder they form into gangs or syndicates. They do it for their own protection. But sadly, then the protectors become the oppressors."

"Drummond!" Casey shouted. "I'll see you at the Rat's Nest when you have something to tell me."

Casey walked away. I wasn't sorry to see him go. The other journalists looked on, hopeful, until I ruined their optimism with a shake of my head.

"You other reporters might as well leave too. You know the routine. When I have something to tell you, I'll tell you all together."

Max Hinton from the *Republican* and Joe Snead of the *Delaware Gazette* groaned a bit, but they knew they could trust me not to play favorites with the press or to accept a bribe for information. And as I told Casey, I didn't want Miss Dugan's family to learn about her death from the newspapers. I had a very delicate situation here. It required me to control the flow of information so that the population wouldn't panic. However, the gathered crowd, once they dispersed, would spread the news fast enough by word of mouth, a system of communication that exaggerated the truth and invented rumors. Casey's Ripper theory would no doubt be repeated and accepted as fact.

Matt rejoined Adelia and me. "What did you find?"

"The murder weapon," I said. "A razor."

"So any man in the city could've killed her," Matt said as a morbid joke.

"It has an ivory handle. Not every man owns one of those."

Adelia said, "Didn't Mr. Carswell say that Miss Dugan's father owned a barbershop?"

"Yes, but why leave the razor behind? Why leave the note behind?"

"I have a new theory," Matt said.

"All right, let's hear it."

"I think the killer is somebody who wants to pin the murder on somebody else. Her father runs a barbershop. Maybe her boyfriend is a barber. So the killer leaves a note and razor behind to make us think a barber did it."

"Very possible," I said just to appease the policeman.

A black wagon labeled, *Coroner's Office*, finally arrived, pulled by two horses and with two men dressed in black riding in the driver's seat. The man not holding the reins dismounted first. He was the county coroner, Dr. Jeff Miles. The doctor was a round little man with a fleshy face and a moustache that covered his upper lip. Like his predecessors, Dr. Miles was a political appointee, but unlike former coroners Dr. Miles actually had medical training from Jefferson Medical School in Philadelphia.

"I read about you," he said to Adelia after introductions were made. "Good luck trying to change the world. Jefferson Medical School has some female students who want to be doctors."

I then shook hands with the wagon's driver. He told me his current name was Bill Travers, but I had known him under a variety of aliases. Bill had had a series of occupations over the years, some honest and some not so honest, and one that he had excelled at. Yet that wasn't unusual. Men without employable skills did about anything to avoid starving. To Bill's credit, he was always on the lookout for respectful work.

"It's nice to see you again, *Mr. Travers*," I said. "So you finally found a job that suits your best talents."

"Yeah," Bill said with an uneasy laugh. He had a couple front teeth missing. "I'm legitimate now."

"Does Dr. Miles know about what you used to do for a living?" I asked.

The coroner chuckled. "Of course I do. That's why I hired him."

Dr. Miles, Mr. Travers and I enjoyed a good laugh. Matt and Adelia wanted in on the private joke.

"I've arrested Mr. Travers on several occasions for stealing corpses. It's quite a lucrative business. When the poor, the insane or criminals die, they're buried in cheap wooden coffins in Potter's Field. Body snatchers dig up the fresh graves, remove the lids to the coffins with a crowbar, pull out the bodies, toss them onto a wagon, and then sell the corpse in the dark of night to medical colleges in Philadelphia for anatomy classes."

"Like Jefferson," Dr. Miles laughed.

"*Ja*," Adelia said. "My literature professor at Illinois State said the practice of body snatching is what inspired Mary Shelley to write her novel *Frankenstein*."

As I suspected, Adelia was college educated, another rare trait for a woman. And she had an interest in literature. Since Adelia was reluctant to talk about herself, I realized I'd have to wait for moments like this, when she'd reveal something about her background through general conversations.

"Unbelievable," Matt said, shaking his head. "The things people do for money."

"We're too hungry to care about morality," Bill said with some anger in his tone. "And you're not one to talk, copper. How much do you make from bribes and intimidation?"

Matt glared at Bill, but did not reply. Even though the new Police Commissions Law guaranteed merit-based hiring and standards for promotion, Wilmington police were paid only $60 a month. My salary was comfortable, but I too once struggled as a policeman and I had to pay my way to promotions. Thirteen years ago, I "donated" $300 to my former Chief's "retirement fund" so he'd recommend my upgrade to detective. Regrettably, I earned the money from street gamblers in exchange for ignoring their illegal boxing matches in the neighborhood I patrolled. Right or wrong, it was a fact of life in municipal government.

Bill Travers opened the two rear doors to the coroner's wagon and retrieved a few sheets and a haversack. He stood by while Dr. Miles did a preliminary examination of Katie's body.

I used the opportunity to light up a cigar and think. "I hope you don't mind if I smoke."

"Oh, no," Adelia said. "I love the smell of a good cigar or pipe."

"Then we'll get along splendidly," I said, puffing. "Did you get everything you need?"

"*Ja*." She showed me her second sketch. Adelia used shadowing to detail Katie's sunken cheeks and dark eyes. She drew Katie's shoulder-length hair to show its realistic resting place. She even drew the way I folded back the burlap. She did all of this in a rather clinical, emotionless manner which surprised me. Like the Chief, I expected, if not fainting, a greater reaction than what Adelia demonstrated. Such a

43

dull response seemed strange to me. I personally had a difficult time accepting the brutal slaying of this young woman because Katie didn't deserve such a fate, and it probably happened because her killer panicked and feared the repercussions of what I suspected Katie told him.

Adelia smiled. "If I may offer an opinion, the killer must be mentally unstable. What he did is so cruel and violent. A normal person wouldn't have done this."

"Why would *anybody* have done this?" Matt said.

I blew smoke. "I suspect, Detective Bern, Officer Ormond, that when it's all over with, we'll discover that the person responsible for Miss Dugan's murder is quite sane, and their motive is a very simple and common one."

Adelia's eyes widened, clearly surprised by my casual assumptions. "How can you say that? How can you be so sure? What's the motive?"

"You'll see," I said, not wishing to reveal my suspicions.

"You won't tell me? I'm your partner."

"Please be patient." That made my partner groan and Matt back off, not wanting to get involved in what he perceived as our personal squabble. "All will be revealed in good time."

I continued to smoke while Dr. Miles wrote some notes in a small book and then gave Mr. Travers permission to wrap the corpse. With the help of two policemen, the driver placed Miss Dugan inside the Coroner's Wagon and shut the doors. Dr. Miles joined us.

"How long do you think she's been dead?" I asked the coroner.

"She was probably killed between midnight and two o'clock," Dr. Miles said. "I'll do a more thorough examination in my office. It's obvious what killed her. I'll see if anything else was going on."

"Like a baby," I whispered.

Dr. Miles nodded. "Yes, sir. Sadly, that may be the case. I'll send the results to your office as soon as possible."

Adelia asked, "Why would you assume she's with child?"

I shrugged. "That's what I meant when I said the motive is probably something very simple. I'm guessing she's pregnant out of wedlock and she was killed by the father of the baby because he had to keep the affair secret."

"So he's probably married," Matt said. "And very recognizable."

"How shameful," Adelia said with a hint of self-righteousness. "Too bad we can't hang him twice."

"When you do this job," I said, "you need to leave your morality at home. Citizens, especially men, generally have three lives, a public one, a private one and a secret one. In our society, reputation and public perception are most important. People will commit all sorts of crimes just to avoid embarrassment or the exposure of that secret life. I arrested an embezzler who stole more than a $100,000 from the Bank of Wilmington. His public perception was that of a devoted Methodist, a good husband and father. In private, he was a regular visitor to opium dens and he needed the money to feed his habit and keep up appearances."

"So it's all a disguise?" my partner groaned. "Each person I see standing here is wearing a mask of propriety?"

I nodded. "That's a good way to describe it. Our killer is wearing a mask too."

"Even you?"

I wore a mask of confidence because I couldn't reveal my raw emotions to public spectacle. The citizens expected me to be calm and tough in the face of tragedy. I took a long drag on my cigar, slowly releasing the smoke. "Never mind. Let's get back to work."

Adelia, Matt and I said goodbye to Dr. Miles and Mr. Travers. With their departure, and with only a large blood stain left on the road, the citizens began to disperse. Each one of them was now free to tell their own version of what they saw and what they believe happened, and their gory details would rival anything printed in the newspapers.

"Let's search the grounds," I said. "Look for spots of blood that might indicate in which direction the killer fled. See if there's any Baby's Breath in the area. Or perhaps a torn piece of clothing, anything that the citizens might've obscured while they stood around."

"Unfortunately," Adelia said, scanning the ground with her eyes, "there are so many footprints in the road that it's impossible to tell which ones might belong to the killer."

"And there's no wheel marks except those from the Coroner's Wagon," I said, glancing at the ground. "No horseshoe marks. They must've walked here, but why?"

Adelia and the officers spread out over the Bush property and searched for anything that might be out of place. I inspected the exterior of the mansion. Built of Brandywine stone, a bluish rock, the house stood two stories high with five windows on the façade and dormer windows in the roof. There were three entrances. Each one of them had a solid oak door that was bolted shut. I peeked through each first floor window, but only saw white sheets over furniture. The walls were covered in various types of paper, mostly light-colored grays and whites with delicate landscape motifs. There were no flower gardens around the house, only shrubbery that was no longer neatly trimmed.

"I found something," Adelia said. She reached under a bush and held up what resembled a glass gin bottle, rectangular in shape, about nine inches tall with a short neck. Its label had the emblem of an Indian tribesman complete with feathered headwear. Above him were the words: KICKAPOO INDIAN SAGWA. Beneath him the label read: CURE-ALL FOR STOMACH AILMENTS. "It's some kind of patent medicine," she added when Matt and I reached her. "It still has something inside."

"It's a worthless cure-all," Matt said with disgust. "No doubt sold by some quack doctor."

I discarded the butt of my cigar. "Have you ever seen this brand before?" I had little experience with patent medicines because I was raised to believe in home remedies. Jane was like my mother in that regard. And fortunately, I was blessed with good health and have rarely been taken to the sick bed. I did agree with Matt that such elixirs had a bad reputation and were generally the product of unscrupulous men just looking to cheat people out of their money.

"No, sir," Matt said. "My wife might've. She goes to the apothecary and sometimes buys them. She swears they work, but I think it's all in her head."

I pulled the cork, and then put my nose to the open bottle and took a sniff. I couldn't identify the smell, but it was sweet. Matt and Adelia did the same.

"It doesn't smell bad," my partner said. "It's almost like jasmine."

I shook the bottle to stir up anything that might've settled on the bottom, but the liquid stayed clear. Finally, my curiosity got the best of me and I took a sip.

"How's it taste?" Adelia asked.

"It's interesting," It had a gentle sting that lingered on my tongue, probably from some spice I couldn't identify. "I feel the throat burn common to alcohol, but it's not like any liquor I've ever tasted."

"Well," Matt said, "if the label's correct, you're now cured of any stomach problems."

"I don't have any stomach problems," I said. "Good find, Detective Bern. We'll hold onto the bottle as possible evidence. The person who killed Miss Dugan might drink it."

"Or it's ordinary litter," she said, "left by some poor drunk hoping there's enough alcohol in it to get intoxicated."

"I've never known a drunk to leave anything in the bottle."

"True." Adelia nodded her head. "My father never did."

I looked at my partner, surprised that she had revealed a private tragedy in front of Matt and me. Culturally, it simply wasn't done. Families did their best to conceal unsavory elements about their household from becoming public knowledge because such information could be used to shame the offender, to extort money or to ruin reputations.

Adelia and I, and the police, searched the grounds for another half-hour, finding nothing of interest.

I thanked Matt and his fellow officers for their help.

"We better get going," I said to Adelia. I was anxious to return to City Hall to inform Chief Francis of our initial findings. Afterwards, my partner and I would have the unpleasant task of finding and informing the Dugan family about what had happened. It was a duty I loathed. No one should hear the news that their loved one had been murdered, especially from strangers who would now infringe upon their lives at a most tragic time.

CHAPTER 8

"Chief's at the morgue," Molly said after we returned to City Hall. "A Mr. and Mrs. Dugan came here looking for their daughter. Of course, Chief didn't know who the victim was, but he escorted them to the county courthouse to make the identification."

"All right," I said, relieved that I'd been spared the duty of informing the family, "we're off to the courthouse." I handed Katie's purse with its coins and the typewritten note, wrapped razor and bottle of Sagwa to Molly. "Please put these in the safe. They're evidence."

"I certainly will."

When Molly took the items from me, she grinned and her fingers lingered against the back of my hand longer than what would be normal for such an exchange. Poor girl, I thought, she was really trying. I pulled away feigning a smile, and in so doing, continued to delay the inevitable confrontation Molly and I would have.

I asked my partner, "Have you ever been to a morgue before?"

"*Ja*," she said as we headed for the stairs. "I had to identify my father's body. My mother was too upset to handle it. I didn't want to do it either. I was only *thirteen*. I couldn't believe she made me do it."

"How did he die, if you don't mind telling me? Alcohol?"

"Partially," she replied as the stairs creaked under our feet. "He was beaten to death in a pub over a wager. He lost some stupid bet and refused to pay. But if it hadn't been that, it would've been the alcohol. He spent more time in taverns than at work or home."

"Sounds like Detective McDonald." We reached the first floor. "Was your father's killer ever prosecuted?"

"*Nej*, they didn't press charges because they couldn't determine who threw the first punch. They let him off on self-defense. I thought it was unfair, but the injustice is what drew me to be interested in law enforcement. What made you become a policeman?"

"I couldn't find anything else that fit my nature." I was pleased that Adelia revealed more about herself and showed interest in me. Perhaps she wasn't as unapproachable as I thought.

"What does that mean?"

I opened the back door for her and we stepped out into the warming temperatures. "After the war, I tried shipbuilding, conducting and hauling freight, but doing the same thing day after day had no appeal for me. I actually missed the intensity of the battlefield, the uncertainty of it all. Police work is the closest thing I found to army life. There's long stretches of boredom, interrupted by seconds of fear, and then the emotional excitement I get once I survived the ordeal. It's really strange, but getting close to death makes me *feel* alive."

Adelia nodded. "I can understand that. I think I might have that in me, too." I led her away from the livery stable and saltbox. "Aren't we riding bikes?"

"No. The courthouse is only four blocks away, but we still use the back door to avoid the reporters."

We walked north toward Sixth Street and past the rear of James T. Mullins & Sons, a four-story clothing store for men and boys that specialized in something new — ready to wear clothing. Most citizens, or I should say women, bought fabric and made garments for themselves and their family. Mullins still did custom fittings, but it hoped to revolutionize their industry by having pre-made clothes that a man or boy could try on, and if it fit, buy it. I owned a couple of suits from Mullins, but Kennard's at 623 Market Street was more to my style and affordability.

Once on Sixth Street, we headed to Market.

Adelia asked, "Why did you want to move up and become a detective?"

"The easy answer is that cop pay is terrible," I said, "and I had to fight to retain my job every two years. But like you, it was an injustice, or what I believed was an injustice. A loan officer at Mechanics Bank, John Pratt, served in the war on the Confederate side, which wasn't unusual for men from Delaware even though the state stayed in Union. Well, Mr. Pratt, while serving in Virginia, got married to a girl down there. When the war ended, he abandoned her and came back here. Well, to his surprise she arrived in Wilmington and found him. I think her name was Barbara. Two days later Barbara was found dead in a field near Front Street. There was an empty bottle of poison next to her so the coroner at that time, an incompetent political appointee who could be easily bribed, ruled her death a suicide. I never believed it. I thought that if I were a detective, I'd convince everyone it was murder and get that bastard husband to confess. By the way, he's still alive and living on Madison, but age is catching up to him."

Adelia and I turned north onto Market Street and joined other people on Wilmington's main artery. We walked slightly uphill at a brisk pace, passing such businesses as James Belt the Druggist,

Charles Smith's Marble and Granite Dealer, an office for the Delaware First Insurance Company, T.W. Bye's Sewing Machines and another druggist, Smith and Painter.

At Eighth and Market, an open streetcar stopped. A few passengers disembarked while a few more got on. The motorman waited patiently for the last person to get on board, an elderly lady with a large, flowery hat. Once she was settled in her seat, the motorman rang a bell and the trolley continued its journey north at ten miles an hour.

I pointed across the street at the Wilmington Institute because it had a library on the second floor. "And it was also the original home of the Delaware Historical Society."

"You should write a travelogue," Adelia said.

I winked. "What makes you think I haven't? But let me know if I'm boring you. People aren't always interested in what I have to say."

"Oh, no, I don't feel that way at all. You have great pride in your hometown and I see that you enjoy talking about it. It's a wonderful trait, and maybe someday I'll come to love the city as much as you do."

I stopped walking and pointed at Wilmington's crown jewel, the Grand Opera House. "About twenty years ago, some of our more influential citizens decided that it was time to champion the idea of an elite theatre to symbolize Wilmington's arrival as a cultured town on par with other eastern cities. Thanks to the efforts of the Free Masons, we have this magnificent replica of the Paris Opera House that the Masons also use as a temple and meeting place." The building's ornate façade, which incorporated some Masonic symbols such as the all-seeing eye on the third floor pediment, was actually cast iron painted to resemble marble. Near the entrance to the four-story theatre was a broadside that advertised Frohman's Company production of *Lost Paradise,* a drama starring Alexander Fusco and Mildred Crane. Another poster announced an upcoming political rally organized by Delaware's former U.S. Senator Thomas Bayard. I pointed at a window on the third floor. "The Historical Society called this place home for a while too." Then I grew somber. "My wife loved theatre. The first performance she and I saw together was Buffalo Bill Cody and his Wild West Show. Her favorite shows were comedy acts." Then I hoped to ingratiate myself with my partner by stating, "We also attended a speech given by Elizabeth Cady Stanton."

Adelia smiled. "Did you attend her speech by choice, or did your wife force you to go?"

I laughed, and we resumed our walk. "I went willingly. Stanton's progressive ideas resonated with the women in the audience, but most of the men were ready to tar and feather her."

"Except for you? What's your opinion about stage performers? Do you consider actors and stage shows sinful?"

"No, I don't," I replied as we passed the nine-story Equitable Building. "I know a lot of people do, but I don't see the harm. Are you *that* pious?"

"I'm confused. I was raised Catholic and believe in its teachings of what's right and what's wrong, but I can't agree with how the religion affects my gender and I don't believe its condemnation of stage performers is fair. We hear about the scandalous things they do, the drunken parties and such, but should we condemn all of them over the behavior of some of them?"

I let her question hang in the air because after crossing Tenth Street we stood in the shadow of the second most impressive building in the city, the New Castle County Courthouse. The two-story granite and marble structure, with a square clock tower in front, occupied the center of a city block called Courthouse Square. The Courthouse opened in 1881 to mark the transfer of the county seat from New Castle to Wilmington.

Adelia looked up at the clock tower. "It's a magnificent building. It rivals anything you'd find in Chicago."

A red brougham hitched to a single black horse was parked curbside on Market. The driver wore a black suit and top hat and sat with his hands in his lap loosely holding the reins. I looked through the window of the conveyance and saw no one seated on the red upholstery. I wondered why such an expensive coach was in front of the courthouse. The wealthy never had cause to enter the building. They had their lawyers take care of any legal issues. So who could it be?

CHAPTER 9

I led Adelia inside the courthouse. There were all types of citizens, from the clean and educated to the dirty and illiterate. They loitered on a marble floor that ran the depth of the building and captured rectangular spots of sunlight that penetrated through the tall and wide windows. Along each side of the central hall, equally spaced marble columns supported a high ceiling and the upper floor. Behind and between the columns were glass doors that led to various offices. I escorted Adelia past the Levy Court, Recorder of Deeds, Register of Wills and County Treasurer to a set of stairs.

At the cellar level, Adelia and I found Chief Francis in the hall trying to console a sobbing gray-haired couple in front of the door to the County Morgue. I could only assume that Miss Katie Dugan was now officially identified by her parents. Adelia and I had no choice except to join the unhappy gathering.

"Mr. and Mrs. Dugan," Chief said, sounding relieved, "this is Detective Drummond and Detective Bern. They'll be conducting the investigation. We'll get justice for your daughter, you can count on that. Now, I have business upstairs, so I leave you in their capable hands. Again, my sincere condolences."

I doubted the Chief had any business upstairs, but it was a good excuse to get away and have us take over. Yet Chief's departure created an awkward silence. After all, Adelia and I were strangers. We were intruding on the Dugan family at a most tragic time. However, for us to do our job and meet the Chief's deadline of Election Day, we needed the grieving couple to cooperate because time was critical. The longer a murder went unsolved, the greater its chance to stay unsolved.

"I'm sorry," I said, "but I do need to ask you some questions."

"Not here," James Dugan said, wiping his eyes with a handkerchief. He was a stocky gentleman in a tight pinstripe suit. He had thinning brown hair, a moustache and bushy eyebrows that needed a trim. "Our words echo in this hallway and I don't wish to be overheard. Let's go outside."

Adelia and I agreed. We escorted James and his wife Emily from the building to a bench that was sandwiched between two small elms off the east side of the courthouse. It was a pleasant, park-like setting in a gentle breeze, too tranquil for the business at hand. I noticed that the red brougham was no longer in the vicinity. The coach and its occupant probably had nothing to do with Miss Dugan, but being aware of my surroundings and noticing something out of the ordinary, and the possibility of being followed, was a normal reaction in my profession.

Emily lowered her round body, which had been squeezed into a gray shirtwaist and skirt, and sat on the bench with a groan. She had gray and white streaks in her shoulder-length hair and patted her green eyes with a handkerchief she kept balled up in her little hand. "My God, I can't believe this is happening. What're we to do, James? What're we to do?"

Mr. Dugan sat next to his wife and put an arm around her shoulders. "We must be strong. We have no choice but to bear this pain and not question God's Will."

"We knew something was wrong, didn't we?" Emily said to her husband. "We just knew it was going to be bad news. Katie's never been away over-night."

"Yes, my dear," James said, fighting back his own tears. Men weren't supposed to cry, especially in public so he suppressed his body's need to grieve, something I fully understood. "We knew something was wrong."

"I know this is a difficult time," I said, trying to do a delicate balancing act between being the sympathetic investigator while pushing the couple to talk freely and honestly, "but I have to ask you some questions. I hope you understand."

James looked up with brown eyes that revealed his inner torment and aroused my compassion. "What do you want to know?"

I choked down my emotions and the dark memories of my own losses. "First, let's get some personal information, please. Where do you reside?"

"1111 Lancaster Avenue," James replied and Adelia took note.

"Do you have a telephone?"

"City 569."

"I understand you operate a barbershop. Is that correct?"

"Yes, sir. My shop is at 213 Broom Street."

"How old was Katie?"

"Eighteen."

"Do you have other children?"

"We have two other daughters and a son. The eldest daughter is married and living with her husband in Kennett."

"Katie was found by the Bush estate at Sycamore and DuPont. Do you have any idea who might've done this to your daughter and why she'd be in that part of town?"

James shook his head while looking at the ground. "No, sir. I don't understand any of it. I can't imagine who hated her enough to do what they did or why she was out in the country."

"Did Katie have any enemies?"

"None that I know of," James said, his voice weak. "She was a sweet girl."

"My girl was a good girl," Emily said, raising her head to show me her tearful round face. "She was a good girl."

"If not an enemy, did Katie have difficulty with anybody?"

"A lecherous old man was after her," James said with disgust in his voice. He raised his head and looked at me. "His name's Albert Stout. He works for Charles Warner Shipping and lives at 505 Broom Street, with his *wife and daughter*. When Katie was fourteen, she was hired out as a servant girl to this man and his family. She left his employment after just two months because he tried to take advantage of her."

"Yes, he's *no* gentleman," Emily said.

"Can you please elaborate on the incident that caused her to quit her employment?" I asked.

James squirmed. "Must I?"

"Please, sir, I only ask so that I have a clear understanding."

James lowered his voice. "Katie told me that Mr. Stout asked her to reveal her chest. He said he wanted to see a nice, young bosom."

"Disgusting," Emily said with a moan.

"I agreed with my daughter's decision to leave his house. I then confronted Mr. Stout in his parlor, right in front of his wife. I told him that if he ever came near Katie again, I'd shoot him and have a clear conscience about it."

"I don't blame you, sir. Did he stay away?"

"I haven't seen him, but Katie and my other children think they've spotted him near the house on occasion."

"Did you ever confront him again?"

"No, sir. I had no real proof."

"He might've killed her," Emily said. "Some men go insane when they can't have something they really want. And only an insane person would've done this. Oh, I'll never get over seeing my Katie lying on that cold slab with that horrible wound." She put the handkerchief over her mouth and sobbed. "My poor baby."

I swallowed my own inner turmoil and pressed on. "Mr. Dugan, I assure you that Detective Bern and I will question Mr. Stout. Can you think of anyone else who might've wanted her affections but were rebuked, a disappointed suitor perhaps?"

"Richard Riley liked her," James said. "The feeling wasn't mutual. They were friends, nothing more. I know he wanted more."

Emily calmed down enough to say, "Katie and Richard went to the Sacred Heart Fair Tuesday night and again last night. That's why she was out."

Adelia looked up from her notes. "Where's that?"

"Ninth and Madison," I said. "It's an annual fair in the German part of town that helps raise money for their church and school."

"My entire family often went," James said. "But we decided to skip it this year."

I tried to lighten the mood with some levity. "I mostly went for the beer." Nobody was amused, so my words fell flat. Adelia even frowned at me like an old, disapproving schoolmarm. I tried to salvage the situation. "But the rides and games of chance are good, too."

James looked at me. "So what happened to Mr. Riley? Did you find him?"

"Me?" I shrugged. "I didn't know about Mr. Riley until just this minute. Do you have an address for the gentleman?"

"I don't remember it, but he works as a barber inside the Clayton House. I almost hired him for my shop a year ago. That's how he met Katie."

"A barber? Why didn't you hire him?"

"I had a more qualified applicant, an older gentleman who had more experience and better skills. Mr. Riley struck me as lazy."

I nodded. "I assume you're familiar with Wostenholm razors?"

"Absolutely," James replied.

I borrowed the pencil and notepad from Adelia and wrote out I*XL on a piece of paper, and then showed it to James. "We found this etched on the blade that was used against your daughter. Is it Roman numerals?"

"No, sir," James replied in a shaky voice. "It means *I excel.* It's their company motto for excellence."

"Oh, I see," I said, returning the pencil and pad to my partner. "The razor had an ivory handle. Do you have such razors in your shop?"

"No, sir. An ivory one would be an unnecessary expense."

"Would Mr. Riley have such a blade?"

"If not personally, he probably does at his shop since the Clayton caters to a wealthier clientele."

"I don't think Mr. Riley did it," Emily said. "He loved Katie and wanted to marry her. We weren't going to permit it, of course, because Katie didn't want it and the man's not Catholic. Her happiness was all that mattered to us."

"Where were you two last night?"

"My wife and I were home with our other children. My friend George Beeson paid a visit. We played cards."

Emily sat straighter and sighed. "Wait a minute, James. Remember? George said he saw Katie when he closed his shop."

James' eyes widened. "That's right. He did say he saw Katie after he locked up."

"What time was that?" I asked. "Did he mention if Mr. Riley was with her?"

"George closes his butcher shop at nine," James stated. "He said Katie was alone, and that she almost got hit by a streetcar. She was reading something in her hand that distracted her."

"When Mr. Beeson told you she was alone, weren't you concerned? Didn't you wonder what had happened to Mr. Riley?"

"It wasn't unusual for Katie to be out alone," James said. "Or spend time with Richard and then visit someone else. Katie had our full trust. She'd been out late before, just never all night. So we weren't too concerned when we went to bed, but come morning and she hadn't come home, that's when we realized something must be wrong and went to the police."

"Where can I find Mr. Beeson?"

"His butcher shop is at the corner of Lancaster and Van Buren."

I told Mr. and Mrs. Dugan about the typewritten note found in Katie's purse. "It stated, 'Meet me Wednesday night at the same place and time.' Did Katie routinely go out on Wednesdays? If so, where did she go? Who did she visit? Did Mr. Riley send her notes?"

"No, sir," James said. "Mr. Riley telephoned from the hotel when he wanted to see her. I can't think of anyone who sent her notes. And she went out most nights, including Wednesdays, so I don't know what to tell you."

"Would Mr. Stout send her notes?"

"He wouldn't dare," Emily said.

"Then," James said, "maybe our Katie had a suitor we didn't know about."

Emily sobbed. "So whoever wrote the note killed her?"

"That's a possibility," I said. "Did Katie act different lately?"

"Different?" James said. "What do you mean?"

"Well, like a woman in love?"

Emily nodded and wiped her nose. "That must be it. George said Katie seemed very happy last night. She even kissed him on the cheek after he yelled at her for not looking before she crossed the street. When I heard that, I laughed. Katie didn't like George."

"Anything else? Did Katie change her routine? Did she stop doing something she enjoyed? Did she act differently toward either of you? Did she change the way she behaved at home or out in public?"

"Church," Emily said, revealing bloodshot eyes.

"Oh," James said, "that's right. Our family attends St Joseph's. About a month ago, Katie stopped going. She insisted on staying home. Naturally, this led to some friction in our house. We argued about it. We asked her to explain her refusal to worship with us. She never gave one and got really angry when I demanded an answer."

"She also insisted on washing her own clothes," Emily said.

"Did she give you a reason for this?"

"No, sir," James said. "We thought she was just testing her independence. Young people are apt to defy their parents occasionally and try things on their own."

"And a friend of ours," Emily said, "Mrs. Crenshaw, heard from her son Michael that he saw Katie go inside the Opera House a few times. According to Michael, Katie seemed to be part of a group that included older ladies and gentlemen he didn't recognize." Then Emily spoke with disgust. "I confronted Katie. She told me they were friends who asked her to join them at the theatre. She didn't see the harm. She even said she liked the shows and didn't see anything wrong with them. I told Katie that decent people don't attend the theatre, that her behavior was shameful. It's just shameful that she'd be seen associating with *theatre*-goers."

I ignored Emily's condemnation. After all, everyone was entitled to their opinion and Emily's seemed to be in the majority. Religious leaders routinely preached against any type of live performance, except their own. "Do you know what shows she attended?"

Emily groaned. "No. What does that matter? She knew we didn't approve."

"So you never found out what brought on this change of behavior?" I wondered how the Dugans could be so naïve. I wanted to ask them if they thought their daughter was with child, but that might offend them and they'd stop talking. Then again, I didn't yet have proof of Katie's pregnancy. "Did you suspect something?"

"No," James said. "We don't know what caused it. It just seemed like another way that she was defying our wishes. I guess we raised a rebel. We also found literature in her bedroom from the National Woman Suffrage Association."

"Which I immediately threw out," Emily said, and Adelia groaned. "Katie was a sweet girl. We thought her sudden change in behavior was strange, but for the sake of peace in our home, we didn't press her. Maybe we should have."

"Maybe," James said, shaking his head and lowering his eyes. "It seemed like she just wanted to be all grown up and not treated like a child anymore, make her own decisions, find her own way, do things for herself. It's quite typical of young ladies her age."

James was making excuses. Perhaps he and his wife *had* suspected something, but just wouldn't admit it, or they didn't feel comfortable enough to tell detectives they just met. A baby born out of wedlock was a parents' worst nightmare and the scandal would shame the family and cause the Dugan barbershop to lose business.

"Do you have any Baby Breath's around your house?" I said.

"Baby's Breath?" James said. "What's that?"

"It's a flower," Emily said. "No, Detective. We don't. What an odd question."

"I found some on Katie."

"Oh. I don't know where she would've gotten it. Detective, is there anything else? I'm exhausted. I'd like to go home. Our other children will need our comfort, and we have a funeral to arrange."

"Well," I said, not ready to release them just yet, "did Katie have her own bedroom?"

"Yes, sir," James said.

"We need to search it."

"Whatever for?" Emily said, sounding offended. "Don't you have to show us a warrant or something before you can come barging into our house?"

Adelia said, "Only federal officers are bound by such restrictions."

Emily looked at me and declared, "I'll not have a man rummaging through Katie's things. It's not decent."

"I'll do it," Adelia said. "You need to understand, Mr. and Mrs. Dugan, there might be something in her possessions that will help us find out who did this. Don't worry I'll treat her things with the utmost dignity and respect."

"Thank you," I said to my partner.

"Can we arrange it for another time?" James asked. "It'll be difficult enough at our house today."

"All right," I said, willing to be flexible under the circumstances, "but it'll have to be soon, and please don't touch anything or change her room in anyway."

"Fine," Emily said with some anger in her tone.

I handed Mr. Dugan my calling card. "Thank you for your time. If you think of anything that might help us in our investigation, don't hesitate to call. We'll talk to Mr. Riley and Mr. Stout, and your friend Mr. Beeson. You have my word that we'll do our best for Katie."

Mr. and Mrs. Dugan nodded and then stood with some difficulty, weighed down by their emotional burden. When I shook hands with James, and saw the man's pleading bloodshot eyes, I sensed that James wanted to say something, but the words stuck in the man's throat. My eyes watered and any words of comfort I might've offered stuck in my throat as well.

As Mr. and Mrs. Dugan left to wait for a Market Street trolley, they had to delay crossing the road because the red brougham I spotted earlier went by at a casual speed. The vehicle's passenger was visible through its side window, but silhouetted to where I couldn't identify the person inside except that it appeared to be a man. The driver was the same black-suited individual, and in my opinion, he glanced at me on purpose. Our eyes met.

A chill went up my spine.

CHAPTER 10

I stared at the brougham as it continued south on Market and wondered who owned it. The obvious choice would be a member of the wealthy DuPont family. However, Wilmington had other rich families, some of whom had earned their fortunes before the French emigrants arrived in 1802. It would be futile to question any of them because the elite were above the law, operating in their own social circle, and if any of them complained about me to the mayor, I'd be out of work.

Adelia spoke with compassion. "You were really kind to Mr. and Mrs. Dugan while trying to pressure them at the same time. I hope someday I can talk to people like that. I think I'm too harsh. And your theory that Miss Dugan was with child looks pretty good. A young lady doesn't just stop going to church and start washing her own clothes without a good reason."

"Miss Dugan probably felt too guilty to sit under the cross. She felt *dirty*. Along with washing her own clothes she probably bathed more often."

"Maybe she was forced against her will."

"That's possible too. She might've felt too ashamed to report it to her parents or the police. Or she might've wanted it, but afterwards hated herself and wanted to wash away all memory of it."

"Drummond!"

I flinched. Casey had crept up behind us. Adelia jumped as well. One of her hands went over her heart while the other grabbed my arm. Even though there were a couple layers of cloth between my arm and her hand, my body reacted as if it had been skin to skin contact. It suddenly felt like a hot summer day and my forehead perspired.

Adelia quickly removed her hand. "Oh, sorry."

I wanted to tell her it was all right, that it was understandable under the circumstances, but I had somehow lost the ability to articulate words and found myself appreciating the contact.

Casey came around and stood in front of us. "Now can you tell me the name of the victim and her parents?"

I took a deep breath and finally spoke. "I'll tell everybody at the Rats' Nest."

"Oh, come on. Why do you play it so straight? Nobody else does."

He removed his bowler hat and turned on the charm while addressing Adelia. "It's nice to see you again, Detective Bern. Can you tell me anything?"

"No statement at this time."

"Oh, come on." Casey flared his hat around and stomped his feet. "I know a lot of my readers would like to hear from you, the city's first lady detective, now actively working a murder case. With my connections, I can make you famous. I can make you the leading suffragette in the state, which would make you a political force to reckon with. What do you say?"

"No, thank you," Adelia said, and Casey frowned.

Casey still flung his hat around. "Jack the Ripper has come to Wilmington, and I'm going to say so in writing."

I sighed, tired. "Utter nonsense."

"Come to my desk," Casey said, taking a step toward Market. "I'll show you what they're writing in New York. It's really interesting, *and* compelling. Don't say nonsense until after you see what I've collected." He turned to Adelia. "Surely, you must be curious."

"Why do you say that," Adelia asked, sounding indignant, "because I'm a woman?"

Casey put his hands up. "No, no, no. I didn't mean that at all. *Please* come to my desk. I can substantiate my Ripper theory."

"We don't have time for that," I said. "We have interviews to conduct. I'm not wasting time on your insane theories."

Casey stomped his foot. "It's *not* a theory, it's *fact*! Let me show you. And if I can convince you that it's true, then it'll help your investigation. Come on, Drummond. Come on, Detective Bern. Just give me a few minutes of your time. Your interviews can wait a few minutes." He put his hat on and clasped his hands together. "Please."

I knew Casey wouldn't stop promoting his crazy idea until we obliged. So Adelia and I followed the reporter for six blocks south to the offices of the *Every Evening* at Fifth and Shipley Streets. The four-story building had plenty of tall and wide windows, and had been built about ten years prior. Next to the entrance was an engraved plaque depicting a father reading the paper by the fireplace, his wife seated in a chair nearby and a son and daughter seated on the floor at his feet. Above the image was the paper's motto and origin for its name: *Printing the news that's fit to read to your family every evening.*

The first thing Adelia and I encountered upon entering the building was noise. The ground floor was mostly rows of desks occupied by accountants, auditors and salesman. However, the commotion from the upper floors caused by printing machines, typesetting and men running about to do their job, drifted down to the first floor.

Casey led us to an elevator, and then operating the crank, he worked the device to get us to the third floor. He shoved the grating aside and hurried ahead, leaving Adelia and me to walk without the Vulture's company past the telegraph office and composition room. We then maneuvered past twelve desks belonging to journalists and copy editors, most of them pounding their fingertips on typewriter keys. We caught up to Casey at his roll top desk near a glass door marked Editor-in-Chief, Gilbert Cameron.

"Here's the folder," Casey said over the ratta-tat-tat of typewriter keys while Adelia and I sat. He pulled out newspaper clippings from the *New York Editorial* and read one of them aloud. "*On the morning of April 24, 1891, a woman's body was discovered in a cheap hotel in New York City. Her stomach had been cut out and her intestines thrown around the bed.*" Then he whispered, still quoting. "*Even more shocking, all of her female organs were gone. The victim had been a known bowery prostitute named Carrie Brown and she was seen going to her room with a man around 10:30 the night before she was found dead. The killer scrawled a message on the wall to taunt Chief Inspector Thomas Byrnes, 'Okay, catch me Boss.' New York City detectives are speculating that Jack the Ripper has arrived in America.*"

I frowned. "Speculating isn't fact."

"I'm not done yet," Casey said.

He put the clipping down and showed Adelia and me a few more. He summarized. "Over the next eleven days, three more brutal murders took place within a few miles of each other. Each victim was a prostitute, and her body ripped open in a similar fashion to the Ripper murders. And like the Ripper murders in London, the New York murders just stopped. New York's Chief Police Inspector Byrnes then received a taunting letter from someone claiming to be Jack the Ripper."

"*Claiming* to be," I said in my best skeptical tone. "Still not fact."

Casey went on, undaunted. "This person wrote that he was bored with the incompetent New York police department and had decided to move on to another city." Casey put the clippings down and looked at us intensely. "Did you hear that? He decided to move on to another city. New York isn't that far by train. So he *could be here in Wilmington!*"

"No, sir. There's two things wrong with your theory. Like I told you, Miss Dugan wasn't mutilated like the Ripper victims and she wasn't a prostitute."

"How do you know she wasn't selling it?" Casey said, desperate to keep his theory alive. "Why was she out late last night and way over by the Bush estate?"

I then violated my — tell every reporter at the same time clause — because I had to stop Casey's wild speculations. "There's another thing wrong with your theory. Miss Dugan was meeting her lover. She had an unsigned note in her purse for a rendezvous. The Ripper never sent love notes to his victims."

Casey frowned. "I don't believe you. You never tell me anything without including all my colleagues at the Rats' Nest. You made it up just to shut me up, and because you can't stand to be wrong about something. Where's this note?"

"At our office, it's evidence."

"Detective Bern," Casey asked, his eyes pleading, "is this true? Is there a love note?"

She nodded. "*Ja*. Detective Drummond is telling you the truth."

Casey frowned, but remained determined. "Maybe the Ripper has changed his routine to make us think he's not here."

Even Adelia chuckled at that.

"Your theory has no merit," I said. "Stick to supporting reform movements instead of writing fiction."

Casey sighed, and finally sounded defeated. "Damn you, Drummond. I was so hoping to have the story of the decade."

"Sorry," I said with a chuckle, but I wasn't really sorry. Casey and I had a strange relationship. We weren't friends, but we weren't enemies. Casey had sarcastically nicknamed me 'the Biking Detective' a few years prior in an article about, in his opinion, the incompetent and corrupt city police. *However*, he went on to write, *the only one of any merit is Detective Drummond, the biking detective.* I then defended our police force in an interview for the *Wilmington Daily* where I had called Casey The Vulture for the first time. "Stick to helping the progressives. Let's go Detective Bern. We have people to interview."

Casey slumped in his chair, obviously displeased that I shot holes in his Ripper theory. Then he sat up, excited again. "What about the letter sent to the police inspector?"

I had to admit that Casey had caught my attention when the Vulture showed us the newspaper articles from New York. It was intriguing to speculate about the Ripper being in America because Ripper-style murders had been committed in that city and a taunting letter was sent to their police inspector. "Casey, you know as well as I do that criminals are known for copying the exploits of other felons. The killer in New York is not the Ripper, but somebody copying him and probably hoping for Ripper-style publicity, or he's doing it to pay homage to the Ripper. One thing is for certain, Miss Dugan's death, while brutal, does not fit the Ripper's modus operandi."

CHAPTER 11

Adelia and I decided to interview Mr. Albert Stout first simply because we assumed he'd be at work and his place of employment was only a few blocks from the *Every Evening*. The Charles Warner Company was the largest passenger and shipping firm along the Christina River. The company's business office at Second and Market was inside a brick structure that advertised the firm on the south side of the building in bold white-painted letters: JOHN WARNER SHIPPING COMPANY, FOUNDED BY JOHN AND CHARLES WARNER IN 1794. WITH FREIGHT SERVICE TO PHILADELPHIA, NEW YORK AND BOSTON.

"Lower Market Street," I said as we walked past storefronts for John Moore Clothing, Boston Boot and Shoe House, Lichtenstein Dry Goods and C.F. Rudolph Jewelers, "still retains buildings that went up prior to my birth." The old brick structures could use a good cleaning and a couple had roofs that appeared ready to cave in. The brick sidewalk was uneven, blown up by roots from trees that had long since been cut down. "This location was prime real estate in my youth, but since then the heart of Wilmington has moved uphill."

"Looks like a lot of bars here," Adelia said. She wasn't wrong. Lower Market was also popular for drinking establishments because the location put them in close proximity of the thirsty men who worked the docks or railroad. Taverns stood on each block, on both sides of the road, and sometimes adjacent to each other. Their proprietors were generally unscrupulous men who aimed to quickly take a man's earnings while distilling a vile, water-downed brew. The businesses were also segregated. Colored men had their own bars. White men had their own places, and then they divided themselves even more. Those of Irish or German descent congregated at their favorite spots.

I held the door open for Adelia and we entered the Warner shipping office to the sound of typewriter keys. Seated at a desk and pressing those keys was a young man in a plain suit with cuff protectors on his shirtsleeves and a banker's visor on his head. He sat near an unused potbelly stove, a clean cuspidor, a large safe and a wall of filing cabinets. I pointed at an advertisement on the back wall that announced the upcoming World's Columbian Exposition in Chicago.

The theme of the World's Fair in Jackson Park was to commemorate the 400th anniversary of Christopher Columbus' arrival in the New World.

"That's another reason I left Chicago," Adelia said. "It's bound to be a madhouse with all the people they're expecting."

Another reason, I thought? She hadn't told me the main reason.

The clerk stopped typing and looked up. "May I help you?"

Another young man entered from a back room and wrote some entries in chalk on a large blackboard that kept track of the company's ships and their time of arrival and departure.

"Yes, you may." I introduced myself and Adelia and our desire to see Mr. Warner. "He knows me."

"Mr. Warner is a very busy man," the clerk said as if he owned the place. "What is the purpose of your visit?"

I told him. The clerk's brown eyes nearly popped out of his skull at the word murder.

"Wait here," he said, visibly shaken. He disappeared into a side room, but quickly returned in the company of a short man with black hair who wore a well-tailored white shirt, brown vest and black stripped trousers.

"Hello, Detective Drummond," John Warner said as he and I shook hands. John had gained a noticeable belly since the last time I had seen him. "It's been a long time, sir. I don't think we've spoken since my father's retirement."

"How is your father?"

Mr. Warner smirked. "He's as grumpy as a bear. My poor mother now belongs to four whist clubs just so she can have an excuse to get out of the house." He bowed to my partner. "It's a pleasure to meet you, Miss. I remember reading about you in the papers. Welcome to Wilmington. I hope you find this city a bit more progressive than Chicago."

Adelia smiled. "Thank you, sir, but unfortunately many of the same prejudices persist in the population here. I'm hoping that with time I can alter people's perceptions."

Mr. Warner nodded, and released an uneasy, "Yes." Then he addressed me. "My clerk tells me you're here to investigate a murder? Is that true?"

"Yes, sir, that's correct," I said. I then told him about Miss Dugan and why Adelia and I needed to interview Mr. Stout. "And we'd like to keep the conversation confidential. The newspapers haven't printed anything yet, but word of mouth is already spreading."

Mr. Warner rubbed his hands together. "Oh my, Detective Drummond, that is troubling news. You don't think Mr. Stout is involved in such a terrible thing? He's been such a good and loyal employee, a good family man."

"No, sir," I said, trying to put John at ease. I assumed he was more concerned about negative publicity in the newspapers affecting his business than he was about Mr. Stout's welfare. "I'm sure he's not involved, but we have to check with everyone who knew Miss Dugan and narrow down the possibilities."

"Of course," Mr. Warner said. He then ordered his clerk to find Mr. Stout. The young man practically flew out the door. "Let's wait in my office."

I smelled the basket of peaches before I saw them, next to a pitcher of water and on top of Mr. Warner's immaculate mahogany desk. I took a deep breath and attempted to further ingratiate myself with my host. "Oh, I just love peaches."

"Me, too," Mr. Warner said with a big smile. He pointed at a pair of wooden chairs in front of his desk. "Please sit down and help yourself." John took a peach and sat in his leather chair beneath the painting of a wooden sailing vessel, *Philadelphia*, one of the first ships in the company's fleet. "They're my favorite fruit, especially in pies. You'll have to come to dinner soon, Detective Drummond, Detective Bern, my wife bakes an excellent peach pie." He winked, laughed and patted his stomach. "I'm afraid I've been eating too many of her pies lately."

I took a peach and sat. Adelia did likewise and asked, "Are they grown locally? Do you ship a lot of them?"

Mr. Warner almost dropped his peach. "My dear lady, I can forgive your ignorance because you're new to the state, so let me enlighten you. There's some four million peach trees in Delaware, primarily below the canal, with the first commercial orchard started by Mr. Isaac Reeves of Delaware City some sixty years ago. There were peach trees in the state before that, but the fruit is so perishable it couldn't be shipped very far without spoiling. That is until the Chesapeake and Delaware canal opened, followed shortly thereafter by railroads. The canal runs between Delaware City and Chesapeake City, Maryland, and it reduces the shipping miles between Delaware City and Baltimore by almost three-hundred miles. So we can now send peaches to thousands and thousands of more people in less time. We also ship them to Philadelphia and New York. Unfortunately, this is the last batch for the season and they're not as full and juicy as the ones we get in August and September."

Adelia twirled her peach in her hand. "I can therefore assume that the state has Peach Barons?"

I was surprised Adelia knew the word barons and what it meant, but I shouldn't be. She was proving to be a well-educated woman, but did her intelligence just come from books? I wanted to know more about her life experiences and hoped to discover more about her background in due time.

Mr. Warner chuckled. "Yes, we do indeed. Major Philip Reybold was known as the Peach King. And in southern New Castle County, if you ever travel that way, you'll see the so-called peach mansions built by the farmers that struck it rich. Most of the houses are big, ornate structures that sit in the middle of what had been a corn or wheat field before the trees were planted. Some people resent them for showing off their wealth in this matter, but I say why not? They deserve it. It's nice to see farmers get a break for once. May I ask you a personal question?" Adelia nodded. "I don't envy you your line of work. It's nasty business. It's certainly not something I'd expect a woman to be doing."

"You needn't concern yourself about me," Adelia said, placing the peach in her lap and taking out her notebook and pencil. "I am more than capable."

"No doubt," Mr. Warner said. "But I am curious. Why did you choose this profession?"

"Please, sir, we'll be asking the questions."

Mr. Warner glared at Adelia, and for a moment I thought he might order us to leave. I doubted any woman, especially one in such a lowly profession as police work, had ever talked to him in such a manner. Fortunately, Mr. Warner was well-versed in the act of being a gentleman and suppressed his anger with humor. "I've been properly rebuked."

I released an uneasy laugh, and thought it best to get to the purpose of our visit. "Since Mr. Stout has yet to arrive, can I ask you a few questions, Mr. Warner?" He agreed and Adelia prepared to write. "How long has Mr. Stout been in your employ?"

"A long time. I think he started as a boy."

"Have you had any trouble with him, any reason to mistrust him?"

"No, sir. Like I said, he's been a good and capable worker, a fine employee."

"What's his position with the company?"

"He's one of my freight agents."

"So his job has a lot of responsibility?"

"Yes, sir. We ship and receive a lot of goods by boat and rail, mostly coal, lumber and limestone. Albert is one of my top men, making sure the process goes off smoothly. The better he does his job the less I have to worry, and believe me, there's plenty to worry about in this business. Only yesterday I had to remove two ships from service for leaking water. Another steamer needs a new engine. We have so many contracts to meet."

"Do you ship gunpowder?" Adelia asked.

"Yes, but not from these docks. The DuPonts have their own piers at Edgemoor and Marcus Hook, which are north of here. Wilmington City Council banned the company from ever bringing their black powder through town after the explosion of '54."

"I remember it well," I said. Three covered wagons carrying 450 kegs of gunpowder exploded in the middle of the city, killing the five men hauling the wagons, fifteen horses and badly damaging nearby buildings. "I heard it all the way out at my parents' farm, some five miles away. Then of course we had to ride into town and see the damage for ourselves. It seemed like every window in the city had been blown out."

"Did they ever find out why it happened?" Adelia asked.

"No," Mr. Warner said. "But let's face it the drivers weren't always the most intelligent. One of them probably lit a cigarette and tossed the match into the wagon."

"That *was* the rumor," I said. Incredibly, smoking was permitted at the DuPont Gunpowder Mills, at least outside the buildings. "Now, let's get back to Mr. Stout. You said he's a freight agent. So he's not involved in the passenger side of the business?"

"Correct, sir, just freight."

Adelia asked, "Are you friends with his family? Do you associate with them outside of business?"

John replied while looking at his peach. "I've met his family here at the office, nothing more. We don't associate off hours because we don't share the same society."

"Oh," Adelia said, "can you elaborate?"

I answered. "If I may, it means that Mr. Warner lives on Delaware Avenue and Mr. Stout lives on Broom Street." Then to John, "I'm showing Detective Bern around the city and educating her along the way. We haven't been to Delaware Avenue yet."

I heard the door open in the outer office. A moment later, a husky gentleman in blackened overalls crossed the threshold.

CHAPTER 12

I assumed the gentleman who just entered Mr. Warner's office was Mr. Stout. He kept his distance because he had soot on his face and in his uncombed wheat-colored hair, but what struck me the most about the man was his large and thick walrus-type moustache. It hid his upper lip and each end reached to the middle of his cheeks.

"You wanted to see me, Mr. Warner?" the man said. "Please forgive my appearance. We just sent off a coal barge. The boy said it was important so I didn't take the time to clean up."

"That's fine, Mr. Stout," his boss said. He then introduced us.

Albert's hazel eyes darted between Adelia, Mr. Warner and me like a frightened cat. "Detectives? Why would detectives want to see me? What's this about?"

"They have some troubling news," Mr. Warner said. "Please sit."

Albert remained standing. "Oh, dear, has something happened to my family?"

"Oh, no, sir," I said, "nothing like that. I believe you knew a young lady named Katie Dugan."

Albert put his hands up. "I've done nothing wrong, sir, I assure you."

I suppressed a laugh. "I'm not accusing you of anything."

"Oh," Albert breathed a sigh of relief. "Then what's this about?"

"Please sit," I said. Albert looked nervously around the room before settling on a chair by the door. "I'm sorry to tell you this, Mr. Stout, but Miss Katie Dugan was murdered last night. Detective Bern and I have been assigned to conduct the investigation into her death. We're interviewing everyone who knew the young lady or saw her in the past few days."

Albert stared without blinking his eyes. His face and body seemed frozen in place. I have seen plenty of reactions to tragic news, including such bad acting from possible suspects that I knew the person was guilty of the crime immediately. However, Mr. Stout's motionless form made me wonder if Albert had died in the chair.

"Sir," I said. "Mr. Stout? Did you hear me?"

Adelia asked, "Do you understand?"

Albert's eyes slowly filled with tears. He then bowed his head so we couldn't see his face. "Miss Dugan? Murdered? That sweet girl?

No, it's not possible."

"Yes, sir," I said. "I'm afraid it's true."

"I don't believe you, sir," Albert said in a less than convincing voice. I sensed that Albert's heart knew it was true, but his mind and mouth claimed otherwise. Had he been expecting this news? "It's not possible. Why would anyone harm that sweet girl?"

Adelia sighed, impatient. "That's what we're trying to find out."

"Please, Mr. Stout," I said, "I know this is upsetting, but we have some questions to ask and we'd appreciate honest answers. Where were you last evening?"

"Oh," Albert moaned. He looked at his boss. There was a streak down each cheek from tears that had flowed through the soot on his face. He looked at the ceiling, then the floor. His voice struggled. "I was at the Sacred Heart Fair with my wife and daughter."

"Really?" I said, intrigued. "Did you see Miss Dugan? She went to the fair as well."

"Yes, sir." Albert pulled a dirty handkerchief from a pocket in his overalls and wiped his eyes and cheeks. "I saw her. She was with Mr. Richard Riley."

"So you know the gentleman?"

Albert was smug. "I know *of* him. We've never been properly introduced."

Adelia said, "How do you know *of* him if you've not been introduced?"

Albert took a long moment to answer, almost as if he had to invent a response. "I asked some people at the fair if they recognized the man with Katie. One gentleman did."

I sensed it was a lie. "How did it make you feel to see Katie with another man?"

"How did I *feel?*" he said, his eyebrows raised. "What kind of question is that?"

"Answer the detective," John said.

"Yes, sir," Albert said to his boss. "I felt fine about it."

Another obvious lie, I thought. "I understand you once employed Miss Dugan as a house servant."

"That's true," Albert said, sobbing. "But that was four years ago."

"And she left your house," I said, "after just a couple months because you tried to take advantage of her."

"No, sir!" Albert jumped to his feet. "That's an absurd lie. I'll kill the bastard who told you that."

"Sit down, Albert," John said, obviously startled. "Keep your wits

71

about you."

Albert again looked around like frightened cat, eyes wide. He appeared to be weighing his options, calculating whether he should stay or flee. If he left, I had a conviction. Finally, Albert decided it was best to remain and answer questions. He took a deep breath and released it slowly.

"Are you all right?' John asked him.

"Yes, sir," Albert said. He lowered his bulky frame back into the chair. He tugged on his fat moustache. Then he tried to laugh. "It was just a misunderstanding. I assure you. It was a very hot day and Katie, eh, Miss Dugan, was cleaning our bedrooms on the second floor. The upstairs is so much hotter than downstairs. I told her it would be all right if she unfastened some of the buttons of her blouse to help her cool off."

"Did you ask her to show her bosom?" I said.

Albert pounded a fist on the arm of the chair. "That's *not* true, sir!"

"Mr. Stout," John said in a stern voice, "please remain calm and answer the detective's questions. The quicker they conduct their business the quicker you can get back to *your* business."

"Yes, sir," Albert said, cowering. Then to me, "I don't remember everything I said."

"She was only fourteen," I said.

He looked away. "I am aware."

"Albert," John said with disdain. "I'm surprised at you. You're a married man."

"Again, sir, it was a misunderstanding."

"Have you seen Miss Dugan since she left your employment," I said, "other than last night?"

"No, sir," he said rather quickly, another lie. "I was warned by her father not to come near her, even though I hadn't done anything wrong. I thought it best to do as he said."

"But you saw Miss Dugan last night with Richard Riley. Was that a coincidence?"

Albert again hesitated before answering and looked toward the ceiling. I got the impression he was rehearsing different responses in his mind and weighing the possible consequences of what might arise from his each answer. Such calculating behavior did not sit well with me and only increased my suspicions. "Yes, sir, it was a coincidence. I had no idea they'd be there."

That was a lie. "Did you greet them?"

"No, sir. I saw them from a distance when I was at the ball toss game. You know the one I mean. You toss a ball at the opening of a milk jug from about eight feet away, hoping to get the ball to land inside the jug. I was showing off for my daughter, Jill. She's twenty-two and not married. I was hoping someone would notice her at the fair, but that didn't happen. And I didn't get any balls in the jugs, neither. I suspect the opening to the top of the jugs is smaller than the ball. I've heard that these carnival games are rigged. You should investigate *that*, sir, and arrest *them*."

I ignored Albert's tirade. "Is that the only time you saw Mr. Riley and Miss Dugan?"

"No, sir," he replied with more candor. "Later in the evening, I was standing in line to buy ice cream when I saw Mr. Riley walking really fast by himself. I wondered why Katie wasn't with him. Why was he in such a hurry? What kind of gentlemen abandons a lady at a public event?"

"Did you go after Mr. Riley?"

"No, sir. My wife and daughter were expecting ice cream. I watched him leave the fairgrounds and wondered what happened, and hoped Katie was all right. Now I know he must've killed her. Why else would he run from the fairgrounds?"

"It's not prudent to assume someone guilty of murder without evidence, Mr. Stout. Please don't spread rumors."

"So you don't think he did it?"

"Miss Dugan wasn't killed at the fairgrounds."

"Oh, where then?"

"On DuPont, near Sycamore."

Albert's eyes widened and he tugged again on his moustache. "But that's all the way out by the Bush estate."

"Yes, sir, it is. Do you have any idea why she'd be out there at night?"

Albert sighed, and then spoke so low only he could hear. He seemed to be trying to comprehend the information.

"Please, Mr. Stout, I can't hear you. Do you have any idea why Miss Dugan would be by the Bush estate in the middle of the night? The coroner believes she was killed between midnight and two."

Albert shook his head. "No, sir, I can't imagine why she'd be out there. There's no street lamps, no trolley service."

"So you're familiar with that part of town?"

Albert coughed like someone who had been caught in a lie and needed to make up a quick story. "My wife and I were invited to the Bush house once. The old man held a gala in honor of Felix Darley."

"I'm jealous, sir," I said, my suspicious nature only getting worse because I suspected another lie. I told Adelia, "Felix Darley was a prolific illustrator for *Harper's Weekly*, and he did a number of illustrations for fiction authors, like Washington Irving's *Rip Van Winkle* and *The Legend of Sleepy Hollow*. He died four years ago at his home in Claymont." I turned back to Albert. "That must've been quite an event and quite an honor for you and your wife."

"Oh, yes, sir," Albert said, his voice shaking, "indeed it was."

"Do you remember what time it was when you saw Mr. Riley leave the fair?"

Albert thought for a moment. "I'm not certain, sir. I prefer not to keep track of the time when I'm off the job. My duties here are so regimented by a time schedule, making sure shipments go and arrive preciously on the minute they're supposed to, that when I have a chance at leisure activity, I leave the watch at home."

"I can understand that," I said, disappointed.

Adelia put her pencil down and asked, "What did you do after attending the fair?"

"Went home to bed."

"And your wife and daughter can confirm this?"

"Of course they can." Albert seemed offended. "I'm innocent, ma'am."

"It's *Detective* Bern. Are you happy in your marriage?"

Albert reacted as expected, indignant. "*That* my dear detective is a very personal question and you have no right to ask it."

"It's *Detective Bern*. From what I've heard, it's apparent that you're not happy at home. Katie's parents think you're a lecherous old man who was after their daughter, that what happened between her and you was more than just a *misunderstanding*. Now, an older man chasing a young woman is nothing new, but it does look suspicious in a murder investigation. If we find out that you've been lying to us, or holding back information, it won't look good for you."

"Why are you treating me like this?" Albert said, his nostrils flaring above his big moustache. "I've answered your questions. I've done nothing wrong."

"I think a lot more happened between you and Katie than what you've stated. You're squirming and tugging at your moustache. Is it a nervous habit? Why are you nervous? What're you hiding from us or not telling us?"

"I'm not hiding anything."

"I have a feeling you are."

Albert smirked. "You women and your *feelings*."

"Albert," John Warner said, "do you have anything more to add about what happened between you and Miss Dugan?"

Albert dropped his shoulders, defeated. "Oh, all right, all right. After Katie refused to unbutton her blouse, I cornered her in the bedroom. I insisted that she kiss me or I wouldn't let her leave. I didn't know my wife was in the hallway. She heard Katie protest and came into the room. I had to deal with my wife's anger, followed shortly thereafter by Katie's father."

"Can't say that I blame them," John said. "I'm very disappointed in you, Albert."

"God as my witness," Albert said, raising a hand. "That's it. No more. I did not kill Katie. Why would I? I loved her."

John groaned. Albert put his face in his hands and shook with sorrow.

I let him weep for a moment and then asked, "Do you know of any other suitors besides Mr. Riley?"

"No, sir," Albert said into his hands.

"Were you envious of Mr. Riley?"

Albert lifted his wet face and emphasized each word. "I was not, sir."

"I find that hard to believe. He was with Katie and you weren't."

"Katie didn't like him *that way*."

"How do you know that, sir, if you hadn't seen Katie in the past four years and only learned of Mr. Riley's name last night?"

Albert froze again, this time caught in a lie that he quickly had to rectify. "What I mean to say is that I heard rumors that she wasn't interested in him as a husband."

"Rumors? Mr. Dugan stated that his children have spotted you around their house on occasion. Have you been following Katie, spying on her?"

"Albert," John said, his voice rising, "this is very troubling. Were you spying on the young lady?"

Adelia said, "Did you ever go with her, or follow her into the Grand Opera House?"

Albert squirmed. "What're you talking about?"

"We heard Katie liked the theatre. Did you go to shows with her, or follow her into the theatre?"

Albert shook his head. "Don't be ridiculous."

"Does that mean yes or no?" Adelia asked.

"No."

I asked, "Did you spy on her?"

"No, sir."

I didn't believe him. "Mr. Stout, did you look for Katie after Mr. Riley left her?"

Albert shook his head. "No, sir. I escorted my wife and daughter home and we went to bed. Besides, I had no idea where Katie went after she left Mr. Riley."

"After *she* left Mr. Riley?" Adelia said before I could.

CHAPTER 13

Even Mr. Warner caught Albert's slip of the tongue. "*She* left Mr. Riley?"

"Earlier," I said, "you stated you saw Richard hurry from the fairgrounds and you wondered why *he* had abandoned *her.* Are you sure you didn't follow Katie?"

"If you weren't such a good and loyal employee," John said, losing his temper, "I'd release you right now. You have darkened my business with a murder investigation, and your character has come into some serious questioning."

"I apologize, sir," Albert said, squirming now as if the chair was on fire. "My wife and daughter wanted to spend time in the Agriculture Tent, looking at some giant pumpkins. I told them I wasn't interested, so we parted temporarily. I used the opportunity to follow Katie and Mr. Riley. I was curious, that's all, and I kept my distance. Well, they spent time watching children on the merry-go-round when something seemed to come between them. They started arguing. Mr. Riley was really upset. I don't know why. I was too far away to hear. Then after a few minutes they came to some sort of truce. Mr. Riley entered a water closet. Katie waited for a moment, and then left him. She headed to the rear of fairgrounds. I followed. She stopped at a medicine show and bought a bottle of their elixir."

"Medicine show?" I said. "Do you remember the name of the medicine show, or was it the only one on the premises?"

Albert thought for a moment. "I believe it's the only one at the fair. It was an odd name. Let me think. I'm picturing their banner in my head....Kickapoo! That's it. Kickapoo Medicine Show."

My heartbeat pounded faster. "What happened after she bought the bottle of their medicine?"

"Katie left the fairgrounds and disappeared into the night toward Tenth Street. I returned to my wife and daughter. Then, as I said, they wanted ice cream. I saw Mr. Riley leave in a hurry. I escorted my wife and daughter home. We *went* home to bed."

"Detectives," John said to me in a calm voice, "how was the young lady killed?"

"Her throat was cut."

"Dear God."

"Mr. Stout," I said, "at any time during the evening did you see anything in Katie's hands? Did she read anything or carry anything other than the bottle of elixir?"

Albert leaned back. "No, sir. I don't remember anything in her hands. And after she bought the tonic, she put it in her dress pocket."

"Did you see anyone approach her? Did somebody hand her something?"

He shook his head. "Not that I saw."

I nodded, and then turned to my partner to see if Adelia had any additional questions.

Adelia said, "Is your address 505 Broom Street?"

"Yes, ma'am, I mean, Detective Bern."

"We know it's a long walk from the Sacred Heart Fair to Sycamore and DuPont, but how far is Sycamore and DuPont from *your* house?"

"I didn't kill her."

"I didn't say you did. I merely asked a question of geography. I'm new to the city and not that familiar."

Albert glanced around the room before answering. "I'd have to walk four blocks west and then five blocks south."

"That's not far," Adelia said. "Is your wife at home?"

"I assume she is."

"May we call on her?"

"What for? She can't tell you anything."

"Please, sir. May we call on her?"

"Oh, I get it," Albert said, nodding. "You want to look around my house. You want to go through my things and find something you can use to pin Katie's murder on me, even though I'm innocent. And if you don't find something, you'll plant evidence against me. I've heard about this sort of thing, corrupt police, just looking to get a case off their hands, so they implicate an innocent person. Then I'd have to bribe my way out of being arrested. You don't fool me."

"That's not our intention."

"You might be a woman, but you're still a copper, just a thief in uniform."

"Albert," John said, "that's enough. May they call on your wife or not?"

The freight agent bowed his head. "Go ahead. I'll warn her to expect you."

I wondered if I should send Adelia on ahead by herself to talk to Mrs. Stout while I kept an eye on Mr. Stout so that he didn't telephone his wife. If Albert was guilty, I didn't want him telling Mrs. Stout what to say, and what not to say, and fabricate an alibi. However, since Adelia was new to the job, and might get lost finding Broom Street, I decided to ignore my concern and take the risk.

"That'll be fine," Adelia said in a calm voice. "Thank you."

I stood and handed Albert my calling card. "Please be available if we need to talk to you again. And if you think of anything that might help our investigation, don't hesitate to call."

Albert accepted the card without looking at it. He sobbed. "Poor Katie."

"Mr. Warner," I said, "as always it was a pleasure seeing you, sir. Give my regards to your father and to your wife. Thank you for your time and your hospitality, and of course, for the peaches." He started to stand. "Don't get up, sir. We'll see ourselves out."

A moment later, Adelia and I stepped outside and we were greeted by the long blast from the horn of a paddle wheeler. The steamship was announcing its imminent departure from the Warner pier a couple blocks away. From my vantage point, I saw the ships' upper deck laden with passengers and the steam escaping its central smokestack.

I took a good, healthy bite into my peach and savored its sweet juicy taste. "That was a good question about the distance from Mr. Stout's house to the murder scene. Nine blocks isn't that far."

"That's what I was wondering," Adelia said, also biting into her peach. "He could've left his house after his family went to bed."

"But if Mr. Stout was jealous of Mr. Riley," I said, "or any other suitor, he had four years to kill Katie. Why do it now, and why at Sycamore and DuPont?"

"The circumstances changed." Adelia had some peach juice on her chin and I was tempted to wipe it off with my handkerchief, but did not. "Let's assume Katie was with child and Mr. Stout found out about it. That might've changed his image of her. Perhaps he worshiped her from afar. Maybe to him she was a sweet and pure young lady that he hoped one day to possess. But when he discovered she was going to have a baby out of wedlock and fathered by another man, she was no longer this sweet and innocent girl, but a common trollop. It was too much for him to bear."

I sighed. "Katie was no longer Baby's Breath."

Adelia's eyes widened. "Exactly."

I smiled. "Did you study psychology in college?"

Adelia nodded. "I did indeed, along with literature."

"I thought so. Well, I don't have any book learning like you when it comes to psychology, but my years of experience have been an education in itself. I do agree with you about older gentlemen. We do have a tendency of putting pretty young women up on a pedestal."

"Are you speaking from experience?"

I laughed. "That's none of your business, Detective Bern."

She nodded. "I have another thought, and it's too dreadful to comprehend. Officer Ormond wondered if someone was trying to put the blame for Katie's murder on a barber. What if the unknown suitor is Mr. Stout? What if *he's* the father? To avoid scandal and deflect blame, he kills Miss Dugan and sets up Mr. Riley."

"It's definitely plausible," I said, finishing the peach and dropping the pit to the ground. "But the thought of Katie and Mr. Stout together is difficult to imagine. And there's something else in Mr. Stout's testimony that bothered me. He said he tried to kiss Katie. Mr. and Mrs. Dugan never mentioned it. Didn't she tell them? I'd think Mr. Stout trying to force himself on their daughter would be an even more severe reason for quitting his employ. Mr. Dugan could've had him arrested."

Adelia shrugged. "Maybe Katie told her parents and they just forgot to tell us. *Or* Katie didn't tell her parents because she didn't want Mr. Stout arrested. Like I said, maybe they were secretly seeing each other and she felt a need to protect him. Maybe they pretended to hate each other in public but something was going on in private. I don't know. I'm just guessing. One thing's for certain, Mr. Stout was quite nervous and not forthcoming. He's definitely a suspect, if you ask me."

"On that, Detective Bern, we can agree."

CHAPTER 14

Adelia and I walked a short distance uphill to the northeast corner of Fifth and Market to Wilmington's largest and most opulent hotel, the Clayton House. We entered the five-story Clayton between the entrances for Artisan's Savings Bank and First National Bank of Wilmington, the two businesses that had paid for the hotel's construction.

The hotel's lobby gave a sampling to the opulence of the 105 rooms upstairs. The Registration Desk was mahogany and it ran the length of the back wall, staffed by gentlemen in identical pin-striped suits and bow ties. A grand piano resided next to a mural depicting the Swedish colonists coming ashore and meeting the native Lenape people in 1638. There were a dozen high-back chairs and four sofas upholstered in red velvet strategically placed throughout, and some of them were occupied by men reading a newspaper and smoking either a cigar, cigarette or pipe. The portrait of former United States Senator and Secretary of State John Clayton, the hotel's namesake, hung above a large marble fireplace.

"It's warm in here," Adelia said.

"Yes, steam heat."

I escorted Adelia toward the rear of the first floor, past the telegraph office, a Lady's Waiting Room, and then the Dining Hall. The door to the barber shop was open. We stepped inside and my nose captured the musky cologne they must apply heavily to every customer. Three barbers wearing identical wool suits with narrow lapels, white shirts and bowties stood next to their empty black upholstered chairs. They smiled at me, hoping I was a customer.

I introduced Adelia and myself. "We're looking for Mr. Richard Riley."

"I'm Mr. Riley," the barber at the first chair said. He was a tall and lanky gentleman. His brown hair was combed back and slicked down with plenty of oil. He pushed his spectacles up higher on his nose. "Why would a pair of detectives need to see me?"

"May we speak in private?"

Mr. Riley shrugged, and then followed Adelia and me to some chairs outside the Billiard Room, next to a passenger elevator. The Clayton had been the first building in the city to have an elevator.

"I understand you attended the Sacred Heart Fair the last two nights with Miss Katie Dugan. Is that correct?"

"That's correct. Why do you ask?"

"Well, sir," I said softly, trying to keep the conversation from being overheard by passing hotel guests, "there's no pleasant way to say this. I'm sorry to inform you, but Miss Dugan was murdered last night."

"What?" Richard said with a mixture of shock, disbelief and sorrow. His reaction seemed genuine and less suspicious than Mr. Stout's. "Murdered?"

"I'm sorry, sir. She was found this morning by the Bush estate at Sycamore and DuPont. Her throat had been cut."

Richard shook his head. "Dear God. No. It's not possible. Is this a joke? If it is, sir, it's in very poor taste. Are you really with the police department?" He looked at Detective Bern, who was poised to take notes. "I never heard of a woman detective."

I handed Richard one of my calling cards. "I can assure you, sir, this is not a joke."

Richard read my card. "Dear God, Katie."

"You seem to be one the last persons to see Miss Dugan alive," I said "Last night, she left you at some point. Can you tell us what happened?"

Richard removed his spectacles. He pulled out a handkerchief from a vest pocket and wiped the lenses instead of his own eyes. He looked at Adelia and swallowed hard. He spoke in a quivering voice. "We were at the fair until, I guess, around ten o'clock when she left me without any explanation."

"You're not sure of the time?"

"No, sir." His voice was still shaky. "I don't own a watch and really don't pay attention."

"Go on."

"Well, sir," he said with his spectacles still in his hand, "I thought we were getting along splendid. I tried to think if I had done anything to offend her, but I didn't. It made no sense. I arrived at her house on time. We had a pleasant talk on the streetcar. Tuesday night we spent time eating and sampling all the desserts, especially the apple pies. She loved apple pie. Last night, we were more interested in the rides and games. So we wandered around the fairgrounds and speculated on how many of the carnival games were dishonest. We had a good laugh about that. Then while we watched children on a merry-go-round, Katie announced she had to leave. I asked why. She just said, 'I have to.' I asked her to wait until after I used the water closet, that I'd take her home. She agreed, but when I finished my business and came back out, she was gone."

"What did you do after that?"

"At first, I didn't believe it. I looked around for a bit, just to make certain she was gone. The more I looked, the madder I got, I can tell you. I took out my frustrations at the shooting gallery. I fired that pellet gun at those metal animals again and again just to burn off steam. I'm not afraid to tell you I wished they were Katie. I was really mad."

"Did she give you any hint about where she might've gone?"

"No, sir."

"Has she ever walked out on you before?"

"No, sir."

"What did you do after the shooting gallery?"

"I got drunk."

"Did you go to a tavern or drink at the fair?"

"At the fair." Richard paused to dab his eyes. "I only had four or five beers, so I wasn't *that* drunk when I decided to leave. However, instead of going home, I went to a friend's house and slept there. Mr. Milton Ferrell at 800 Madison Street, Room 4."

"When did you arrive at Mr. Ferrell's place?"

"Well, I was at the shooting gallery for a while. I must've gotten to my friend's place by midnight. Look Detectives, I didn't kill Katie. I was mad at her, but I didn't kill her. I loved her. I wanted to marry her. I wouldn't have harmed her in any way."

Adelia said, "Did you notice any strain in the relationship between Katie and her parents?"

Richard tilted his head and his eyes squinted at Adelia, signaling to me that Richard was near-sighted. "Well, detective, I hate to disclose private matters."

"Please, sir, it's necessary to our investigation. Did you notice anything?"

Richard finally put his spectacles on and sighed. "Katie and her parents disagreed over religion and theatre. Katie didn't understand why the church was so hostile to actors when all they did was entertain people. I was never present at any of these exchanges, I'm just repeating what Katie told me when we were together and she talked about such matters."

"Did you share Katie's opinion about the theatre?"

"I have no opinion. I've never attended the theatre."

"Katie *has* attended the theatre," I said. "You didn't go with her?"

"That's correct, sir; I had no interest."

I nodded. "That strikes me as odd. You wanted to marry the lady. You could've taken her on dates to the theatre, yet you did not?"

Richard shrugged. "Correct, sir. I had no interest." Then he looked down. "And it's a point of embarrassment for me. Theatre tickets are not cheap. I'm not a big wage earner."

I sympathized, but pressed on. "Miss Dugan was seen at the Grand Opera House in the company of some older men and women. Did she ever mention the names of these people?"

Richard shook his head. "No, sir. I just listened to her complain, nothing more. And if she mentioned any names, I don't remember them."

Adelia asked, "Whose idea was it to attend the fair?"

"Katie called me. Which was unusual, but she said she needed to get out of the house and have some fun, and the fair looked like what she needed."

I looked at Adelia. She nodded, seemingly in agreement with my opinion of Mr. Riley's testimony, that it seemed trustworthy. I would've preferred a better time-line, but I saw no reason to press him further. "Mr. Riley, may we see your work station?"

"My work station? Why?"

"Please."

Richard shrugged and agreed, so the three of us returned to the barber shop. There was now a customer in the third chair receiving a shave. The middle barber sat in his chair reading the *Morning Herald,* which reminded me that I needed to make an announcement at the Rat's Nest. On the other hand, it was nice to operate with relative freedom. Once the public learned about Miss Dugan's murder, fear would grip the city, and fanning those flames would be Casey Moran. If I was a betting person, I'd put money on Casey still printing his Jack the Ripper theory and standing behind it as the truth. Frightened citizens, easily manipulated by such propaganda, would rally for justice and put pressure on the police department to solve the crime immediately.

Adelia and I inspected the drawers and marble counter space behind Richard's chair and in front of a gold-trimmed mirror that ran the length of the back wall. Richard had what would be expected of a barber, some shaving mugs and brushes, a team of scissors and combs, a bottle of West End Cologne, Fistfighters Beard and Moustache Wax, Rowland's Macassar Oil, three ordinary straight razors and a leather belt for sharpening.

I pointed at a mahogany box about eight inches long and four inches wide. "What's in that?"

"That's where I keep my Wostenholm," Richard said casually. "The best blades ever made. I only use it by customer request."

This was too easy, I thought. If the razor was missing, I had my man. Then again, Richard hadn't reacted like a guilty man when I told him the news about Miss Dugan. "May I open it?"

"Certainly."

I controlled my enthusiasm and lifted the lid. The box's interior only had red velvet over a molded indentation that I suspected would fit perfectly the razor stored in the police safe.

CHAPTER 15

"What?" Richard said, his eyes wide. "Where's my Wostenholm?" He was near panic. He looked around the counter space and then at his fellow barbers. "Do either of you have my razor?"

The middle barber looked up from his newspaper with daggers in his eyes. "Why would we take your razor when we have our own? You probably took it home with you."

"No, sir." Richard pointed at the empty box. "I didn't take it home. I never do that. I don't understand. It was here yesterday when I shaved Mr. Cullen. Somebody must've taken it."

"Well," the third barber said, "it wasn't me."

"May we see your razors?" I asked the other barbers.

They opened their boxes without protest. Both contained a Wostenholm with an ivory handle similar to the one found under Miss Dugan.

I turned to Richard, "Did your blade have an ivory handle?"

"Yes, sir."

"Do you own a typewriter?" I asked.

"What? A typewriter? No."

"Did Miss Dugan show you a note before she left you?"

"A note?" Richard said, more perplexed than ever. "What're you talking about? I don't believe this is happening. I never saw any note. I don't own a typewriter. Where's my razor?"

"I'm sorry, sir, but you'll have to come with us."

"What? *Why?*"

"I'm placing you under arrest for the murder of Miss Katie Dugan."

"Me?" Richard said, his arms flaring. His spectacles nearly slipped off his face. "No! I didn't do it! You're insane!"

"Miss Dugan was murdered by a Wostenholm with an ivory handle," I said. "The same type of razor that is now missing from your station and in our possession." I picked up the mahogany box. "If the razor we have fits this case, it must be yours."

"But I didn't do it! I loved Katie. I'd never do such a thing. Someone must've come in here and stolen my razor."

"How easy would it be for someone to do that?"

"Very easy. We're only busy in the morning. The rest of the day, if there aren't any customers, we wander around the hotel, get something to eat or take walks outside. Anyone can come in here then and take something."

Adelia stated the obvious. "But they took something from *you*."

"Right. Don't you see? Someone's trying to put Katie's murder on me. You're playing right into their plan by arresting me. And think about it. If I had killed Katie with a razor, wouldn't I have blood on my clothes when I woke this morning? I didn't. I went home at first light and gave my clothes to Mrs. Tesler. She's my landlady. She can tell you. Her boardinghouse is on Fourth Street, at Washington. You can't miss it. My friend Mr. Ferrell can speak for me too."

"I'm inclined to believe you, sir," I said, "but until we can confirm your alibi, I'm placing you in custody."

"Well, you're making a terrible mistake. I didn't do it."

"Please, sir, come along peacefully."

I did not handcuff Mr. Riley because he seemed harmless and we only had to travel a half block to City Hall. However, after we left the hotel through a rear door and headed north on King Street I could've used a muzzle on Richard's mouth. The barber stressed his innocence loud and clear to every citizen we passed. "I didn't do it. Innocent man here. I'm being arrested for something I didn't do. They'll probably torture me and claim I confessed." Naturally, Richard got the attention he wanted. Citizens stopped and looked. Fortunately, most of them recognized me and knew my profession so they didn't interfere.

Officer Hinder placed Mr. Riley in one of City Hall's two basement jail cells. The ten-by-ten foot lockup had a hard earthen floor, a wooden bed frame with slats and a chamber pot. The cells usually held drunks and vagrants, so a well-dressed barber was certainly an unusual sight.

"It stinks down here," Richard said from the other side of the iron bars. I agreed. It did have a dank and earthy smell. "If I catch pneumonia I'm filing a lawsuit against you and Detective Bern and the entire city."

"Oh," I said as Officer Hinder left us, "you won't be here long enough to catch pneumonia."

"Why's that?"

"Because we're going to torture you into a confession," I said with a smile.

"I have no doubt that you will. That's why I said it."

"Try and relax, sir. Once we confirm your alibi, you'll be released."

"You better be telling the truth. I don't have enough money to bribe my way out."

I cringed. Yes, there was plenty of corruption and an out-of-control patronage system in city government, but I hated it when somebody unfairly included me in with the bad. Citizens could trust me. "I'm a man of my word, Mr. Riley. As soon as Detective Bern and I confirm your alibi, you'll be out of here. If you've lied to us, then get ready to stay for a while."

Adelia and I climbed the stairs to the second floor. She said, "He's right, you know."

"What do you mean?"

"We're playing right into Mr. Stout's plan by arresting Mr. Riley."

"First, we don't know that Mr. Stout's guilty. And holding Mr. Riley until we confirm his alibi is just a precaution. This way I know where he is."

We said hello to Molly, and then informed Chief Francis about the arrest of Mr. Riley.

"Great job, you two," Chief said from behind his desk. "You wrapped that up fast."

"Don't celebrate yet. We're not sure he did it. He has an alibi. We're on our way to verify it right now, so we'll let you know."

"Is it a *good* alibi?" Chief asked, stroking his chin hair.

"It appears so."

"Oh," Chief said, disappointed. "Do you have other suspects?"

"One other," I replied. "You said I could use whatever manpower I needed. I need someone to follow a gentleman named Mr. Albert Stout."

Chief nodded. "I'll assign Officer Frank Swenson. He's new and eager."

"Have him report to me as soon as possible."

"I will. Good luck. I know the *two* of you will solve this in no time."

Adelia actually smiled at being included, but if Chief Francis hoped to get on her good side, he still had plenty of work to do.

CHAPTER 16

Before Adelia and I checked on Richard's alibi, we crossed Market Street and caused quite a stir when we entered the Rat's Nest. Never had a place been more appropriately named. Adelia's first reaction was to almost vomit at the stench caused by the numerous cigar, cigarette and pipe smoking that went on among the lowly journalists. Even with a few windows open, a cloud of smoke floated just beneath the ceiling. That smell was coupled with beer. Not only were the men drinking while seated on chairs or at tables, but so much beer and stronger spirits had been spilled over the years that it had absorbed into the planking. As for the reporters — except for Casey — they weren't the best of citizens. Most of them would sell their mother for the right price. They generally had minimal education and wore a rag-tag collection of moth-eaten suits and sack pants, or homespun clothing, and they usually went unshaven for days. Some smelled as if they hadn't bathed in weeks.

Adelia and I left the front door open to cast more light on the interior and to announce our presence. Upon seeing us, Casey and his fellow journalists shot out of their chairs, pulled out their little notebooks and practically fell over each other to hear what we had to say. I told them the name of the victim and her parents. Some were too drunk to write it down properly. I summarized Miss Dugan's manner of death, the location of the crime, and asked for the public's help in solving the case. The journalists then bombarded the two of us with questions, mostly about suspects — did we arrest anyone? — and possible motives. We said nothing more on the subject. I did not want Mr. Riley or Mr. Stout's names publicized when the gentlemen might be innocent.

Back outside on the sidewalk, Adelia took a big refreshing breath. "Don't ever take me in there again. I'm very sensitive to smells. How can you stand it?"

I laughed. "I guess my nose isn't as good as yours." I then caught sight of the red brougham parked in front of the Clayton House. My eyes weren't the best, but from my half-block distance it appeared to be the same top-hat wearing driver. I made a gesture with my head toward the hotel. "I wonder."

"Wonder what?" Adelia said. I gestured with my head again and she glanced down the street. "There's that coach again."

"Exactly. It was at the courthouse before we were. It rode by after we interviewed the Dugans. Now it's at the Clayton *after* we were there. I suspect we're being followed."

Adelia sounded nervous. "Really? Why?"

"I think whoever killed Katie probably has money and influence and he can't risk being exposed. Such a person will be anxious to know what we know and when we know it, and he'll probably step in to stop us if he feels we're getting too close. Please be alert and aware of your surroundings at all times."

"Who do you think is following us?"

I shrugged. "I don't know, but it's a little unnerving."

"You? You're nervous?"

"Of course. I don't like the idea of somebody watching us."

"But if they *are* watching us, they're not keeping it a secret. So do you really think they're a threat?"

"I don't know. That's the other troubling thing about this. Whoever they are, they're not shy about letting us know they're in the vicinity. I earlier saw the outline of a man's head inside."

"*Ja,*" Adelia said, excited. "It looked like a man's head. Shouldn't we tell the Chief and ask him to assign some officers to accompany us?"

"We don't have the manpower for personal bodyguards. And we assume the risk when we joined the police department." And deep down, I didn't trust Chief Francis. He was a political appointee. Therefore, he owed allegiance to the businessmen and ward leaders of Wilmington and not to his officers. "I don't mean to scare you, but I thought watching your back went without saying."

A small group of men and women walked by, so Adelia whispered, "*Ja,* you're right. But remember, I only had a desk job before, looking over financial ledgers and trying to catch embezzlers. I've never worked outside, chasing down murder suspects, so I guess I wasn't thinking about it."

"Well," I said in the most comforting voice I could muster, "please don't worry."

Adelia's resentment ignited. She pulled out her derringer as if to remind me that, "I don't need a *man* to protect me."

I put my hands up in a mock surrender. "I believe you. However, as a gentleman, I won't be comfortable letting you fend for yourself."

Adelia put the gun back her pocket and then dropped the tough suffragette exterior. "What about at night? I'll be alone then."

That was true. As someone who usually worked cases without a partner, I never had to concern myself with another officer's safety. On the few occasions where I was assigned to work with McDonald, well, McDonald was a man and expected to take care of himself.

"If you don't mind, I will sleep by your front door."

Adelia's eyes went wide. "Oh, I can't have a man at my place. Mrs. Tenny, my landlady, will throw me out."

"Even if I tell her I'm there for your protection?"

Adelia shook her head. "That won't matter. She already told me when I rented the room that she's very suspicious of men and won't believe any story they tell her."

"Then stay at my house," I said. "I know it won't look proper to a great many people, especially my neighbors, but I'll explain it's for your own protection. I have extra rooms. I stay downstairs anyway and you can have upstairs."

Adelia stared at me with those blue eyes, a look that showed her uncertainty about my offer and her curiosity about my motivation. Could she trust me? How many men had crossed her path and betrayed her trust? She then backed away and spoke in a frustrated tone. "Oh, I can't think about this now. I'll think about it later. Let's go confirm Mr. Riley's alibi."

CHAPTER 17

And so we did. Adelia and I retrieved our bicycles and rode six blocks to Mrs. Tesler's Boardinghouse at Fourth and Washington. Richard was right. We couldn't miss it. The white house had an odd, triangular design with a porch around the entire first floor. The property was surrounded by a four-foot-high wrought iron fence. A sign by the gate read: MRS. TESLER'S DIVINE HOME FOR SINGLE MEN.

Adelia and I left our bicycles on the front lawn and stepped up to the entrance. I used the doorknocker. Shortly thereafter, a short, pear-shaped woman with gray hair answered. She wore an old cotton dress with a floral print that had frayed sleeves, and around her neck were a couple of beaded necklaces of little value. "Oh, hello," she said with a beaming smile, but her blue-gray eyes looked tired and glazed over by what I suspected was an alcoholic haze. She also had too much powder on her face, like someone desperate to cover the wrinkles. "I'm sorry, I don't rent to couples."

I said, "Oh, no, ma'am. We're not looking to rent. I assume you're Mrs. Tesler. I'm Detective Drummond and this is Detective Bern."

"Oh, go on. There ain't no such thing as a woman detective."

Adelia sighed in disgust. "If you read newspapers, you'd know that I'm real. We're investigating the murder of Miss Katie Dugan that took place last night. May we come in and ask you a few questions about one of your tenants?"

Mrs. Tesler looked Adelia up and down suspiciously. It was only then that I noticed the head of a cane held between the small fingers of the landlady's right hand. "Oh, dear," she said, practically swooning, "a murder, that's very upsetting. And you suspect one of my tenants?" She stepped back. "You must be mistaken. I only rent to the finest of gentlemen. But if you insist on seeing me, then please come into the parlor."

Adelia and I stepped into the vestibule and then followed the slow-moving Mrs. Tesler to a bright room off the central hall. The red curtains on either side of two tall and narrow windows were tied back, allowing in daylight that revealed a threadbare sofa and two high-back chairs arranged on an old carpet. Editions of *Harper's Magazine* and *Collier's* were displayed on a dusty table.

"Can I get you something to drink?" Mrs. Tesler said, leaning on her cane with both hands. "Would you like some tea?"

We both shook our heads and declined her offer.

"Please sit," Mrs. Tesler said, gesturing at the sofa. Adelia and I obeyed. The landlady sat with some difficulty in a chair opposite. She laid the cane next to her, folded her hands and placed them in her lap, striking a regal pose and then speaking in a formal tone. "Now why would you suspect one of my tenants of something as ghastly as murder? I run a respectable boardinghouse."

"I'm sure you do, ma'am," I said. "One of your tenants, Mr. Richard Riley, was at the Sacred Heart Fair the last two nights with Miss Dugan. Well, the young lady was killed sometime around midnight last night. We have Mr. Riley in custody, but he has an alibi. We're here to confirm it."

Mrs. Tesler released a dainty laugh. "That's absurd, sir. He's no murderer."

"Yes, ma'am. Did you know Miss Dugan?"

"No, sir," Mrs. Tesler replied with her nose high. She continued to speak in a formal voice, appearing to behave more sophisticated than she actually was. "We were never properly introduced. Mr. Riley talked about Miss Dugan often, and always in a radiant manner. He loved her. He wanted to marry her. And he's a perfect gentleman, sir, just perfect. No vices. He pays his eight-dollars a month on time. He helps me with the upkeep of this place, which is no easy task. Ever since my dearly-departed husband left it to me, it's been a struggle. Most of my tenants just come and go like I'm not here. Not Mr. Riley. He's been like a son to me. He wouldn't harm anyone."

Adelia took out her notepad and pencil and asked, "How many tenants do you have?"

"Six, counting Mr. Riley. They're all hard working, respectable men currently at their jobs and doing very well."

"Did Mr. Riley tell you he was taking Miss Dugan to the fair?" I said.

"Yes, he did. Like you said, they went last night and the night before. But last night," she leaned in closer and whispered, "if it's not impolite to say so, I think he was going to propose marriage."

"What makes you think that?" Adelia said.

Mrs. Tesler sat back and grinned like she knew a big secret. "An old lady like me can tell such things. Oh, I had such high hopes for him. I would've hated to lose him as a boarder. But sadly," her voice trailed off.

"Did Mr. Riley give you clothes to wash this morning?" I said.

She nodded. "He did."

"Was there anything unusual about them?"

"Unusual?" she said, her eyebrows raised. "No, sir. Just that they were badly wrinkled, like he had slept in them. He said he had, spending the night at a friend's house."

"No stains of any kind?"

"No, sir. His clothes were wrinkled, nothing more."

Adelia asked, "Where are the clothes he asked you to wash?"

"Hanging on a line in the backyard. They should be dry."

"So if there had been any blood on them, it's too late to see."

Mrs. Tesler folded her arms across her chest. "Blood? Dear God, Detective Whatever-your-name-is, are you accusing me of lying for Mr. Riley?" She pointed a finger at Adelia. "I told you there was nothing unusual about his clothes except that they were wrinkled. Had there been blood on them, then by God I would've mentioned it. No matter how much I like Mr. Riley, I won't have a murderer under my roof."

I said, "We meant no offense. We need to be thorough and I understand that some of our questions may sound accusatory. They're not meant that way."

"Yes," Adelia said, "I meant no harm."

Mrs. Tesler nodded, folded her hands again and placed them in her lap. "That's better."

"May we have a look at Mr. Riley's room?" I said.

"His room?" Mrs. Tesler said, looking down her nose. "What on earth for?"

"Please."

"There's nothing in there but a bed and dresser and his clothes. He lives very simply."

"Nevertheless. May we have a look?"

Mrs. Tesler shrugged, and started to get up. I put a hand under her arm to assist her to her feet. She took hold of her cane and then led us upstairs to a rear bedroom. "I'm sure he'll be terribly angry with me for this."

Adelia and I searched Mr. Riley's room, which was exactly as the landlady had described. He had a bed with a blue cover and pillow, a five-drawer dresser with an oil lamp on top and an oak armoire. The drawers contained only a few undergarments, some socks, shaving supplies and a comb. The armoire had a couple suits, shirts and pants.

"Plain and simple," I said, closing the armoire.

"I told you that," Mrs. Tesler said at the doorway.

Adelia opened the single drawer to Richard's nightstand and pulled out four books. "Interesting, *The Works of Edgar Allan Poe* by John Henry Ingram."

CHAPTER 18

Adelia flipped through the pages of the four books and found underlined and circled passages in some of Poe's short stories and poems. I have never read Poe, but at least knew he was an author of fictional stories that leaned toward the macabre.

"Did you know Mr. Riley liked to read Poe?" Adelia asked Mrs. Tesler.

She shrugged. "No, I did not, but so what? Plenty of people read Poe. I don't. His writings are too strange. Now, are you convinced that Mr. Riley's innocent?"

"We are," I said to appease the landlady, but also because I believed it. Until I had solid evidence, much of my work as a detective was based on hunches, speculation and a gut feeling about something or someone. Richard Riley hadn't struck me as a killer. Nevertheless, until Adelia and I solved the case we had to keep Mr. Riley in our thoughts. Sometimes hunches and gut feelings were wrong.

"I'm glad to hear it," Mrs. Tesler said. She pointed a finger at me. "I'll testify in court if I have to. So please release him right away."

I handed her my calling card. "Yes, ma'am. Thank you for your time."

Mrs. Tesler, however, wasn't through with Adelia. She blocked the doorway and looked at Detective Bern with a condescending expression on her face and spoke in a rude manner. "In all sincerity, Miss, why would a woman be a detective? Are you perverted?"

"What? I beg your pardon."

"Do you get your excitement from other people's misfortunes? Why would a woman burden herself with the horrors of the world unless she has some strange deficiency of the brain?"

"Why would a woman just stay home and raise children, and then be left alone as a widow forced to rent rooms to single men? Why only single men? Are *you* perverted?"

Mrs. Tesler revealed a fake smile. "My dear, it's a woman's job to marry and raise a family and then face whatever life brings."

"Well," Adelia said, pointing at herself, "it's not *this* woman's job. Stand aside."

Mrs. Tesler and Adelia had an intense staring contest that seemed to last a couple minutes, but was actually only a few seconds. And it was the landlady who blinked first. Mrs. Tesler stepped into the hallway. Adelia hurried past her and headed downstairs.

"She's rather odd, isn't she?" Mrs. Tesler said, acting like she and I were co-conspirators.

"Excuse me, ma'am," I said just to get out of there. "Goodbye."

I hurried downstairs. The front door was open. Adelia was already on her bicycle and waiting for me by the gate. She appeared mad enough to hit something and I wouldn't blame her. I then got a lesson in how difficult it was for Adelia to be Adelia.

"I expect men like Chief Francis to treat me rudely," she said when I reached her. "I expect all men to treat me rudely because they don't know what to do with an independent woman. They've never met one. They have no experience. They've been raised to treat women as weak and stupid. It's all they know. So maybe I can understand how men act around me.   But to get such treatment from another woman is astonishing." Her face was red and I saw the veins in her neck.

"You'd think women would want to emulate me," she continued, "or at least support me and encourage me. Don't they realize I'm trying to elevate our place in society? Don't they realize I'm trying to get men to treat us better? Can't they see that I'm an example of what a woman can achieve? I'm saying to every woman that we can have *more*!"

"Reformers agree with you." It was all I could think to say. I didn't know how to calm her down, or if I should even try. "Change is difficult, Adelia, and it takes time. People are slow to accept new things."

She stared at me for a long moment. She took a deep breath and released it slowly. "Thank you for calling me Adelia."

CHAPTER 19

Even though Mrs. Tesler's testimony was enough to clear Mr. Riley, we still wanted to confirm Richard's portion of the story that involved his friend Milton Farrell. We learned from Milton's landlady that the young man wasn't home, but should be clerking at the Stuart General Store around the corner at Fourth and Monroe. The business occupied the first floor of a four-level tenement.

We left our bicycles against the building and stepped inside. A bell jingled upon our entrance. My nose picked up a collection of wonderful smells from the store's vast inventory. Bags of coffee beans, rice, sugar and salt were stacked separately on the floor. There was a barrel of pickles and one of apples near a pot-bellied stove, and a keg of tobacco. Glass display cabinets contained a variety of cheeses, cakes and pies. On top of the cabinets were a stockpile of soaps, and rolls of wool, calico and denim. Shelves along the walls were well stocked with boxed, jarred and canned goods of all sorts.

Two young gentlemen, one with blond hair and the other black, wore dirty white smocks and were busy assisting female customers who carried wicker baskets to hold their purchases. When I could interrupt one of them, I introduced myself and Adelia and asked for Mr. Ferrell.

"That's me," the blond said.

Adelia and I talked to the skinny young man out on the sidewalk and beneath a red and white striped awning.

"You're both detectives?" Mr. Farrell asked next to our bicycles. "What's this about?"

I told him the reason for the visit. Mr. Farrell reacted to the word murder by putting both hands over his mouth. "Mr. Riley claims he spent last night at your place. Can you confirm that?"

Mr. Farrell uncovered his mouth and spoke with enthusiasm. "Oh, yes, sir, yes, sir, of course I can. Richard most definitely slept at my place."

"What time did he arrive?"

"A little before midnight. He pounded on my door, woke me up."

"Was he sober?"

Mr. Farrell chuckled. "He smelled like beer. He was all right, though, in complete control of himself, but angry. He said Katie left him at the fair, and that he should stop wasting his time with her, that she was never going to marry him."

"Has he spent the night at your apartment before?" Adelia asked.

"A couple of times."

"Have you been friends for very long?"

Mr. Farrell shook his head. "Our fathers are friends. So that's how we know each other. The four of us go fishing on the Brandywine sometimes." He chuckled. "Richard even introduced me to his cousin hoping I might be interested in her, but I'm not ready for that."

"Did Mr. Riley have any blood on him?" Adelia asked.

"Blood?" Mr. Farrell sighed in horror. "Good God, no."

I asked, "How did he act this morning?"

"I didn't see him this morning. When I woke, he was already gone."

I looked at Adelia. She had no further questions. As expected, it was a short interview. "Thank you." I handed the clerk my calling card. "I think we have what we need. Don't hesitate to contact me if you think of anything that might help us."

"Yes, sir. I will, sir, miss. You must know Richard didn't do it."

"Thank you again for your time."

After Mr. Farrell returned to the store, Adelia mounted her Colombian. "I guess we have to release Mr. Riley."

"Yes, You can't argue against those testimonies. They seemed fully sincere."

"But don't you think it's interesting," Adelia said, now using her own gut feelings, "how quickly Mr. Riley pointed out his alibis? Right after we accused him of killing Miss Dugan, he thought clearly enough to tell us about the lack of blood on his clothes and sleeping at his friend's place. He was getting arrested for murder. Wouldn't most people be too upset to think so fast and to think so clearly?"

"What's your point?"

"Well, maybe Mr. Riley killed her, but hid a change of clothes at the Bush estate. He might've known about the other suitor and knew the rendezvous point. So when Katie left him, maybe he spent time at the shooting gallery, maybe he didn't. He then hurries to the Bush estate. He waits. He kills Katie when he gets the chance, puts on fresh clothes and tosses the bloody ones into the river."

"I guess it's possible, but I'm skeptical. He would've kept the razor, cleaned it and put it back in its box. And I don't think he had enough time to amuse himself at the shooting gallery, and then travel from the fair out to Sycamore and DuPont, kill Miss Dugan, change clothes and get to his friend's place by midnight. Remember the coroner thinks Miss Dugan was killed between midnight and two. Richard was at his friend's place around midnight. Of course, Dr. Miles could be wrong about the time of death. It's not an exact science. We'll need to confirm with Mr. Beeson what time he saw Katie in front of his butcher shop. Then when we visit the fair tonight, we'll talk to whoever runs the shooting gallery and whoever we can talk to at the Kickapoo Medicine Show. Hopefully, somebody can confirm Richard's whereabouts, and somebody at the medicine show will remember selling a bottle of their medicine to a young lady in a green dress. Maybe Katie said something to them that'll prove useful."

"We're going to the fair?" Adelia said, putting her hands together and showing some childish excitement.

"Of course we are. But we still have interviews to conduct."

CHAPTER 20

George Beeson's storefront was typical of most butchers in the city. Fresh cuts of beef and ham were displayed in the window, while complete carcasses of chicken, rabbit and squirrels hung outside beneath a red and white stripped awning. A couple of hungry dogs salivated by the Dutch doors.

Adelia and I hopped off our bicycles, both a little winded from the eight-block ride, and we leaned them against the side of the building. Inside, the smell of beef blended with the aroma of sawdust that covered the floor behind the counter to capture any splattered blood. Two butchers, both heavy-set gentlemen and sweating, wore red-stained white smocks over their cotton work clothes. They stood behind a counter chopping meat against well-worn butcher's blocks to fill orders for three lady customers. The countertop also had scales to weigh purchases, plenty of knives and cleavers, and rolls of white paper. Under the counter, inside glass cases were various cuts of steak, liver, tongue, ham, chicken, pork, rabbit and sausages. When I could, I interrupted the proceedings and asked to speak privately with George Beeson.

"I'm Mr. Beeson," the heavier-looking man said. George had a full head of black hair and a round face with sagging cheeks. He removed his smock, used it to wipe his forehead and then stepped out from behind the counter. "I need to leave, so I'll have my assistant wait on you and your wife after he finishes with Mrs. Kane."

"I am *not* his wife," Adelia said in an irritated tone while taking out her notebook.

I sighed, wishing Adelia would be less sensitive. People meant no harm when they confused us with a married couple. After all, a man and woman out together were expected to be spouses.

Mr. Beeson glared at Adelia. "Excuse me, then, whoever you are. I'm on my way to comfort a family who has received some tragic news."

"Yes, sir," I said in a whisper, "that's why we're here. I'm Detective Drummond. This is Detective Bern. We're investigating the murder of Miss Dugan. May we speak outside?"

Mr. Beeson's eyes watered and his lower lip quivered. "Very well," he said in a soft voice. Once on the sidewalk, he chased away the dogs and used the smock to wipe his face again. "Oh, it's so unbelievable. It's just horrible, isn't it? I just saw Katie last night. She was so happy, so happy. I ask you, sir, what kind of a world is it when a young lady can't walk the streets?"

"Can you tell us about your encounter with her last night?" I asked while Adelia took notes.

"I was closing the store."

"What time was that?"

"At nine," Mr. Beeson said. "I always close at nine."

"Then what?"

"I was on my way to play cards with Mr. Dugan. I locked the door to my business and then heard the loud c*lang, clang, clang* of a trolley's bell. I looked toward the street and there was Katie, right there." He pointed. "She was face to face with the bright headlight of an approaching streetcar. My heart jumped into my throat, I can tell you. I thought she was about to get run over. But she managed to pull up her skirt and run out of the way. The driver cussed at her. I yelled at her to be more careful. I asked her why she was in the middle of the road. She didn't answer me. Instead, she came over and kissed me on the cheek. I was surprised, I can tell you. She never liked me. She always said I smelled of raw meat, blood and cigarette smoke, and that I only talked about livers, hearts and kidneys."

"Did you find out why she was in the middle of the road?"

"She was reading something in her hand, so she wasn't paying any attention. I asked her what the note said. She didn't answer. She kissed me again. I asked her why she was so happy. Did she have a date? But I meant it as a joke. She winked and said, 'I'll never tell.'"

"Before you saw her, Miss Dugan attended the Sacred Heart Fair with Mr. Richard Riley. Do you know him?"

"I met him a couple times at the Dugan house."

"But Mr. Riley wasn't with her when you saw her?"

"No, sir. She was alone, but out-right happy, like I'd never seen her before."

"Like a woman in love?" Adelia said.

"Yes, ma'am. She acted exactly like that."

Adelia corrected him. "It's *miss* or Detective, not ma'am."

Mr. Beeson rolled his eyes and moaned.

I quickly asked my next question to alleviate the tension I felt between Adelia and the butcher. "Are you a *good* friend of the family?"

"Yes, sir, I've known the Dugans for years and I visit them from time to time. I play poker with Mr. Dugan and a couple of his friends. That's what we did last night."

"Was it normal to play cards on a Wednesday night?"

Mr. Beeson frowned. "No, sir. I questioned James when he called me, but he said he had a couple friends in town from Dover that wanted a game."

"How late did you play?"

"Until around one."

"Did Mr. or Mrs. Dugan express any concern about their daughter being out so late?"

"They mentioned it, but Katie's been out late before. Besides, they just figured she was having a good time at the fair. James hoped so, although Emily doubted it because Katie didn't see Mr. Riley as a potential husband. Emily thought Katie was wasting her time going out with Mr. Riley when she could've been seeing other men with better prospects."

"And Mr. Riley's not Catholic."

"Yes, sir. That was a matter of contention as well."

"We've learned that Katie liked the theatre. Do you know who she attended shows with?"

"I heard about that too, sir." George wiped his face again. "But no, can't say that Mr. or Mrs. Dugan knew who these people were. Katie refused to tell them their names. I got the impression she wanted to protect them from her parents."

Adelia asked, "If Mrs. Dugan thought Katie was wasting her time with Mr. Riley, did she mention any other gentleman she felt would be a better match?"

Excellent question, I thought.

Mr. Beeson replied, "No, eh, miss. I think Emily was just wishing out loud. I don't think Katie had any other suitors."

"After you played cards, then what did you do?" I asked.

"Went home to bed. Is there anything else? I'd really like to get to my friend's house and provide whatever comfort I can."

"Yes, sir," Adelia said. "Was it normal for Katie to be in this part of town alone?"

"Yes, miss, her house is only three blocks from here."

"Oh, forgive me. I'm new to Wilmington and still learning the streets. Have you seen her walk by your shop before, going in the direction she was going?"

"Well," the butcher pondered this query, "I can't say that I have. She's come alone to my shop before, but I'd have to say that was the first time I ever saw her pass by without coming in."

"All right," Adelia said, finishing up her notes. "Thank you."

"Thank you for your time," I said, giving Mr. Beeson my calling card.

After George left us, I looked at my partner. I could tell by the smirk on her face that she had the same thought I did.

"Mr. Beeson closes his shop at nine."

"Richard said Katie left him around ten," Adelia said.

"Richard either made an honest mistake about the time."

"Or he lied."

CHAPTER 21

Seeing and smelling all those meats at Mr. Beeson's butcher shop made us realize we hadn't eaten anything except a peach since our own breakfast. So we stopped at a small café on Broom Street that I liked operated by a large German man named Henkel who believed all food should be boiled. He arrived in the United States with his parents when he was twelve, so he had a thick accent when speaking English. As he escorted us to a window-side table, Adelia asked him if he missed his homeland.

Henkel grinned, an expression that revealed a missing tooth. He spoke in a deep baritone. "Not anymore. Meeting you, beautiful lady, has restored my light."

I laughed as I sat. "I never knew you could be poetic."

"Hey," he said with another grin, "I'm more than just a cook."

Henkel left for the kitchen. A barmaid who couldn't have been more than ten or eleven years old arrived with a one page menu. I ordered a beer.

"Vodka," Adelia said, seated across from me. The barmaid looked panicked because women never ordered liquor, but Adelia wasn't serious. She laughed. "No, my dear, just a glass of water, please."

"Do you like fish?" I asked after the server departed.

"I love fish. Any food from the sea."

"Good, then try the sturgeon. It's caught right out here in the Delaware." I lit a cigar and enjoyed a good, long drag that was as enjoyable as the tobacco's aroma. "Umm, that's good."

"Did you always smoke cigars?"

"I tried cigarettes in college. I was still a naïve farm boy, and it was my first time away from home, so I was willing to try anything to look older." I laughed. "Then I tried chewing tobacco right after I entered the war. But that didn't appeal to me. My fellow volunteers then introduced me to pipes as a way to socialize around camp, to relax and think. And believe me, there was plenty of time to think. When we weren't drilling or fighting, army life was extremely tedious and boring. I didn't try cigars until I earned a decent living."

"So you went to college? Which one did you attend, and for how long?"

"Yes, I attended college," I replied, almost embarrassed to admit it, "but only for a year. My father saw that I was an inquisitive boy, interested in the world around me, not just the natural world, but anything related to the past. So during the winter months he made me attend Brandywine Academy. I did well too, which surprised me. I liked being outside, not stuck inside a school, so I never thought I'd be good at book-learning. He then had this crazy idea that I should attend college and become a history professor. 'Ain't no future in being a farmer,' he said. 'Be a gentleman.' So I attended Delaware College in Newark. It's about twelve miles south of here."

Adelia frowned. "Only one year? What happened?"

I shrugged. "I met Jane working as a secretary at the college. Then the war broke out. I enlisted. Jane and I got married. I left for the fighting with other young men who believed in the glory of the battlefield and the righteousness of our cause." I chuckled, recalling my patriotic fervor for the Union and my foolish determination to defeat the rebs single-handedly. "I don't regret my decision, but after my first battle I questioned my sanity."

The barmaid returned and served Adelia a dirty glass of water and me a mug of beer that tasted as if the lager had been brewed in Henkel's bathtub.

I made a face and yelled loud enough so that the proprietor heard me in the kitchen. "I thought Germans knew how to ferment grain."

"You want better," Henkel shouted back, "go to Hartmann and Fehrenbach."

"I will!" I said with a laugh. Then to Adelia, "Hartmann and Fehrenbach, and Joseph Stoeckle's Diamond State are the top breweries in the city, both owned by Bavarians who know what they're doing."

"I heard that," Henkel yelled.

 Adelia and I ordered sturgeon.

She said, "I think you should've stayed in college and become that history professor. You would've been a great teacher."

I shook my head. "No. I made my choice and I can live with it. Besides, being a detective is like being a historian. A historian does his research and draws conclusions from the evidence collected and then writes about it. A detective looks for clues and forms conclusions from the evidence presented. They're very similar."

Since I had provided some personal background, I hoped my partner would do the same. I was anxious to learn more about this lady, yet still reluctant to ask her questions directly. I had to remain on her good side and not encourage the wrath of the suffragette, who seemed to come out around men of authority, or when people questioned her independence, or if they associated me as her husband. However, Adelia said nothing, so all conversation ceased and I sat there glancing at her and experiencing an awkward silence.

Through the window glass, I heard the clump, clump, clump of a striding horse and the sound of four coach wheels against the brick road. I looked out just in time to see the red brougham and the silhouetted head of a man seated inside. I never saw the driver, but I assumed it was the same coach we had spotted before. I didn't alert Adelia, wanting to spare her.

The barmaid returned and delivered a plate of boiled sturgeon to both of us. Adelia grabbed her fork and knife and appeared ready to tear into the fish, and then acted as if she suddenly lost her appetite, and sat back.

"What's wrong?"

"Nothing," she replied, sounding shameful.

"Then eat."

Adelia approached the plate carefully, almost as if she expected the fish to still be alive and possibly attack her. But once she cut a piece and ate it, she dropped the façade of propriety and tore into the meat. She ate like a ravenous dog and I worried she'd consume everything— even the bones — in a matter of seconds.

I let my fish get cold because I felt something more important was in front of me. "Why didn't you tell me you were so hungry? We could've stopped for something to eat earlier."

Adelia regained her poise, and in a very lady-like demeanor, dabbed her mouth with a cloth napkin. She looked directly at me. "There's no need to concern yourself about me, Detective Drummond. I eat when you eat. I'll sleep when you sleep."

"Stop acting so tough." Then in a compassionate voice, "You've known starvation, haven't you?"

Adelia's hid her face, afraid or ashamed to show weakness. "You see a lot, don't you, Detective Drummond?"

"You can call me David, remember? The way you ate that fish reminded me of when my regiment came across some starving Confederate soldiers. They surrendered in exchange for food. We didn't have much, just some cornbread, but they devoured it with the same look on their faces."

"I'm sorry."

"There's nothing to be sorry about. I went a couple of days without eating in the war, but that was the extent of my suffering. I was fortunate to grow up on a farm. We had a few years when draught or infestation ruined most of our crops, but we always had some eggs from our chickens and milk from our cows, as well as livestock to butcher."

Adelia nodded. "After my father died, my mother couldn't find work. We actually ate rats to survive. Then she....I went hungry again after I divorced my husband and nobody would hire me for anything."

"You started to say something about your mother. Your father died, and then your mother did what?"

Adelia drank some water. She took a deep breath, tried not to sob, but failed. "I've never told anyone this, and please don't repeat it. I still don't believe it happened. It's almost like a bad dream instead of reality. But my mother sold my sister and brother to a couple that didn't have children. I was fifteen. I ran away from home before she could sell me, and then lived on the streets. I never prostituted myself, but I certainly considered it, and men offered. Then I made the stupid decision to marry just to have a bed and food. Yet in many respects, Ian was a good man. He encouraged me to attend college, but the more I learned the more I resented being controlled. I attended Pinkerton after we divorced."

In my line of work, and from my experiences, I knew how poverty twisted the hearts and minds of human beings, causing them to do unimaginable things society wouldn't consider normal. I have seen people at their worst. So I was rarely surprised by anything I saw or heard. However, Adelia's revelation left me dumbfounded. "Your siblings were sold?"

Adelia nodded. "I have no idea where they are or if they're even alive. As for my mother, I don't care. I hope she's dead." She looked at me with wet eyes. "Please don't tell anyone."

I felt a strong urge to leave my chair and embrace her, to let Adelia cry on my shoulder. Then I questioned the motivation behind this feeling. Why did I want to take her into my arms? Was it because I was a kind gentleman helping a lady in distress? Or was something else happening to me? Had I become infatuated with this woman and longed to show it with a gentle embrace? Was my heart healing? "You have no reason to be embarrassed or ashamed. I won't tell anyone."

Adelia smiled. "Do you like me, Detective Drummond?"

I was taken aback by her question. Was Adelia so perceptive that she could read my thoughts? Was she experiencing the same feelings? "Pardon?"

Adelia gave a dismissive wave. "Oh, I don't mean as a man and woman, but as a person. I know I can be difficult to get along with. I was always different. I've always been too independent. As a girl I demanded that my parents send me to school. They thought I was the devil for wanting to be educated. But school was unpleasant. Home was unpleasant. So I retreated into my own world of books and developed a superior attitude that comes out sometimes. I thought, if people don't like me, then I won't like them. I didn't need them anyway. I could survive on my own. Yet Pinkerton only accepted me because a local newspaper forced them to. They set me up as a challenge, to prove to men that a woman could get through the training, even though Kate Warne came before me. So I ask you, David, do you like me as a person?"

I cut into my cold fish and leaned forward, "Yes, Adelia. I like you."

CHAPTER 22

After our meal, we rode a short distance to 505 Broom Street. Albert
Stout's Victorian home might've been grand in its day, but it currently
needed a loving hand. Some shingles were missing on the side of the
mansard roof. A few bricks had at some point fallen from atop the
chimney. Two of the second-floor windows had only one shutter.
There was a shallow wraparound porch with white columns where the
paint had peeled, exposing the wood to the elements. Shrubbery that
bordered the property hadn't been trimmed in some time, and a
sapling sprouted from the middle of one bush.

"Be careful," I said because the porch's floorboards sagged with
every step I took toward the front door.

A rotund woman in a blue woolen dress opened the door before
Adelia and I had a chance to use the doorknocker, an obvious indicator
that Albert telephoned his wife and prepared her for our visit. She
must've watched for us from a window, and since Adelia and I had
spent more time at lunch than I had expected, Mrs. Stout had plenty of
time to stew, and her face showed it. She wore an unwelcoming scowl,
a clear warning that our interview would be unpleasant.

I tried kindness. "Good afternoon, ma'am."

"No need for pleasantries," she said, putting a hand up and showing
me her fleshy palm. "I know who you are and why you're here. I
should send you away, but you'd only come back. So let's get this
over with, shall we? Come in."

Mrs. Stout invited us into the parlor. The curtains were closed,
restricting the amount of light in the room. A couple of chairs, a table
and a sofa were arranged near the fireplace, but nothing was displayed
on the mantel or on the wall above it. In fact, there were no paintings
or portraits, just bare walls. No book shelves. I had never been in a
more drab room in my life.

"I assume you're Mrs. Stout?" I said.

She folded her arms across her large bosom. "I am. So you suspect
my husband? That's ridiculous."

"May we sit?"

"No, I don't expect you to be here long."

"All right. Your husband denies any involvement in Miss Dugan's
murder. We're here to confirm his alibi for last night."

"Look detective, my husband's an idiot, a very mousy man, and a dozen other things, but he's no murderer."

"Well, we have to investigate all possible suspects."

"I know this is a delicate situation," Adelia said in a pleasant tone, trying to appease Mrs. Stout with a feminine voice. She removed her notebook and pencil. "We don't want to take up too much of your time, but whose idea was it to hire Katie?"

Mrs. Stout's chubby face grimaced. She released a deep and frustrating sigh. "If you must know, *that* was regrettably my idea. I brought that girl into the house. She wanted a job. I wanted this ghastly place to be clean."

"You're not happy here?"

She moaned. "Good God, no. There's only three people living here. We don't need such a big house, but Albert's parents left it to him, so we stay. The place gets so dirty so fast, and so blasted cold in winter. Everything's so old. Albert really can't afford it. My daughter is ashamed to bring suitors over because it's not presentable. I do what I can, but my old bones can't stand for very long."

"And yet you've chosen to stand through our interview."

"Look, miss, you're a guest in my house. I expect you to act accordingly."

"Then act like a hostess. How long have you and Mr. Stout been married?"

"A very *long* time," she said with a tired sigh. "Twenty-three years."

"Has he worked for the Warner Company all that time?"

"Yes. He started as a mail boy when he was sixteen. His father got him the job."

"How long did Katie work here?" I said.

"Katie worked for us just a couple months." She seemed totally bored. "But of course, you already know that from speaking with my husband. And you know why she left our employ." She closed her eyes for a moment. "Disgusting business. I was upstairs and I heard Katie protest. I entered the bedroom and found my husband pressed up against her. He had her face squeezed between his hands, forcing her lips to touch his. Oh, it was absolutely shameful, a man his age trying to take advantage of a young girl."

"I can imagine you were very angry and hurt." Adelia said.

"Yes, it was positively indecent."

"But you and your husband must've reconciled."

"We have an understanding."

"What does that mean?"

Mrs. Stout frowned. "It's personal, something between a wife and husband."

"Well, can you please elaborate?"

Mrs. Stout looked at Adelia with a condescending gaze. She might claim her husband wasn't a murderer, but Mrs. Stout looked capable of putting a knife in my partner. "We have separate bedrooms. We're not the first married couple to come to this arrangement and we won't be the last."

Adelia nodded. "Has your husband ever been violent?"

"He has struck me on occasion, usually when he's drunk."

"Then Mr. Stout could've gotten mad enough to kill?"

Mrs. Stout huffed. "Nonsense. Like I said, my husband's a mouse. He came home with me and our daughter after we attended the fair. We went to bed. He didn't kill that poor girl."

I asked, "Did you and your husband attend an event for Felix Darley at the Bush estate?"

"Yes."

She answered so quickly that I suspected she had been waiting for the question and had been instructed by her husband on how to reply.

I moved on. "What type of razor does your husband use?"

Mrs. Stout's eyebrows went up. "Razor? What an absurd question."

"Katie was killed with a razor. May I see your husband's razors?"

"Nonsense," Mrs. Stout said, waving a hand. "They're old and dull, just like him, too dull to even slice melted butter."

"Please."

Mrs. Stout stared for a long moment, then sighed. "If it'll get you out of my house quicker, follow me."

Because of her weight, the stairs were a slow and difficult climb. She took one step at a time, leaning heavily on the railing and not advancing to the next step until both feet were on the same level. When she reached the second floor, she bent forward and paused to catch her breath.

"That's his room," she said, pointing at the first room on the left.

Albert had an ordinary bed with wool blankets. An oil lamp and clock set on the nightstand. A chest high dresser had a large wash basin and pitcher on top. Next to them were four volumes on *The Works of Edgar Allan Poe* by John Henry Ingram.

CHAPTER 23

The volumes of Poe's writings were pinned between two porcelain book ends shaped like ravens. A framed lithograph of Mr. Poe's likeness hung on the wall next to an oval mirror. If Mr. Riley and Mr. Stout had never been formally introduced, then how did the two men both have the same volumes of literature? Had Katie presented them as a gift? Was there some other connection Adelia and I had yet to uncover?

"I see your husband enjoys reading Poe," I said as Mrs. Stout entered the room.

"Yes, my husband likes Poe because he seems to enjoy reading dark and morbid stories."

"Mr. Stout didn't seem dark and morbid when we met him," Adelia said. "Do you like Mr. Poe's writings?"

Mrs. Stout's eyes bulged and she leaned heavily on the door jamb. "Good God, no."

I noticed the binding on one book was loose and something was folded within the pages. I picked up the volume. A newspaper article fell out. It was from the *Delaware Ledger*, dated December 26, 1843. The headline read: MR. POE SPEAKS AT NEWARK ACADEMY.

"Where's that?" Adelia said, reading over my shoulder.

"It's on Main Street in Newark," I said. "The Academy is a boys' preparatory school that pre-dates the American Revolution and is part of Delaware College."

Adelia nodded. "Please read it aloud. I'm curious."

I did.

Mr. Poe granted the good people of this fair town a well-received lecture in the Academy's Oratory on the night of December 23. The audience filled every seat available, not only to listen to Mr. Poe, but to escape the shivering cold night. Two pot-bellied stoves tried their best to keep everyone warm. Mr. Poe is best described as a portly gentleman with uncombed black hair, sunken cheeks and an unruly moustache above what appeared to be a permanent frown. He wore a black overcoat with two buttons missing, and the rest of the buttons looked ready to pop, so the garment was obviously too tight and too small for his frame. After everyone exchanged a greeting of Happy Christmas, Mr. Poe looked about the room with round black eyes that appeared lifeless to this reporter. He then retrieved papers from beneath his overcoat and announced, 'My theme tonight is American Poetry.' For the next hour, Mr. Poe spoke in a voice the audience had troubling hearing, but his central theme was a criticism of American poets. He chastised them for not studying their craft, for failing to provoke vivid imagery and imagination in their pieces. Mr. Poe was especially hard on Reverend Rufus Griswold's book *Poets and Poetry in America.* He called it, 'A bit of trivial nonsense.' When Poe finished, he looked at the collected crowd and said, 'Thank you for attending my lecture tonight and tolerating my mild criticism.' The audience laughed, and then applauded before heading for the exit. I, your reporter, tried to get a personal interview with Mr. Poe, but he claimed to be exhausted and had an early train to catch for Philadelphia.

Mrs. Stout put her hands on her hips. "What does my husband's interest in Mr. Poe have to do with your investigation?"

I looked at Adelia, hoping to communicate with my eyes that she shouldn't say anything. She didn't. "Nothing, Mrs. Stout," I said. "We were just curious. May I look in his dresser drawers?"

"Good God," she said with an impatient wave. "Go ahead if you must."

The top drawer contained two non-descript straight razors, cologne, hair and moustache wax, a folded towel, a snuff box and twenty dollars. The other drawers only contained folded shirts and undergarments.

"Your husband has an impressive moustache," I said. "It must've taken him many years to acquire it."

"He's had a moustache as long as I've known him."

"How did you meet?" Adelia asked.

"We were introduced by a mutual friend."

"Does your husband frequent the Clayton House?" I asked.

"He speaks of it. Why?"

"What does he say about it?"

"It has a bar, doesn't it? What man doesn't go to a bar?"

"Has he ever received a shave and haircut at the hotel's barbershop?"

Mrs. Stout thought about it for a moment. "I don't know. He might've. He usually goes to Moore's Barbershop around Market and

Third since it's closer to work and cheaper."

"But he has gone inside the Clayton House?" I said.

"Yes, why does that matter?"

"Do you know a gentleman named Richard Riley?"

"No, the name is not familiar."

Adelia said, "How long has it been since you and your husband shared the same room?"

"So we're back to that subject, are we? Look, I didn't want any more children. We buried two babies. I don't ever want that pain again. And I'm too old."

"I understand," Adelia said. "Has Mr. Stout been unfaithful?"

The daggers returned to Mrs. Stout's eyes. "You really are impertinent."

"I know." Adelia's devilish smile made me grin. "Does your husband have a mistress?"

Mrs. Stout grinned sardonically. "He doesn't need a *mistress*."

"What do you mean?"

"Oh, don't be naïve. We wives know all about the *parlor houses* and where they are."

"Oh." It took only a second for her face to go from pale to crimson. "And you're all right with that?"

"I have to be. But it does infuriate me, though not for the reasons you think. He could be spending that money on making improvements to this house instead of spending it on some soiled dove."

"So his sharing a bed with a total stranger doesn't bother you?"

"What choice do I have? Divorce isn't permitted, especially for Catholics, and it's not practical. Divorced women end up on the street."

It was the first time since entering the house that I felt sympathy for Mrs. Stout. She had long ago compromised on her marriage and accepted the fact that to survive she'd defend her husband no matter what, and not from love and devotion, but desperation. If her husband went to jail, Mrs. Stout would lose her only source of income. Fear motivated her to protect Albert.

Adelia forged ahead on a subject polite society pretended didn't exist. "Do you know which house your husband frequents?"

Mrs. Stout's eyes went wide. "Really? You seriously asked me that?"

"I did," Adelia said without batting an eye. "Do you know which house your husband frequents?"

Mrs. Stout looked ready to vomit. "Why does that matter?"

"How do you know your husband didn't leave the house after you and your daughter retired to bed last night? You have separate bedrooms. Your husband could've gone out without you knowing about it. He could've murdered Miss Dugan. Or he could've visited a parlor house. We need to confirm his whereabouts around midnight."

Mrs. Stout groaned. She glanced at me as if she sought an ally against Adelia's invasive questions, but I agreed with my partner's reasoning. Mr. Stout could've left the house, followed Katie, or known where Katie would be, and killed her in a fit of rage with Mr. Riley's razor.

"If you must know, Albert takes comfort at Miss Mabel's on French Street, behind the Grand Union Hotel."

"Oh, all right," Adelia said, writing it down. "Thank you."

"Is there anything else, detectives?" Mrs. Stout said. "Your visit has left me exhausted."

"One more thing," Adelia said. "Is your daughter available to talk to us?"

"She is not. She's at Mrs. Hebb's School for Young Ladies learning secretarial skills that I hope she never needs. She's not plain. She can certainly attract a husband, but nobody sticks around long enough after they've seen this house. Is there anything else?"

Adelia looked at me. I shook my head. "Thank you. I think that's all."

Mrs. Stout had an easier time escorting us down the stairs and out the front door. I started to say goodbye, but Mrs. Stout clearly made her feelings known. "Good riddance to bad rubbish." She slammed the door.

"Well," I said, attempting humor, "that went better than I expected."

Adelia didn't laugh. "Was I too rough with her? Are you upset that I dominated the interview?"

"No, it shows you're gaining confidence. And it's all right to upset some people. After all, we're investigating a murder. We can't act like we're at the social club, but you need to know when to pry and when to hold back. Sometimes tactful is better, like with Mr. Warner. You offended him when I didn't think it was necessary. Fortunately, he didn't throw us out, which he could've done. It's really a matter of how to read people, psychology again. Mrs. Stout, for example, even though she acted upset was actually very willing to talk to us because she's lonely and hates her husband."

"That was my impression. Where should we go next?"

I smiled. "Miss Mabel's, of course"

"Oh, right," Adelia said with some hesitation. Then she had to justify the action to herself. "I suppose we have to go there if we're going to confirm Mr. Stout's whereabouts around midnight. It's all part of the investigation, right? So it shouldn't be sinful for us to go there because it's part of the job."

I patted her on the shoulder. "There's no need to be nervous, Adelia. If you don't want to go inside Miss Mabel's, I can conduct the interview alone."

Adelia blushed. "Nervous? I'm not nervous. It's just that I've never been to a brothel."

I feigned a cough. "Oh, well, me neither."

Adelia stared for moment, no doubt wondering if I had been truthful or not. Then her expression broke down and she burst out laughing.

CHAPTER 24

Adelia and I pedaled a few blocks south on Broom and then east on Front Street for another nine blocks. After we crossed Washington Street we entered the Warehouse District. Storage buildings of brick lined both sides of the gravel road in close proximity to the wharves on the Christina River and the depot for the Philadelphia, Wilmington, and Baltimore Railroad. Only the strongest of work horses had any value here, necessary to haul the freight wagons. And only the roughest of men were seen. These dirty, muscular and sweaty brutes practically broke their backs every day loading and unloading supplies necessary to keep the factories going. A few of these men paused in their work to stare at Detective Bern. A woman riding a bicycle was indeed a rare sight in this part of town.

Adelia and I arrived at the Philadelphia, Wilmington and Baltimore Train Station, which occupied the entire block between French, Walnut, Front and Waters Streets. The three-story depot resembled a Gothic castle, a unique architectural style for the city. A group of men and women waited on the south side of the station beneath an overhead shelter for an approaching northbound train, its large Baldwin locomotive blasted its whistle to warn people to stay clear of the tracks.

By day, this area of Wilmington was the noisiest spot in the city. Mixing with the sound of arriving and departing trains was the commotion caused by manufacturing railroad cars and steamships at Jackson and Sharp, Harlan and Hollingsworth, Pusey and Jones, and their assorted maintenance shops. The mammoth machinery and furnaces required to produce the steel and iron kept the noise level high and had numerous smokestacks spewing black from dawn into the night. The factories employed thousands of muscular men, both white and colored, Americans and immigrants, who went home each evening covered in sweat and grime.

"Wilmington has about 200 trains arriving and departing daily," I said as the latest locomotive pulled into the station. I spotted some journalists waiting for people to disembark. "Along with the Rat's Nest, Adelia, you'll see reporters loitering about the depot. They'll meet every train hoping to get a story from the crew, or from the passengers, because these people might've heard about something that happened down the line, and they also bring in newspapers from other cities."

Now that it was safe to proceed, Adelia and I walked our bicycles across two sets of rails. We stayed on French Street and crossed Second, passing the Grand Union Hotel, a guesthouse that had been "Grand" in its day, but now operated as a low-class boardinghouse with a German-owned bar on the first floor. Miss Mabel's establishment was another half-block up and in a set of row homes that appeared no different than any other group of homes in the city. There was no outward sign or advertisement to alert someone as to which door provided access to the parlor house, everyone just knew. Well, everyone except Adelia.

"Why does this trade exist?" she asked after we leaned our bicycles against the brick façade. "Help me understand. It's illegal, isn't it? Yet nothing is done about it."

"Yes, it's against the law. However, it's generally tolerated by citizens and ignored by the easily-bribed police. Chief Francis, like the police chiefs before him, doesn't enforce prostitution laws as long as the trade doesn't disturb the peace or injure someone. Occasionally, we do conduct a clean sweep of the parlor houses when some religious leader wants us to shut down 'palaces of sin' for the sake of people's souls, or when a man in public office wants to show his constituents that he's morally just. Raids are good for newspaper headlines, and might get a politician a few extra votes, but for the most part they're a waste of time and effort because there's a demand. When there's a demand, there's a supplier. It's no different than the opium trade. It's illegal, but people want it, especially rich people."

"So none of you men can control your baser instincts?" Adelia asked, descending to her self-righteous tone.

"In my opinion, prostitution flourishes even in little Wilmington because in our society the male pursuit of sex is lengthy. A woman is won by marriage and the wedding day comes after an extended courtship that could be as long as a year or more. If the lady is taken to bed before the exchange of vows, she's considered common and vulgar, a 'chippie,' and therefore not the right girl for a wife. After marriage, men in Mr. Stout's situation or those with similar reasons, seek prostitutes because it's quicker and easier than finding and hiding a mistress."

Adelia shook her head in disgust. "I guess I'll never understand. It's a wonder you men aren't all dead by the age of twenty. You're all out there looking for thrills, risking bodily injury, and possibly catching some horrible disease. Is it really worth it?"

I shrugged, not willing to debate Adelia when there was work to be done. "Let's save this argument for another time." I used the doorknocker to Mabel's business and the door opened immediately. A gray-haired Negro gentleman wearing a full black suit, white shirt and bow tie invited us into the foyer and closed the door. I introduced myself and my partner and stated the purpose of our visit. "May we see Miss Mabel?"

"Wait here while I fetch her." He disappeared into the back of the house.

Miss Mabel's business actually occupied two houses. The connecting wall between the homes had been removed, creating a large foyer and double parlor with matching crystal chandeliers and white marble fireplaces, each with a gold-trimmed mirror above the mantle. A woman in a nightgown sat next to a well-dressed gentleman on one of three red upholstered sofas. Another man relaxed on a divan with a lady who wore only a chemise. Three other gentlemen sat at the bar, drinking beer and smoking cigars while talking to a lady bartender who wore a tight corset that lifted and revealed almost all of her breasts. A heavily-framed painting of a female nude hung on the wall behind the bar. A piano sat idle.

I almost laughed at Adelia's reaction. Like most people when it came to sexual taboos, my partner couldn't help but be intrigued while acting appalled. Adelia blushed, embarrassed that I caught her staring, but her eyes soaked in the bawdy environment, remembering every sordid detail.

Adelia whispered. "Don't these men have jobs?"

"Yes," I said, keeping my voice down as well, "but they're able to get away. Are you offended by this place?"

"No, I suppose not, but no matter how desperate I was, I had the fortitude to resist this fallen occupation."

"Some feel they have no choice."

"Oh, they have a choice," Adelia said loud enough that those at the bar turned to look at us. "Or they'll have choices once they stop acting like slaves and make a place for themselves at society's table."

I whispered, "Face facts, detective. A woman with no husband or family to take care of her has very few options. You know that. Same goes for poor girls turned out by their families, or young immigrant girls who tried, but failed to find honest work in the mills or factories. So they end up on the streets. Miss Mabel's is a far safer and cleaner alternative than the houses on the east side of the depot in an area referred to as the 'Coast.' There, lawlessness is the rule, and even the police are afraid to go, especially after dark."

The Coast was home to the most miserable people in the city. These individuals, mostly destitute men, sought refuge each night in the dankest bars and brothels imaginable almost as a death wish. Patrons drank water-downed liquor that might be laced with any number of narcotics, meant to induce a sleepy haze that made the victim easily susceptible to pick-pockets, or roaming bands of brutes that just enjoyed beating people. Any new arrival to Wilmington was warned by train conductors not to wander over to the Coast. Even so, especially young men looking for a challenge to test their manhood, went anyway and usually regretted it.

"And it's all right with you that girls end up like this?" Adelia whispered. "I thought you were sympathetic to women."

"I am, but I can't change the world by myself. Regrettably, that's the way it is, and the way it's been for centuries."

"That doesn't mean it has to stay that way."

"Then join the reformers," I said, tired of fighting with her because I really couldn't defend what I was saying. "Miss Stanton's National Woman Suffrage Association could use you."

Adelia nodded. "Maybe I will."

Mabel, a tall and skinny brunette, with a pale face and large bags under her brown eyes, appeared in a flowery gown she might wear to a society function. "It's nice to see you again, Detective Drummond."

Adelia couldn't resist. "She *knows* you."

I feigned a cough. "I've investigated a few theft cases, nothing more."

"I read about you in the newspapers," Mabel said to Adelia. "It's a pleasure to meet you. Welcome to Wilmington. Are you a crusader against vice?"

"I'm not a crusader *yet*." Then she got down to business in a very direct manner. "First things first, Detective Drummond and I are investigating the murder of Katie Dugan that took place last night around midnight. We have a suspect in mind who is said to frequent your establishment and we're attempting to find out where he was at the time of the lady's death. Do you know Mr. Albert Stout? Would any of the girls know him?"

Mabel grinned. "Our clientele rarely give us their real name."

I described Mr. Stout physical size, and then added, "He has a big walrus-type moustache."

"Oh, yes." Mabel acted like she wanted to spit. "He's been here a few times."

"And you don't like him?"

"He's a baby. And he's perverted."

"How so?"

"He always wants the youngest girl I have. I never take in any girl under sixteen. He's asked me to bend the rules. He wants me to telephone him the minute I get a fourteen-or fifteen-year-old. I told him he'll never get that call from me."

"Does he have a favorite girl?"

"He did. He liked Jennifer, but she found herself a man willing to marry her and they moved to Boston about six months ago."

"How did he react to that?"

"He moaned about it for a while. Lately, he takes whoever's available."

"Was he here last night?"

"I don't believe so, but of course we don't keep records."

"Were *you* here last night?" Adelia asked.

"I was. I'm pretty certain he didn't show up. Is he claiming he was here?"

"No, ma'am.," I said. "He's claiming he was home after attending the Sacred Heart Fair."

"Well, sorry, I can't help you. I'd really like you to catch whoever killed that girl. That's just God-awful."

"You don't consider what you do *God-awful?*" Adelia asked.

Mabel revealed a sarcastic smile. She has been down this road many times with reformers, clergymen, politicians and upset wives. "No, miss, I do not consider what I do God-awful. I provide a service that keeps these girls off the street and gives them something to live on until they can find a husband or family member to take them in. And don't give me that holy-holy about it being sinful. Prostitution's in the Bible. And another thing, quite frankly, it keeps men from molesting girls in public, and they behave like perfect gentlemen in my house. They're actually better behaved here than they are in their own homes, where most of them beat their wives and children. My house is more *civilized.*"

Adelia looked like she wanted to argue, but kept quiet, possibly to consider Mabel's point of view.

"Miss Mabel," I said, "is there anything else about Mr. Stout that you can remember? Does he have a temper? Did he ever talk about Miss Dugan or the author Edgar Allan Poe?"

Mabel shook her head. "No, other than the fact that he makes my skin crawl. I don't know much else to tell you. He pays well." Then Mabel touched my arm and grinned. "How old are you, if you don't mind my asking?"

"Soon to be fifty," I said.

"What?" Adelia said. "You're almost fifty! Well, I guess you'd have to be if you served in the war, but I never thought you were that old. You certainly don't look it."

I grinned, not believing her. "Thank you, I think. Yes, I'm old."

Mabel caressed my arm. "You look pretty good for a man your age. No offense, Detective Drummond, but if you're ever feeling lonely, stop on by. You have my *personal* invitation."

"Well," I said with a smile, and avoided looking at Adelia, "thank you Mabel, but I think I'm too old for this sort of thing."

She playfully slapped my arm. "Nonsense. You get with one of my girls and you'll feel like a new man. Best thing for you right now. I sure was sorry to hear about your wife."

I swallowed hard and took a deep breath to suppress my emotions. "Thank you, Mabel. You're very kind, but work is the best thing for me right now."

And it was. As I hoped, getting back into the city and busy with an investigation had restored my spirits. Adelia's feminine presence also contributed to my improving mood.

"I understand." Mabel said. She turned to Adelia. "My invitation extends to you too, miss, if your tastes run in that direction."

Adelia's eyes almost shot from her skull. "They do not."

"No offense, dear. We don't judge."

Adelia turned and left in a hurry, slamming the door.

Mabel laughed. "I guess I scared her."

CHAPTER 25

I rejoined Adelia on the sidewalk in front of Miss Mabel's. My partner's face burned red. She was clearly upset and embarrassed by what transpired inside. I was tempted to laugh and tease her, but something told me that Adelia would shoot me with her derringer if I did.

She mounted her bicycle and put up her best professional façade. "Now what?"

I mounted my Victor. "Let's visit the manager at the Grand Opera House, Mr. Williamson. Since it's late in the day, and the busy hours for the theatre are about to commence, I expect the manager to be in the building and available for questions. It's a long shot because Mr. Williamson only makes an effort to know people who can benefit his theatre, but maybe these people Miss Dugan accompanied were people of influence."

Adelia agreed. We rode to the Grand Opera House and rested our bicycles in front of the broadside for *Lost Paradise*. We entered the building through a folded wooden door in the middle of seven cast-iron arches that made up the façade on the ground level. The narrow vestibule and red-carpeted hallway was currently void of citizens yet well-lit by two 6-light glass chandeliers. The ticket booth was located in the wall on the right and near three doors that led into the theatre.

"Is Mr. Williamson in?" I asked a young man seated inside the booth. "Tell him it's Detective Drummond. He knows me. I need to speak to him."

While waiting for the boy to return, Adelia commented on how much more at ease she was in the Opera House than at our previous location. "Although, that place was pretty fancy too."

"Wait until you meet Mr. Williamson. He's the cleanest and most organized man I've ever met. Everything about Mr. Williamson is clean, even the shows he promotes. He proudly boasts that the Opera House is high-class entertainment, and that they only do plays, events and concerts that every man, woman and child in Wilmington can attend without fear of a harsh word spoken."

Adelia laughed and proclaimed, "So it's exactly opposite from the last place we visited."

I agreed and we waited a few minutes more. Then the boy from the ticket booth appeared in the hallway and escorted Adelia and me up a circular staircase and into Mr. Williamson's balcony-level office. The theater manager was a portly gentleman with a receding hairline and round brown eyes. He wore an immaculate pin-striped suit and cherry-red necktie and sat behind an oak desk in the middle of the room. As expected, the office was free of clutter and dust, and minimal use had been made of the space.

"Detective Drummond," Mr. Williamson said with a grin. He stood, and came out from behind his desk and extended a hand. I shook it. "What can I do for you and your lady?" He gave me that conspiratory smile known only between men, an expression of good luck and happy to see I was with someone. "Free tickets to a show?"

"No, sir," I said, "nothing like that." I wasn't sure how much Mr. Williamson knew about my life over the past months, nor was I interested in telling him. I introduced Adelia and stated the reason for our visit. "Did you know Miss Katie Dugan?"

He sighed. "You mean that poor girl was a patron of this theatre?"

Adelia said, "She was. She was seen accompanied by a group of people we have yet to identify. Did you know her?"

Mr. Williamson frowned and shook his head. "No, I'm sorry. I don't recognize the name. I assume she wasn't from the upper layer of society?"

"No, sir," I said. As a theatre owner, Mr. Williamson associated with, and flattered immensely, any patron of the arts that had money. For his business to survive, he needed more than just the revenue generated by ticket sales. He needed well-to-do citizens to donate funds that covered some of the larger expenses, such as repairing plumbing or electrical issues and fixing leaks in the roof. "Miss Dugan's father operates a successful barbershop. But Miss Dugan did enjoy your theatre."

Mr. Williamson shook his head. "Such a tragedy, then. I'm sorry I can't help you."

I handed Mr. Williamson my card with the usual instructions. He again offered a pair of tickets to tonight's performance of *Lost Paradise*. "Mr. Fusco and Miss Crane are excellent. You won't regret it."

"Thank you, no," I said. "We're attending the Sacred Heart Fair tonight."

"Oh, well, another time then."

Adelia and I returned to our bicycles. For safety reasons, and because it was only two blocks between the Opera House and Sixth

Street, we walked our bikes among the pedestrians to within view of City Hall beyond Mullins & Sons.

Joey was at his usual location pitching the latest edition of the *Every Evening*. "Young lady murdered on DuPont Street next to the Bush Estate. Read all about it." It always amazed me how fast newspaper companies produced their product, considering how much labor was needed to assemble all the individual letters of type from the bins in the composition room, spell the words onto plates that were then inked and pressed against flat sheets of paper.

Joey had a small crowd of excited men and women around him, citizens anxious to buy a copy of the three-page folio. Then, after the initial shock of the tragedy wore off, public outcry would put pressure on Adelia and me to find the culprit. I could already imagine the fearful wails from the citizens, especially those inspired by Casey Moran who had little regard for the police department: "The people of this city aren't safe in their beds."

I left my bike with Adelia and hurried to Joey, giving him two cents for a copy of the *Every Evening*. The city's most popular newspaper cost a penny more than other Wilmington dailies, but the citizens were willing to pay it because the paper presented the news without partisan politics. "Thank you, Joey."

I returned to Adelia and showed her the headline: *YOUNG LADY MURDERED!* I perused Casey's two-column story, which contained the details Adelia and I had given to the press earlier at the Rat's Nest, along with my revelation about the rendezvous note that I hadn't told the others. I was certain to hear about that indiscretion from other journalists, especially those accusing me of secretly admiring Casey Moran. The Vulture's article then named the suspect in custody.

"What?" I exclaimed, practically ripping the newspaper in half.

CHAPTER 26

"I don't believe it," I said to Adelia. "How did he get Mr. Riley's name?"

If that wasn't bad enough, the Vulture wrote his article to insinuate that Mr. Riley was guilty of the crime without actually stating it. Then, to stir up emotions even more, he gruesomely exaggerated the horrible circumstances of Miss Dugan's death, even comparing it to the style of Jack the Ripper.

"Damn him," I said. Our job was difficult enough without propaganda generated by a journalist who was out to make his own headline. The newspaper reading public generally accepted what they read as the truth. Since they were already suspicious of the police and authority in general they were more willing to believe a lie in the press than the truth from the mayor or police chief.

The remainder of Casey's article was filled with journalistic outrage and a call to moral order that made me laugh.

The people of this city must now rely on Detective Drummond, of whom we have written about in the past and labeled the Biking Detective, and, believe it or not, his cohort, a female investigator Detective Bern. She comes to us from Chicago and was featured in this newspaper last week. We now put our trust in these two individuals to bring justice for the victim and her family. But, ladies and gentlemen, such a brutal attack warrants the question, are we witnessing the degeneration of our society, the human being at its most cruel and diabolical, in desperate need of God's guidance?

"Unbelievable."

Adelia and I returned our bicycles to the saltbox and then hurried inside City Hall. Molly greeted us when we reached the second floor, but I stormed past her and rushed into the chief's office with my partner right behind me.

My boss was seated at his desk. I clenched my fists. "How did Casey get Mr. Riley's name?"

Chief Francis looked up and spoke in a pensive voice. "Oh, I told him."

I considered using my fists against my boss' face. "I *told* you he might not be our man. And he *isn't*! His alibi checks out."

Adelia then surprised me. "Mr. Riley might still be our man."

Chief Francis perked up at this news. "How so?"

"There's a timeline discrepancy we need to clear up."

I faced my partner. "It's not enough to hold him. It could be a simple mistake."

Chief stroked his chin hair. "Well, do what you need to do. But the fact that Casey printed a name will keep some of the pressure off of us."

I calmed down a bit because Chief Francis had a point. If the public knew that we had a suspect in custody they'd relax. However, in exchange for temporary relief on the police department, Mr. Riley's life had been irrevocably damaged. Again, perception was seen as reality. The publicity from the newspaper article would compel Richard's employer to dismiss him, and he could have difficulty finding another job. His landlady might be forced to evict him, despite her good-natured feelings.

"We're going to the Sacred Heart Fair," I said to my boss. "I hope to get a sense of what Miss Dugan experienced last night. Maybe we can find somebody who remembers seeing her, and we need to interview whoever's running the Kickapoo Medicine Show."

"Well," Chief said with little enthusiasm, "good luck." We started to leave, but my boss asked Adelia to step outside because he wanted a private word with me. After she closed the door behind her, Chief whispered, "Have you found out anything about her? Why is she here?"

The Chief's inquisitive nature would've been satisfied had he asked me his questions this morning and had I known the answers. However, my attitude toward Adelia had definitely improved. I treated her like any other partner, and even appreciated the new investigative techniques she had brought to our working relationship. Now, even though I had learned a great deal about Adelia's background, I wasn't going to reveal any of it. What she had said to me was spoken in confidence and I wasn't going to betray her trust. "I haven't learned anything. She's been all business. And she resents any effort to get personal."

"Oh, I guess you don't want to encourage her temper by pressing the issue."

"Yes, sir, maybe after she's been here awhile, and gets more comfortable around us, she'll talk about herself. Maybe if you treat her better she'll be more friendly."

Chief grinned. "I don't know if I can do that. At least she's pretty to look at."

I agreed with his latter statement and then excused myself to reunite with Adelia in the hallway. She followed me to the telephone that hung on the wall next to Molly's desk.

Molly was about to put a sheet of paper in her typewriter. "Who are you telephoning?"

"I'm going to yell at Casey."

I lifted the phone's hand-held receiver from its perch, put it to my ear and turned the crank a few times to alert the operator. The central exchange for the Diamond State Telephone Company was in a building at Third and Market. All calls were sent there first and then operators re-routed them to other subscribers. The phone company had initially hired boys as operators, but they had proved to be rude and obnoxious, so ladies were hired.

When I heard a female voice on the other end of the line, I spoke into the mouthpiece and told her to connect me to Casey Moran at the *Every Evening*. "I'm not sure of the number," I said, "but you must have it in your directory." She did. She put the call through, but someone else answered.

"May I speak to Casey? This is Detective Drummond."

"You're too late, Drummond," a male voice stated. "You know the issue has hit the streets."

"Who is this?" I said.

"It's Charlie Dalton, you old bat. Casey figured you'd call to chastise him. You know he don't care if the guy's innocent or not. It's good copy."

"Damn. Well, you can tell Casey that I'm releasing Mr. Riley. He has a legitimate alibi. So thank you very much for ruining a man's life."

"Who cares?" and the phone went dead.

I hung up the receiver with a little more force than necessary.

"Hey," Molly said, scolding me like one of her children. "Don't break it."

I rubbed Molly's back to appease her. "Sorry."

Molly looked up with a genuine tenderness in her eyes, the same way my wife had looked at me. I was tempted to kiss Molly on the cheek, just as a friendly gesture, and she would've welcomed it, but if I kissed her I'd be a cad. I'd give her false hope, especially when the temptation to stare at Adelia had been getting stronger throughout the day.

Adelia and I went to the basement with Officer Hinder.

Mr. Riley was already standing and holding onto the iron bars. "Detectives, have you come to let me out of this rat hole before I catch my death?"

"They have," Officer Hinder said, showing the key to the cell's lock.

"But first," I said, "I have to apologize. The chief of police gave out your name to a reporter for the *Every Evening*."

"I know," Richard said, pushing his spectacles up the bridge of his nose. "Some little man came by earlier with this officer and said he wanted to talk to me. I told him to go to hell. Excuse me, miss. He didn't seem to care if I was innocent or not."

"I'm sorry. Chief should've kept his mouth shut and waited until after we checked your alibi. Your friend and landlady were most helpful."

"Yes," Adelia said, pulling out her notepad. She flipped through the pages until she found what she was looking for. "We have a question about what time you left the fair. You said Katie left you around ten and then you were at the shooting gallery and got to your friend's place around midnight."

"That's what I said."

"Well, Katie was seen walking in front of a meat shop by the shop's owner at nine o'clock. The time is accurate because the gentleman always closes his shop at nine."

"Well, I told you I don't have a watch. So maybe I was a little off about the time."

"A *little* off? It's an hour difference."

"So what? Do I have to account for every second?"

"When you're suspected of murder, you definitely do"

"I didn't kill her," Richard said, his jaw tight. "I'm only guessing at the time." Then he turned to me. "You know, I'll probably lose my job over this. It's not the kind of publicity the hotel wants."

"I am sorry," I said.

"That doesn't help."

Adelia said, "I'm still not satisfied about the time."

Richard adjusted his spectacles again, "Well, I don't know what to tell you. Katie must've left me earlier than I thought. I must've been at the shooting gallery longer than I thought."

"Is that the best you can do?"

"Yes, damn it."

"That's enough," Officer Hinder said. "Are you sure you want to let this man out?"

I nodded. Adelia wasn't satisfied, but she consented to releasing Richard.

A short while later, Adelia, Richard and I stood in front of City Hall. Joey was still hawking his newspapers to a swarming pack of citizens, but the pile of *Every Evenings* at his feet was almost gone. "Young lady murdered by the Bush estate."

Richard cringed. "Does he have to yell it?"

I was about to say goodbye to Richard when I heard a male voice call my name. Two men I hadn't seen before waved at me while they dodged a hansom and crossed Market Street. When the men arrived, they were sucking air, but determined not to let a little thing like breathing interrupt their cause. "Bill Kendel, junior reporter for the *Morning Herald*," one said, and the other gave his name as Terry Fine, junior for the *Gazette*."

I put a hand up. "Oh, newcomers. It's nice to meet you, gentlemen." I started to introduce Detective Bern and Mr. Riley and then thought better of it for Richard's sake. "I have nothing to say."

Bill Kendel pulled out his notepad. "Come on, Detective Drummond, has the suspect confessed yet? How did Casey get a name? Did he pay for information? Did he make another *contribution* to the chief's retirement fund?"

The mention of Casey's name reminded me of the phone call I had made to the Vulture that Charlie Dalton took instead, and how unfair Casey's article was. "I'll give you an update." The two reporters practically drooled on themselves. So as an act of revenge against the Vulture, and to help new and aspiring journalists get their big break, I again violated my tell-every-reporter-at-the-same-time-rule. "The suspect has been released. He has a solid alibi."

"Great." Terry Fine said, writing in his notebook.

Mr. Kendal looked at Richard suspiciously. "I know she's Detective Bern. Who are you, sir?"

Richard stared down the man. "None of your damn business."

"Well, excuse me." Then he asked me, "Do you have another suspect?"

"We're looking at everybody who knew the young lady."

"Can you provide any names?" Mr. Fine asked.

"Sorry, I can't. That's all, gentlemen."

The two reporters thanked me and scrambled across the street to make sure the next edition of their morning newspapers alerted readers to Mr. Riley's freedom. Then more journalistic outrage would ensue. I could already imagine the headlines and the harassing questions. *If the suspect was innocent, where's the real killer? When will he be caught and prosecuted? The people of Wilmington need to know! The Detectives should be fired and replaced with someone who will move quicker and give us the killer yesterday.*

I extended a hand to Mr. Riley. "Well, best of luck to you, sir. I will be happy to speak to your employer if it will help."

Richard said, "I had a lot of time in that jail cell to do some thinking and I want to help you. I loved Katie. I can't rest without finding out who killed her. It has to be someone who knows me and knows I work at the barbershop. Please let me help you."

"I don't know. It won't be pleasant, and you'll probably hear things about Miss Dugan you won't like."

"I'm already hearing that damn newsboy yelling about her murder. What could be worse than that?"

I kept my voice down for discretion. "We don't have the coroner's report yet, but I believe Miss Dugan was killed because she was with child, and the father of the baby is probably the man who killed her. And like you said, her killer probably stole your razor in an attempt to implicate you."

Richard's eyes watered. "No. Katie was a good Catholic girl."

"Her behavior changed in recent weeks. She stopped going to church."

Richard let that bit of news sink in for a moment. "So she stopped going to church. I stopped years ago. Katie would never succumb to any man before marriage."

Adelia was rude. "And you say that because she never surrendered to you?"

Richard's face turned an angry red. If Adelia had been a man, he might've struck her or challenged her to a duel. "I will not discuss such matters with you. It's positively indecent."

"Relax," I said. "The coroner is examining Miss Dugan and will provide a report after he's finished. Then we'll see if my suspicions are correct."

"Well, you're wrong, sir. She wouldn't do such a thing, at least not willingly. Poor Katie. Do you have a suspect?"

My partner said, "Mr. Stout."

I cringed. I didn't expect Adelia to reveal a suspect's name like that. Her Pinkerton training should've emphasized confidentiality when it came to criminal investigations. However, since Adelia had been doing so well I decided to overlook this lapse in judgment.

"Mr. Stout? I've heard that name before."

"In what context?"

Richard thought for a moment. "Katie said it. She talked about some old man that's been spying on her for years. Did you interview him?"

"We did."

"And what did you find out?"

"We'll keep that to ourselves for now," I said, cutting off Adelia just in case she chose to reply.

"All right, will you please consider letting me help you?"

"I don't know. It could be dangerous. Whoever killed Miss Dugan won't hesitate to come after us if they feel threatened."

Richard stood tall. "I assume the risk, sir. Don't worry about me. I can't stay home when I know someone is out there who killed Katie and is trying to get *me* sent to prison. Besides, once my boss reads my name in the papers, I'll have all the free time in the world. No plea from you will change that. Please let me help."

"What do you think?" I asked Adelia. "Is there room for him?"

"We're heading to the fair," she said. "He was there with Miss Dugan the last two nights. He could provide some insight."

I considered her point, and Richard's pleading face. My decision was a foregone conclusion. "All right, Mr. Riley. You may join us, but you've been warned."

CHAPTER 27

By seven o'clock the sun was replaced by a waning moon, stars and a few small passing clouds. Electric streetlamps provided dim illumination along Market Street, and some of the city's other main arteries, but not on every block, so for safety reasons bicycles were no longer practical.

Adelia, Richard and I paid our nickel fare and hopped on board a well-lit, twelve bench open vestibule trolley at Market and Sixth Streets. Unfortunately, we had to stand in the center aisle because all the seats were stuffed with dirty working-class men who had just ended another hard day at the docks, shipyards, factories or mills. Eventually, they'd arrive home, spend a little time at the dinner table with their families, sleep and then wake in the morning to do it all over again, except on Sunday. Looking at their exhausted expressions, I could easily sympathize and understand why labor unions were pushing for a 40-hour work week. Most factory workers labored from seven in the morning until six or seven at night, six days a week.

We got off at Ninth Street and then we waited under a streetlamp with a few other people for a westbound car. I stood there, taking glances at Adelia and actually regretting my decision to have Richard join us. Not because of the possible risk to his health, but because I wanted to spend the evening alone with Adelia. I could make our trip to the fair both work related and pleasure. But would she welcome my attention? She was a strong and independent woman who called marriage evil.

The westbound trolley arrived, ablaze in electric light inside and out. We paid the fare to the motorman and climbed onboard. We still had to stand in the center aisle and share the ride with workers, but some of the passengers were children with their parents and they were all decked out in their best outfits.

Oh, to be a child again, before my mother passed away and my father turned angry from it. We never attended fairs or circuses because my parents and I, and our hired hands, had to work hard on the farm and we needed to make every penny count. Yet after my morning chores I had been free to explore the land and admire the various insects, birds and small animals that thrived in and around the Drummond Farm. Those moments had been my favorite. Some other memories weren't so good. If I misbehaved, father had plenty of switches available from our willows. My parents had a small cemetery by the barn where they had buried two baby sisters I never knew. I was the only child to reach maturity and I hadn't taken that responsibility lightly. I had every intention of taking ownership of the farm, keeping it successful and caring for my mother and father as they grew old. Destiny, however, had other plans.

CHAPTER 28

We heard the babble of voices and the mechanical music from the carnival rides a block before we reached the fairgrounds. The children stood up, stared ahead with wide eyes at the bright lights, and then bounced up and down on their feet. "Come on, mama. Come on papa."

Adelia's wide-eyed expression resembled the look on the children's faces. "I've never been to a fair before."

I smiled. "I never would've guessed."

When the car stopped, the boys and girls grabbed hold of a parents' hand and rushed from the trolley, pulling their mother or father along. Once that commotion subsided, the three of us followed the flow of adults off the streetcar and we joined an influx of people coming from a variety of directions but all heading for the front gate. Electric light, most of it temporary and strung between trees, illuminated the block-sized area and reflected off Sacred Heart's stained-glass windows, brick walls and flat-topped steeple.

I sniffed the air. "Smell that sauerkraut."

Adelia inhaled. "I'm hungry."

"Me too," Richard said.

"Didn't they feed you in jail?" I said as we joined the line for the ticket booth.

Richard groaned. "The jailer gave me something in a bowl he called soup. It was just hot water with a couple rotten vegetables in it. A starving dog wouldn't eat it."

"All right, we'll get some food first. And some beer."

"Oh, yes," Richard said, adjusting his glasses. "The Germans know how to brew beer."

"Which do you prefer? Diamond State or Hartmann and Fehrenbach?"

"Diamond State."

"You know," I said with a smile, "you and I just might become friends."

When we reached the ticket booth, a lady seated inside announced, "Twenty-five cents each."

I paid. "Compliments of the Wilmington Police Department."

We entered the crowded fairgrounds and followed our noses to two steaming cauldrons of fermented cabbage tended to by women in sweaty, cotton work clothes. They also stoked cooking fires that roasted bratwursts. To wash the food down, Joseph Stoeckle's Diamond State Brewery had an open wagon of tapped beer barrels readily available.

"Hallelujah!" I shouted.

Adelia bought a plate of bratwursts over sauerkraut, collected some utensils and searched for a place to sit among an assortment of picnic tables. "I'm not partial to beer, so I'll hold you a place."

After Richard and I purchased plates of food and steins of beer, we joined Adelia on a long bench at a wooden table with a young couple who barely acknowledged our presence. They were too busy staring at each other and putting forkfuls of food into the other's mouth, chewing and swallowing together. They kissed and smiled. They performed the ritual again.

"They should be more discreet in public," Richard said over the clanging noise from the carnival games and rides.

I removed the last cigar from my vest pocket and lit it. "Oh, I don't know, after listening to Mrs. Stout talked about her marriage those two are downright refreshing."

"I can agree with that," Adelia said.

"I hoped Katie and I would've been like that," Richard said.

I took a long drag on my cigar and remembered how affectionate Jane and I were. Best part about our relationship was that over time we became friends. We married fast, during the rush to war and the concern that I might not survive. When I returned home Jane and I were almost strangers to each other. Yet we re-discovered our love and I looked forward to a long and healthy relationship, and to growing old with her. Whenever I was around Jane, I felt at peace. She had a self-reliance, a confidence that made her womanly charms unnecessary. Men naturally flocked to her. So it was to my credit, and amazement, that Jane kept seeking my company and agreed to marry me. Now after months of mourning, I was experiencing feelings for another woman. It didn't mean that I missed Jane any less; it was simply proof that my heart was healing. However, I needed to be careful. Were these feelings for Adelia genuine or just a physical reaction to the first woman to come into my life since Jane's tragic departure?

Ignoring his food, Richard stared at the ground. It took me a moment, but I realized why. The young couple reminded him of his freshly ripped open heart.

I patted him on the back and raised my stein. "To Miss Dugan."

Richard looked at me and I saw the pain of Katie's death in his eyes, a raw and festering wound that I identified with and it convinced me of his innocence. No actor was that good.

Richard nodded, raised his stein and tapped mine. "To Miss Dugan." We drank. "Thank you." He cut his bratwurst with a knife. "So what did Mr. and Mrs. Stout say?"

I smoked and summarized the testimonies presented to Adelia and me by the unhappy pair. Then I added, "There are holes in Mr. Stout's story. He might've slipped out of his house and gone to the rendezvous location. We just need to prove it. And when we told him where Miss Dugan was found, he knew the area. He said he once attended a gala for the artist Felix Darley. I don't think given Mr. Stout's social status that he would've been invited to such an event."

Adelia stopped eating. "You didn't mention that before."

"I know," I said over the carnival noise. "I've been thinking about it. Mr. Stout is working class. He wouldn't normally be invited to Dr. Bush's house. He might've read about it in the Society Column. And when I asked Mrs. Stout if she attended the gala, her response was an obvious lie."

"So you think there's another reason he's familiar with the location?" Richard said, eating his bratwurst and downing it with beer.

"That's my suspicion," I replied, doing the same while holding a cigar. "Like I said, he might be familiar with the area because he knows it's the rendezvous point. Otherwise, what reason is there? There's nothing else around there until they start building next year. And if he was a member of the Wilmington Gun Club he would've stated so instead of making up the Felix Darley story."

Adelia turned to Richard. "I am curious. Were you going to propose marriage to Miss Dugan last night? Your landlady thought so."

Richard paused. "I considered it, but I hadn't bought a ring yet. Something told me she might've said no."

Adelia wasn't tactful. "She would've said no, according to her parents. And they weren't going to allow it anyway because you're not Catholic."

"Well then, I guess it's a good thing I didn't go to the expense."

"We found something interesting in Mr. Stout's bedroom," my partner said. "Apparently, he likes the writings of Edgar Allan Poe. He even has a portrait of the man hanging on his wall and a newspaper article about when Poe spoke at the Newark Academy. What's interesting is that we found the same collection of Poe's writings in *your* room. Is that a coincidence?"

Richard swallowed a mouthful, and then slowly pushed away what was left on his plate. "You were in my room?" His voice was angry, but he calmed. "Of course you were. How stupid of me. My landlady let you in, didn't she? You had no cause to go into my room. You were only supposed to talk to her about my clothes."

"Do you and Mr. Stout share an interest in Poe?"

Richard sighed. "I don't give a damn about Mr. Poe *or* Mr. Stout. Katie gave me the books about a year ago. She said I'd enjoy them, and that I'd like certain passages she circled. I told her I don't read fiction, but she insisted. She called them a gift, so I accepted them. I stuck them in my nightstand and that's where they've been ever since."

Now I was curious. "Did you ask her why *she* reads Poe?"

Richard's demeanor calmed as it appeared he was recalling a pleasant memory. "Katie enjoyed being scared. She claimed her life at home was so regimented and boring that she'd go out at night and stay out late because it frightened her. She liked dark and secluded places and not knowing what might be around the next corner."

"Interesting," I said. "Did she ever ask you to scare her?"

Richard's eyes widened. "Good God, no." He sipped some beer and glanced at our affectionate table-mates. They were locked in a good ten second kiss. "Oh, wait a minute. There was this one time when Katie and I were walking at night by the depot and Katie asked me to take her to a tavern at the Coast. I refused. That was no place for a lady, and I didn't need that type of thrill in my life. Then she told me to go on up Market Street and hide in an alley. Then when she comes walking by, I was to jump out and scare her. I did. She loved it."

Adelia pushed Richard's plate of food back to him. "There are people who find pleasure in taking risks. Detective Drummond is such a person."

"I am?"

"Yes, sir. You told me you only feel alive when you come close to death. That's why you miss the battlefield. That's why you became a policeman. Miss Dugan must've had the same trait. But for a woman, it's not acceptable, so I'd imagine she had an extremely difficult time suppressing it."

"Do you think she followed a stranger out to the Bush estate?" Richard said, adjusting his spectacles.

I finished my beer and shook my head. "No, her killer was someone she knew. There were no wounds on Miss Dugan's hands to indicate that she fought off her attacker. And remember, the murderer is cunning enough to try and pin the crime on you. This was planned in advanced, so it's no stranger."

Adelia asked, "When Miss Dugan gave you the books, did you ask her where and how she got them? Did she buy them at a bookstore? Did she get them from Mr. Stout? Maybe she and Mr. Stout were seeing each other?"

Richard nearly gagged. "You're making me ill. I can't imagine Katie spending any time with such an old man."

"Is there a literary society in town that's dedicated to Poe's work?"

Richard shrugged. "Like I said, I don't read fiction, so I wouldn't know, and Katie never mentioned one to me."

I said, "We can check the City Directory or the Social Column in the *Every Evening*."

Adelia looked around and asked Richard, "Are tonight's festivities similar to last night?"

Richard finished his last bite of sauerkraut and looked around. "There are more children here than yesterday, but it's just as loud."

"Do you know the pastor here?" I said, finishing my meal as well.

"No, sir. I don't attend Sacred Heart. For personal reasons, I don't really belong to any particular church."

I interrupted the young couple at our table and asked them if they knew the church's current pastor. They did not. I then walked around and asked several people. An elderly lady was kind enough to escort us to a booth near the front steps of Sacred Heart, where a man and woman handed out Bibles and church literature. There were also two collection baskets, one for donations to the church and the other one for the widow of policeman Charles Schultz.

"Who was he?" Adelia asked.

"He was an officer in the Ninth Ward," I replied. "Not this past winter, but in '91, Officer Schultz was in pursuit of two safecrackers on 21st Street near Tatnall. He ordered them to put their hands up. They shot him. One bullet grazed his head, but a fatal shot hit his gut. He lingered for a while at Delaware Hospital, but died leaving a wife and five children."

We each donated a dollar to the widow. The man in the booth thanked us. He was a tall and skinny individual who wore a full suit and bow tie, so I was surprised when our escort introduced him as Father Sylvester Joerg.

CHAPTER 29

"I'm the pastor, choir director and Sunday School teacher," Father Sylvester Joerg informed us in a German accent. Then he tried humor. "And I sweep out the place." I introduced Adelia and Richard, and then explained our circumstance. He mourned. "Such a dreadful thing. I read about it in the newspaper. How can I help?"

"Can we ask you a few questions?" I said.

"Certainly, but not here. How about we walk and talk?"

We agreed, and Adelia pulled out her notepad and pencil.

"Can you start by giving me some background on your church?"

"Absolutely," Father Joerg replied as we walked. "Bishop Becker dedicated the Church of the Sacred Heart on September 2, 1883. The church was established through the efforts of Father Wendelin Meyer. It is said that during construction he slipped medals of St. Benedict between the bricks."

"The stained-glass windows are very beautiful," Adelia said.

"Thank you," the priest said. "We have fifty stained-glass windows in all. They're magnificent, aren't they? And we can seat a thousand people inside the church. You are all welcome to join us for service."

"Thank you," I said. "And congratulations on the fair. It appears to be a success."

"Oh, it is," Father Joerg said as we moved by a stage that had children in lederhosen performing a traditional German dance. "People have been very generous. We've had wonderful weather and raised almost $200 for the church and school." Then the priest returned to the subject of our meeting. "I don't envy you your task, detectives. To think that sweet girl was here last night, among our friends. Do you have any suspects?"

I lied to keep our investigation confidential. "No one at this time. Mr. Riley was here last night with Miss Dugan, but he's not a suspect. Did you know Miss Dugan?"

"No," Father Joerg replied, waving to a couple who greeted him. "Her family name is not familiar. They must attend a different church."

We passed a booth where a young man was selling copies of the *Freie Presse*, a German language newspaper, for a penny a copy. It had a bold headline and I wondered if it announced the murder of Miss

Dugan.

Adelia said, "Do you know Mr. Albert Stout?"

"Yes, miss. He belongs to our church. His father came from Bavaria. Why do you ask?"

"Miss Dugan was once employed at his house as a maid," she said. "We interviewed him earlier and he claims he was here last night and saw Miss Dugan from a distance."

"Yes, Mr. Stout was here. I talked to him and his family briefly. Surely, you don't suspect him?"

"It's just routine questions," Adelia said. I just looked on with a smile, amazed at how quickly she took over the questioning. "Is Mr. Stout an honorable man?"

Father Joerg sounded shocked by the question. "Of course. He's a good man."

We arrived at the ball toss game that Mr. Stout described. A three-tiered platform with a row of six glass jugs at each level set beneath a canopy. A banner across the front read: *Four Throws for a Nickel, Win a Cash Prize.*

"Are the games honest?" Richard said.

"Honest?" the priest said, "of course they're honest. We wouldn't allow them on the grounds otherwise."

"I meant no offense, sir. Katie and I wondered if the games were honest."

"Yes, they are."

"Mr. Stout didn't think so," Adelia said. "Take this game for example. Is anyone winning at the ball toss?"

"I believe some have."

We watched a young man toss a ball underhanded toward the top openings to the glass jugs. Each ball, even when it looked like it might make it through the opening, bounced off the top of the bottle.

My partner said, "Mr. Stout suspects that the ball's diameter is wider than the mouth on the jugs."

"I'll have someone look into that. If it's true, we'll have them removed from the fair and ban them from ever returning."

I smiled. The priest couldn't be that naïve. Everyone knew carnival and circus games were rigged. If the priest was sincere about kicking out cheaters, he'd have no event.

The four of us resumed our walk and soon arrived at the ENGLEWOOD SHOOTING RANGE. The temporary wooden structure had a slanted ceiling that advertised the name of the business and announced 3 SHOTS FOR 5c or 16 SHOTS FOR 25c.

Participants stood behind a three-foot-high wooden wall and aimed a pump action .22 rifle at small cast iron images of rabbits, squirrels, wolves, foxes, birds, bears and deer on six tiered rows against a painted forest background. When a pellet hit the target, a *ting* sound was heard and the image fell.

"This is where I went after Katie left me," Richard said.

I pointed at a bearded man who operated the game. "Was here he last night?"

"He was."

We approached the operator and I said, "Sir," I gestured at Richard, "do you remember seeing this gentleman last night?"

The man shrugged. "I must've had over a hundred men here last night. You can't expect me to remember just one of them."

"So you have no recollection?"

"That's correct."

"Well," Richard said, "I was here."

"And so was I," the man said with a sneer. "What of it?"

"You have no cause to be rude," Father Joerg said.

"Thank you anyway," I said, and we walked away.

"Why was he so rude?" the priest said.

"Most carnival people are naturally shy around police," I said.

"You didn't introduce yourself. How did he know you were police?"

"I know you said the games are honest, but most carnival and circus shows are run by con men and they have an instinct for policemen."

"So he just knew you were police without having to be told?"

"We must all have the same look or give off the same smell. I don't know what it is. They just know us on sight."

We walked to a circular gazebo that revolved around a center hub and played a loud, tinkling music. Near its outer edge, metal poles were equally spaced, and each one supported a wooden horse, uniquely painted in a different color and style. As the structure spun, the horses rose and dipped slightly on the poles, bringing smiles to the children sitting in the saddles and delight to their parents, who stood beyond the device's perimeter.

"The merry-go-round," Richard said. "This is where Katie said she had to leave."

"Did anyone approach her?" I asked.

"I didn't see anyone."

"Miss Dugan had a typewritten note on her about meeting someone last night. While it's possible she might've gotten it earlier in the week, it's also possible that she came to the fair expecting to receive the note and somebody slipped it to her. I'm sorry, Mr. Riley, but she might've just used you as a means to get here. You said she telephoned you, which was unusual. Once she received the note, she needed to leave."

"Detective Drummond, you're not helping my disposition."

A man at the controls brought the merry-go-round to a stop and the children got off. Another group, including a few adults, climbed into the saddles, and the operator turned the machine back on. The whole spinning device, with its loud and clanging tune, reminded me of a life-sized music box not that different from those my wife owned. They were still displayed on our fireplace's mantel in the parlor. Her favorite had a toy ballerina.

I finished my cigar just as our walk reached the back of the fairgrounds. To my delight we came upon the real reason why we came to the Fair.

CHAPTER 30

Bunting across the front of the canopy read: KICKAPOO INDIAN MEDICINE COMPANY SHOW. Across the front of a temporary stage, another banner read: SAGWA OIL SALVE, WORM KILLER AND COUGH CURE. LONG LIFE AND GOOD HEALTH GUARANTEED. USE INDIAN SAGWA. There was a stack of crates on stage behind two Caucasian gentlemen who paced back and forth pitching their magic elixir to a small crowd while looking ridiculous dressed in Indian deerskin clothes and feathered headdresses.

The taller of the fake Indians was the loudest. He held up a bottle of their Sagwa yelling, "I make no idle claims, ladies and gentlemen. Our remedy has been proven to work by medical science. One bottle of our Sagwa and you'll feel like a new person. It'll take care of *all* digestive discomforts. Ladies, it'll make that uncomfortable time go a lot smoother. I guarantee its results."

"It cures my stomach pains," a tall gentleman in the front row hollered a little too dramatically. He held up a dollar to the salesman, who took it quick. The shorter salesman then pulled out two bottles from the top crate and handed them to the customer. I had my suspicions, of course. Medicine shows were notorious for planting shills in the audience who pretended to be enthusiastic customers but were actually part of the deception. I was tempted to call out the gentleman and ask him to drink the Sagwa, but decided against it.

"You've made a wise decision, sir," the taller salesman said. "You're on the road to better health. Come on now, how about the rest of you? You won't regret it."

"Well," Father Joerg said, "do you have any further need of me?"

"I don't think so." We wished him well. "Thank you for showing us around. You were most kind."

"Godspeed," the priest said, and he left.

I asked Richard, "Did you buy a bottle of their medicine last night?"

"Never."

"Did Katie buy a bottle?"

"No, sir."

"Well, Mr. Stout claims Miss Dugan bought a bottle after she left

145

you, and a nearly empty bottle *was* found near her."

"That doesn't make sense. Katie was smarter than to fall for this chicanery."

I made eye contact with the taller Kickapoo salesman and waved at him to join us at the front of the stage. He removed a couple bottles from the crates and came toward us. He leaned forward, holding the headdress to keep it from falling.

"You won't regret purchasing a bottle of our miracle elixir."

"We're not customers." I introduced myself and Adelia and asked for a private word.

The salesman handed the bottles of Sagwa to his shorter friend and then sat off the edge of the stage, away from the audience. "What's this about?" he asked, removing his headdress and combing his thin black hair with his fingers. He had dark eyes and a scar down the bridge of his nose, and another one on his cheek, my guess from a knife fight. I wondered what criminal activity he had been involved in before he found *legitimate* work with a medicine show. "We have a license. We're not breaking any laws."

"What's your name?"

He grinned. "Call me Professor Vincent."

Adelia laughed. "*Professor* of what?"

"Of miracle elixirs. How can I help you?"

I answered. "We're investigating the murder of a young lady named Miss Dugan who was here at the fair last night with this gentleman," I gestured at Richard. "She was killed around midnight."

"Murder? Why come to me? We're a legitimate business conducting legitimate sales. We're not involved in anything illegal, and we're certainly not involved in any murder."

"After leaving Mr. Riley, Miss Dugan was seen by a witness buying a bottle of your Sagwa, which was then found near her body."

"Well, Sagwa isn't poisonous, if that's what you're implying."

"She was killed with a razor."

"Then why bother us?" He started to get up. "Look, mister, I have to make a living. You're holding me up."

"You'll leave when I'm done asking you questions. Do you remember selling a bottle of your tonic to a young brunette in a green dress, say just before nine o'clock? She may have acted like she was in a hurry."

Professor Vincent thought about it, and then his eyes went wide. "I did! She was quite a beauty. And she was in *quite* a hurry. She rushed the stage and demanded a bottle." He smiled proudly. "She was probably a returning customer. I took her money, gave her a bottle and asked her why she was in such a rush. She said, 'I'm late. The Count's waiting.' "

CHAPTER 31

"The Count?" It had to be a nickname. I searched my memory, recalling two decades of criminal aliases because lawbreakers rarely provided their real names. Even boys as young as five years old who were in street gangs were more popularly known by their monikers than by the name their parents gave them. "I don't know who that could be. Are you certain that's what she said?"

"Yes, sir. That's what she said because I yelled after her, 'what's this Count got that I don't have?' She didn't answer me. I don't think she heard me."

I asked Richard, "Did Katie ever mention somebody named the Count?"

He shook his head. "No, sir."

I turned back to Vincent, "Did you see a gentleman last night with a thick walrus-type moustache?"

"A walrus moustache? No, sir."

"What's in your Sagwa, other than alcohol?" Adelia asked.

"A special mix of herbs and spices and plants from the Indian nations."

"Can you be more specific?"

"It has burdock root, mandrake root, licorice, dandelion root, rhubarb root, senna leaves, aniseed red cinchona bark, yellow dock root, aloes, alcohol glycerin, and water."

"And all that comes from the Indian nations?" Adelia said.

"Yes." Then he gave us a story he probably repeated hundreds of times to potential customers. "Our founder, Texas Charlie, was in the Indian nations and dying from some unknown illness when an Indian medicine man gave him what he called Sagwa to drink. Within a day, Texas Charlie was cured. He begged and begged the medicine man to tell him the ingredients. Once he did, Texas Charlie started our company with the goal of bringing the best health possible to all Americans."

"And to con people out of their money," Richard said. "Does the medicine man get any money from the sale of Sagwa?"

Professor Vincent grinned. "What do you think?"

Adelia asked, "Have you ever *been* to the Indian nations?"

The salesman frowned. "No, but that's where we get our

148

ingredients."

I said, "I'm not familiar with those ingredients. Is it possible that one of them acts like a drug and causes delusions, or makes people act violently, such as peyote or opium?"

"*No, sir,* I can assure you there's no opium or intoxicating drug in it." He laughed. "We leave the opium trade to the Chinese. What's peyote? I'm not familiar with it, but it's definitely not an ingredient. You're not going to blame this girl's murder on our patent medicine, are you?"

"That's not my intention, sir. I've read about certain tribes who use native plants, such as peyote, to commune with the spirit world and induce visions during their religious ceremonies. It is possible that under the influence of such a drug, people can act irrationally and do things they wouldn't normally do."

"The same is true of alcohol."

"Yes, sir, it is. And your product does have some alcohol in it. If Miss Dugan didn't drink your medicine last night, then it's highly probable her killer did. He drank most of it. Maybe it influenced him, maybe it didn't. Then for some reason, it was left at the murder scene."

"Someone else could've left it there days ago," Professor Vincent said. "We've been here all week and our product is available in any drug store. You're just guessing."

"Yes, sir, I can't be sure, but I have to explore every possibility." I handed Professor Vincent my calling card. "Thank you for your time. You've been most helpful. If you remember anything that might help us, please contact me."

"Are you sure you won't buy a bottle?"

"No, sir."

"Well, you can't blame me for trying." He stood and put his headdress back on, and then returned to selling his magic elixir to a gullible public.

"Now what?" Richard said.

I stretched and yawned and looked at Adelia. "Home to bed. It's been a long day." I didn't expect any argument, and I didn't get one initially. However, as we headed for the exit the situation brought up an uncomfortable reality. "Detective Bern, it's time to think about where you're going to sleep tonight."

"Don't you have a home?" Richard asked.

"It's not that," I said. "We suspect someone is watching us."

"Someone is watching you? You didn't tell me that."

"We told you there would be risk. Do you want out?"

"No. Who is it? Do you know?"

"We keep seeing a red brougham wherever we go, so we think somebody's watching us. It's either that or it's a big coincidence, and I don't believe in coincidences." I turned to Adelia. "For safety sake, I don't want you spending the night alone in your apartment. I offered to sleep on your floor. You said your landlady won't allow a man in the building, no matter how honorable my intentions. So I offered my house. I sleep downstairs. You can have the upstairs."

"But it won't look proper," my partner said. "I can't be seen going inside your house."

"I've had witnesses live with me in the past,"

"Yes, when you had a wife in the house with you. You're a widower now. If I go in your house, what will people think? What will they say? It's not decent."

"Well, I won't have you spending the night alone and scared."

"I'm not afraid. You can escort me home, but that's *it*! I'm no dandelion. I can take care of myself. Remember, I have my little companion in case there's any trouble."

"I'm sorry. As a gentleman, it's my code of honor to make sure you stay safe." I wanted to add that as a man infatuated with her I couldn't let her be alone. However, I couldn't confess that yet, not until I knew how Adelia felt about me and not with Mr. Riley staring me down.

Adelia folded her arms across her chest. "*Nej, nej, nej.* I don't need your help."

The argument continued as the three of us reached the exit and headed for a busy trolley stop.

Richard said to me, "I understand your concern about Detective Bern, but are you *not* concerned about me? I'll be going home alone, sleeping alone."

I wanted to slap him. "Mr. Riley, I don't believe you're in any danger, but if you feel frightened in any way, you may stay at my house too."

Mr. Riley did as I had hoped. "No, sir. I'll be fine."

"Good man. Detective Bern, we'll stop by your apartment for your things. Then you'll come to my house."

"No, no, no."

"Stop arguing. This is the way it *must* be."

"Ha!" Adelia was quite aware of what was expected of gentlemen in our society. Yet she was obsessed with proving to the world that a woman could survive independent of a man, that a woman was capable of doing any job a man did, and possibly doing it better. However, Adelia could only prove her point if she acted alone. If she accepted my assistance it meant that she gave in to the perception of feminine weakness, a trait intolerable in her eyes, but necessary under the circumstances.

"I'll put you in handcuffs if I have to. Here's your choice. Spend the night in jail or at my house. It's for your own safety. Don't worry about what the neighbors think. *I'll* tell them what to think."

Adelia folded her arms across her chest and frowned. "All right, all right, you win."

CHAPTER 32

I carried Adelia's trunk of essentials into my house and turned on the lights. She followed. It was only then that I noticed my home's state of disrepair and its musty smell. The walls in the front hall, parlor and dining room were covered in decorative paper that hadn't been replaced in years so their colors had faded. The floorboards in the hall had a couple of warped pieces that must've been there before, but were only now blatantly obvious to my eyes. There were some cracks in the ceiling. The mahogany railing on the stairs was no longer shiny and bright, but a dull stain. This wasn't a house to bring a woman I hoped to impress.

I said, "Be careful on the steps, the carpet's a little loose."

I flung Adelia's trunk over my shoulders and led her upstairs, past the closed door to the bedroom where I had laid with my wife and the reason for my self-imposed exile to the first floor. After Jane's funeral, I spent too many nights waking up in a terrible sweat, my heart racing and expecting to find her in the bed next to me. Each time, when I realized Jane wasn't there, I was unable to get back to sleep and cussed at the world.

I put Adelia's trunk on top of another trunk at the foot of the bed in the spare bedroom used by my son and his wife when they visited. Adelia entered behind me. She wrung her hands in a nervous fashion, avoided eye contact and seemed anxious for me to leave.

"I have indoor plumbing," I said just to break the awkward silence. "It's at the end of the hall. Like I said, I live downstairs. If anyone's thinking about coming after us tonight, they'll have to get past me."

Adelia nodded. "Thank you, Detective Drummond."

Her formal reply made it clear how she felt. "Well, see you in the morning for breakfast. Goodnight."

"Goodnight." As I headed for the door, she stopped me with a question. "Oh, wait. I forgot to ask you about our plan for tomorrow."

I stood on the threshold and thought out loud. "First, we'll go to City Hall. Hopefully, Officer Swenson will be around so we can have him to watch Mr. Stout. But more important, I'm hoping the coroner's report will be waiting for us on Molly's desk. Dr. Miles, knowing the urgency of the situation, should've concluded his examination. Other than that, we need to pass the word around to see if anybody recognizes the name the Count. Right now, that's our only solid clue as to who Miss Dugan was secretly dating."

Adelia nodded. "Well, we know the Count, whoever he is, won't come walking into City Hall and confess to the crime, so we'll need somebody to turn him in. You'd think somebody in this town would be able to identify someone with such an unusual moniker."

"But if that somebody's a friend, he won't turn him in. We need somebody who knows the Count and doesn't like him."

"Do you think the Count is the person in the red brougham?"

I nodded. "It's quite possible, or the Count hired someone to follow us."

Adelia smiled, and seemed more relaxed. "Goodnight, then."

I said goodnight and went downstairs in a much better mood than I had been when Adelia and I arrived at my house. Adelia had been so paranoid when we approached my front door, believing everybody in the neighborhood was watching us, that she hid her face. Most houses, I pointed out, were dark because it was quite late and everyone had gone to bed.

My parlor, a room that had been the center of living and for receiving guests, was now my place to sleep and dress. My bed was a divan built of birch with gray upholstery and situated by the fireplace. A couple pillows and blankets were piled on it. I removed my suit and undergarments and hung them in an oak armoire, and then put on a woolen nightshirt that covered me to my wrinkly knees. I sat on the divan and instead of lying down or thinking about the identity of the Count, I considered the woman upstairs and how much I was taken with her in just one day. There was no denying the fact that my vision kept drifting in her direction. I experienced yearnings I hadn't felt in some time. As a woman, Adelia's physical appeal was without question, but she did nothing to flaunt it. There was nothing flirty or manipulative about her behavior. She wore no cosmetics. No perfume. Her hair was kept in a style that made her appear older. Intellectually, Adelia had more schooling than me, and even formal training as a detective. She challenged me mentally and at times intimidated me because of her independent nature. As a detective, Adelia started tentatively, and then with each interview she gained confidence and at times took over the investigation, sounding like a true veteran of the streets. So as a trainee, Adelia excelled faster than expected. I couldn't have asked for a better partner. Yet I craved more.

I heard the *click* from the lock on Adelia's bedroom door. In my quiet house, at that late hour, the sound was like the crack of doom, and an indicator of the separation between the two of us. Not that I would've intruded on her. I was too much of a gentleman for that, and our society had a strict code of conduct between the sexes. Even so, people sometimes violated the code and escaped retribution. But no, Adelia made it clear she had no interest in romantic entanglements, with me or any man. She was all business and I was left with a helpless feeling that any affection I may desire would go unfulfilled.

CHAPTER 33

It happened again. I woke in a cold sweat, out of breath, my heart pounding. A ray of sunlight shone through the closed curtains at one of the parlor windows. My first thought was that somebody was trying to break into the house. Was Jane safe? Then I looked around and realized I was on the divan in the parlor. Jane wasn't here. Adelia was upstairs. It was a dream, and this one was violent.

The War Between the States had been over for almost thirty years, yet in dreams I still relived the spectacle as if it were currently happening. I heard the air-piercing whistle of bullets as they zipped by my head, heard the thunderous blast from exploding cannonballs and firing artillery. I watched men fall in agonizing and twisted forms. Most of them never knew what hit them. Some, however, survived the initial strike from a bullet or shrapnel. Their horrified screams and cries for help were excruciating memories. Yet for me, the worst sound was the high-pitched scream from horses. The poor creatures found themselves thrust into a deathly barrage with no knowledge of what might befall them, much like the infantry on both sides of the battlefield. We were just fodder to some bigger political struggle our nation should've had the common sense to avoid. So why did I dream about battle? Weren't dreams supposed to be fantasies, or pleasant images of beautiful meadows, ocean voyages, or women?

My breathing and heart rate relaxed. I threw off the covers and sat on the edge of the divan. My muscles ached from head to toe. I must've ridden my bicycle several miles yesterday, and then walked a few miles more. All that physical activity after being inactive for months took its toll. *I'm getting too old for this.*

After my morning toilet and shave, I put on undergarments, a white shirt, gray vest, trousers, suspenders and a gray frock. I put some money in my pants pocket. I stuffed a compliment of handkerchiefs into a vest pocket and then slipped into black socks and shoes.

I called up the stairs to Adelia, and then prepared some oatmeal and coffee.

Adelia soon appeared in the kitchen, and I caught myself smiling. I fought an urge to embrace her. "You look very nice this morning." She wore a blue shirtwaist and skirt. However, her hair was tied up the same and she wore the same boots.

"Thank you, Detective Drummond. I slept very well. I didn't realize how tired I was. We had a busy day. Did you sleep well?"

"I did. I'm even a little sore today."

Adelia and I ate quickly, both anxious to get to City Hall. When we stepped outside, we were greeted by a chilly wind that rustled the green and some yellow-gold leaves on two elms that fronted my property. The trees, along with others on the street, occupied a thin strip of land between the roadway and the sidewalk, and they competed for space with poles that supported telephone and electric wires.

Wilmington was a city of trees. From a high point in Rockford Park, anyone looking downtown would see a leafy canopy broken up only briefly by a church spire or tall building.

Then the red brougham with its black horse and black-suited driver passed as casually as any coach might do on a morning ride. I thought to holler after it, but my partner summed up the obvious.

"And now the person in that red coach knows that I spent the night in your house. Why won't they come forward?"

I sighed, and felt my gun under my suit. "They will when they feel the timing is right."

"David! Good morning!" my neighbor James Whittier exclaimed. He was no doubt on his way to his accounting job at the Wilmington Water Company. Of course he stared at Adelia and revealed that look of curiosity that told me if I didn't explain her presence he'd start the whispered conversations about a tryst. So I introduced Adelia and casually stated she was in my house as a necessary precaution while we investigated Miss Dugan's murder. James nodded. He appeared to believe me, but citizens were notorious for interpreting events for themselves and choosing a seedier explanation.

After James left, Adelia asked, "Do you think he'll cause trouble?"

"He might."

The two of us walked in and out of shade cast by the trees that lined Jefferson and stepped on the occasional dead leaf. "I told him the truth, but gossip is a favorite way to pass the time."

"I know some incantations from the old country that would lock up his lips."

I laughed. "Are you a witch?"

"*Ja*, my parents told me their village had a few witches. But in Sweden, they don't burn witches at the stake like they did here in America. In Sweden, they're cherished. They're called upon for potions to help cure the sick, to get a lover, to strike at enemies. We're a very superstitious people."

"So if I want to get someone to fall in love with me," I said with a grin, "you know the formula? What do I have to do?"

Adelia smiled and nodded. "*Ja*. My mother taught me some of the spells. Do you want the potion? I can make some. Do you have someone in mind? If it's Molly, you won't need any potion. She's already willing to be courted."

We turned onto Sixth Street with a few other pedestrians and headed toward Market, but my enthusiasm for the day was gone. The conversation proved Adelia had no idea how I felt about her. So to cover my disappointment, I chastised her. "I can't believe someone as intelligent as you believes in witches and potions. I thought you'd know better than that."

Adelia smiled and shrugged. "What can I say? I have many facets."

I smiled at that. "Do you believe in ghosts too?"

"I'm not telling you. You'll laugh at me."

"No, I won't. Tell me."

"Well, I do believe in ghosts, and I'll tell you why. Just after my dad died we stayed at my Uncle's farm in Elmhurst. He asked me to go outside one night and get some firewood. There was a cord of wood by the barn. While I was collecting the wood, I saw a light. I looked and saw my dead grandmother. I dropped the wood but stayed right there and stared at her. Her name was also Adelia. I was named after her. She told me I should stop worrying about my mother and my siblings and do what I want with my life. I shouldn't feel obligated. But if I stayed I'd only become like them, producing babies with an alcoholic husband and dead before I'm forty. She said I should do whatever it takes to leave, and not feel guilty about leaving. There was no future there for me. So I did as she said. But my grandmother was right. I couldn't be me if I had stayed."

"If you had an Uncle to live with, why did you end up hungry?"

I waited for an answer, but she refused to elaborate.

"I admire you. It takes a lot of courage to leave home. You're a remarkable woman, Adelia. I hope you don't mind me saying that."

She looked at me with wet eyes, and I sensed a deep pain was being suppressed, yet I saw a hint of tenderness. "No, Detective Drummond, I don't mind you saying that. Thank you."

We arrived with a few other folks at the corner of Sixth Street and Market and stood next the Security Trust and Safe Deposit Company. After a streetcar passed, Adelia and I crossed Market and then walked in front of Mullins & Sons. A group of boys had gathered in front of two display windows to watch a store clerk change the clothes on the male mannequins. The boys giggled and appeared curious to discover if the models were anatomically endowed. When they saw they weren't, the boys expressed bitter disappointment by banging on the glass and yelling at the clerk. "Fraud."

Joey was in his usual spot hawking the latest edition of the *Morning Herald.* Newsboys could be good sources of information. They hung around pool halls, dice games, prostitutes, petty criminals, and might even deliver messages for Western Union Telegraph. Surprisingly, newsboys were also well-informed about the coming and goings of society's upper crest because well-to-do gentlemen gossiped or complained during a shoe-shine. A few other wealthy men were known to spill secrets when drunk inside seedy taverns, opium dens, brothels and gambling houses.

Joey tapped his chin. "Well, Detective Drummond, let me think about that for a minute." I waited patiently, as did a few men who hoped to purchase a newspaper. "Sorry. I don't know nobody that's called the Count, but I'll ask around."

"Thank you, Joey. I appreciate that. I assume Molly bought a paper?"

Joey frowned. "No. What did you do to her? She was all mad this morning and said that if Detective Drummond wanted a newspaper, he can buy it himself. Did you go and break her heart?"

"I didn't do anything," I said, placing a penny in the palm of Joey's dirty hand. He gave me a copy of the four-page *Morning Herald* for Friday, October 21, 1892. Like every other newspaper in the city, the bulk of the publication was advertisements. Only the first page was devoted exclusively to news. The front page had the headline I expected. *SUSPECT RELEASED IN THE KATIE DUGAN MURDER.* Bill Kendle's article vindicated Mr. Riley, proclaiming the gentleman had a solid alibi, quoting me and Detective Bern. "Let me know the second you hear anything."

Joey promised he would.

I gave the newspaper to Adelia and pointed at the headline. "We're certain to hear from Mr. Moran, but I don't care."

"Maybe today we'll find the evidence we need against Mr. Stout."

I agreed. We entered City Hall, said hello to Officer Hinder and then hurried upstairs.

Molly looked up from her desk. "Oh, it's you two," she said in total contrast to her behavior yesterday. "The Coroner's Report arrived a half-hour ago."

CHAPTER 34

"So it's here?" I said, my enthusiasm back again. "Where?"

"In your office." Molly said.

I almost ran to the room, but paused to ask Molly, "What happened to good morning?"

Molly frowned. "What's good about it?"

"What's the matter? Did I do something to upset you?"

"*No.*" She folded her arms across her chest and glared at Adelia. "You didn't *do* anything."

"I'm sorry, Molly, but I don't have time or patience right now to discuss whatever it is I did to upset you. Has the Chief read the report?"

"No. He's not here. He went out to help the ward leaders buy votes among the Irish and the Negroes."

I stared at Molly, surprised by her candor. "Boy, you are in a foul mood this morning. Did something happen at home? I've never heard you talk like this."

"No, nothing happened *at home.* I don't think I like men anymore."

"Good for you," Adelia said, but Molly ignored her. "Did Chief leave a message or say anything we need to know before we resume our investigation?"

"No, Detective *Bern*," Molly sounded as if the words left a vile taste in her mouth. "He was disappointed that you let your suspect go. He did call Officer Swenson and told him to see you. I don't know when the constable might get here."

"That's all right. Thank you, Molly."

Adelia and I entered the Detective's Office. I quickly spotted the sealed envelope from Dr. Miles on my desk and grabbed it. "Well, here we go." I broke the seal, removed the report and skimmed over the coroner's autopsy results. "Just as I thought."

"With child?"

"Yes."

My partner bowed her head. "So the murderer killed two."

"He did indeed."

"What about suicide, Detective Drummond? I thought about it last night. Here's an unmarried lady about to give birth to a bastard child. She might've been despondent, knowing the shame she'd bring to her family. Maybe she went to that isolated location so no one would see her and try to stop her."

I considered Adelia's theory, and then voiced my opinion. "I guess she could've cut her own throat, but I doubt it. The wound was so severe and across her entire throat. Most suicides by razor are done at the wrists."

"I guess that's true. But now I'm wondering if Mr. Stout is guilty. He doesn't strike me as a man of means. Yet someone rich enough to own an expensive brougham is watching us. Mr. Stout doesn't have that kind of money. It must be a DuPont, right?"

"Not necessarily. We have a lot of wealthy families in this city and they generally live on Delaware Avenue. There's *old* money. That would be the Bayards, the Bancrofts, the Leas, the Canbys, Gilpin, Tatnalls, and Shipley. Those families made their fortunes as millers along the Brandywine long before the DuPonts arrived. Then there's new money from coach, car and shipbuilders such as Job Jackson and Joshua Pusey. You met a member of the Warner family yesterday. They have over a hundred years of profits from shipping. So there's a lot of possibilities."

"Don't go in there!" Molly yelled from the hallway.

Casey Moran appeared on the threshold. "Is that the coroner's report?"

"I'm sorry, sir," Molly said, standing behind him, "he just won't listen."

"What're you doing here?" I said. "Too crowded in the Rat's Nest?"

"Yes," he replied, stepping into the office. "I saw that grave-robber Travers come in here and leave about thirty minutes ago. So what's the report say?"

I was morbidly sarcastic. "Miss Dugan was killed by a razor."

Casey groaned. "I know that. What else does it say?"

"Not until after I inform her family," I said.

"I can pretty well guess what it says," Casey said. "Just confirm my suspicions. I have a deadline."

"I don't care about your deadline. This is a private matter and you know the protocol. Go crawl back inside with the other rats."

"I understand you let Mr. Riley go. It made my article last night worthless. My boss wasn't happy."

"I don't care, Casey. You overstepped your boundaries and now you've jeopardized an innocent man's livelihood."

"That's a pity, really. Is there another suspect?"

"When I know, you'll know," I said. I took three Henry Clay's from my cigar box and put them in a vest pocket. I stuffed the coroner's report back in the envelope and waved at Adelia to follow.

"Wait," Casey said as we hurried past him.

CHAPTER 35

Adelia and I rode our bicycles southwest to 1111 Lancaster Avenue. The Dugan house was an impressive three-story green Victorian with the typical mansard roof, a corner turret and front porch. However, windows were shut and curtains closed. The front door was slightly ajar so that anyone paying their respects could enter without using the heavy brass knocker that would certainly disturb the solemn household. White crepe and ribbon had been tied to the doorknob, the tragic symbol that a young person had died.

Adelia and I stepped into the vestibule. James Dugan stood in the parlor in front of a green upholstered sofa and shook hands in a lethargic manner with a white-haired gentleman who expressed his condolences. James appeared to have little strength. He probably wanted to be somewhere else, anywhere else. People meant well when they came to share grief, but it was a custom I loathed. Every well-wisher only reminded me of my emotional pain and physical loss. I wanted them to stay away and leave me alone. Their presence and their words did not bring comfort.

Father Milford, a young priest from St. Joseph's, appeared from the back of the house holding a glass of water. He had bags under his brown eyes and pitch-black hair he greased flat to his scalp and a narrow moustache above thin lips. His white vestments hung like drapes from his bony shoulders. We exchanged a silent hello.

"Thank you for coming," James said to his visitor. "Your friendship has always been valuable to me and my wife."

The man walked past Adelia and I without saying a word or making eye contact. I spoke softly when I introduced my partner to Father Milford.

"It's a pleasure to meet you," Adelia whispered. Then she asked me, "How do you know Father Milford?"

"I met him at Wilmington Hospital during my wife's illness." I faced the priest. "How is Father Donaghy? I hear he's leaving St. Joseph's."

"He's leaving next year," Father Milford said after taking a sip of water, "once he's satisfied that the parochial school will be in good hands."

"I'm sure the Irish workers will sorely miss him. He gave them a sense of home."

"And I don't?"

"I didn't say that," although he was right. Father Donaghy came from Ireland and understood the immigrant laborers at Henry Clay Village far better than Father Milford, a native to Wilmington and someone who has been described as stoic and aloof. From my brief encounters with Father Milford, I had to agree.

Adelia, Father Milford and I approached Mr. Dugan.

"I am sorry to disturb you, sir," I said, "but we have the Coroner's Report. Where is your wife? She should hear the results with you."

"She's upstairs lying down," James said. His tired eyes looked at me. "I've heard some conflicting news about a suspect. Did you arrest Mr. Riley or not? I can't believe he's responsible."

"We arrested him," Adelia said, "but his alibi checked out, so we released him."

"Good," James said, looking at her with an odd expression. Perhaps he was surprised the way she spoke as if she were in charge of the investigation. "Is anyone else suspected?"

Adelia answered, "Nothing definite yet, but we're looking at Mr. Stout."

James nodded. "If he's responsible, I'll live to regret the fact that I didn't shoot him years ago."

"Yes, sir. Are your children home?"

"No," he replied. "I sent them away to be with friends. I thought it best under the circumstances. Excuse me. I'll get my wife."

James held onto the banister and labored up the stairs.

I turned to Father Milford. "Has the funeral been set?"

"Tomorrow at noon. It'll be a simple ceremony, with the family and some friends. I assume you two will be there."

"We will," Adelia said, "but it may not be so simple."

"How so?"

"The newspapers have greatly publicized this case. A lot of people might attend just to show support for the family."

Father Milford nodded. "You may be right. Our church isn't very big. Have either of you been to St. Joseph's?"

"I just moved here and haven't had the opportunity," Adelia said.

"Well, then," Father Milford said with a smile, "let me extend my invitation, although your profession will probably alarm some of our parishioners."

"And you too, I assume?"

Father Milford feigned a cough and then spoke to me in a

condescending voice. "As for you, Detective Drummond, you did not allow me to administer Last Rite's to your wife, or accept my counsel in any way. What is your faith?"

"Personal," I said, which got me a snide look from the priest. "But I have been to your church."

"When? I don't remember seeing you."

"I battled the fire in '66 that destroyed the original building. It was one of the first things I did after coming home from the war."

"Well, thank you for that. But in '66 I was just a baby."

Adelia asked, "How long have you been at St. Joseph's?"

"Only a couple of years," he said. "Seminary School before that."

I turned my attention to a collection of Cabinet Cards on the fireplace mantel. One in particular caught my eye. It stood in the center and measured eight inches by ten and must've been a family portrait taken years ago. The black and white image showed Mr. and Mrs. Dugan standing proudly behind three daughters with Emily cradling what I assumed was their infant son.

"Do you know which child in this photograph is Katie?" I asked the priest.

Father Milford joined me. "I'm not sure." He pointed at smaller individual portraits. "These are more recent. This is Sara, the oldest. She's married. This is Victoria. She's younger than Katie was. This is Katie. And this is their son Harold, the youngest at twelve."

Miss Dugan's youthful beauty made it obvious why any man would want to seduce her. Had she surrendered willingly or been forced? Either way, scandal would've followed had she made the indiscretion public. Then add to the fact that the illicit affair had produced a baby, Katie and her lover faced a serious problem that her lover chose to eliminate in the worst possible manner.

James returned with his wife, who wore a long black dress and had a handkerchief in her hand. She walked hunched forward.

"I was just admiring your photographs," I said.

Emily didn't seem to hear me. "You have news to share?"

"Please sit."

"Is it all right if Father Milford remains?"

"It's fine with me. As the family priest, he'll find out about my news anyway."

I opened the envelope while the unhappy couple occupied the sofa and the priest took a neighboring chair. Adelia and I remained standing. "I have with me the Coroner's Report, compiled after Dr. Miles performed a full autopsy on your daughter." I removed the report, paused, and then spoke with compassion. "We know the motive behind Katie's death. She was with child."

CHAPTER 36

The Dugans and Father Milford barely moved or reacted to the news of Katie's pregnancy.

"Do you understand?" I asked.

Finally, James squirmed. He kept his face down. He spoke in a low voice. "No. It's a lie. It's not possible."

Emily's face turned red and her eyes watered. "No, our sweet girl would never bring such shame to our house."

"I'm sorry," I said, "but the medical evidence is clear."

Emily sobbed. "Then it wasn't some unmarried man who killed her. It was someone who wanted to hide his shame."

"Albert Stout," James said in a quivering voice. "You go arrest that bastard right *now*!"

"It's not that simple, Mr. Dugan. He has an alibi. Can I assume Katie never told either of you about her condition?"

James reacted as if I had insulted him. "No, sir. We weren't told. We never suspected."

I turned to Father Milford. "Did she confess it to you?"

"Father," Emily said, looking at him with wet eyes, "did Katie tell you?"

The priest reached from his chair and took hold of Emily's hand. He spoke in a sympathetic voice. "All I can say is that Katie did not come to me for confession."

"My poor baby." She dabbed her eyes with her handkerchief. "Why didn't she come to us? She could've told us. We would've been angry, but we wouldn't have thrown her out in the street. Oh, James, think about it. That's why she stopped going to mass. She was too ashamed. Why did she think we weren't approachable?"

"Please, dear," James said, his cheeks wet, "don't reproach yourself. It's too hard."

"As for Mr. Stout," I said, "he told me he attended the Sacred Heart Fair with his wife and daughter Wednesday night, and that it was a coincidence he was there when Katie and Mr. Riley were. He admitted to following them, but never approached them. After the fair, he went home and straight to bed. I'm not sure if he's been completely truthful."

"Does Mr. Stout sleep in the same bed with his wife?" Emily said.

Adelia said, "He does not."

"Since he sleeps alone, he could've gone out without being noticed and then followed Katie."

"Yes, ma'am, we've considered that."

"Do you know anything else about Mr. Stout that might help us?" I said. "All I know is that he's unhappy in his marriage, works for Warner and reads Poe."

"Reads Poe?" James said.

"Yes, sir, are you remembering something?"

James nodded. "When Katie worked for them, she mentioned that Mr. Stout would come home sometimes at mid-day and scare her by reading one of Poe's stories. She mentioned a tale about an old man who had been murdered and his body put under floorboards, but the killer still heard the dead man's heartbeat and it drove him to confess. There was another story about somebody put behind a wall, and a scary poem about a raven. I'm not sure what the titles were to these stories because I'm not that familiar with Poe's work. Is it possible to keep this indiscretion from becoming public? Our girl is dead. Why shame her in the newspapers?"

"I can keep it secret," I said, "but newspapermen have a way of finding these things out. They bribe a family member or someone in the Coroner's Office."

"Doesn't anyone have scruples?" Emily said

"Not when it comes to something like this. You know people love scandal."

"Well, you keep after Mr. Stout," Emily said. "I'm sure you'll find something that proves he's responsible. I can't imagine my Katie giving herself willingly either. That must be why she became more distant and insisted on washing her own clothes. He must've taken her by force and threatened her somehow not to talk, and she felt ashamed and dirty."

"I can assure you, ma'am that we will keep after Mr. Stout. Do either of you know anybody referred to as the Count?"

The Dugans and Father Milford looked puzzled, and then denied knowing anybody by that name.

"Why do you ask?" Father Milford said.

"We came across the name while talking to someone at the Sacred Heart Fair. Now, Mr. and Mrs. Dugan, may we look at Katie's room?"

"Oh, must you?" Emily said. "I know you told us you were going to, but is it necessary?"

"I'm sorry," Adelia said, "but it *is* necessary. I will treat her things

167

with the utmost care and respect."

James looked at his wife, who nodded reluctantly. He then groaned and slowly rose to his feet. "I'll be back shortly, my dear. You stay and visit with Father Milford." Then he addressed Adelia and me. "I'll show you the way."

James labored up the stairs again. Adelia and I followed close behind. I was tempted to wrap an arm around her waist, but refrained. As it were, we bumped arms. I apologized.

At the top of the stairs, James opened the door to the first bedroom on the right. "Please be gentle with her things and leave the room as you found it."

Adelia was sympathetic. "Of course we will. I promise you."

James left. I crossed the threshold behind my partner and entered a truly feminine room that was both childish and blossoming womanhood. There was a pink blanket on a lacy canopy bed, a travel trunk at the foot of the bed, a nightstand and an oak armoire. There were dolls piled on a corner chair. The wallpaper depicted a summer meadow, with bunnies at play and deer grazing. I could imagine Katie seated at her vanity, where she would've applied cosmetics to her eyes, cheeks and lips and then admired her creation in an oval mirror.

I waited by the door while Adelia opened the mahogany armoire, exposing Miss Dugan's dresses, shirtwaists, skirts, undergarments and nightgowns. I cleared my throat. "Let me know if you need my help."

"I'll handle the clothes," Adelia said. "I don't think the family will object if you look around the bed and her nightstand."

I lifted the blanket and peeked underneath, but saw only a white sheet. I patted down the pillows. I looked under the bed. "Not a speck of dust. I think they cleaned recently."

"Maybe so," Adelia said. She was eye-balling each article of clothing and squeezing them with her hands. "Nothing here yet."

Katie's nightstand had an oil lamp, a clock and a hair-brush. I opened the drawer. It contained a Bible, some handkerchiefs, another hairbrush and a few thin books related to *Ladies Manners and Etiquette.* Under the books were some thicker volumes including *The Works of Edgar Allan Poe* by John Henry Ingram.

CHAPTER 37

"These looks familiar," I said, holding up the four books for Adelia to see. "Should we assume that Mr. Stout gave them to her before Katie quit her position?"

"And then she held onto them for four years? From a man she despised?"

"Then how do you explain their presence?" I lifted the book covers on each volume and skimmed over the pages. "The binding is relatively loose. She must've read them a lot. Do you really think she might've liked Mr. Stout?"

"Women don't always make smart choices when it comes to men. Katie was young and naïve, easily fooled by sophistication. I was stupid enough to get married."

Adelia judged Miss Dugan as inexperienced without having known the young lady. However, from the testimonies heard so far, I suspected Katie had experience with men and her need for thrills signaled a strong passion for life.

"Hallelujah," Adelia said. She'd found a half-empty bottle of Kickapoo Sagwa in one of the dresser drawers. "It was hidden under some slips."

I put the books back in the drawer and joined my partner. "So we can assume Katie drinks it. Not the killer."

"Maybe for morning sickness, since it's supposed to cure stomach ailments."

I nodded. "All right, let's assume Miss Dugan drank it for morning sickness. We have another bottle of the medicine by the Bush estate. Let's assume that's the bottle she bought at the Sacred Heart Fair. She told Professor Vincent she had to hurry. The Count was waiting. So she didn't buy the bottle for the Count. She bought it for herself. How did it end up under shrubbery?"

Adelia pondered my question. "Maybe she was standing by the house when she took a drink and had just put the cork in the bottle when the killer surprised and scared her. She dropped the bottle and took off running, but unfortunately, he caught her by the persimmon tree."

"That's possible. Why didn't Mr. Beeson see her carrying the bottle?"

"She put it in a dress pocket."

"Yes, of course," I said, feeling stupid. I opened a travel trunk at the foot of Katie's bed. It contained only folded blankets and pillow covers. "Nothing here."

Adelia put the bottle of Sagwa back where she found it, but continued to search. "Maybe she kept a diary."

"Great idea. Something only a female would think of. I'll definitely inform Chief Francis that you've been an asset to this investigation."

Adelia looked at me and I thought she was about to cry, but she stifled any emotion. "It's been a pleasure learning from you, sir." Then she pointed at me. "See I was right. I told you that you'd make an excellent professor."

I helped raise a son to be a man, but never did I experience the surge of pride that went through my body because of my partner's sentiment. This emotion made me wonder what my life might've been like had I become that history professor. I might've influenced hundreds of students who would've remembered me fondly for my scholarship and paternal presence. Until that moment, I never regretted my decision to leave Delaware College and join the war, but perhaps I had made the wrong decision.

Adelia searched the bedroom for another half hour. No diary was found, or anything else of interest.

"It's too bad Mr. Dugan sent the children away," I said. "Sometimes a sibling has a lot to say. They might even know who Katie was seeing, if Katie confided in one of them. But my guess is she didn't tell them. Otherwise, they might've told their parents."

"Maybe. Now what?"

I held up three fingers. "Unmarried ladies in trouble have three options. They marry the father of their baby." I put one finger down. "We can rule that out. And because Katie was murdered, she must've decided against an abortion, which proved to be a fatal decision." I put a second finger down. "So that leaves an orphanage."

CHAPTER 38

"The Home for Friendless and Destitute Children is the best and largest orphanage for white children in the city," I told Adelia as we rode our bikes north on Adams Street toward Ninth. "There are a couple of other poor and overcrowded orphanages in the city, run by churches, but I'm guessing Katie would want to leave her baby with the best one." The mansion-size building came into view from a block away. It was constructed originally as a boarding school, but that endeavor failed. As we approached, I developed an uneasy feeling in the pit of my stomach. "Where is everybody?"

The property was usually teeming with boys and girls at play and under the supervision of staff members, but no children were visible. No games of tag, nobody on the swings or seesaws. No adult stood watch from the porch. No little faces peered out from the many windows in the hope that my partner and I might be a married couple looking to adopt.

"So this isn't normal?" Adelia asked.

"No. Something's wrong."

As a policeman, I assumed the worst. Maybe someone poisoned the children and staff members. Perhaps a teacher or caregiver went insane and killed everybody. Adelia and I could be walking into a bloody mess. But what other explanation was there? I had never seen the yard void of children. Even in winter, boys and girls came outside wrapped in their coats and created a raucous noise that could be heard for blocks.

"What could've happened?"

We left our bicycles by the gate to the perimeter fence and entered the grounds. *Dear God, let there be a good explanation for this.* I approached the front door tentatively and turned the knob. "It's locked. It's never been locked before."

Adelia peeked in a window. "I don't see anybody. There's no furniture"

"What? How can that be?"

"Wait, I see somebody."

I put some strength behind the doorknocker. Impatient, I pounded my fist against the wooden door. I heard a female voice yell, "Hold on. I'm coming."

I heard the click of the lock and the door opened. "Detective Drummond," Mrs. Granger said, stepping onto the porch and giving me a quick embrace. The caretaker was a heavyset and gray-haired widow whose sailor husband had been lost at sea thirteen years ago. He left her little money, and as a charity worker, she barely earned enough to survive. Her situation was most evident in her clothes. She owned only two dresses, a gray cotton one for cold weather and a blue one for summer. The gray one had a torn pocket. "It's so good to see you."

I introduced Adelia. "What's happened?"

Mrs. Granger ignored my question and focused on Adelia. "So, you're the lady detective the mayor hired to satisfy the reformers. No wonder the old guard is upset. Not only are you destroying their notion of a woman's limitations, but you're a beautiful lady proving you can do a man's job." She patted my partner on the arm. "Good for you. I'm so glad to know you."

"Thank you, the pleasure is all mine."

Mrs. Granger winked at my partner. "I'm sure you don't need any advice, but I'm going to give you some anyway. Don't listen to anything bad they write or say about you. In fact, don't read the newspapers. You stick to your convictions." She pointed at me. "And you can learn a lot from this gentleman. You have a great teacher and a kind-hearted soul."

"Yes, ma'am, I know."

I couldn't wait a second longer. "Mrs. Granger, what's happened here?"

She frowned. "Come inside and I'll tell you."

We stepped into an empty hall where children once played. Parlors to the left and right, rooms once used to greet adoptive parents or receive unwanted children, were absent of furniture and rugs. The white walls were bare, with cleaner squares and rectangles marking the former locations of landscape paintings and portraits of the orphanages' top benefactors. Even the bust of founder Mrs. Gause, which had had a prominent location on a pedestal by the front door, was gone.

Mrs. Granger released a deep sigh. "Our funding was cut." Her voice echoed. "We weren't getting the donations we once received. The repair bills to keep this house going just kept rising and rising. So the trustees decided to shutter the place and put the property up for sale. The children have been moved to New Castle or Claymont."

"Oh," I said, relieved but still troubled by the news because it meant Wilmington had one less facility for abandoned or orphaned children. There were already enough boys and girls struggling to survive. Even if one of them wanted to make a better life, their options were limited and sometimes worse than staying on the streets. Some children disappeared, kidnapped and transported to other cities to become prostitutes, while others slaved away in garment factories or sent down coal mines, or forced to work on ships. It was a sad fact of life that the upper crust and our government officials pretended didn't exist. "I was really worried when we rode up and saw nobody here."

"It was decided at the last board meeting. The actual removal of the children and furnishings took place eight days ago. I would've told you, but you were out of town."

"I assume you went to the benefactors and asked for more money, and they turned you down."

Mrs. Granger nodded. "Some of them had the nerve to ask me if they could see the books, as if they didn't trust our accounting. One gentleman, who I won't dignify by mentioning his name, told me it was time the children fended for themselves. They shouldn't rely on charity."

I sighed, disgusted. The lack of compassion for homeless children was spurred by the fact that our society didn't view childhood as a separate or developmental stage of life. Children were seen and treated as small adults. The belief was that if a child lived on the streets, then that child chose to live on the streets. Reformers knew that to get homeless boys and girls into safe houses or orphanages they had to defeat this misconception that children were responsible decision-makers. It was a monumental task, but one Casey Moran and his reformers were willing to accept. "I'm sorry to hear that it's come to this. You did such great work for our unfortunate ones. So what're *you* going to do?"

Mrs. Granger sighed, "My son asked me to live with him in Lancaster. It's time. And I'll enjoy my grandchildren. Besides, I was never going to get rich doing this line of work."

"Money was never your motivation," I said with a hug. Mrs. Granger loved children and believed it was her mission to keep the prisons and workhouses from gaining any more victims. "You and everybody that worked here can take great pride in the service you provided."

"Thank you," Mrs. Granger said with teary eyes. "Now that the formalities are out of the way, I can only assume you're here because the murdered girl I read about in the newspaper must've been with child and you're wondering if she stopped here to discuss adoption."

"Yes, ma'am," Adelia said. "Miss Katie Dugan."

"Follow me." Mrs. Granger led us toward the back of the house. Our footsteps echoed on the wooden floor. "My office is the last room to get cleaned out. We're trying to decide what to do with all the paperwork and ledgers."

"I have a good friend at the Historical Society who might take them," I said. "He's currently cataloging the files from the old almshouse and insane asylum."

CHAPTER 39

In her office, Mrs. Granger walked past her roll top desk to a stack of cardboard boxes against the back wall. She lifted the lid off the top container and pulled out a black ledger book that had 1892 embossed on the cover.

"All visitors," Mrs. Granger said for Adelia's benefit, "had to write down their name and address upon arrival because we had to prove to the General Assembly that we got enough foot traffic each year to warrant public funds. Did her parents know she was expecting?"

"No," Adelia said. "Or so they say."

"You don't believe them?"

"Their reactions seemed genuine, but I can't believe they didn't suspect something."

"Maybe her father killed her?" Mrs. Granger said. "That's been known to happen."

"No, ma'am, he was home playing cards when she was killed."

"But," I said, "Mr. Beeson said it was unusual for them to play cards on a Wednesday night. Mr. Dugan could've hired someone and paid to have it look like Mr. Riley did it. I don't believe it, but it's still something to consider." Adelia nodded. "Mrs. Granger, do you know anyone who goes by the moniker the Count?"

Mrs. Granger almost laughed. "The Count? What an odd name. No, David, but I'll ask around. I assume he's a real suspect?"

"He is."

Mrs. Granger put the ledger on top of her desk and turned pages until she found the beginning of the current month. "All right, I assume the young lady came in recently. Sometimes girls give a false name because they're embarrassed or just want to ask general questions."

Mrs. Granger, Adelia and I read the short list of handwritten names starting on October first. Each entry included the time of their visit. As we read the list, the majority of names were married couples, such as Mr. and Mrs. Jones, Mr. and Mrs. Wellington and so on.

"It doesn't say if they adopted or not," Adelia said.

"Not all couples came here to adopt. Sadly, some came here to surrender their children. I couldn't deal with those. The kids scream, the mothers cry, but the parents are so poor they don't see any other way. Their kids are starving and practically naked." She then leaned close to Adelia and whispered in a respectful tone. "In case you didn't know it, David was one of our benefactors. He gave some money, but his real success was getting children off the streets. Unfortunately, some of the urchins are so blasted independent they can't stand our rules so they leave after a few days. Even with winter coming on, they'd rather live by their own resources, or in the gangs that have become their family."

Adelia nodded and asked me, "Do you share an affinity with orphans, Detective Drummond?"

"No, but after years of working as a policeman in our poorer neighborhoods, I couldn't help but sympathize with them." I laughed. "I wanted to adopt all of them, but my wife wasn't in favor of it."

We returned to reading the names under October and discovered five single women. No Katie Dugan, but we looked for variations on Katie's name, such as anagrams and similar-sounding names.

"How about this?" I said, putting my finger on a name from October 9 — at 2:15 p.m. "Katherine Douglas. Do you remember her?"

Mrs. Granger thought for a moment. "I was at a meeting with the trustees at that time. Unfortunately, it was the meeting where they announced they were closing the place. Mrs. Pleasance was in charge. She would've counseled any young lady that came in, but she's already moved to New York."

"Anyone else?"

Mrs. Granger tapped her chin while she thought. "Wait! Anna Belle Sanders. Why didn't I think of her before? She's a young lady who for some insane reason wants to be a nun." The caretaker laughed. "Sister Margaret at the House of Visitation sent her to us so Anna could perform a week of charity work as part of her indoctrination, or whatever nuns-to-be call it. She was here that week. She helped prepare and serve meals. She helped make the beds and manned the front desk. She might remember this Miss Douglas."

CHAPTER 40

Adelia and I rode four blocks north on Adams Street, then turned north onto the most beautiful promenade in the city, Delaware Avenue, home to Wilmington's wealthier people not named DuPont. Beautiful Norway maples lined both sides of this wide thoroughfare, between the sidewalk and brick roadway, and some of their leaves had started to turn blood-red.

I spoke as I pedaled. "In a couple weeks, the autumn colors will be at their peak. I'll take you to Rockford Park. From that vantage point, you can look back into the city and see all the reds, golds and yellows."

"I look forward to it."

I smiled. Did she realize she just committed to a date?

Adelia and I passed some impressive three-and-four story mansions of varying architectural styles. Victorian homes had the usual mansard roofs, bay windows, turrets and large front porches. There were Italianate homes, with heavy bracket cornices, central gables and Palladian windows. A few others were in the Queen Anne style, high-hipped roofs, gables with bargeboard trim, tower, and turret. Most exterior walls were either brick, terra cotta, Brandywine granite, Chester County serpentine or brownstone, with stucco or slate for roofs. Some homes had stained-glass windows. They all had spacious yards with well-trimmed bushes and trees and bordered by black wrought-iron fences. At the curb, they had an iron hitching post for horses and a marble stepping stone to use when alighting from a carriage.

"Do you know the families that live in these houses?" Adelia asked while riding.

"Most of them, but even knowing them, I still can't use the front door. They live by a strict code of conduct. Someone like me, a lowly policeman, would have to use the servants' door and even the butler would look down his nose at me."

We turned onto Harrison Street and arrived at The House of Visitation Convent and School. It was a large brownstone set on a two-acre lot and surrounded by a stone wall. Adelia and I dismounted our bikes at an open iron gate and took a winding walkway past dormant flower gardens and statues of former priests and nuns.

"Can I ask you a personal question?" Adelia said.

"You can ask," I replied, happy that she was curious about me. "I won't be offended."

"Do you have a religion? I only ask because of the way Father Milford treated you."

"I don't attend any formal church. I'd say Nature is my church. As a boy I loved to be outside. I still do. I'd much rather walk among the trees and animals than sit on a pew and hear somebody tell me about the wonders of the world. But I'm nervous about going into this convent."

"Why?"

"Well, I was raised Catholic by my Scottish parents until my mother died. My father stopped attending mass, so I never went back. I didn't complain. All the pomp and circumstance that surrounds the church and its rituals frightened me as a child. The priests were intimidating figures in their dark robes, and I didn't understand Latin. However, for me, the most frightening aspect were the nuns. Cloaked in black from head to toe, they looked like images of the Grim Reaper minus the scythe. They often stared at me as if they were waiting for a reason to discipline me. I never saw one smile, and they were generally old and plain. My father once yelled at a group of nuns, 'Good thing you're married to Christ. No living man would want you."

"He sounds like a bitter man."

"He let his grief consume him, something that *won't* happen to me."

"What happened to him? Is he alive?"

"No. He entered the war after I did, so I wasn't around to stop him. The damn fool. He was too old for that sort of thing, but the recruiters didn't care. I fully believe he joined the army hoping to die. He got his wish at Antietam. I was stationed at Fort Delaware when I got a telegram that he'd been killed and his body had been sent home. I claimed his body and buried him in the Wilmington and Brandywine Cemetery."

Adelia nodded, satisfied, and then returned to the subject at hand. "Are you familiar with this order?"

"Yes," I replied as we arrived at the front door. "The nuns are part of the Order of the Visitation. I believe it was founded in France."

"So you're familiar with them even though you're afraid of nuns and don't attend church?"

"Churches are a big part of the city's history." The doorknocker sounded like a thunderclap. "I'm as familiar with them as I am any neighborhood or industry. And even though the nuns scared me, I do give them credit for teaching me to read and write when I attended Sunday School at St. Mary's, which was on Lancaster Pike near our farm."

" *Was* on Lancaster Pike," Adelia said.

"It's gone now. They tore it down about eight years ago. The cemetery's still there. I don't know what they're going to do with it."

The door opened. We were greeted by a blue-eyed nun in black who was not old or plain.

CHAPTER 41

"Hello, are you Sister Margaret?" I asked. She nodded. "I'm Detective Drummond and this is Detective Bern. We just came from speaking with Mrs. Granger at the Home for Destitute Children and she told us that you sent Miss Anna Belle Sanders there to work for a week earlier this month. We're investigating the murder of Miss Katie Dugan. We believe the victim stopped at the orphanage to inquire about adoption for her baby while Miss Sanders was there. We'd like to ask Miss Sanders a few questions. May we speak with her?"

Sister Margaret looked me up and down, and then stepped aside. "Please come in." She closed the door behind us and we stood in a dark corridor. The few sticks of furniture were simple wooden chairs and benches, and crucifixes hung on the walls. In fact, this morbid depiction of Christ was displayed in the adjoining parlors, either as a painting, drawing or statuette. No wonder this religion gave me nightmares. "Did Miss Anna Belle meet Miss Dugan?"

"That's what we'd like to know." A couple elderly nuns walked by and glanced at us suspiciously. They nodded their heads. We nodded back. "And if she did, we'd like to know if she remembers anything about it."

Sister Margaret nodded. Apparently, nodding was the top form of communication. "Wait here." She headed to the rear of the house. Her long habit scraped against the floor and her footsteps echoed.

Adelia looked around and whispered, "So austere." Although my partner kept her voice low, a nun heading for the stairs paused and glanced our way as if she had overheard the comment and resented it. "I do hope this girl can help us."

I agreed, and we waited. The quiet time gave me an opportunity to reflect on my "religion period." As a little boy, I had succumbed to the faith's teachings of Jesus, the saints and apostles and believed in the general goodness of people. However, I was also taught to fear God and his retribution should I misbehave. Those stories about turning people into salt or being eaten by whales or killed in floods had definitely left an impression. Therefore fear, not love, had made me the perfectly behaved child. I was too scared to be anything else. I wondered what would've happened to me had my father continued to attend church after mom died. Would he still have sent me to

Brandywine Academy and encouraged me to attend college? Would I have turned out differently had I not attended church at all?

Sister Margaret returned. A young lady in a white robe and hood walked behind her, head down and eyes to the floor. "This is Anna Belle Sanders," she said. The young lady did not speak or raise her head. I wondered if she was shy or had to behave this way. Sister Margaret offered the adjoining room for our interview. "Would you like some tea?"

"No, thank you," Adelia said, retrieving her notebook and pencil. "We don't expect to be here long."

Sister Margaret frowned and directed us to a pair of benches in front of a stone hearth. "Please sit and ask your questions."

I spoke to the woman in white. "Miss Sanders, we just talked with Mrs. Granger at the Home for Friendless and Destitute Children. She said you were there for one week earlier this month."

"Serving her charity duty," Sister Margaret said. "As a postulate, Anna Belle will be performing several duties to test whether or not she is worthy of becoming a nun."

"Do you remember October ninth?" I asked. "Did you meet a young lady who signed her name as Katherine Douglas at 2:15 in the afternoon? I realize that's a difficult thing to answer. I'm sure you met a lot of people. However, we're investigating the murder of Miss Katie Dugan and we believe she might've used the name Katherine Douglas when she stopped at the orphanage to inquire about adoption for her unborn baby. She was with child when she was killed, and not married. Do you remember anything about that day? Do you remember Miss Douglas?"

Anna Belle had yet to raise her head and look at me. I wondered if she heard me or if she could talk.

"Do you recall the young lady?" Sister Margaret said. "Answer the detective. It's all right."

Anna Belle finally lifted her head and looked at me with hazel eyes. She had a fair and delicate complexion, with a straight nose and small mouth. Strands of blonde hair poked out from under her hood. She spoke in a soft voice. "October ninth? I did meet a lot of people, all good people. It's difficult to remember just one of them, but if it's the girl I think it is, I remember her because she's the first woman I ever met who was going to have a baby without a husband."

"What do you remember?"

"She was nice at first," Anna Belle said. "Later, she got cross with me because I stared at her. I apologized. I couldn't help it. Like I said,

I had never met a woman who wasn't married and having a baby. I thought about all the horrible things my mother would've called her, or done to her. My mother would've *killed* her. But this lady wanted to see Mrs. Granger. I told her she wasn't available, that I was just minding the front door until she returned from her meeting. Mrs. Pleasance was there, but she was busy watching the children. So I told this lady she could wait, but I didn't know for how long. She didn't stay."

"Did she tell you she was with child? How did you know?"

"She wasn't alone."

Adelia and I slid to the front edge of the bench, excited.

"Who was with her?" I asked. "Do you remember his name? What did he look like?"

Anna Belle smiled. "How did you know it was a *he*?"

I shrugged. "Lucky guess."

"He wouldn't give his name. He was a tall fellow with a thin moustache, but it was hard to see all of his face because he wore a nice coat with a big, turned-up collar. He held the collar up in front of his mouth. His bowler hat was a size too big because it came down almost over his eyes. He refused to remove it. I guess he didn't want anybody to recognize him."

"What else do you remember about him?" I asked, my heartbeat pounding. "Even the littlest thing could be significant. How did he act?"

"He wasn't very nice. I asked about the purpose of the visit. The man wanted to know why we needed that. I told him it was for our log-book, that we recorded all visitors because it showed our benefactors that their donations were definitely helping people. He said he wanted to learn about adoption. He wanted to know what happens to babies left at the orphanage that come from unwed mothers. As soon as he said that, the lady looked away in shame, so I figured she was with child. He seemed more interested in himself than the lady or the baby. He wanted to know if the real names of the parents were necessary. I told him we'd appreciate having the birth certificate. He asked if we'd publish the parents' names in the newspapers or gossip about it. I assured him everything was confidential, but I don't think he believed me. He said everybody has a price. He asked several more times when I expected Mrs. Granger to return. I again said I didn't know. He got frustrated. He moaned and groaned, grabbed the lady by the hand and they walked out."

"Did this man identify himself as her father, brother, lover?"

Anna Belle blushed. "He never said."

"How did he talk? Did he have an accent? Did he have an unusual walk?"

Anna Belle frowned. "He talked down to me, like I was some lowly servant."

"So he sounded like a rich person. He must've been educated."

"Oh, yes, sir. He spoke in a very formal way, like rich people do that went to college. Am I helping, sir? I sure hope I am."

"Yes, you're helping a lot. Do you recognize the name the Count?"

Anna Belle shook her head. "Oh, no. I never got any names except Katherine Douglas." She looked at Adelia. "I never heard of a woman detective before. It must be exciting."

"I'd say it's very challenging."

Anna Belle smiled. "Is Detective Drummond kind to you?"

"Anna Belle," Sister Margaret said, "it's not your place to ask questions."

"Detective Drummond is the only man ever to treat me as an equal."

"Where are you from?" Anna Belle asked, ignoring Sister Margaret's frown.

"From Chicago."

"Oh, that sounds so exciting. Why would you leave that big city for little Wilmington?"

Sister Margaret said, "Anna Belle! They are not here to answer your questions."

Anna Belle frowned. "I envy you."

"Miss Anna Belle!" The nun stood and turned to me. "Are you finished with her?"

I looked at my partner, who nodded. "I think we have what we need, Sister."

The nun pointed toward the back of the house and addressed Anna Belle. "Go to your room and wait for me."

"Why?" Anna Belle said, pouting like a child. "Stop treating me like a baby."

"We have to discuss your tendency to envy others. It is not an acceptable trait."

Anna Belle blushed, obviously embarrassed about being yelled at in front of guests, yet her eyes glared at Sister Margaret like a prisoner might hate their jailer. Slowly, deliberately, and with malice in her voice, Anna Belle said, "Yes, Sister Margaret." She bowed slightly to Adelia and me and spoke in a pleasant tone. "It was nice meeting you, detectives. I hope you catch the person who did this awful thing."

I handed her my calling card. "If you think of anything that might help us, please don't hesitate to call."

"Oh," Anna Belle said with a big smile. "I certainly will." She glanced at Sister Margaret. "If they let me."

Anna Belle shuffled from the room.

Sister Margaret escorted Adelia and me to the door. "I do apologize for Anna. She's young."

"She doesn't want to be a nun," I said. "Anybody with eyes can see that."

"I'm beginning to think you're right. It's not a vocation for everyone." She opened the door and walked outside with us. "Godspeed."

We said goodbye and returned to our bicycles. After Adelia mounted her Columbian, she said, "So, are we assuming Katherine Douglas was Katie Dugan?"

"We are. And the Count must've been the man with her. Which means some well-to-do gentleman, or the son of a well-to-do gentleman was the father of her baby and he had to hide that fact."

"So the Count could be living in one of those mansions," Adelia said, gesturing toward Delaware Avenue.

"It's a distinct possibility," I said, mounting my Victor.

CHAPTER 42

Since Adelia loved seafood, and it was time for lunch, we rode to the finest restaurant along Delaware Avenue, the Logan House, at the intersection with DuPont Street. The three story green-painted tavern and hotel opened in 1864 and it stood in a planned neighborhood referred to as Forty Acres. One hundred fifty homes had been built under the direction of developer Joshua Heald and the Wilmington City Railway Company, the owners of the city's streetcar system. The Railway's storage barns, repair shops, main offices, central hub were adjacent to the Logan House.

"It's named after General John Logan," I said after a waitress escorted us to a table near a crowded bar, tended to by a large Irish gentleman who kept the drinks coming at an impressive speed. The tavern was always busy because of the heavy foot traffic coming from the trolley station, or from train passengers because the Baltimore and Ohio Railroad Depot was on the opposite side of Delaware Avenue. "He was a Union officer I met but never served under."

"I can't imagine fighting in a war," Adelia said over the commotion while looking over the menu. "You must be really brave."

"I'm not brave. I had thousands of people, in uniform and out, supporting me. True bravery is when a person stands alone against incredible odds, much like you."

Adelia blushed. "I'm not brave."

"Yes, you are. You're the bravest woman I've ever met. Much like Thomas Garrett was the bravest man I had ever met. Thomas helped runaway slaves continue north at his home at 227 Shipley Street, in full view of the law and anyone else who didn't like it. He got arrested many times. He was sentenced to pay crippling fines, but he never wavered in his determination to aid those poor souls. When he died, Wilmington held the largest funeral procession in its history. Thousands of citizens, white and Negro and me, attended. He was buried at Wilmington Friends Meeting House at Fourth and West Streets. Someday, like the fight against slavery, everybody will see the righteousness of your cause, Adelia, and you'll be vindicated. So don't lose heart."

My partner was near tears. "Thank you for that. I only hope I live to see it."

We ordered a meal of terrapin soup, clams, and biscuits, and then the conversation died. I hoped that Adelia would say more, perhaps reveal more about her background, and answer the question of why she came to Delaware. However, the noisy atmosphere didn't lend itself to a free exchange of ideas without having to shout, so we ate quickly and got back to business.

"I want to talk to a friend of mine who runs the historical society," I said at our bicycles. "I have a few questions he might be able to help us with, and he has contacts among the elite who might know who the Count is."

Adelia and I pedaled to Market Street, between Ninth and Tenth Streets. We dismounted our bicycles in front of a one story brick building with a gambrel roof that had been a Presbyterian Church, but was now home to the Delaware Historical Society. We entered and found no one in sight. We passed a row of portraits. "Delawareans from the Revolutionary War period," I said. We came upon a display of Civil War memorabilia, such as Union and Confederate uniforms, regimental flags, various guns, knives, canteens and cooking utensils.

We reached the back of the building and stepped through the open door to the curator's office.

CHAPTER 43

"Hello, Thomas," I said to a heavily bearded man with a wide nose who sat at a roll-top desk by a closed window. "Didn't you hear us come in?" It was a stupid question. When Thomas Hillary was immersed in his work, he was deaf and dumb to his surroundings. "We could've robbed the place."

Thomas looked up. His eyes went wide. "David." He got up, but had to maneuver around stacks of newspapers, books, and open boxes of paperwork. His tweed jacket was unbuttoned, revealing a white shirt that had a small coffee stain. We shook hands enthusiastically. "It's so great to see you. How are you? Is everything good? The last time we spoke you were off to spend time with your son and his family. Are they well? Did you get the rest you needed?"

"I did. I'm well, thank you. My son and his family are good."

"Great." Thomas said. He stepped back. His brown eyes scrutinized Adelia while he continued to speak to me. "I assume you're chasing whoever murdered that girl I read about in the *Every Evening*. Poor thing. I know you'll find the guilty person in no time." He smiled and bowed to my partner. "And this must be Detective Bern. I read about you, too. I'm pleased to make your acquaintance."

"Mr. Thomas Hillary has been the society archivist for the past ten years," I said. "He knows everything there is to know about Delaware and its past."

"Even more than you?" Adelia said. "That would be impressive."

Thomas said, "Yes, David is my top pupil." He pointed at a gray horsehair sofa that had a large tea stain in the middle. Thomas drank a lot of coffee and tea and it was obvious from his clothes and furniture that not all of it went down his throat. "Please sit. How can I help? I know your boss and the good people of this city are anxious for a resolution."

"What do you know about medicine shows?" I asked while we sat. I removed a cigar from my vest pocket and lit it. "I suspect they're run by charlatans."

"I'd say that's a fair assessment." Thomas handed me a small bucket of sand he kept by his desk, and then sat. "They peddle what they call patent medicine or miracle elixirs. They're supposed to cure everything a human being could suffer from, but it's usually just alcohol and worthless herbs. The salesmen use exotic language to promote the stuff, such as saying their product is a timeless remedy from the Far East, or the deepest parts of Africa, or from the Indian nations, places none of us have been, or even heard of, so nobody can verify the claims they're making. Yet the more fantastic the claim, the more people buy it."

"Are you familiar with the Kickapoo Medicine Show?"

"Yes, they're one of the biggest patent medicine companies in the country. And Kickapoo is an actual tribe, somewhere in Texas, I believe. However, the company is based in Connecticut, so I doubt there's anything really Indian about it."

"Could their patent medicine contain opium or peyote," I asked, "or some other drug that induces violent behavior or hallucinations?"

"Anything's possible. Why do you ask?"

"Miss Dugan's murder was extremely violent. The man who killed her was full of rage, a type of elevated anger you don't normally see. I've had a couple of cases where a man killed his girlfriend or wife because she planned to continue the pregnancy, but nothing like this. He nearly severed her head from her shoulders. Detective Bern found a bottle of Kickapoo's Sagwa near Miss Dugan's body, and another in her bedroom, so she might've consumed it for morning sickness."

Adelia said, "I think that's the more plausible explanation."

Thomas leaned forward and whispered, "So Miss Dugan was with child."

"She was. Please don't repeat that."

"You have my word."

As a life-long bachelor, Thomas had no one living with him who might tempt him to break his vow. I always struggled at home to keep my mouth shut. My wife hated my occupation except when I had gossip to spill. Despite my best efforts, she could tell by my facial expression when I was hiding something. So she'd beg and beg until I revealed news I should've kept discreet. Fortunately, Jane had been better at keeping secrets than I was. Whatever I told her never went outside the house.

Thomas said, "Take the Sagwa to a chemist, one who is familiar with opium and peyote."

"I'll keep that in mind," I replied, blowing smoke. "I know you, along with Mr. Porter and Colonel LaMotte, do a lot of fundraising for the society among the upper class. We suspect Miss Dugan's killer is a gentleman in good standing, perhaps someone referred to as the Count."

Thomas thought for a moment, and then shook his head. "No, I've never heard it."

"Please ask around. We really need to find out who has this name. Detective Bern and I also found volumes on the writings of Edgar Allan Poe among the belongings of our victim and suspects. One of our suspects has a newspaper clipping about Mr. Poe speaking at the Newark Academy."

Thomas raised a finger. "Yes, your suspect must have a copy of the *Ledger* piece that was written about the event. Poe did give a lecture at the Academy. I believe it was on December 23, 1843. I came across it while researching the pirate William Neub, who supposedly left a treasure buried around Aiken's Tavern, also in 1843."

I took and long drag and smiled. "I was born in 1843."

He teased. "You're really old."

"But younger than you," I said with a wink. "Did Mr. Poe ever speak in Wilmington?"

"No, sir."

Adelia said, "Mr. Hillary, do you know when Mister Poe died?"

"1849 in Baltimore. Some believe he was murdered."

I said, "Well, maybe we can look into that after we catch whoever killed Miss Dugan. Do you know if there's a literary club in town dedicated to Poe's work?"

Thomas shook his head. "Not that I know of, but that doesn't mean there isn't one. I prefer to read alone in quiet solitude as opposed to being involved in those social clubs."

"Does the Dugan family have a notable history in our state?"

"No, the name is not familiar."

We socialized for a few more minutes. I mentioned the closing of the orphanage and that they needed a home for their records. Thomas agreed to contact Mrs. Granger. Then Adelia and I said goodbye and mounted our bicycles. There was a sudden commotion in the street. The red brougham raced by. The driver used the whip to keep the horse at a gallop. A few pedestrians had to jump out of the way. They yelled at the driver as the vehicle kept up speed, not slowing down until it went another two blocks, far enough away so that I wouldn't give chase.

"Who could it be," Adelia said, "and why are they letting us see them?"

"I don't know, but we'll find out soon enough."

CHAPTER 44

"It sounds like this case will take some time," Chief Francis said to Adelia and me, his voice signaling disappointment and criticism. He got up from behind his desk, rubbed his beard and then cast his eyes in my direction. "Is she helping or hindering?"

"*She?*" I said.

"You can speak to me directly," Adelia said in a calm voice, but her hands were clenched into fists. "I'm standing right here."

"Detective Bern has been a great asset," I said.

Chief looked at me. "So you still want to work with her?"

"*Her?* You mean, Detective Bern? Yes."

"I don't know," Chief said, shaking his head. "You normally wrap up cases by now. What's going on?"

I couldn't believe my ears. "What're you talking about? It's only been *one* day, and this one's complicated. We can't rush it. The pieces will fall into place."

"Before Election Day?"

I sighed, frustrated. "Yes, sir, we'll do our best to meet your deadline. I'm sure your job is safe. The ward leaders will certainly bribe enough drunks and vagrants to vote over and over again so everyone gets re-elected. Besides, if you're not satisfied with our work, you can always replace us with McDonald. I'm sure he's sober enough to do a better job."

I smiled. Telling Chief to replace us with McDonald was a hollow threat and he knew it. Half the time, the man couldn't find his own house let alone solve a murder case that was front-page news. When he did work, McDonald preferred to chase down burglars and pick-pockets because they'd bribe him to avoid arrest and McDonald used the money to pay for his drinks at the Ebbitt or gamble on cockfights in its courtyard.

"I can't replace you with McDonald," Chief said. "He resigned. He doesn't want to work with a woman."

I laughed. "He isn't working with a woman. *I am*, and happy to do so."

Adelia smiled at my compliment, but said to the Chief. "Am I supposed to feel guilty that McDonald resigned?"

I answered. "No, no you're not. That's his choice. But so what? It's no great loss. He spent more time at the Ebbitt anyway. He was everything that's wrong with our department. And the police department won't achieve any respect among the citizens until every officer like him is removed. He won't be missed."

Chief reluctantly agreed. "Yes, but now I'm down a detective."

"So hire somebody."

"It's not that easy." Then he snapped his fingers. "Oh, I do have a bit of good news. City Council approved a $200 reward to whoever solves the case. That should motivate you."

I clenched my jaw and spoke through my teeth. "I was already *motivated.* I don't need some reward from City Council to spur me into action. Reward or no reward, we're going to find the person responsible. And where the hell is Officer Swenson? You promised him to me."

Chief shrugged. "I don't know." Then he returned to the reward, sounding like he'd appreciate the money in his own pocket. "Two hundred dollars is a nice incentive."

"I told you I don't give a damn about the money."

"Chief," Adelia said, "we believe we're being watched by someone who owns a red brougham, or somebody hired this person who rides around in a red brougham. Do you know anybody who has such a coach?"

Chief stroked his beard. "Are you certain they're watching you?"

I said, "Yes, we noticed them yesterday. I don't believe they're a threat because they're making their presence known, but as a precaution Detective Bern is staying at my house. I thought it best under the circumstances."

Chief revealed a devilish grin, resembling a child who just heard a dirty word for the first time. I stared him down, daring him to say something he'd regret.

Adelia repeated her question, "Do you know anyone who owns a red brougham?"

Chief shook his head. "Sorry, no."

"Do you know anyone called the Count?"

"The Count?" Chief said, looking puzzled. "Is that some sort of alias or real name? Is he a suspect?"

"We believe it's a nickname," I said, "and yes, he's a suspect."

Chief shook his head. "No, I don't recognize it."

I took a deep breath to calm my temper. "Please spread the word to all of our constables that if anyone recognizes the name the Count they should come and see Detective Bern or myself."

Chief nodded. "I'll do that. Is that all?"

"It is."

"Then get back to work."

CHAPTER 45

Adelia and I did so gladly. We passed Molly at her desk and entered the Detective's Office. McDonald's old roll-top was closed and cleaned, with the chair neatly tucked. I headed to the window and lifted the glass to let in some cool autumn air. However, with it came the noise from Market Street. The crates on a heavy conveyance wagon bounced with the bumpy road. The clump, clump, clump from horses' hooves had a rhythm all their own. The bell from a streetcar clanged. Some citizens called out to each other.

I looked across the street and swore I saw Casey Moran's pitiful face staring back at me through a window at the Rats' Nest. I wondered if he knew about the $200 reward. He probably did. He might go after it himself. Then if he solved the crime he'd proclaim himself a hero and shame the police department.

Adelia said, "Thank you, Detective Drummond, for defending me against the Chief. You didn't have to, but it's appreciated."

I sat on the window ledge. "I know I don't have to. I just don't understand the Chief. Sometimes he acts like my best friend and other times he acts like we're enemies. He's never had any cause to doubt my work or criticize my results." I sighed and looked below at three women crossing the street. "How do you women do it?"

"Do what?"

"Look at those ladies," I said, pointing at a trio. "They're squeezed into those tight dresses from neck to feet. It's a wonder they can breathe. That one's wearing a hat with so many ribbons and bows on it that it's as tall as a building. How does she keep it on her head and keep her balance? That other woman has so many feathers in her hat that she might fly away."

"I don't know. I'll never understand the need for such ornamental displays, but it *is* the fashion."

"I guess so," I said, still upset by the Chief's behavior. I stepped away from the window. At my desk, I opened the cigar box and removed a Henry Clay. "All right, let's solve this damn thing." I lit the cigar, smoked and paced the room. "Katie was with child and obviously killed for that reason, probably by this person named the Count, who feared being exposed. The Count probably took Miss Dugan to the orphanage earlier this month. He's described as tall with a thin moustache, well educated, probably has money and is married or very well known. The murder weapon was a Wostenholm razor with an ivory handle. It came from Mr. Riley's work station at the Clayton Hotel. So this unidentified man knows Mr. Riley, or knew he'd make the perfect scapegoat as Miss Dugan's jilted lover. So the razor was left at the scene to make us think Mr. Riley did it. Fortunately for him, he has a good alibi."

"I still question the time discrepancy."

"I know you do." I puffed on the cigar. "But I'm convinced he's innocent. Miss Dugan had in her purse a typewritten note that indicated a rendezvous at a place Katie was familiar with. Maybe the Bush home was the rendezvous point, but it's been locked up since March, so maybe it wasn't. Perhaps it was Delamore Park. There were no wheel marks in the road except those from the coroner's wagon. No horseshoe marks either. Miss Dugan and her killer must've walked there. The typewritten note is further evidence that her lover had to be discreet. He didn't want his handwriting recognized. Yet the note was also left at the scene. Why? The killer, if he intended to frame Mr. Riley, would've left the razor, but should've taken the note, unless he couldn't find it in the dark because Miss Dugan dropped her purse. Officer Ormond said he found it near her, not on her. You found a bottle of Sagwa under shrubbery next to the Bush home. It appears Miss Dugan drank it for morning sickness since you found another bottle in her bedroom. She had Baby's Breath placed on her body. The flower wasn't found on the Bush property.

"Miss Dugan liked to be frightened." I continued, smoking and pacing. "She liked taking walks in the dark. She read Poe because of his scary stories. Mr. Riley has a collection of Poe's work, but claims never to have read a single word. Miss Dugan has the same collection of Poe's writing, so does Mr. Stout. Mr. Stout appears to be the real Poe enthusiasts since he even has a picture of the author on his bedroom wall. How does this interest in Mr. Poe's writings fit into our investigation? And who's watching us?"

"Does walking around the room and summarizing out loud help you think?"

I stopped pacing and faced her. "Oh, yes, very much so. I used to do it with Molly or at home with my wife. Does it bother you?"

"Oh, no, I didn't mean to imply that. But listening to you, it seems you've covered about everything, but none of it makes any sense."

My feelings for Adelia didn't make any sense either. Should I tell her? If I did and she rebuked me, as I expected her to, it would make the rest of our time together quite uncomfortable. She might even march into the Chief's office and resign.

The telephone rang in the hall

CHAPTER 46

Molly answered the phone, then entered the Detective's Office and spoke like a jilted woman. "Oh excuse me, David, eh, Detective Drummond, but there's a *lady* on the telephone for you. She says her name's *Anna Belle*."

"Anna Belle? Oh, right, from the convent."

Molly seemed stunned. "You're taking a call from a nun? That's a first."

"What's wrong with you? It has to do with our case." I went into the hall. Molly left the conical-shaped receiver hanging. "Hello, Miss Sanders. Did you remember something that'll help in our investigation?"

"Oh, no," Anna Belle replied as Molly retook her seat at her desk. She leaned toward me, obviously trying to eavesdrop. "I didn't call you about that. I was wondering if you could help me get out of this place."

I sighed, disappointed and surprised. "Get out of there? The convent? Shouldn't Sister Margaret help you with that?"

"Oh, she is," Anna Belle said. "She'll let me leave the order, but I don't have any place to go."

"Oh," I sighed, wondering why I had to get caught in the middle of this. "Miss Sanders, don't you have family?"

She sobbed. Her voice cracked. "No, sir. I only came to the convent because I couldn't think of any other way to be safe and off the streets."

"So what do you expect me to do?"

"Can I stay with you until I decide what to do?"

Molly snickered. She had obviously overheard the tinny sound of Miss Sander's voice coming from the receiver. "You just can't help yourself, can you, David. All these women just fall at your feet."

I coughed, and not from smoking my cigar. "Well, Miss Sanders, for propriety's sake, you must know I can't be seen taking a young lady into my house, even for a short while. It wouldn't be proper, no matter how innocent it is." Of course, I took Adelia into my house and my neighbor was probably gossiping to everyone he knew. They in turn tell everyone they know. The entire population of Wilmington must've heard about it by now. "I'm sorry. It just wouldn't be proper."

A short and stocky gentleman wearing a city police uniform passed me and headed into the Detective's Office.

Anna Belle said. "I'm really sorry to bother you. It's just that you seemed like such a nice man. Detective Bern said such nice things about you. I thought if anybody could help me, you could."

Her words and tears tugged at my heart, but I couldn't save the whole world. "That's sweet of you to say, Miss Sanders. When do you have to leave the convent?"

"Sister Margaret would like me to leave as soon as possible, but I asked for a few days."

"All right, let me see what I can do. You must know I'm very busy right now. Please be patient."

"Oh, thank you, sir."

I ended the call with Anna Belle and telephoned Mrs. Mary Yates, who lived along Delaware Avenue near Thirteenth Street. Mrs. Yates was involved in philanthropic endeavors. Her favorite charity was the Women's Benevolent Society, an organization that helped poor women find employment and housing, or get schooling, or helped them relocate if they had family in another town willing to take them in. Like many wives in her social status, Mrs. Yates took care of her family, spent her husband's money, entertained friends who stopped by her mansion, and she eased her conscience by participating in one or more charities. Some ladies on Delaware Avenue didn't give a damn about social causes and were only involved in charities because it looked good in the society column. Not Mrs. Yates. She was a kind soul that I had known for many years.

Fortunately, Mrs. Yates was home. I spoke to her after her butler interrogated me about the purpose of the call. "Thank you for contacting me, Detective Drummond. Miss Sanders sounds like the perfect candidate for our organization."

Mrs. Yates used the word organization instead of charity because the word charity was as repulsive to the poor souls of Wilmington as any cuss word. The less-fortunate had pride, a fact that surprised the wealthy. This pride kept many public schools from being filled. Public schools were often referred to as "pauper" schools because if a child attended one the parents were admitting to their low social status.

"I'll send someone to the convent to bring her to me," Mrs. Yates said. "We'll take care of her."

I thanked her, and then hung up the telephone.

"That was a very nice thing you did," Molly said. "I apologize for the way I've been behaving."

I put the cigar butt in a bucket of sand by her desk and rubbed her back. "Perhaps when this is all over, we can have a nice long talk."

Molly smiled, got up and wrapped her arms around my waist. It was a rather awkward situation, so I loosely put my arms around her, not wanting to send the wrong message by hugging Molly too tightly. She sobbed. "Why can't life be the way you want it?"

"Am I supposed to answer that question?"

Molly backed away and rubbed her eyes. "No, David. You don't have to answer it. It can't *be* answered. It's just the way things are."

"I'm sorry if I've done anything to upset you. It wasn't intentional. But I was sincere when I said we'll have a nice long talk. All right?"

"Yes, thank you."

I released her and returned to the Detective's Office.

The policeman that passed me in the hall approached and shook my hand. He had the classic Swedish features: pale skin, blue-gray eyes, sandy-colored hair and a small upturned nose. "Officer Frank Swenson. Chief says you have an assignment for me?"

"Yes, where have you been? We need you to keep an eye on a murder suspect."

Frank's eyes almost popped from his skull. "Murder?"

I wrote down Mr. Stout's home address and place of employment and handed the piece of paper to Officer Swenson. "He's a big man with a thick walrus-type moustache. You can't miss him. He has a wife and grown daughter. Keep an eye on him and report back a couple times a day, or when you feel it's necessary. Use the phone or stop by and leave notes on my desk, or with Molly."

"Will do, sir," Frank said with enthusiasm. Most police work was dull, just walking the streets and chasing down drunks, so my assignment was a welcomed reprieve. "You can count on me, sir."

"Count?" I said. "Since you're out there on the streets, do you know anybody, or have you heard of anybody referred to the Count?"

Frank paused for a moment. "No, sir. I can't say that I recognize the name, but I'll check into it for you. If I find out who it is, will I get promoted?"

I laughed sardonically. The little man was more devious than I thought. "Are you implying, sir, that if you discover who it is you won't tell me unless I promise a promotion?"

"You're very wise, sir."

Adelia couldn't refrain herself. "You little bastard. Can't you just do your job like you're supposed to?"

"He is," I replied. "Well, if you hear of anybody going by that name, let me know immediately and I'll talk to Chief about a promotion. It's in his hands anyway. I don't make the decision. Also, for this job, don't wear your uniform. Put on ordinary work clothes or homespun. You're going to hang around the Warner Company wharf, so you need to blend in without drawing attention to yourself. Can you do it? Can you start right now?"

Officer Swenson shook my hand with some force, sealing the deal. "Indeed I can, sir."

He bowed to Adelia and then left.

CHAPTER 47

I heard Mr. Riley in the hall asking Molly if I was in.

I shouted. "Come in." He did. Richard wore an ordinary pin-striped suit. "I hadn't expected to see you again."

"No offense," Richard said, glancing at Adelia and me, "but I had hoped never to see either of you again."

"What brings you here?"

"Well," Richard said putting his hands behind his back, "I went to work this morning. My fellow barbers were reading about my release from jail in the *Herald*. They were satisfied. Nobody said anything more about it. I did my job. I'm about an hour from finishing my time when Mr. Pyle shows up at the shop holding last night's copy of the *Every Evening*. Well, he was surprised to see me because he doesn't read the *Herald*. 'It's a Democratic rag,' he says. We show him the *Herald* article. Even so, he tells me the hotel can't afford this kind of publicity. I tell him over and over again that I'm innocent, and that Detective Drummond says so too. It didn't matter. He released me from my employment."

"I'll talk to your boss."

"No," Richard said, adjusting his spectacles. "I'm not asking you to do that. It was a degrading job anyway. No man should have to bow down and kiss the ass of another man just because he's got money. They're no better than me. I can't tell you how many times I shaved one of those arrogant bastards and had to fight the urge to slit their throats."

My mouth fell open. "What?"

Richard realized what he just said and reacted horrified. "Oh, dear God, forgive me. What am I saying? I didn't mean that. I can't believe I said that." He put his face in his hands. "Oh, forgive me, please forgive me. How could I say such a thing?"

Adelia stared at Richard with a suspicious look on her face. She wasn't convinced of the barber's innocence because of the time discrepancy, and now his comment about slitting throats made her more concerned that he might be guilty.

I let the tension in the room relax before I asked Richard, "What can we do for you?"

He showed his red face and sighed. "Well, like I said, I've been discharged from my job at the barbershop. And I can't rest until we find out who killed Katie. So I'd like to continue to work with you until we catch the person responsible."

I saw the pain and sincerity in Richard's eyes. It still looked genuine. However, if he did kill Miss Dugan, it would be best to keep him at our side where we could watch him. I looked at Adelia. She didn't object. "All right, let's continue."

"Thank you, sir," Richard said. He shook my hand and bowed to my partner. "Did you learn anything new since last night?"

I told Richard what happened at the orphanage and the convent. "Unfortunately, this tall man that we suspect is the Count covered his face. Miss Sanders said he had a thin moustache and sounded educated and well-bred. Does he sound like anybody you know because he certainly must know you?"

"It could be anybody. Most of my customers are well educated with moustaches."

"Yes, but this is a customer that knows you dated Miss Dugan, and probably knows she wasn't interested in marrying you."

Richard shook his head. "I'm sorry. I can't think of anyone. But you're not certain this Katherine Douglas was Katie. You're just guessing it was her."

"Yes, a lot of what we do is guess work. We have to look at all possibilities. Draw any number of conclusions. Then eliminate some as we learn more."

"Well, if it was Katie and the father of her baby, it sounds like we need to interview every rich man in the city."

Out the corner of my eye I saw Molly standing on the threshold with Joey the newsboy and another boy in ragged clothes. I had a feeling that Joey's presence was going to benefit our investigation immensely. He never before came inside City Hall.

"Hello Joey, bring your friend."

"This is Fingers," Joey said of his dirty and barefooted companion. Then he realized he had said too much. "I mean, this is Kirk."

Kirk had all ten fingers so I assumed the nickname meant the boy was a good thief, probably a pickpocket. Kirk removed his cap, revealing a gaunt face that aroused my sympathies.

"Pleased to meet you, Kirk. When's the last time you ate, son?"

"Oh, I ate," Kirk said, twirling his cap nervously.

"When?"

"I had something yesterday. I bought it with money I *earned*."

"I don't doubt that, son. And there's no cause to be nervous. Is there something you need to tell me?"

Joey nudged Kirk. "Go on, tell him."

"Well, sir, I hang around Tenth Street Park with some members of me gang, the Happy Valley Boys." He stuck his chest out and spoke proudly. "We were up to our usual, making sure no boy from in town came out to our territory. Just after dark on the night that lady was killed, I was sitting on a bench by the reservoir when this swell in a fancy black coat comes up to me and asks if I'd like to earn ten cents now and ten cents after the job's done. Of course, I tells him yes. He asks me to go to the fair at Sacred Heart and deliver a note to a pretty lady in a green dress who should be at the merry-go-round in about fifteen minutes. I was to do this in secret. If she's with anyone, I make sure her company doesn't know about the note. He gives me the dime and the piece of paper and tells me not to read it. Shoot, that don't matter anyhow cause I can't read, never did learn my A-B-C's. He tells me to hurry. The lady's expecting me, so off I went."

I tried not to appear too anxious. "Did this man have a thin or fat moustache?"

Kirk scratched his neck. "I don't know, sir. It was night time. There wasn't much light, and he had his collar up and his hat way down low."

Adelia whispered, "So Katie went to the fair that second night expecting to hear from her lover. Sorry, Mr. Riley."

Richard cringed.

I whispered, "Perhaps Miss Dugan and her gentleman friend parted ways when Katie told him about the pregnancy and her decision to keep the child. So when Katie gets the note, she interprets it as a reconciliation, except it's a trap." I asked Kirk, "Do you remember anything else about him? Did he talk with an accent? Did he walk with a limp? Did he carry anything?"

"He had an umbrella with him, but it weren't raining."

"Anything else?"

"Well, I delivered the note like he told me. I was real sneaky about it and careful. The gentleman with this lady never saw me."

"*I* was that gentleman," Richard said, his voice raised.

Kirk looked at Richard. "Hey, you do look like him. Anyway, when I went back to the park, the louse was gone. He didn't pay me my second dime. But later, I saw him with this lady all wrapped up into each other and kissing on a bench by the pump station." He made a face. "Oh, it was disgusting. But I wanted my second dime, so I waited until they were done. The lady walked down Harrison Street.

The man walked toward the hospital. I stopped him and asked for my dime. He got all mad, said he never made such an arrangement, to stop begging, but he paid me."

I nodded. "Thank you, Kirk. What made you think I'd be interested in this information?"

"I was visiting my friend Peter. He's a bootblack. His customer, some old gentleman with a cane, was reading the newspaper while getting a shine. He said a lady in a green dress was killed. I got to wondering if it was the same lady in a green dress that I gave the note to. If it was, I don't want no part in no murder. So after the old man gets his shine, I tell my story to Peter. He tells me that Joey was spreading the word that you were looking for information to help catch whoever killed this lady. So I tell Joey and he takes me to you."

I nodded and smiled. "Thank you, son. You've done a good deed." I reached into my pants' pocket and gave Kirk and Joey 25 cents each. "Here you go. You and Joey get something to eat."

They clutched their coin and grinned. "Oh, thank you, sir."

After the boys left, Adelia asked, "I assume Tenth Street Park is somewhere on Tenth Street?"

I opened one of my desk drawers and pulled out my copy of the city directory. A street map was included in the middle of the book. "Tenth Street Park is right here," I put my finger on the seven acre park between Jackson and Franklin Streets and home to the Cool Spring Reservoir. "It's about a mile from here and near the Wilmington and Brandywine Cemetery."

Then an idea struck me, and I slammed the book shut.

Adelia flinched. "Hey, I was looking at that."

I waved at her and Richard to follow me. "Come on."

CHAPTER 48

Like a bloodhound that just picked up a fresh scent, I had renewed energy. I could've run to Delaware Hospital at Fourteenth Street, between Jefferson and Washington, but instead the three of us took a half-filled streetcar to our destination.

"The hospital opened a few years ago," I said as we left the trolley. "And it's only a couple blocks from Tenth Street Park."

"Why are we going to the hospital?" Adelia asked for the third time since we left City Hall.

"I won't say yet. I think I'm right, but I need to investigate. If I *am* right, you'll discover my suspicion right along with me."

I also neglected to point out that it would be the first time I'd been to the hospital since Jane died, and that I had real trepidations about going inside. My wife, like most people, did not trust hospitals. The perception, right or wrong, was that hospitals did more harm than good. I certainly saw incompetent doctors during the war, but it was thirty years later and physicians were better trained. Nevertheless, Jane insisted on visiting her own physician, a drunkard named Silas Kendall. He listened to her chronic cough and prescribed Mrs. Winslow's Soothing Syrup, something I later found out was normally given to teething babies. Then Jane coughed and tasted blood. It finally convinced her to enter the hospital. After being interviewed by a physician for more than an hour, he determined that Jane had consumption. As soon as we heard the news, we looked at each other and knew it meant goodbye. I'd be losing my sweet Jane and having to go on without her. It wasn't right. I had been at death's doorstep so many times and came away unscathed. How was it that I survived and good people like my Jane did not? I knew of several cruel and unscrupulous men who had died peacefully in their sleep. If anyone deserved to die young, they did. Yet they flourished, free to harm people and ruin lives while good people suffered and died before their time. It certainly wasn't fair.

The three of us approached the hospital entrance. Adelia sensed my anxiety. "Are you all right?"

I took a deep breath. "Yes, I'm fine."

We entered the hospital and I smelled the various cleaning solutions the staff used to keep the tile floor shining. The odor ignited memories of all my visits here during my wife's final days. The painful recollections were so strong that every impulse in my body signaled a desire to flee. For the sake of self-preservation, I had to get out of there. But I couldn't. For Katie Dugan's sake, I conquered my fears and pressed on.

The patient's waiting area had one sickly man coughing into his handkerchief and a young couple that appeared healthy, but wary of the ill gentleman. A long counter was manned by a couple of nurses in gray uniforms with full-body white aprons and caps. One of the nurses, Alice Moore, a silver-haired lady with a bright smile, immediately recognized me.

"Detective Drummond," she said softly. She came out from behind the counter and gave me an embrace. "It's so good to see you. What brings you back?"

I introduced my companions. "We're investigating the Miss Dugan murder."

"Oh, dear God. We were just reading about it. Isn't it just awful? What can I do to help?"

"Can you confirm that Father Milford was here Wednesday night?" I said.

"Father Milford? He's here every Wednesday night."

"Did you see him this past Wednesday?"

Alice raised an eyebrow. "What're you trying not to say? Do you suspect the priest? If so, you better go to confession right now and beg for forgiveness."

"No, ma'am. We're investigating everybody who knew Miss Dugan and confirming their whereabouts at the time of her murder. Do you remember what time Father Milford was here?"

Alice frowned. "I believe I saw the good Father around eight when I visited a patient in the Children's Ward. I saw him other times up until ten o'clock when he left for the evening. Of course, I was busy with patients so I couldn't keep track of him the whole time."

"Did he act the same?" I asked. "Did he behave like he normally did? Was he tired? Was he sweating?"

"He's always tired and sweating." Nurse Moore looked me up and down as if she didn't recognize me. "You should be ashamed of yourself for suspecting a man of God."

"He's not a suspect. If he was here, then you're confirming his innocence. Is there anyone else on staff who worked Wednesday evening?"

The nurse hesitated for a moment, still shaming me with her eyes.

"Let's go upstairs."

The four of us took the steps. For me, heading to the second floor made me relive the painful days and nights of visiting Jane in the Women's Ward. I still couldn't believe she was gone. In the end, the hospital couldn't do anything for her except keep her comfortable with various sedatives, mostly laudanum. I watched her body deteriorate for nearly a month before she took her last, agonizing breath.

The four of us passed through an open door and entered a room with twelve beds, half of which were empty and the other half occupied by children. Alice approached a bony nurse with a large nose who sat at a table near a window.

"Mary," Alice said, "may we speak with you for a moment? You worked Wednesday evening, right?"

"I did," she said in a soft voice.

"Did you see Father Milford?"

"Yes."

"At what times?" I asked.

"Time?" Mary said, tilting her head. "I started at eight. He was here then, talking to Timmy." She pointed at a boy lying in bed with a cast on both legs, each limb elevated in a sling. "He said goodbye to me around ten. I didn't see him other than that."

"So, is eight to ten his regular time to be here?"

"It is," Mary and Nurse Moore said simultaneously. Alice added, "But you must know he wouldn't be involved in anything like murder. He's a priest, for God's sakes."

"Murder? Alice, who are these people?"

"Thank you," I said to the ladies. "Thank you both for your time."

"I know you're in mourning, Detective Drummond," Alice said, "but that don't give you any right to cause a scandal."

I sighed, frustrated. "I'm not trying to cause a scandal. I'm looking to eliminate all possible suspects, and you did that by confirming Father Milford's whereabouts." Then I added, "And I didn't thank you enough for the care and kindness you showed my wife. You were Jane's angel in her time of need. Thank you for all you did for her."

Alice blushed, her anger disarmed. "Oh, I was only doing my duty."

"It was more than duty," I said with a gentle embrace. "Thank you."

I had the nurse in tears by the time we left the hospital.

On the front drive, Adelia said, "You *do* suspect Father Milford."

"Think about it," I said, as we walked toward Fourteenth Street and our trolley stop. "Father Milford's tall. He speaks in a formal, almost arrogant voice. He has a thin moustache. And other than a married man, or a prominent figure in society, who else would be ruined by a bastard child?"

"A priest," Richard said.

"Exactly. What if Father Milford is the unknown suitor? What if he's the Count?"

"What made you think of him?" Adelia asked.

"I knew Father Milford came to the hospital every Wednesday evening because I saw him here during my wife's illness. He even talked to me on occasion about administering Last Rites. Kirk said the man who gave him the note walked away toward the hospital. And the hospital is a perfect cover if Father Milford needs an alibi. He visits the sick. He's seen by the patients and staff. When nobody's looking, he slips out of the hospital and goes over to Tenth Street Park. He gets Kirk to deliver the note. He returns to the hospital. He's seen by the staff and patients. Then at the allotted time, he slips out again and visits Miss Dugan for few minutes on the bench by the pump house. Afterwards, Father Milford returns to the hospital to complete his time and is seen again by the patients and staff until he leaves at ten."

"But Miss Dugan was killed around midnight to two in the morning," Adelia said. "And she was out by the Bush estate. Why did she walk all the way out there?"

"Father Milford used his time at the hospital to set the stage for Miss Dugan's murder. He lures her to the bench at Tenth Street Park. This is their regular rendezvous point. While they're together, he probably tells her she doesn't have to go through with the adoption. He'll leave the priesthood and they'll get married. She's happy. They've reconciled. He then convinces her to meet him again later at Delamore Park. They meet and go for a pleasant walk under the stars in a relatively unpopulated part of the city. Katie's agreeable to this because they can't be seen in public together. They've been sneaking around during their entire relationship, and have probably been around the Bush house before. And we've already heard that Miss Dugan enjoyed walking at night, and enjoyed being scared. Maybe she liked being around the Bush house because it's closed up and rumored to be haunted. Perhaps Father Milford used that rumor to frighten her in a playful way, like pretending to see the old man's ghost. Miss Dugan is enjoying the game, but her stomach bothers her so she pauses to take a drink of Sagwa. Father Milford pulls out the razor. She realizes it's not a game anymore, drops the Sagwa, runs toward DuPont Street, but

Father Milford catches her and kills her under the persimmon tree."

Adelia looked skeptical. "That's a pretty fanciful tale."

Richard said, "I don't know, maybe that's possible. How can we find out if the priest calls himself the Count? Just ask him?"

"Why not?"

"Why would he admit it?" Adelia asked.

"Dear God," Richard said, "if you're right, we won't have to wait for a trial and the gallows. I'll kill him myself."

I put a firm, but sympathetic hand on Richard's shoulder. "No, you won't."

"But all you have is speculation. It's nothing but speculation."

"Yes, you're right. It's speculation. But priest or not, Father Milford is a man, with the same faults as any other man."

"You just want him to be guilty," Adelia said, "because you and your father are anti-Catholic."

I glared at her, grit my teeth and spoke harshly because she deserved it. "Detective Bern, I realize you show a tendency to have an undisciplined mouth, but when you're wrong, you're *very* wrong. This has nothing to do with religion. This has *everything* to do with arresting a murderer, be he a street bum, a politician, a doctor, lawyer, saint, or priest."

Adelia gave me a cold stare, but she eventually said, "I'm sorry. That was wrong of me. I apologize for offending you."

I smiled. "You're forgiven."

Richard said, "So, we're still no closer to finding out who killed Katie because it's all guess work."

I nodded. "Don't despair. I think we're terribly close."

CHAPTER 49

Adelia, Richard and I hopped on a streetcar in front of Delaware Hospital and returned to City Hall as the late afternoon sun dipped closer to the horizon. We needed to make our evening report to the Chief, and to see if Officer Swenson left any messages. If he had, and depending on the contents of that note, our investigative work for the day might not be over. Spurred by City Council's reward offer, maybe a cop or citizen knew somebody called the Count and that information awaited us. Then we planned to get supper and a good night's sleep. We had Miss Dugan's funeral at noon tomorrow.

When we stepped from the trolley at Market and Sixth Streets, there was a gathering of ladies and gentlemen on the sidewalk in front of City Hall. A few of them held signs that read: "Citizens Action Committee." Another placard read: "A Killer Roams the City," and "Demand Action Now." These citizens, and the curious onlookers they attracted, pushed Joey and his newspaper business closer to the Clayton House, where its proprietor, Mr. Pyle, was certain to object. Newsboys have tried in the past to set up shop in front of his hotel, only to be chased away because Mr. Pyle claimed that the business of selling newspapers obstructed people from entering the Clayton or its neighboring banks. Truth was he hated the little urchins. Like all upper crust society, Mr. Pyle pretended that poverty didn't exist.

Naturally, the protestors attracted every journalist in the city. Each one of them had a notepad and pencil out and spoke to a man or woman marching in the action committee. I didn't see Casey, but he had to be somewhere.

"We'll go around back," I said. "Mr. Riley, wait here."

"No, I'm going home. I need to prepare myself for tomorrow."

"What about dinner?" I said, knowing full-well that his departure meant Adelia and I would dine alone. "The police department's paying."

"Thank you for the offer," He looked at the protestors. His eyes watered. His voice cracked. "I've had enough for one day, and tomorrow will be worse."

I patted Richard on the back as a sympathetic gesture, trying to reassure him that I understood. "All right, sir, we'll meet you at the church."

Richard removed his spectacles and wiped his eyes with the back of a hand. He appeared ready to say something, but the words stuck in his throat, so he just nodded and returned his eyeglasses to their resting spot on his face.

Adelia and I said our goodbyes to Richard. My partner and I then circled around back and entered the rear of City Hall. We greeted Officer Hinder, who told us everyone had left for the day. I wasn't surprised. Chief Francis and Mayor Willey probably exited the building the second the protestors arrived. Like most politicians, they were public servants in name only. When they were really needed, nobody could find them.

Adelia and I went upstairs. There were no notes on Molly's desk or in the Detective's Office.

"That's disappointing," Adelia said in our office. "I still have energy to burn."

I agreed. "Do you have any ideas?"

She shook her head. "Reluctantly, no. Are you going to get someone to watch Father Milford?"

"I'll talk to the Chief about it tomorrow."

"Do you think the Chief will attend the funeral?"

"There won't be anything controversial about attending Katie's funeral, so he'll be there."

"You know, you have a cynical streak."

I nodded. "When it comes to politics, yes I do. I hate how these men take advantage of the citizens to stuff their own pockets while doing as little of their actual job as possible."

"Does the Chief ever do any real police work?"

I laughed and shook my head. "No. He's a figurehead, just like the mayor's a figurehead."

Adelia shook her head. "Then how does the city survive?"

"Business. Businessmen actually run it. Politicians are their tool. Hungry?"

Adelia said she was, so we returned to Market at Sixth. Dusk prompted the protestors to disperse. Streetlights came on, and it was proving to be a fine and comfortable autumn evening. I took a deep breath to savor the refreshing air, and my mood was enhanced by the prospect of sharing another meal alone with Adelia.

I directed her north. Wilmington's main thoroughfare was busier than usual because stores stayed open later on Fridays. There were a higher number of horses and coaches tied to posts along the curb. More pedestrians walked the sidewalks. There was additional trolley service. Even so, we still had plenty of room to maneuver.

Adelia and I crossed Seventh Street, and after passing the real estate firm Heald and Company, we entered Jasper's Café, a small and relaxing place with the usual bar in front and tables in the back. A young lady about thirteen or fourteen escorted us to a table in a dark corner along the back wall.

"I assume you've eaten here before," Adelia said as we sat and received our menus.

"Many times. It's basic fare, but good."

For the first time in a long time I felt I had a healthy appetite and ordered a beef steak and beer. Adelia requested mutton chops and a cup of hot tea. After the girl left, Adelia squirmed in her chair and looked around at the other diners.

"I know you're anxious to continue the investigation," I said, "but sometimes it's nice to take a break and enjoy a quiet moment. It's a good time to think and reflect on what we've learned. Hopefully, we'll find out something at the funeral. Keep your eyes and your ears open. Murderers have been known to show up at the service for their victim, mixing in with the mourners. I expect Father Milford to be there because it's his church. I'm curious to see if Mr. Stout attends, or if the person in the red brougham makes an appearance."

"Do you think this person in the coach is an accomplice?" Adelia asked as the girl returned with her tea and my mug of Diamond State.

"I don't think so. If he were an accomplice, we'd be dead by now."

"That's comforting."

"Like I said, he'll introduce himself when he feels the time is right. For now he's probably hoping we chase the wrong people." I sipped my beer and studied Adelia. She still squirmed in her seat, appearing uncomfortable in her surroundings. I finally asked the one question plaguing my mind. "May I please know why you came to Wilmington? Of all the cities in this country, why did you leave Chicago and come here? There had to be more progressive cities where an independent woman like yourself would've been more welcomed."

Adelia stopped squirming. She stared at me while stroking her cup of tea, warming her fingertips. "I'm reluctant to say because you already have enough to worry about."

"What do you mean? Please tell me."

Adelia looked around at the other diners before whispering, "As I said I left home fearing my mother might sell me. She got the idea from my Uncle, the one we lived with where I saw the ghost of my grandmother. I should've left right away, but didn't. When I did, I headed to Detroit, to a Swedish community I had read about. I thought I'd get a job there. I didn't get a job, but met my husband. I attended college. I tried to live with him. He was a good man. We eventually divorced. He kept begging me to take him back. I did, but it was hopeless. I needed to get away. Once I graduated from Pinkerton, they told me about the job here in Wilmington. Ian still wanted me back. He just wouldn't accept the divorce. So I took the job here believing he'd never think to look for me in a small city on the east coast. I hopped on a train and came here with just my one trunk of clothes and a couple dollars in my pocket."

"But there's a Swedish community here too, so he might use that to track you down."

"I doubt it. The fact that there's a Swedish community here is a coincidence."

Then an unnerving question popped into my head. "Are you worried this man in the red brougham is watching *you* and reporting back to your former husband? If so, you should've told me about this from the beginning."

Adelia shook her head. "I admit the thought *did* cross my mind, but Ian doesn't have the money to afford a spy. Even if he did, I know he would want it done secretly so he could just show up and surprise me. He'd never do anything this elaborate."

Adelia sipped her tea. I stared at her delicate hands and how she held the cup to her lips. I imagined those fingertips caressing my body and I suddenly broke out in a sweat. I was about to confess my feelings when the girl returned with our meals.

After the waitress left, Adelia said, "I'm sorry. I was hoping not to burden you with my personal issues. You have enough of your own. I thought we could just concentrate on work, but I see that's not possible. There are gaps in the investigative process. To fill those gaps we can't help but share personal experiences."

I finally took a chance. "And share personal *feelings*."

She appeared perplexed. "What do you mean?"

I shrugged. "Well, I feel foolish." I put my heart out on the ledge. "I'm at an age where I shouldn't act this way, but I'm hoping we can develop a relationship beyond work."

Adelia sat back and frowned. "Oh, I was afraid you might approach this subject. I'm not so blind, Detective Drummond. I know when a man's interested in me. The eyes don't lie. You've been a perfect gentleman and a perfect mentor."

"But?"

Adelia looked at her mutton. "I'm sorry."

"Never mind," I said, no longer wanting my beefsteak. "I understand. We'll work together, nothing more. You have my word as a gentleman."

She looked at me with wet eyes and repeated, "I'm sorry."

"Me too."

CHAPTER 50

I achieved a few hours of sleep after we returned to my house, although it was anything but restful. We hardly spoke during the walk from the restaurant, except Adelia promised to remove herself from my house as soon as the Katie Dugan case was over. I just grunted. Her statement was quite obvious. Then throughout the night I was tempted to go upstairs and drop the gentlemanly façade and either release my temper or seduce her. I played out both scenarios in my head. Each one ended with Adelia running out of my house.

I woke at dawn with less muscle soreness and dressed in my best black suit, vest and cravat, clothes not worn since my wife's funeral. No sign of Adelia, and I didn't yell up the steps that I had made coffee and oatmeal. So I ate and drank alone at my kitchen table and turned my attention to the murder case. The more I thought about it, the more I suspected Father Milford. He was the Dugan family priest so he had opportunity to socialize with Miss Dugan and fall in love with her. She obviously had a gift for getting men's affections, with Albert Stout and Richard Riley already in her court.

Someone knocked on my front door.

"Oh, good morning, David," my neighbor James Whittier said, shivering on my porch. A cool and damp fog had settled over the area. "I'm sorry to disturb you so early, but I found this young lady walking back and forth in front of your house. She has your card and says you know her."

James moved out of the way. Anna Belle Sanders stood behind him with a beaming smile. She still wore the white robe from the convent, but its hood was down, so her blonde curls fluttered in the chilly morning breeze.

"Thanks, James. Miss Sanders, what're you doing here? Didn't you speak with Mrs. Yates?"

"I did. She's a nice lady, but I want to be with you."

"What?"

James feigned a cough and flashed that devilish smirk that told me he'd be gossiping about this as soon as possible. *Now Detective Drummond has two women in his house! And one of them is underage.* "Perhaps I should leave you alone."

I was polite. "I'll talk to you later, James. Thank you for helping

214

her."

I grabbed Anna Belle by the arm and sat her on a wicker chair on my porch, in full view of the departing James and anyone else nosy enough to watch. I scolded her like a parent to a child. "Miss Sanders, you can't stay with me. It's not proper. You must understand."

"But I want to." She started crying "I can't go back to my family. I'm scared to live on my own. I can't live on the street. I won't prostitute myself. I don't have anywhere to go. There's no place for me."

"Mrs. Yates has a place for you. She will help you."

Anna Belle made a face. "She wants me to learn how to sew. I don't want to be a seamstress, working dawn to dusk in some old factory for pennies a day."

"It's not like you have a lot of options. And you don't have to be a seamstress the rest of your life. It's only a start. You can always move onto something else later. What do you want to do? I'm sure Mrs. Yates can arrange training for a different vocation."

Her eyes pleaded. "Can't you marry me? I'd be the best wife in the whole world."

"Miss Sanders, you can't be serious. I'm almost fifty."

"So? You're the only nice man I've ever met. That's the truth."

"You should marry someone your own age."

She pouted. "I don't want to marry anybody my own age. They're all brutes. Even my own father and brothers treated me like a slave. When I complained, they threw me out."

I sighed. "I know it's tough for women, believe me, Miss Sanders I do. I see it every day. But Mrs. Yates is a good lady. Her organization has other nice ladies that help girls like you. Give them a chance."

Anna Belle sat back, folded her arms across her chest and pouted. "No. I want you to marry me. I don't care about your age. I'll be a good wife. I'll give you great children."

I suppressed a laugh. "Miss Sanders."

"Stop calling me that. Call me Anna."

"Miss Sanders, you're being ridiculous. I'm too old to start another family. You need to think clearly. Mrs. Yates is your best course of action. I'm sure if you talk to her, she'll be as accommodating as possible. Please, believe me and trust me on this."

Anna Belle continued to pout. "You don't like me either. Nobody likes me. I should just jump off a bridge."

"Miss Sanders," I sighed, frustrated. "It's not that I don't like you. You're very young. You're not sure what to do. Take my advice and go back to Mrs. Yates."

Anna Belle sobbed for a few minutes before surrendering. "All right, fine. I don't like it. Mrs. Yates probably won't take me back. She's probably mad at me for running out of her house. I can't go there and face her alone. Will you come with me and speak to her for me?"

I sighed, frustrated because I should be concentrating on my murder investigation. I had a funeral to attend. Then again, what choice did I have? The young lady had turned to me for help and I hadn't the heart to turn her away. "All right, but we have to hurry. I need to be someplace at noon."

Anna Belle sprang from the chair and wrapped her arms around my chest and squeezed me tight. She wasn't wearing a corset. I got a good feel of her body pressed against mine. The embrace lasted longer than I thought proper, so I forced her arms apart and stepped back.

Anna Belle revealed a seductive grin. "See. I'd be a good wife to you."

I ignored her and went back inside for my frock coat and a couple cigars. I wrote a quick note to Adelia explaining the situation and that I'd meet her at the church. In a strange way, I was almost glad Anna Belle provided an excuse for my early departure. I wasn't too anxious to see Adelia, to watch her come downstairs and sit at my breakfast table and wonder what might have been possible for the future. Chances were good we'd mumble good morning, avoid eye contact and struggle to find something positive to say. Maybe later I'd have a better attitude.

Maybe.

CHAPTER 51

It took a half hour to cover the twelve blocks to Mrs. Yates' Victorian on Delaware Avenue near Thirteenth Street. For reasons of protocol, I knocked on the back door. Then, I needed all my charms to convince the arrogant butler to let us inside. He reluctantly agreed and escorted us to the sitting room instead of the parlor because in Delaware Avenue mansions, parlors were for show. They were decorated like family museums, and like any room in a museum, guests could look but not touch. Mrs. Yates' parlor displayed a Chippendale sofa upholstered in red velvet, with matching chairs and a settee. Magazines such as *Home Journal, Illustrated American* and *Lippincott* were neatly spread on a mahogany table set between two tall windows covered by maroon drapes. A Steinway piano, next to the marble fireplace, was a fashion necessity whether anyone in the family played or not. The walls were covered with expensive paintings and family portraits, and a gilded mirror hung above the mantle.

The sitting room, across from the parlor, had a smaller fireplace, tinier paintings, less expensive chairs and tables, a grandfather clock, and bookcases filled with books and magazines that a guest could actually touch and read. It was also the place where guests waited at the mercy of the hostess. Mrs. Yates could either receive us or instruct her butler to dismiss us from the house. If the latter happened, Anna Belle and I had no recourse except to obey.

"I don't like it here," Anna Belle whispered as we waited on a divan. "It's too fancy."

"There's no need to be intimidated by your surroundings. When Mrs. Yates appears, please show her the respect she deserves. What she's doing is very admirable. Most people in her station aren't this generous."

The pendulum bob of the grandfather clock ticked, ticked, ticked the seconds away. Minutes passed. I squirmed. I perspired. I seriously worried that I'd have to take Anna Belle to Miss Dugan's funeral and then home with me. The thought of having this young lady in my house along with Adelia was certain to spread scandalous talk that would ruin my reputation among the citizens and they'd probably call for my removal from the police department. Of course, my neighbor might already be ruining my reputation.

Ten minutes later, still no sign of Mrs. Yates. I tried to remember if there was another benevolent society in the city that catered to homeless women, but couldn't think of one.

I finally heard footsteps in the hall. They could belong to the butler or another servant sent to dismiss us. So I waited with anxious anticipation as each step drew closer to the sitting room. Fortunately, it was Mrs. Yates. Her dignified presence appeared on the threshold with her gray hair pinned up high, and she wore a flowered taffeta gown meant for a woman half her age.

"Hello, Detective Drummond," she said, allowing me to kiss her powdered cheek. "It's a pleasure to see you again." Her brown eyes scrutinized my clothes. "I'm sorry, has someone died?"

"Yes, ma'am. I'm attending the service at noon for the murdered girl, Miss Dugan, at St. Joseph's."

Mrs. Yates only nodded, and then glared at Anna Belle. The young lady stood with her head down and clasping her hands in front of her. She prepared to receive a sound verbal beating, but women of Mrs. Yates stature rarely showed their true feelings. From birth, girls born into upper society were trained not to display emotions, especially anger, so they learned to control their outward behavior while fuming inside their expensive gowns. "Young lady, I'm not accustomed to wasting my time with people who don't appreciate what I'm trying to do for them. If you want my help, you need to show respect."

Anna Belle was demure, a part she played well. "Yes, ma'am. I got scared, that's all. I'm sorry. It won't happen again."

Mrs. Yates looked down her long and elegant nose. "Very well. I forgive you. Thank you for bringing her back, Detective Drummond."

"You're welcome. Mrs. Yates, before I go, do you know anyone using the name or nickname the Count?"

Her eyebrows pinched lower. "The Count? I can't say that I have. It sounds royal, doesn't it?" Mrs. Yates went over to the bookcase and removed a volume. "Like *The Count of Monte Cristo* by Alexandre Dumas. Have you read it?"

I shook my head and thought about the well-read Adelia. "No, ma'am, but thank you. I hadn't thought about it being a royal title." Wilmington wasn't currently hosting any blue-bloods. Four years ago, the city welcomed a regal contingent from Sweden to commemorate the 250th anniversary of that country's efforts to colonize the New World. The Pusey and Jones Shipbuilding Company now occupied the land where the settlers stepped ashore and erected a fort and village they called New Sweden. The colony fell to the Dutch without a shot fired in 1655 and then the English took over in 1664.

"Well," Mrs. Yates said, "it's understandable that you wouldn't think of it as a royal title. We're in America, after all."

I wasn't sure if Mrs. Yates had insulted me or not, but I made a quick exit, satisfied that I had again helped Anna Belle get on with the rest of her life.

CHAPTER 52

The sun finally burned away the fog, revealing beautiful blue skies and only a few white clouds. I still had time before the funeral, so instead of heading to St. Joseph's, I crossed the street and visited Alfred S. Nones' memorial to Delaware's Civil War dead, the Soldier and Sailor's Monument. It was a marble obelisk topped with the sculpture of an eagle killing a serpent, and it stood on a spit on land formed by the triangular intersection of Delaware Avenue, West Fourteenth Street and North Broom Street. As always, the memorial reminded me of comrades who didn't make it home, and my father.

My father was buried nearby inside the 24-acre Wilmington and Brandywine Cemetery. A plaque by the gate stated the graveyard had been established in 1843. The year of my birth seemed to be a popular year. The founding of the cemetery, Edgar Allan Poe's lecture in Newark, the pirate Neub hiding his treasure, and if I wasn't mistaken it was the same year the insane asylum had opened at the old almshouse. It was all too incredible to be anything other than a coincidence. However, the superstitious Adelia might attribute something else to it.

I entered the Wilmington and Brandywine cemetery and passed a few elms that were dropping their golden yellow leaves. The main path cut a straight line from the gate to the rear of the property and the Soldier's Section. My father rested alongside Union and Confederate soldiers who had come from Wilmington and perished during the war or since. Delaware citizens had been split over the issue of slavery just as the nation had, so both Northern and Southern armies had First-Staters in their ranks.

Death came for Dad by the stone bridge at Antietam. He had been among the few to be transported home for burial. Thousands of other victims of that Maryland battle had just been dumped into large pits and had the dirt thrown over them. After Dad's casket arrived at the Philadelphia, Wilmington and Baltimore depot, I'd made myself fall-down drunk in order to get through his funeral.

"Hello, father," I said to his headstone. It simply stated: *Harold Drummond, beloved husband, father and Union soldier, 1815-1862.* Dad had reserved a nice shady spot by an oak shortly after Mom passed because he didn't want to be buried in any graveyard affiliated with a church. The Wilmington and Brandywine was the only cemetery in town to meet his criteria. Sadly, Mom was not next to him. Her parents had insisted she be buried on their family farm in Odessa. Dad was furious, but he had given in because he was too heartsick to fight them. "I fully understand how you felt. I miss my Jane." I took a deep breath to help suppress my emotions. "I miss the two sisters I didn't get a chance to know. I miss my mother."

I then told my father about my latest case. He'd be surprised that I was working with a citizen and a woman detective. He'd wonder why I needed the help, so I told him about the different perspectives they brought to the case, that it was nice to have someone to formulate ideas with. I did not mention my hurt feelings for Adelia. My father would call that weakness. However, he'd like Detective Bern. Dad respected spirit in a woman. One night, when I was eight or nine years old, Dad had come home drunk and Mom slapped him across the face. "It's either me or the alcohol!" she exclaimed. "You can't have both!" My father stopped drinking immediately and often said he greatly admired Mom for doing what she did. "That's why I married her," he said. "She has spunk."

"Dad," I said, "I think you'd be pleased that I suspect a priest killed Miss Dugan." I imagined Dad with a big grin on his face. "Father Milford dislikes me even though I've never done him any harm. His feelings might come from the fact that he's afraid I'll find out the truth about him and Miss Dugan."

My father, of course, couldn't hear me, but like a lot of people who visited the gravesite of a loved one, I found comfort just in talking. It had been 30 years since he died, and I had long ago reached a comfortable place of acceptance. I wondered how long it would take me to reach that point of comfort with Jane because I was certain not to have 30 more years to live. How would Jane feel if she knew I was interested in Adelia?

I stared at my father's tombstone for a few minutes more. Sadly, no matter how hard I tried to remember all that was good about him, I couldn't change what had turned him into a bitter man. Dad had been pious. As a farmer, he'd pray for good weather and a good crop. He'd pray for health and longevity. He'd pray for my sweet mother when she fell ill. Then, when she took her last breath, he cursed God and flung himself on her bed, and neither the physician nor his friends could console him.

I thought how sad it was that I never had more time with my mother. I couldn't even remember what she looked like. All I had was the image of a sickly person lying in bed.

I said goodbye to my father and walked toward the newer portion of the cemetery, closer to Adams Street and my wife's final resting place. Sadly, without intending to, it was becoming a day of cemeteries and mourning. Even so, I was able to cope with my emotions while my mind was racing with speculation. I felt a resolution to my case was near. I had nothing to base this feeling on. Maybe it was blind hope. Maybe it was the fact that I had a firm suspect in Father Milford and I just needed to confront him. Then with enough pressure, his Christian ethics might provoke him to confess.

CHAPTER 53

I took a trolley to St Joseph's Roman Catholic Church on Barley Mill Road and arrived a half hour before the service for Miss Dugan. The interior of the church must've been full because citizens in their funeral black stood by the open doorway, down the walkway and throughout the adjacent graveyard. I doubted any of these mourners had received a funeral card from the Dugan family. Detective Bern was correct in her prediction that newspaper accounts of the crime and its victim had aroused public sympathy. Thanks to journalists like Casey Moran, who actually printed his Jack the Ripper theory, subsequent articles have created a heighten sense of outrage from citizens, calls for justice, criticism of the police department, and Adelia and me in particular. I ignored disparaging remarks for the sake of my own comfort. I couldn't let public opinion, or Chief's desire to solve it by Election Day, put unnecessary pressure on us. I put enough pressure on myself. Outside of the Dugan family, no one wanted the killer caught and punished more than I did.

I stepped through an open gate to the wrought-iron fence that surrounded the crowded churchyard. My stomach was uneasy. Perhaps a melancholy had gripped me because I looked at more rows of gravestones after having just come from my father and my wife's resting places. I shivered, but the temperature wasn't cold, just cool with a slight breeze that knocked off some orange and gold leaves from nearby trees and blew them across the churchyard. I took a deep breath, then another and followed by yet another. I thought I might vomit or faint or both. How would that look in front of these citizens, a tough city detective passed out on the ground and wearing his breakfast? Yet in contrast to my mood and the morbid surroundings, birds sang happily in the trees.

I glanced at every visible male and female face in an effort to locate Richard and Adelia, but no luck. Perhaps they were able to get a pew. I wondered if Mr. Stout and his shadow, Officer Swenson would be present. I didn't see them either or Chief Francis and Mayor Willey. So I waited with other mourners near an open grave.

To take my mind off the funeral, I lit a cigar and remembered battling the 1866 fire. Actually, it wasn't much of a fight. A hundred or so people stood around while the original church was reduced to smoldering cinders. That church, along with the current Gothic-style building with its tall spire, was constructed with funding from the Du Pont family for the benefit of their workers. The DuPont Gunpowder Mills was only a short distance downhill from the churchyard.

"Did you know Miss Dugan?" I asked a dour woman.

"No," she said, dabbing her eyes with a handkerchief, "but I felt I needed to be here."

I smoked and posed the same question to a man standing nearby.

"No, sir, just come to show my support."

And so it went. Citizens who had no connection to the Dugan family felt an obligation to be present at Katie's funeral. They took it as their civic duty. For now, Miss Dugan had the public's sympathy, but citizens were a fickle breed. Her condition at the time of her murder hadn't been printed yet. After the public discovers she was with child and not married, many of these same people might turn on her. A woman pregnant outside of marriage took the blame for the indiscretion, not the man. Last year, the city had a rape case where the jury declared a man not guilty because the young woman had "loose morals." She was drunk and out late, so the all-male jury reasoned that what had happened to her was her own fault.

A few minutes past noon, the crowd in the churchyard went silent as the beautiful voices of the St. Joseph's choir drifted through open windows and filled the air. *Have mercy upon me, O God, after Thy great goodness.*

Thanks to my early Catholic education, I recognized the hymn: "Miserere Mei, Deus." I heard the choir, yet when their voices went still, I could not hear the funeral sermon. The same was true of everyone around me. So we waited and waited, occasionally passing the time with talk of the weather or how unfortunate that someone so young was being laid to rest. Of course, such talk just led to other stories of death, and the gruesome details. It seemed as if each teller wanted to surpass the previous story in sadness and horror.

Fortunately, no one recognized me. A few citizens asked my name and what I did for a living. I told them I was Alan Krause, using the name of a friend killed in the war, and a shoe salesman. I lied because if anyone recognized my name, I'd be questioned about the case, and I didn't want to discuss it with the public.

It was almost an hour later when I discarded my cigar butt and the citizens standing by the church's front entrance backed away and cleared a path. Father Peter Donaghy, his white collar shining against his black suit, led the way. Father Milford, wearing black vestments and carrying a Bible, appeared second. He was followed by Miss Dugan's coffin, carried by six pallbearers that included George Beeson and Mr. Riley. I was surprised to see Richard in that capacity. He hadn't mentioned he'd be a pallbearer. James and Emily Dugan came next, trailed by what I assumed were Katie's two grieving sisters and brother. I spotted Adelia. No sign of Mr. Stout, Officer Swenson, the Chief, or Mayor.

Men in the graveyard removed their hats and mourners stepped aside as Miss Dugan's casket was carried into the cemetery and placed next to the rectangular hole in the ground near where I had been standing. Katie's parents and siblings took a seat on benches arranged at the gravesite. Father Donaghy, a good half-foot shorter than Father Milford, stood at the head of the coffin. I stared at Father Milford's stoic expression, looking for any sign of remorse, anything that might indicate guilt, but his expression never broke.

I made eye contact with Richard and Adelia and they soon joined me. When it came to Adelia, I experienced an emotion I could only describe as pleasant torture. I felt myself smile. My body warmed. Yet I had to stifle my feelings. Fortunately, there seemed to be no repercussions for having left her alone this morning.

Adelia smiled and whispered, "Good afternoon."

I replied in kind, and patted Richard on the back. "My condolences, sir. How was the service? I couldn't get inside."

"Thank you," Richard's eyes were wet and bloodshot behind his spectacles. "It was a beautiful service."

I felt a pat on my own back. Casey Moran, holding his bowler hat in front of him, circled around in front of me. He nodded and whispered a greeting to Richard and Adelia. "Hey, Drummond," he said softly, "She was with child."

Richard looked ready to punch him. I stepped in between and asked the Vulture, "Is that a statement or a question?"

"I know what the Coroner found," Casey said. "I just want to let you know it'll be printed in today's edition."

"How do you know?" Adelia asked.

"I have my sources."

I said, "You mean you bribed somebody in the coroner's office. The Dugans would appreciate discretion."

"And you know I can't oblige. I have to do my job. Do you have anything new to tell me?"

"About what?"

"Please leave," Adelia said.

Casey looked at Richard and Adelia. "Is there anything you'd like to say? I already got a quote from the mayor and Chief Francis."

"Go jump off the Third Street Bridge," Richard said.

"No, sir, that's not a quote I can use. Good day, then."

Father Donaghy kissed the cheek of each member of the Dugan family. He then addressed the mourners in an Irish brogue. He thanked everyone for attending, "this solemn occasion." He blessed the grave and the cemetery. Then he converted to Gaelic, almost singing his words in a haunting tone of voice that made me wish I understood the language. When he finished, he made the sign of the cross and then stepped back.

Father Milford stepped forward. "We are gathered to commit Katie's body to its resting place and her soul to God, with mercy and compassion to all, and to await the glory of resurrection. Do not let your heart be troubled. For in My Father's house are many dwelling places; if it were not so, I would have told you; for I go to prepare a place for you. If I go and prepare a place for you, I will come again and receive you to Myself, that where I am, there you may be also. Believe in God, believe also in Me. We commit the body of Katie Dugan to the ground; earth to earth, ashes to ashes, dust to dust. The Lord bless her and keep her, the Lord lift up His countenance upon her and give her peace. Amen."

"Amen," filled the air.

Father Milford talked about the unfairness and cruelty of life that would claim someone so young and yet leave other people, evil people to enjoy a long life, something I was well aware of. "We can never truly understand God's plan for us. We can never understand what would motivate someone to take another human life in violation of God's commandment. Please keep your heart pure. Do not let hate consume you. For he that robbed this sweet child of life will be judged and punished."

Was it you? I scrutinized the priest, searching for increased respiration and sweating, facial tics, unusual muscle tension and avoiding eye contact. Too bad I couldn't tell if his heart rate increased. Habitual criminals were masters at hiding their emotions. Father Milford wasn't a career outlaw, so if he was guilty of the crime he was putting on a performance worthy of the actors at the Grand Opera House.

The ceremony lasted a few minutes more while a steady line of mourners laid flowers on and around the casket. I looked to see if anyone dropped Baby Breath's, but no one did.

CHAPTER 54

As we stood along the churchyard fence, Adelia kept her voice low. "I woke this morning with an idea. I went to the library at the Wilmington Institute and spoke to a nice old gentleman named Roger Mecklin. He said Dr. Bush was President of the Raven Society, a literary group dedicated to the works of Edgar Allan Poe, but since the man died, he wasn't sure if the society still met." She retrieved her notebook from her pocket and flipped through the pages. "When I mentioned the Count, he said Poe wrote a short story titled 'Some Words With a Mummy.' It's a strange tale about an Egyptian mummy called Count Allamistakeo who is brought back to life and holds a conversation with the narrator and one other character." She closed her notebook. "I don't know if it means anything or not, but since we're looking for someone nicknamed the Count and we're coming across Poe enthusiasts, I'm just letting you know what I found."

I nodded. "Excellent work, Detective Bern. I'm glad to see you took the initiative. I had an interesting morning of my own. Miss Anna Belle Sanders from the convent came over and proposed marriage."

Richard and Adelia said together, "What?"

As the mourners filed out of the churchyard, I told them what happened. "And Mrs. Yates pointed out that the Count could be a royal title, not a nickname. I hadn't thought of that."

Adelia said, "If we were in Sweden, I'd believe it was a royal title, but here in America I think it's more likely a nickname."

A horse-drawn black brougham and its driver stopped by the gate. Father Milford assisted James and Emily Dugan and their three children into the closed carriage. Once they departed, I had my chance to speak with the priest.

"Good afternoon, Father," I said. I introduced Richard and told the priest he was part of my investigative team.

"I must say, Detective Drummond," Father Milford said in a dull voice, "I'm impressed by your lack of ego."

I wasn't sure if I'd be insulted or not. "I'm smart enough to know the benefits of using resources presented to me. It's a foolish man who lets his ego control his common sense."

Father Milford cracked a smile. "Indeed. Are you close to making an arrest?"

227

"Maybe," I replied. Adelia got ready to take notes. "I was hoping to ask *you* some questions."

The priest groaned and looked down his long nose at me. "If you feel you must."

It was odd how Father Milford, a poor priest, acted like someone who owned a mansion on Delaware Avenue. I swallowed any offense and proceeded with my interview. "What's your real first name?"

His eyebrows pinched together, apparently perplexed by the question. "Kenneth."

"When were you born?"

"March 3, 1866."

"And your mother's name?"

"What're you getting at?" Father Milford said.

"Please, sir, it's just routine questions."

The priest was obviously annoyed. He then spoke as if he were reading a list of ingredients for a recipe. "My mother's name was Katherine. I was born in the almshouse. She died giving birth to me and was buried at the almshouse. Her grave has since been moved to the Wilmington and Brandywine Cemetery. My father raised me. He's deceased, buried on private property. I attended the Brandywine Academy before going onto Seminary School. Detective, all of this is well known to my parishioners, but of course, you don't attend my church."

"We've already established that. What was your mother's maiden name?"

"Pennington."

I was surprised. "Oh. Was she related to Douglas Pennington on the Board of Directors for the Wilmington City Railway?"

The priest cringed. "Yes, sir."

"Why did your mother live in the almshouse if she came from a well-to-do family?"

Father Milford's stoic expression finally showed some cracks when he looked away for a moment and then revealed a pair of mournful eyes. I saved him from explaining.

"Let me guess. Your mother fell in love with a penniless man who left her with child. So her father threw her out of the house, forcing her to live at the almshouse. Am I right?"

Father Milford was blunt, resentful. "You are. Not only was he penniless, he returned from the war having fought on the rebel side."

"I'm sorry."

He seemed to appreciate my compassion and spoke in a more

civilized tone. "Is that all?"

"No," I replied. "Where were you Wednesday night?"

The priest laughed. "Why do I get the feeling that you suspect me of killing Miss Dugan?"

"Did you?" Adelia said.

He smirked. "Don't be absurd. May I ask what evidence you have to make such an accusation?"

"We're not making any accusations," I said. "I'm questioning everybody who knew Miss Dugan. She was killed by someone she knew, someone she trusted, and someone who was very angry at her."

"How can you be so sure?"

"The manner of death."

"Are you sure her killer is a male?"

"Odds are it's the father of her baby."

"Well, detectives, I've taken a vow of celibacy."

"Priests have been known to violate it."

"Well, sir, I assure you that I have not."

"And I have to take your word on that?"

"Yes, you do. Now, if you'll excuse me, there are people in need of my comfort. Is there anything else?"

"You didn't answer my question," I said. "Where were you Wednesday evening?"

Father Milford looked me up and down as if I were a piece of dirt and not worth his time and effort. "Wednesday evening I was administering to the sick at Delaware Hospital. I do so every Wednesday evening. You already know that. You saw me there during your wife's illness."

"Yes, sir, I did. Are you familiar with Tenth Street Park?"

His eyes widened, but he quickly gathered himself and returned to his arrogant tone. "Isn't that where the reservoir is?"

"You know it is."

Father Milford nodded. "You *do* suspect me. I assure you I had nothing to do with Miss Dugan's murder. I resent your attempt to make me a suspect or to suggest that I was intimate with the young lady. May I go now? I do not appreciate being interrogated and having my character questioned by the likes of you."

"Well, it's better that I question you here than at City Hall."

Father Milford softened his tone. "Fine. May I go?"

I purposefully took a long moment to decide, which allowed me time to think of another question. "No. Not yet. Do you ever refer to yourself as the Count?"

Father Milford laughed. "The Count? The Count of what? Don't be absurd."

"Do you know anyone who goes by such a name?"

"No, sir."

Father Donaghy appeared, now wearing a bowler hat on his round head. He saw the stare-down between Father Milford and me. "I'm sorry," the Irishman said, "did I interrupt something?"

"No, Father," I said. "It was a beautiful service. I didn't understand what you said, but I loved it."

Father Donaghy smiled and patted my back. "Well, Detective Drummond, if you ever want to learn the language, I hold classes at my church Monday nights at seven. But you'll have to act fast. I'm planning to return home next year."

"I know." Then I added the following to irritate Father Milford. "I know the mill workers will miss you. You have been an inspiration and a welcomed reminder of their homeland."

"Oh, thank you very much. It's a pleasure to hear such things, and to know my time has been of value."

"Father," I said in a voice full of respect to further irritate Father Milford, "do you know anyone who uses the name the Count?"

Father Donaghy looked at Adelia and Richard. "No, sir. I can't say I know the name. I'll ask my parishioners during tomorrow's services. Maybe someone will recognize it. Are you close to making an arrest?"

I looked at Father Milford. "I hope so."

"Well, I wish you all the best." He and Father Milford headed to a group of elderly ladies that had been waiting for our conversation to end.

Adelia, Richard and I walked from the churchyard. "Damn," I said, "Father Donaghy stopped me from asking Father Milford if he reads Poe or belongs to the Raven Society. Miss Dugan was likely a member of the group and so was her killer. Again, good work Detective Bern. We need to find out who else was part of this literary society. Mr. Stout probably was, and he failed to mention it. We need to question him again."

Adelia said, "If Dr. Bush was President of the society then they probably held their meetings at his house. Maybe the society didn't dissolve after the man's death. Maybe Miss Dugan and her killer still had a key to get into his mansion. That would explain why she was out there."

"I agree." I looked downhill into the tops of trees that hid a village, mills and a river. "But before we go see Mr. Stout, and since we're within walking distance of Henry Clay Village, I want to visit somebody who is usually a good source for information."

CHAPTER 55

Adelia, Richard and I walked downhill on dusty Barley Mill Road toward the Brandywine River, a waterway that I heard long before I saw it because its fast-moving current rushed over a rocky and shallow course and spilled over a low dam.

"Mr. Riley," I asked, "have you ever been down here?"

"No, sir," Richard said as we came into view of the river. "I tend to avoid places that are prone to explode."

"Explode?" my partner said.

"Yes," I replied. "Eleuthere Irenee du Pont, looking to restore the family fortune after they fled France, had training in the making of gunpowder. He was lured to Wilmington by other Frenchmen who claimed the Brandywine would be perfect for operating his manufacturing mills. They were proven correct. The E.I. DUPONT DE NEMOURS GUNPOWDER MANUFACTORY was formed and the company sold their black powder to the U.S. military, mining interests, railroad contractors, canal and road builders. The business struggled at first, but under the leadership of E.I.'s son Henry 'The General,' the company emerged from the Civil War as the largest black powder manufacturer in the world. But making gunpowder is very dangerous. There have been several accidental explosions. The worst one happened just two years ago. Twelve men and a woman were killed."

"I remember it well," Richard said. "It was the main topic of discussion at the barbershop for over a month."

"I was at my desk in the Detective's Office when the first explosion occurred. City Hall shook. I hurried to the window and lifted the glass and saw this dense black smoke rising above the Brandywine valley. Little did I realize the disaster was just starting. The flames from the initial explosion ignited another blast, then another. Six huge explosions took place that destroyed five acres of buildings and homes and severely damaged many more. Some people who feared the end of the world had come ran screaming under my window for the bridge over the Christina and safe haven across the river."

Adelia's voice was shaky. "Now I'm not so sure I want to be here."

"We'll be fine," I laughed. "I hope."

I led Richard and my partner into Henry Clay Village, a town with a narrow Main Street that followed the curve of the river. Breck's Lane and Rising Sun Lane were its only two intersecting roads and they ascended sharply from the riverbank up to Kennett Pike. Along these roads were small wood and stone houses occupied by families who depended on the various mills for their livelihood. Most of the mills were a short distance north of the village, and some were on the opposite riverbank. Since Saturday was a work day, we mostly encountered old men and women and very young children.

"Does everyone of age work?" Adelia asked as our shoes crunched on the gravel surface.

"Yes, it's men only in the gunpowder mills. Women and children are employed in the cotton and paper mills, a much safer alternative."

"No school?"

"There's a school in the village," I said as we passed a series of connecting homes called Pigeon Row and Long Row. "And there's big plans for a new school on Kennett Pike next year, but it's hard convincing parents to send their children to school when they need them to earn money to help the family."

Adelia pointed toward the river. I followed her gaze to a section of rocks in the stream bed where three little boys in ragged clothes were standing on boulders and staring at us. We were an unusual sight, well-dressed in black and our hair groomed, in contrast to the average man and woman of the village who hadn't the money to afford our wardrobe. Adelia waved. The boys returned the gesture.

We then came upon a stone and stucco house with two dormer windows. In the center of the second story facade was an oval stone with 1823 carved into it.

"Charles du Pont once owned and occupied that house," I said.

"Really?" Richard said. "One of *them* lived down *here?*"

"Oh, yes, he preferred to live among the workers. The early DuPonts lived here, or up on the hillside, within view of their mills. It's only the latest generation that has moved along Kennett Pike, with each one of them trying to out-build the other in the size of their mansions."

"I'm curious," he asked, "have any DuPonts been killed in explosions?"

"Two that I know of. Alexis Irenee du Pont in '57. Lammot du Pont was killed a few years ago in a nitroglycerin explosion, but that was at their chemical works over in New Jersey. The company also owns nitroglycerin and dynamite factories."

Richard, Adelia and I arrived at Rising Sun Lane and a covered bridge that spanned the Brandywine and connected the village to homes and mills on the opposite bank. Near the bridge stood a three-story clapboard building that had a first and second floor porch.

"John Miller's Store," I said. "His business occupies the first two stories, with living quarters for the Miller family on the third floor. There's also a pub. It's run by an Irish gentleman who usually knows about everything going on down here. We may or may not learn anything about who killed Katie, but it never hurts to visit with him."

We entered the dimly-lit store. Various aromas from soaps, coffee, teas, sacks of potatoes and leather goods struck my nostrils. I saw rolls of linen, wool, and denim to make clothing. The workers of Henry Clay didn't shop at Market Street retailers because those stores didn't sell the durable clothing needed for mill work. Something made at Mullins, for example, would wear out too fast.

The Miller Pub occupied the back third of the first floor. A couple of white-haired men were half-asleep at the bar and holding nearly empty mugs of beer. Next to them sat a young man who appeared miserable and definitely out of place. He wore a long, unbuttoned gray frock over a gray suit. His black hair was slicked back and he was clean-shaven except for a thin moustache. He sipped something from a mug that was probably stronger than beer.

"Hey, Detective." Scott O' Leary said with an Irish brogue, looking up from his sweeping. He was a thick-necked man with broad shoulders, a wide face and graying hair at his temples. He leaned his broom against the wall and hurried to me, slapping his hand against mine in a mean grip. "Welcome back, old friend. It's good to see you."

I introduced Richard and Adelia and waited for blood to go back into my hand.

"Riley?" Scott laughed, shaking his hand. "Not O'Riley?"

"No, sir," Richard said. "But my paternal grandmother was born in Ireland."

"Then we're practically cousins," Scott said, laughing. He patted Richard on the back. Then he turned his attention to my partner. "And what miracle is this, a beautiful lady detective? Well, that's something I never expected to see. But why not?" He bowed slightly. "I'm happy to make your acquaintance."

Adelia revealed an uneasy smile. She seemed uncomfortable around the boisterous Irishman. "I'm happy to know you, sir."

"Where's John?" I asked of the store's owner.

"Sleeping upstairs," Scott said. "He's not a young lad, you know. What's your desire?"

"Information."

"I figured as much," Scott offered us a seat at a square table offset from the front of the bar. "I know you're partial to the German stuff, Detective Drummond, but how about a good Irish stout? A pint for you, too, Richard? And coffee for you, my lady? Or do you drink?"

The three of us agreed to accept what Scott had offered, so he left to get our beverages. As soon as Scott stepped behind the bar, the well-dressed young man banged his empty mug against the wooden counter top, startling the two elderly men. The gentleman mumbled something in an angry tone but incoherent. Scott put his hands out to the young man in a soothing gesture and retrieved a bottle of Harper's Whiskey and refilled the gentleman's glass. When Scott returned a few minutes later, he delivered our drinks and sat across from me, with Adelia on my right and Richard on my left.

I took a sip of the black beer and enjoyed its frothy warmth as it traveled to my stomach. I then gestured toward the young man, whispering. "He looks familiar, but I can't place him. He doesn't look like your usual customer?"

Scott sipped some beer and then grinned. "I'll ignore that insult to my people, Detective Drummond, because I know you don't realize what you said." He leaned over the table and whispered. "It's Louis du Pont."

CHAPTER 56

"So that's Louis?" I said softly. He was one of the few DuPonts I hadn't met, but I'd heard much about him, and not all of it good, such as being labeled a philanderer. For Adelia and Richard's benefit, I said, "Louis still looks heartsick. He can't still be pining for Bessie Gardner. Bessie married Louis' older brother Alfred, but that was some time ago."

Scott nodded, leaned forward and kept his voice low. "He just wandered in after visiting his brother at Swamp Hall. It's really strange, he and his brother still talk. He said he came home yesterday. He quit law school. So the family's extremely upset with him. And this comes after he took six years to finish Yale. And Alfred seems to be the only member of the family who can reason with him. The rest of the clan has given up."

"What's his problem?" Adelia said, warming her hands on her coffee cup.

Scott shrugged. "He seems to have no direction, no purpose, no desire to join the family business. He's been arrested a couple of times for disorderly conduct and has been caught at gambling halls just throwing away money. He's known to frequent pleasure palaces. He's just not a responsible young man. His brother is trying to get him to grow up."

"I've heard rumors that Alfred's marriage is unhappy," I said.

Scott smiled, "Why Detective Drummond, are you indulging in gossip?"

"No, but in my line of work I hear a lot of things."

"Well," Scott whispered, "a couple of the butlers at Swamp Hall drink here. They say Alfred and Bessie argue a lot and sleep in separate rooms. Also, Alfred's going deaf. That's no rumor. It's the truth."

"That's a shame," I said, picturing Alfred in my mind. Physically, Alfred wasn't an impressive man. His one feature that drew a lot of attention was his big and crooked nose, the result of breaking it as a youth while diving into the Brandywine. Though not physically aspiring, Alfred had intelligence. He attended Phillips Academy in Andover, Massachusetts and then two years at the Massachusetts Institute of Technology. Last year he was made a partner in the family business. "So he's going deaf, but isn't he the conductor for the workers' orchestra?"

Scott nodded. "He is. They have a concert scheduled tonight at Breck's Hall."

Adelia said, "Why is Alfred's home called Swamp Hall? I don't see any swamps around here."

Scott laughed. "It's meant as a joke, dear lady. All the other DuPonts have elaborate names for their mansions, usually French names, so Albert counters with Swamp Hall." He sat back and sighed. "But I don't think the three of you came to visit me to talk about *them*. I hear they're burying that sweet lass today and you don't have someone in jail."

"That's true," I said, taking another sip. "We just came from her funeral. Have you heard anything that might help us?"

"Sorry, no. My people would certainly want to help. Dugan sounds Irish. She could be kith and kin for all I know, but too good to live among us. I'd suspect someone among the upper crust killed her. Ain't too many secrets down here among us plain people."

"That's my thinking. How well do you know Father Milford?"

Scott's eyes went wide. "Why? You suspect him?" He turned to Richard and Adelia. "You agree with him?"

"I do," Richard said, his glass almost empty.

Adelia drank some coffee and shrugged. "I haven't made up my mind yet."

I whispered to Scott. "Miss Dugan was with child. That's not the sort of news a priest would want public."

Scott took a sip of beer and then sighed. "Such a sin, then."

"So, how well do you know the Father?"

"Not well. He doesn't live among us like Father Donaghy. I don't think he likes us Irish, even though he's Irish on his mother's side. I could be wrong. You might see him today. Saturday afternoons he does come around to talk with some of our older folks who can't make the climb on Sundays."

I finished my beer. "Do you know anyone named or nicknamed the Count?"

Scott pondered the question for a while, and then shook his head. "No, I can't say that I know the name."

Adelia asked, "Does the village have any literary groups?"

Scott chuckled. "No time for reading, dear lady, except the newspapers. And lots of us can't read."

We visited with Scott for a few minutes more, mostly discussing the pleasant fall weather, the colorful leaves, the possibility of the different mill workers forming unions, and whether or not trolley service would ever reach the village. "They'd have to widen Main Street for that," Scott said. "And that ain't likely to happen, not with the river on one side and houses already backed up against the hill."

When we left the Miller's Store, Scott wished us good luck in finding the murderer and promised to alert me to any news should he hear something. "You never know," he said in the doorway, "men do talk when they drink."

CHAPTER 57

We headed back to St Joseph's, but I changed our course and took my two companions up Breck's Lane. "Since we were discussing Swamp Hall, I want to show you the house. It's the biggest one down here." It stood three-and-a-half stories tall, with multiple chimneys, a gable roof, and a most impressive eight-window-wide facade with a first floor porch. "Alfred and his four siblings, including Louis, grew up here, although they were orphaned at an early age. I think Alfred was thirteen. Their mother died in an insane asylum. Their father died of tuberculosis. There's a story that the children were going to be removed from Swamp Hall to live with different relatives, but when their uncle arrived, another Alfred they called Uncle Fred, young Alfred met him at the door with a shotgun. Young Alfred argued that with their mother gone for so long at the asylum and their father's lengthy illness, they had already been raising themselves anyway and saw no reason to leave. Uncle Fred agreed."

"All very interesting" Richard said, "but it doesn't help us find out who killed Miss Dugan."

Adelia spotted something out of the corner of her eye. She pointed uphill. "Look."

Father Milford approached. He now wore a black, pin-striped suit and bowler hat, and was frowning.

"What do I have to do to avoid you people?"

"Stop acting suspicious," I said. "When I was talking to you earlier, you made a run for it when Father Donaghy showed up. Why did you leave? I wasn't finished asking you questions."

"I'm not involved in Miss Dugan's death. Now, if you'll excuse me, I'm needed inside."

"Inside Swamp Hall?"

"Yes, there's an elderly aunt who is bedridden."

Adelia smiled. "That's very nice of you to visit her, Father."

The priest bowed slightly. "Only doing my duty."

"I have additional questions," I said.

Father Milford groaned and rolled his eyes. "Ask them please, so I may leave you permanently."

"Do you read Edgar Allan Poe? Do you know anything about a literary group called the Raven Society?"

"No on both counts," the priest said, almost too quickly, so I suspected he was lying. "May I go?"

"Are you familiar with the home of Dr. Bush?"

He released a long and tired sigh. "No, sir. May I go *now*?"

I gave him a mocking wave. "You may. Say hello to Mr. DuPont for me. I haven't seen him in a while and I hope he's doing well."

"I'm surprised, given your lowly profession that you'd ever be in the same room with a DuPont."

I chuckled. "Go to hell, Father."

CHAPTER 58

Adelia, Richard and I stepped down from a trolley at Market and Sixth Streets in front of Mullins & Sons. A white-haired gentleman in a black frock coat was holding a pince-nez in front of his eyes and examining a tweed coat on a mannequin in the display window. Joey was at his usual spot, hawking the latest edition of the *Every Evening* to a small crowd that gathered on the sidewalk in front of City Hall. "Read all about it. Murdered girl was in delicate state."

There it was. Miss Dugan's condition at the time of her killing was now public. Citizens couldn't wait to give Joey their two-cents and grab a copy of the newspaper. Once again, they displayed their love of scandal and their hypocrisy in matters of sex. Venery was as well known among the population as alcoholism and opium addictions, but it was taboo to discuss it in public, and in conservative families it wasn't mentioned at all. If a couple violated the societal rules governing carnal knowledge, it was the female who suffered most, and as I suspected, poor Katie was bound to be vilified by those who loved to judge others.

"More on the Miss Dugan murder. Read all about it." Joey yelled as he masterfully collected customers' pennies and handed them a newspaper from the pile at his feet. I made eye contact with Joey. He shook his head. He had nothing new to tell me.

We circled around Mullins's and entered City Hall through its back door. Joseph Hinder told us everyone had gone home. Saturday was still a work day, but very few city employees stayed until the usual six o'clock.

The three of us went upstairs. I found a note on Molly's desk in her handwriting, so I assumed it was taken from a telephone call. *Mr. Stout did not attend Miss Dugan's funeral, but instead reported for work. I will continue to follow, Officer Swenson.*

So Adelia, Richard and I turned right around, headed downstairs and out the rear exit. We maneuvered back to Market Street at the Clayton Hotel and hurried downhill toward the Warner Company's busy pier. In doing so, one of my earliest memories came to mind, the day I rushed to the riverfront to greet the last whaling ship that ever docked at Wilmington. The whaler had been away for three years procuring whale oil for lamps. The ship's captain gave me some whale's teeth that I still have, displayed on the mantle in my parlor.

The three of us walked by several stores, crossed Water Street and passed the Holly Tree Inn. "It's the only lunchroom in town that doesn't serve alcoholic drinks," I said.

"You'll see more of that," Adelia said in her superior tone. "The Temperance Movement will prove successful one day."

I gagged. "Don't you dare take away my beer."

Richard laughed. "Amen."

After crossing the railroad tracks, we stepped onto the Warner Company pier and joined a crowd of travelers and laborers. Two steam-powered side-wheelers were docked, the *New York* and the *Dorchester*. The *New York* had two decks and a single billowing smokestack and was taking on passengers who wanted to go to Philadelphia or New York. Colored porters assisted travelers by hauling their luggage on hand trucks between family carriages to the steamship. The *Dorchester,* further down the pier, was a single deck, double smokestack vessel used for hauling freight. Dirty and sweating men were unloading sacks of lime from a pair of wagons that belonged to the Eastburn-Jeanes Mining Company of Pike Creek and carrying the sacks on their shoulders into the ship.

I looked for Mr. Stout, but didn't see him. Then for Richard's benefit, I said, "Mr. Stout's a freight agent so he should be somewhere nearby. Look for a large man with a big moustache."

While we searched the faces, Officer Frank Swenson found us. He wore homespun clothes and a bowler hat and hurried to our location. "Oh, Detective Drummond," he said, out of breath, "Detective Bern. What brings you down here? There's no need for you to be here. I'm keeping a good eye on Mr. Stout. I'm a regular hound dog. He ain't seen me neither."

"I'm sure you're doing a fine job. We need to talk to Mr. Stout. Where is he?"

The officer rolled his eyes. "He's on the *Dorchester*. Apparently there's some discrepancy in the ledger over bushels of pumpkins or something. I don't understand it all. But let me tell you, that fellow is a pretty dull man. Up for work at dawn, in bed by dark, stays in his room to avoid his family as much as possible. When he does talk to his wife, he's mean."

"What have you overheard?"

"Well, today, Mr. Stout went to the White's Pharmacy on Front Street during his lunch. He used one of their pay telephones. I got in the booth next to him and listened. I put my ear up close, but not too close that he sees me. Anyway, Mr. Stout spoke to his wife in a very rough manner. He said he wasn't coming home tonight. He wanted to get drunk."

"Did he mention anything about a Raven Society?"

"No, sir. What's the Raven Society, birdwatchers?"

"No, it's a literary group. Go on."

"Well, sir, judging from Mr. Stout's side of the conversation, I guess Mrs. Stout wanted to go back to the Sacred Heart Fair tonight. It's the last night. Mr. Stout said he wouldn't go, that he'd rather get drunk than spend another evening at the fair. She must've nagged him some more, probably about how they never do anything together and how their daughter's going to be an old maid if she doesn't get out of the house and socialize. I figured she said that because Mr. Stout said, 'Face facts, our daughter couldn't attract bees if she was covered in honey."

"Ouch. Has Mr. Stout done anything at work that you found curious or unusual?"

Officer Swenson shook his head. "No, sir."

"Have you heard of anyone referred to as the Count?"

"No, sir. Sorry."

"Officer Swenson, you've done a great job. I'll certainly tell Chief Francis how valuable you've been to this investigation."

He practically jumped up and down. "Really, sir? Thank you, sir."

"Why don't you take the rest of the day off. Spend it with your family. We'll handle it from here."

"Really, sir? That's so kind of you. Maybe I'll take the wife and kids to the fair."

"Yes," I said with a pat on his back, "you do that. Have a good time."

After Officer Swenson left, I wanted to enter the *Dorchester* and find Mr. Stout, but Adelia talked me out of it. She was worried about our safety, and we might lose our way inside the ship. She felt the odds of seeing Mr. Stout were better if we waited on the pier. So I paced like an anxious child anticipating a gift. I sensed a resolution to the case was imminent and every second wasted loitering on the wharf was time postponing my victory. A beer and a cigar always tasted better after solving a case.

"There he is," Adelia said, pointing.

CHAPTER 59

Mr. Stout wore a gray cotton work shirt and denim trousers and carried a clipboard stuffed with papers. He wasn't alone. He had a much younger man at his side.

"Mr. Stout," I said after we hurried to him, "may we have a few minutes of your time?"

We startled him. His eyes darted in all directions. He sounded short of breath. "What? Again? I already answered your questions. I'm terribly busy. Can't it wait for another time?"

"No, sir, it cannot."

"Oh, very well." He handed his clipboard to his companion and ordered the young man to, "Take over."

Because of the noise created by the workmen, the passengers and the churning steam engines, I suggested that we leave the wharf for a quieter spot at the foot of the Market Street Bridge. Mr. Stout agreed. When we reached the bridge, Adelia and Richard sat on a low rock retaining wall and invited Mr. Stout to join them.

"No, thank you," Albert said, preferring to pace and sweat. "Let's get this over with. What do you want?"

I remained standing. "You're a member of the Raven Society, are you not?"

Albert's eyes widened, but he feigned anger. "My wife told me you were in my bedroom. I'd appreciate discretion in regards to our marital arrangements."

"Gossiping isn't part of our job," Adelia said.

Albert studied her with squinted eyes, and then nodded, appearing to believe her. "All right. You saw the portrait of Mr. Poe. You saw the books. You read the article about his lecture in Newark. And I suspect you have somebody following me. Don't deny it. Of course you're spying on me. Can't trust you damn coppers. None of you are worth a plug nickel. So I guess it was only a matter of time before you learned about the Raven Society. It's nothing sinister, I assure you. We *were* a literary group. We met once a month to discuss the works of Edgar Allen Poe. We dedicated each meeting to one of Poe's stories or to one of his poems. We'd read passages aloud. We'd give our interpretations, our critiques. We'd try to scare each other. We ate. We drank. It was always a fun gathering among very respectful people."

"And you met at Dr. Bush's house?"

Albert nodded. "Yes, sir. But we disbanded at our January meeting because the good doctor was in ill health. I didn't agree with the decision. I wanted to keep the society going, pick a new president and decide on a new meeting location, but I was out-voted. The others felt we had run our course."

"That's the real reason why you're familiar with the area around Sycamore and DuPont. You never attended the gala for Felix Darley, did you?"

Albert bowed his head. "No, sir. I read about it in the society column."

"Why didn't you tell us about the Raven Society? What're you hiding?"

Albert put his head down and shrugged. He kicked at the ground like a little boy caught stealing candy who now wished he could put the sweets back. "I was hoping to protect Katie's good name."

"Why? Was she intimate with you *and* Father Milford?"

Albert laughed, a genuine expression I hadn't expected from him. He then looked at me with bloodshot eyes. "I *wish* she had been intimate with me. I got Katie interested in reading Poe when she worked for us. I got her admission into the society. I did all this for selfish reasons, of course. I hoped she'd become interested in me. It was a false hope. She preferred Father Milford, or you Richard, and I suspect several others."

"So Father Milford was a member of the society."

"Yes, but he stopped attending last November."

"Who else is a member?"

"At the end, it was just me, Katie, Dr. Bush and Miss Nellie Neub."

"Neub? Neub? Where have I heard that name before?"

Adelia paused in her note-taking. "Neub was the name of the pirate Mr. Hillary mentioned."

"Yes," Albert said, "Nellie hates that buried treasure story. She says she never got any treasure. I told her she couldn't be related to the pirate because there's no evidence he ever married and had a family. 'Then how do you explain me?' she said. I couldn't, of course. So maybe the old pirate had a family. But that still leaves the mystery about the treasure's location."

I nodded. "Where can I find Miss Neub?"

Albert shrugged. "I wouldn't try to find her, if I were you. She's a grumpy old maid. I believe she moved to New Castle to live with her sister."

"So membership was pretty low at the end. How about before that?"

"We used to have twelve to twenty people at our meetings. Some people attended for a year or two. Some only came a few times. Others just attended once and decided they weren't interested. We were also allowed to bring invited guests."

I jumped on that revelation. "Did Miss Dugan ever invite someone?"

"Oh, she caused quite a commotion about a year ago when she arrived in a fancy coach and got out on the arm of this tall, good-looking gentleman. He had perfect features. He wore the most expensive-looking frock coat I've ever seen. He spoke in a very formal manner."

I was salivating and stressed each word. "What was his *name*?"

Albert thought long and hard. "I don't remember, sir. It wasn't a familiar name. Definitely nobody local. He did say he was visiting from Connecticut."

Adelia looked up from her notebook and asked. "He was just a visitor and yet Katie knew him well enough to ride in a coach with him? Did they act like they were more than just friends?"

"You know, detective, that's exactly what Father Milford and I thought. We suspected something more was going on. They had that certain look, if you know what I mean. And Katie giggled too much that night. Father Milford wasn't happy. I wasn't happy. Neither was Dr. Bush."

Richard put his hands up. "I don't want to listen to any more of this." He pointed at me. "You're accusing Katie of loose morals. You have her intimate with this man from Connecticut, *and* with Father Milford. I won't stand for it."

Adelia said, "We warned you that you might find out some things about Miss Dugan that you didn't want to know."

Richard pushed his spectacles up higher on his nose, and walked away. He stood at a distance where he couldn't hear us but close enough to keep an eye on us.

"Was this the only time this gentleman from Connecticut came to one of your meetings?" I asked.

"Yes, sir," Albert replied. "I think he sensed our disapproval. I don't remember what Poe story we discussed because the meeting dissolved quickly into an angry exchange about how much better Connecticut society was than Delaware society. We wondered aloud why our sweet Katie was in the company of such an arrogant fellow.

We questioned her motives. Maybe Katie was using her charms to move up the social ladder. I guess I couldn't blame her. Who wants to be working class? Mr. Bush was disappointed in Katie as well and he said so. Eventually, Katie and this man got tired of it and left."

"Did Miss Dugan ever invite anyone else?"

"No, sir. Once was enough. Katie was so mad she quit the group for a while. Father Milford convinced her to come back."

Adelia said, "You stated that the Raven Society met once a month? Was there a set date or did you meet anytime a meeting was called?"

"We met in Dr. Bush's library the third Wednesday of the month."

"Third Wednesday?" I pictured the October calendar in my head. "This past Wednesday was the third Wednesday. So even though the society disbanded in January, Miss Dugan still went to the Bush house on the regularly scheduled night. Can you explain *that*, Mr. Stout?"

Albert shook his head, perplexed. "No, sir, I can't. Ever since you told me she was murdered, I've been trying to figure out why she was there, *and* on the third Wednesday. It doesn't make sense. The house is closed, tied up in probate. I haven't been there since the doctor's funeral."

"Did Miss Dugan have a key? Perhaps she held onto one."

Albert shrugged. "I don't think so. Dr. Bush never gave any of us a key to his house, and I was Vice President."

"Tell me about the last meeting."

Albert took a deep breath. "At our last meeting, Dr. Bush didn't look well. It was obvious that age had caught up with him. Our subject was 'The Pit and the Pendulum.' We read passages from the story and had an open discussion about it, like we did probably a hundred times before. It was one of our favorite stories. We drank wine. The more we drank, the louder we got, and we got off topic and talked about all sorts of different subjects. Nothing important, though, just idle talk and some gossip. Then Miss Neub handed us what she called the beginning of a story she was writing about Patty Cannon."

"Patty Cannon?"

"Who's that?" Adelia asked.

"Only the most notorious murderer in Delaware history," I replied. "She was the leader of a gang of outlaws who kidnapped free Negros and then took them south and sold them into slavery. Captured Negros were held in the attic of her tavern until her gang could transport them south. Some of the captives were murdered and their bodies buried in Patty's field. And many a weary traveler who stopped at her tavern regretted it. If the guest had any fortune on him, he didn't have it long.

Some were not only robbed, but killed and buried in her field. Patty reportedly poisoned her husband and beat her own son to death. Her downfall came when she was accused of killing a white slave trader. However, it proved difficult to arrest her, or any member of her gang. Patty's property straddled the Delaware-Maryland border in Sussex County. If Delaware authorities showed up, Patty retreated to the Maryland side of her property. If Maryland officials arrived, she ran to the Delaware side of her land. Finally, the two states coordinated their efforts and Patty was arrested and held at the Georgetown jail. That was in 1829."

"Very impressive," Albert said. "Well, Miss Neub had been trying and failing to be a writer for some time. She's not very good. We didn't feel like listening to another one of her long-winded tales. Miss Neub got mad. That's when Dr. Bush called the meeting to an end and announced that he was disbanding the group. We argued about it. He said he was too old to keep it going and probably wouldn't be around much longer. And he wasn't too keen about all the flirting that went on. He said he recognized it months ago. We thought we'd been pretty clever about hiding it. Shame on us, then, but it was harmless stuff, a bit erotic at times, but we just laughed it off. The old man didn't think any of it was funny. So we lifted our glasses one last time and said our goodbyes. Katie rode in Father Milford's coach. I walked home."

"Well," I said, "Miss Dugan was with child when she was killed. It's being announced in tonight's *Every Evening.*"

Albert bowed his head and spoke in a somber voice, "Then it must've been Father Milford who killed her. You got to believe me, Detective Drummond, Detective Bern. I never stole Richard's razor. Father Milford must've done it. We had lunch together last week at the Clayton House. I saw Mr. Riley's right before we went into the dining room. Father Milford seemed to already know him, or knew what he looked like. He asked me to confirm the gentleman's name."

Adelia was desperate to keep the priest from the gallows. She asked the one question that still put an ounce of doubt in my mind about the priest. "Did Father Milford call himself the Count?"

Albert shook his head slowly. "I never heard him use that name."

"Is there anything more you can tell us about this gentleman from Connecticut?"

"Well, I didn't like him. And not just because he was with Katie. I envied his literary knowledge. He seemed well versed not only in the works of Poe, but in the poetry and fiction of other writers. He quoted passages from memory. That was one good quality."

"What happened to him?" I said. "Do you know?"

"When Katie returned to our group I asked her about the gentleman. She seemed reluctant to talk about him, even sad. She just said he wasn't coming back. So I don't know what happened to him." Albert looked back anxiously at the *Dorchester.* "May I go now? The ship looks ready to depart."

We dismissed him.

My partner put her notebook and pencil in a pocket. "I'm afraid to ask because I think I know what you're going to say, but now what?"

"Isn't it obvious?" I said as Richard rejoined us. "We arrest Father Milford."

CHAPTER 60

As some dark clouds drifted over the city from the south, the three of us walked past the same stores on the way uphill that we had passed on the way down. As we crossed Fourth Street near the Western Union Telegraph Office, the wind kicked up, compelling men and women to hold onto their hats and scurry to trolleys or inside buildings.

"Arresting a priest," my partner said against the noise from the wind, "will make you the most hated man in Wilmington. These people won't care if Father Milford's guilty or not. The Church is seen as infallible. You don't arrest priests. I can't remember when I've seen a priest arrested."

I wondered why she continually defended Father Milford. "I'm aware of the mountain before me. But priest or not, he's still a man and subject to the law."

"We don't know that Father Milford called himself the Count."

"I'm not worried about that. He'd only deny it."

"How will you get Father Milford convicted?" Richard said. "Are you going to stick him in that same disgusting cell I was in until he breaks down and confesses?"

"That's the plan. I'm confident that once we tell him we know all about the Raven Society and his liaisons with Miss Dugan, his sense of moral right will kick in and he'll be consumed with guilt. He'll have no other choice except to confess to cleanse his soul."

I stopped dead in my tracks. There it was. That elegant red brougham with its black horse and black-suited driver was parked in front of the Clayton House. More surprisingly, Chief Francis held its door open while a white-haired gentleman in a full gray suit, and carrying a walking stick, climbed inside.

I raced ahead, leaving my startled companions behind.

Chief closed the door just as I arrived. My sudden appearance startled him. He reacted as if I was a petty criminal threatening the gentleman in the coach. Chief grabbed my arm and shoved me as hard as he could. I stumbled backwards and almost fell. He reached under his coat for what I suspected was a weapon. Then he recognized me. "David! What're you doing?"

The driver slapped the reins and the horse bolted to a gallop, pulling the brougham up Market Street. I ran after it.

"David!" Chief said. "Stop! Get back here!"

The brougham sped away, almost running over a few people. I had no choice except to give up the chase and return to Chief Francis.

"Who was that?" I said, panting.

Adelia and Richard joined me. We surrounded the Chief, who rubbed his beard and acted relieved to see us. "Good. I'm glad you're here. It'll save me the trouble of trying to find you. Let's go inside my office. Who's this gentleman?"

I stepped back. "This is Mr. Richard Riley. He's been helping us with the case. Who was that man in the coach?"

"I'll explain everything in my office," Chief said, still stroking his beard, but his eyes avoided looking directly at me or Adelia. Chief addressed Richard. "I'm sorry, sir, but you can't be a part of what I have to say. Please excuse us."

Since the wealthy ran the city under the guise of our politicians, my suspicious nature sounded the alarm, and I worried that outside interference was about to intrude upon our murder investigation.

CHAPTER 61

I prepared for the worst as we climbed the creaking steps to the second floor of City Hall. I had been down this road before. On three other occasions I was ordered to end an investigation because someone with money wanted it that way. Two cases involving embezzlement were declared unsolved and the banks absorbed the loss. The third case involved the robbery of an architect outside one of the buildings at the Jackson and Sharp Company. His story of "an immigrant" assaulting and stealing his satchel never made sense to me. I suspected something else was going on, but I was ordered to forget about it.

Chief Francis unlocked his office door and led Adelia and me inside. With the curtains closed, the dark interior added to the gloomy atmosphere and my distress. Chief closed the door behind us. "Please sit."

"I prefer to stand." Adelia agreed. "Who was that gentleman? What did he want? He's the one who's been watching us."

Chief Francis went behind his desk, but remained on his feet. "I can't tell you that."

"You said you were going to tell us everything."

"You both have done an excellent job investigating the murder of Miss Dugan—"

"Why do I feel there's a *but* coming?"

"*But*, I'm ending your investigation immediately and declaring the case unsolved."

Adelia threw her arms out and exclaimed, "What? You can't be serious? We're close to making an arrest."

My reaction was less dramatic than my partner's because of my experience in these matters. I was more frustrated and dumbfounded. "Who got to you?"

Chief was insolent. "I hear you've been harassing Father Milford. You're accusing a priest of fathering a child and murdering a young woman. The Catholic leadership is in an uproar. I don't need that kind of aggravation with the election coming up. We can't afford to lose the Catholic vote."

I laughed. "What uproar? I haven't heard a thing. Nobody's bothered me. I realize the Catholic Church has some pull in this city, but that's too weak an excuse. They're only a small portion of the population. I ask again, who got to you? Who was that old man?"

Chief Francis shook his head. "I can't tell you that."

Adelia said, "What if we wait and arrest Father Milford *after* the election?"

Chief shook his head. "No good. We can't make this public — *ever.* You know very well that men of God are untouchable, no matter what they've done."

"Sir," Adelia said, trying her best to be diplomatic, "with all due respect, we owe it to the Dugan family. Their hearts are broken. They need justice to help them heal. They've put their faith in us to arrest the perpetrator. How can you sweep it under the rug?"

"Sorry, I won't allow it and the mayor will back me."

"You're willing to let a murderer go free?" Adelia said as the first raindrops struck the window glass. "What if he kills again?"

"I pray that he doesn't."

"That's noble." She put her hands on her hips and groaned. "I can't believe this is happening."

"I can," I said, scratching my head. "Chief, you wanted this case solved by Election Day. We can solve it by Election Day. The people have short memories. They won't remember that a priest was arrested when they go to vote. And why does that matter? Their votes are already bought and paid for."

"David, you know as well as I do that if a murder isn't solved within forty-eight hours, chances are it won't be solved. Do you have any reliable evidence? Do you have any witnesses? Let's be honest, you'll need a confession to convict. You don't have a confession, and you probably won't get one. It'll be the priest's word against yours and no jury will convict a priest."

"It's been three days," I said, sick to my stomach that all my efforts, and those of Detective Bern, were in vain. "You gave us until Election Day."

"Sorry," Chief said as the large rain drops pounded against the window, "I'm declaring the case *unsolved.*"

I closed my eyes and rubbed my temple in an effort to calm my rising indignation. "Why can't you tell me the name of the person who got into that brougham? We've been seeing that coach all over the city. Who is it? Who ordered you to stop the investigation? Was it a DuPont?"

Chief rubbed his beard and remained silent.

Adelia glared at him. "You're a coward."

Chief Francis glared right back, but held his temper. "I'll make an official statement to the reporters on Monday. The case is unsolved. It's no reflection on either of you. You've both done an excellent job. I'll praise your efforts to Casey Moran and the rest of the reporters, but I'm sorry. This is how it *must* be."

"And that's your final word?" I said, knowing it was. I just needed Chief to say it.

"My final word."

I looked at Adelia, who was near tears. I tried to stop myself, but I couldn't. "I'm sorry, sir, but I'm going to tell the Dugan family how you're forcing us to stop the investigation."

"If you do that, David, I'll have no choice except to dismiss you from the force and you'll never work for the city again. Trust me on this one. I won't be able to save you. The mayor won't be able to save you. Casey Moran and his progressives won't be able to save you."

It took me only a second to decide. "You don't have to dismiss me, Chief, I quit." I turned and bowed to my partner. "Detective Bern, it was a pleasure working with you. I wish you the best of luck."

CHAPTER 62

I strolled the wet sidewalks of Wilmington's downtown under dark skies and in a gentle rain that flattened my hair to my scalp and dampened my suit, yet I hardly noticed, nor did I care. I was tired, both physically and mentally. Alone with my thoughts as if no one else existed, I reflected on my actions. I had quit the only job I liked. Quit for principle sake. The thought of spending another minute in the employ of the city, under the control of wealthy men who could obstruct justice and get away with it, left me sick to my stomach. If only I could vomit this feeling and cure society at the same time.

True, I had been through this before, but in those previous cases only money or personal possessions were taken and the victims agreed with the investigation being cancelled. This was radically different. My victims had no voice. Katie and her baby were brutally murdered so a man could hide his indiscretion. Who were those in power protecting? Was it the Catholic Church? If so, then I was right about Father Milford, but I suspected someone bigger than the church was behind this.

I dried off inside the Clayton House and then telephoned the Dugan family to schedule a private time to come out and visit them. Mr. Dugan insisted on hearing any news I might have immediately. So I told James my suspicion and why the case would be declared unsolved.

James was horrified, but not because I couldn't arrest Father Milford. He hated me because I had had the nerve to accuse his priest. He displayed the outrage that Adelia had warned me about and hung up.

Hungry and disgusted, I entered Clayton Hall's relatively quiet dining hall. It could seat 300 people, but only about a third of that number was currently present, displaying their best etiquette and table manners. A waiter escorted me to a lone spot next to a window that overlooked Fifth Street. I lit a cigar, ordered a Diamond State Beer and a bowl of crab soup, and watched a few pedestrians stroll by wearing raincoats or carrying umbrellas. At that moment, I didn't give a damn about anything. The rest of the world could go to hell. However, I knew that mood wouldn't last. I'd soon feel the need to help my fellow citizens and I'd get involved too deeply, so involved that it hurt. Why did I have this sense of duty and fair play? No one else did. Everybody was in the game of life for themselves, grab all you could and don't leave anything for anybody else. Don't worry about who got hurt. Be immune to all suffering.

That wasn't me. I couldn't act like that.

A short while later, while I drowned my mood in tobacco, beer and soup, Adelia appeared. "There you are."

I looked up, somewhat surprised to see her. I removed my cigar from between my lips and gave a gentle wave. "How did you know to look for me here?"

"I telephoned Molly. She said I should try Grinder's Cigar Shop or the Tiltan Pub. Then she remembered what day it was and that you eat your Saturday dinner at the Clayton."

I laughed at myself. Despite my mood, I had kept to my routine without realizing it. "Molly knows too much." I gestured at the chair across from me. "Please sit."

She did, and a waiter appeared with a one-page menu. I told Adelia to order whatever she wanted, but she settled for water.

"No, you're hungry. Order something to *eat*. It's all right to show that you're hungry. Hell, most of the people in this city tonight are hungry. Order what you want and don't worry about the cost."

Adelia nodded. She was near tears when she perused the menu and ordered lamb chops. After the waiter left, she wiped her eyes on a handkerchief. "Thank you. I'm such a proud fool."

"Yes you are," I said, and gulped down some Diamond State. I stared at her downcast expression and allowed myself a romantic daydream, where I embraced and kissed Adelia in an effort to comfort her. The dream vanished when I remembered she wasn't interested. "What's your salary, if I may ask?"

"Thirty dollars a month."

I shook my head in disgust. "No wonder you're hungry. That's half what a constable earns."

"You know women aren't paid much, no matter what the job."

"Well, now that I've quit, you can go ask the Chief to give you my salary. You're the only detective on the force now."

Adelia leaned forward and stared me down. "I really didn't appreciate the way you ran out on me and left me alone with the Chief. I stood there like a fool. He asked me if you were serious about quitting. I told him you probably were. I wanted to go after you, but Chief said he'd fire me too and that the mayor would definitely have no choice except to support his decision. I guess I got scared. Even though I admire your integrity, I can't afford to lose my job. When I told Molly what you did, she started crying. Did you see the Dugans? You didn't have time to get out there, right?"

I swallowed the last spoonful of my crab soup before replying. "I shouldn't have left you like that. I'm sorry." I took a drag on my cigar. "I was sitting here, not thinking about the case, but thinking about all my failures when it comes to the women in my life. I know poor Molly's been sweet on me for some time, but I don't *feel* anything for her. I couldn't stop my mother from getting ill and dying so young that it turned my father into a hateful person. I couldn't stop disease from taking my sweet Jane. I failed you too, by walking out on you. I never knew Miss Dugan, but I failed her too."

"You're being too hard on yourself. It's not your fault that you didn't get justice for Miss Dugan. You did the best you could." She rubbed her chin and appeared pensive. "So I ask again, did you make it to the Dugan house?"

"No, I telephoned to set up a meeting. You know, Detective Bern, the citizens of this city continue to amaze me. I told Mr. Dugan who I suspect killed his daughter, and why I couldn't make an arrest. I explained the political situation, and used the Chief's line about the Catholic Church. Well, Mr. Dugan reacted as if *I* killed his daughter." I paused to drink another mouthful of beer. "He was horrified that I'd accuse their priest. I pleaded with him to understand our reasoning, and that priests, despite their sanctified place in our society, were still men under their sack cloth, susceptible to the same human emotions as any other man. Mr. Dugan hung up on me."

Adelia nodded. "Then you did all you could, and you can do no more." She reached across the table and took me by the hand. I flinched, surprised by her action, but her contact was sympathetic, not flirtatious. "Take comfort in that. You did all you could. I'll move out of your house in the morning."

I nodded. I wanted her to stay longer, but knowing how she felt, I hadn't the nerve to pursue it. "I didn't do enough. A young lady and her baby are dead, and we're just supposed to forget about it?"

"What can you do?"

"I thought about that while I was walking in the rain. I'll have to tell Mr. Riley that the investigation has been stopped, and the reason behind it. He won't stand for it. Then as private citizens, he and I can join together and continue to look into Miss Dugan's murder. Chief Francis and the mayor won't have any power over us. Perhaps we can get Casey to join us."

"I like that idea," Adelia said as the waiter brought her meal, "but is it practical? Do you really think you'll get any results as a private citizen that you couldn't get as a city detective? You have no leverage. You can't threaten anybody with jail if they don't cooperate. And suppose you *do* find evidence against Father Milford, what can you do with it? The city attorney won't prosecute if the mayor tells him not to. No prosecutor in the county or state will touch it if they have any political aspirations."

She had a point. "You're too damn smart." I sighed, defeated. "But I'm still going to talk to Richard and Casey about it. Now, eat your dinner."

CHAPTER 63

Over the next week, my desire to continue the investigation proved to be foolhardy. Whoever had the power to force Chief Francis to declare the Katie Dugan case unsolved also had the ability to censor the *Every Evening*. Casey's editor refused to print another word related to Miss Dugan and threatened to fire Casey if the reporter insisted on pursuing the matter. "I can't help you or the progressives if I'm unemployed," Casey told me. I reluctantly agreed.

As for Richard Riley, once the reality of the situation took root in his conscience, he succumbed to the inevitable and boarded a train west, destination undecided. "I want to find a place where money doesn't rule an entire city." I told him he'd have to live on the moon. He wasn't amused.

As for me, I should've accepted the reality of the situation, but I couldn't. I followed Father Milford. Why not? I had the time. I had funds in an account at the Bank of Wilmington and profitable investments through the Security Trust and Safe Deposit Company, so I could afford to be unemployed, at least for a while.

Father Milford spent his days administering to the worshippers who stopped in at St. Joseph's and working on sermons with Father Donaghy. He lived at the Clergy House, a residency a half-mile from the church. He visited elderly parishioners in their homes. He did his duty at the Delaware Hospital on Wednesday evening. He held Sunday services. I kept my distance so I wouldn't be arrested for harassing a citizen, but I wasn't far enough away that the priest couldn't see me. We made eye contact on a few occasions. I even gave him a sarcastic wave. I wanted him to know I was watching.

The Western Union Telegraph Offices were the first to alert Wilmington citizens that Grover Cleveland won the presidential election. He garnered almost every state east of the Mississippi, including Delaware, so for the first time in our nation's history a man was re-elected to the highest office in our federal government after having lost the job four years earlier. This historical moment received a few cheers in our local taverns, but for most of the citizens, life continued on as it had without interruption. Wilmington city officials remained the same in all twelve wards, so Chief Francis was happy.

A week after the election, I spent a rainy day on my front porch smoking and relaxing when an unrelated idea popped into my head. Why hadn't I thought of it before? Of all the jobs I'd ever had, I liked being a detective the most. So why not open my own agency? I could work on cases the public hired me for, and maybe along the way I might uncover something related to Katie Dugan. It was a long shot, a real gamble, but it could happen.

So on December first, with a light snowfall outside, I opened the Drummond Detective Agency in a second floor office at 222 Market Street, a building once occupied by Crosby and Hill Dry Goods. Adelia Bern, Molly Delmar, Casey Moran and Thomas Hillary of the historical society attended the grand opening, along with a few other reporters who promised free publicity in their newspapers. Hoping to attract additional business, I made it known that my agency welcomed "female clients."

"Will you be hiring additional detectives?" Casey asked from in front of my desk.

"Yes," Thomas said before I could answer, and gesturing at Adelia, "why don't you give this lovely lady a job?"

Thomas and I have spoken on several occasions since I quit the police department and during those conversations we never mentioned Adelia and I avoided the subject for the sake of my own comfort. Since arriving at my office today, it was clear I still had feelings for Adelia, but nothing seemed to have happened during our separation to change her opinion.

"Detective Bern still has a job with the city," I said.

"You know I'm not happy working for Chief Francis," Adelia said. "I'd gladly join your firm. You only need to ask."

What? Maybe I was wrong. Was there some underlying message in what she said? Women didn't always say exactly what they meant. They were clever at subtlety, but men weren't always smart enough to understand the signals.

I sighed. "Detective Bern, you must realize that working for me will be a financial risk. I'm a brand new business. I can't guarantee that my agency will still be operating a year from now. At least with the city you have steady pay."

Adelia frowned and looked at the floor. "I understand."

The pleasant mood in my office disappeared. Everyone stared at me as if I had stolen a precious heirloom and refused to return it. "I'm sorry, Detective Bern. Perhaps, if I'm still in business come spring, I'll be able to offer you a position."

Adelia smiled, and the others were placated as well.

"Will you still be the *Biking Detective*?" Casey asked.

I grinned. "Of course. My first purchase was a new Victor. It's downstairs."

Everyone laughed and wished me well. Molly gave me a big hug before she left. Adelia shook my hand like a man, but her soft contact was friendly. It also lasted longer than a normal handshake and it made me again wonder if there was a hidden message. Unsure, and not wishing to appear foolish, I let Adelia leave my office without comment.

The next day, my grand opening, and the publicity generated in the newspapers, was overshadowed by the shocking suicide of Louis du Pont.

CHAPTER 64

Louis du Pont, that 24 year old gentleman I had seen drowning his sorrows inside Miller's Store, shot himself in the head in the library at the Wilmington Club, an exclusive male fraternity. None of the five newspapers gave a reason for suicide. The *Every Evening* simply stated, "*An air of melancholy had overtaken the young man, and perhaps he suffered from the same affliction as his mother.* I doubted Louis du Pont had been insane, but his mood at Miller's was definitely morose.

Then an odd thing happened. Suicide within a family as prestigious as the DuPonts usually created a great scandal and journalists beat up their own kind to get the story and to be first with any new revelations. Reporters bribed butlers and maids for information. However, nothing of the sort happened. Newspapers never printed another word about it. Naturally, I got suspicious. To satisfy my own curiosity, I returned to Miller's and spoke to Scott O'Leary. He informed me that Louis' funeral at the DuPont family cemetery happened within two days of his death, and it had been sparsely attended. Louis' older brother Alfred handled all the arrangements. "They seemed to be in quite a hurry to plant him," Scott said.

"I don't like it. Something feels rotten about it. Yet what can I do? If the family's satisfied, that's the end of it."

As the dreary, cold days of December progressed, I went to my office daily and killed time by smoking, reading newspapers or conversing on the telephone when a prospective client called. I spent most of the time staring out the window and watching citizens bundled in coats, scarves, gloves and hats cope with the freezing temperatures and the occasional snowfall. Those who were on foot walked fast to reduce the amount of time exposed to the elements. People alighting from trolleys, cabs or coaches hurried indoors. Drivers draped woolen blankets across their laps while they held the reins and directed their horses. The animals' appeared to be smoking with the steamy puffs of air that escaped their nostrils with each exhale.

As for my business, I got phone calls but no clients. I blamed it on the weather and the approach of Christmas, which caused me heartache. I couldn't imagine spending the holiday alone in my empty house. Fortunately, my son invited me to visit, so I closed up shop and traveled to Chestertown, Maryland and enjoyed Christmas with his family.

Upon my return to Wilmington three weeks later, I learned that Father Milford had left town, taking over a congregation in Boston. I had no solid evidence against him, so I had no choice but to accept his departure. On the plus side, I got my first two clients. A mother of three suspected her husband was gambling away his salary. He was. Then a well-to-do woman suspected her husband had a mistress. He did. I felt so sorry for both ladies that I refused payment.

By February, I could no longer endure sleeping in the parlor and confronting memories in every room of my house, so I bought a Cape Code style home on a small lot on Madison Street. It was primarily a single story house with a bedroom attic under a high-pitched roof. I moved in by the end of the month and put my Jefferson Street house up for sale.

Then as the buds returned to the trees and tulips sprouted, the *Every Evening* announced the collapse of the American economy. The Reading Railroad, a major eastern line, went into receivership. Its bankruptcy wasn't the main cause of the financial depression that gripped the nation, but it fueled an already tentative situation. During the past decade, railroad companies had expanded dramatically, borrowing money at a high rate in order to cover the nation in rails. Meanwhile, a major drought in the mid-west kept farmers from producing and selling enough crops to cover their yearly loans. With railroads overextended and farmers unable to pay their debts, numerous banks failed and a financial panic hit the country resulting in high unemployment and business closures that could soon include the Drummond Detective Agency. My lease expired on May 31. I decided to hold out until then.

CHAPTER 65

Eight days before my office lease expired, I smoked the last cigar in the box on my desk and waited for Adelia. She telephoned while I was at home and asked for a meeting at one o'clock. When I inquired about the purpose of the get-together, she preferred not to say, but that I'd be interested. I wondered if it had something to do with the Dugan case? "No comment," she said. Had it something to do with us? I didn't ask.

At the appointed hour, I watched from my office window as a black barouche pulled by two horses parked in front of 222 Market. The open carriage was a pleasure vehicle only ridden in warm weather, and by people who wanted to be seen. Adelia and Casey Moran were seated together and they faced a young man I didn't recognize.

I put the butt of my cigar in a bucket of sand and waited behind my desk. I was tempted to greet my guests in the hall, but I didn't want to appear too anxious. It wasn't long, however, before I heard footsteps. The doorknob turned. Adelia walked in, followed by Casey and the unidentified gentleman.

Casey carried a leather case. He and I shook hands. "This is Mr. Kyle Baer," the reporter said of his well-groomed and youthful companion. It was easy to see that the gentleman was accustomed to fine living. His pin-striped suit probably cost more money than all my suits combined, and he carried himself with an air of dignity. His black hair was cut close to his scalp and slicked back with plenty of oil and he had full moustache. Was this the man from Connecticut? Was this the Count?

"It's a pleasure to meet you, sir," I said, shaking hands with Mr. Baer. I bowed to my former partner. "Detective Bern, it's good to see you again." I offered everyone a seat, but since I only had three chairs, I remained standing. "Now that the formalities are out of the way, what can I do for you?"

Adelia spoke. "We know you were suspicious about Louis du Pont's suicide. Mr. Moran has been looking into it, along with Mr. Baer. I think they have some interesting points to make, and we'd like to present them to you and see what you think."

"I appreciate that," I said, a little disappointed. I hoped they were bringing me something that would put my agency on page one of the newspapers. I needed business. "You must know any investigation involving the DuPonts is doomed to fail and will never make the papers."

"Hear them out."

Casey opened his case. "No one saw Louis shoot himself and there's plenty of reasons to distrust the official statement. If you'll just give me a few minutes to explain what we all suspect, it'll be well worth your time."

I shrugged. "All right, present your case."

The reporter sorted through newsprint and hand-written notes. When he found what he was looking for, he handed me a page from the *Louisville Courier Journal* of Louisville, Kentucky dated May 16, 1893. "Read the article I've circled in ink." I did. The story had nothing to do with Louis, but announced the death of Alfred Victor du Pont, affectionately known as Uncle Fred. Alfred died of an apparent heart attack while visiting his brother Biderman in Louisville.

I returned the page to Casey and shrugged. "There's nothing new here. The Wilmington papers announced his death last week. What does it have to do with Louis' suicide?"

Casey grabbed the paper from my fingers, obviously displeased with my snide response. "Not suicide, Drummond, *murder.* I'll show you." I guess the Vulture fancied himself a lawyer in a court room presenting his "evidence" to the Grand Jury. He handed me his second piece of proof. "Read *that.*"

I unfolded a copy of the *Cincinnati Enquirer* dated two days after the *Journal* piece and read another article that had been circled in ink. It stated that Uncle Fred had been shot dead by a prostitute at Maggie Payne's brothel on West Park Street in Cincinnati. The woman claimed Uncle Fred was the father of her baby and that he refused to admit paternity or pay support for the child. The bullet penetrated his heart and killed him instantly. Nephew Coleman du Pont, also a regular customer at the exclusive brothel, retrieved the body with a hearse and took Uncle Fred to Biderman's home in Louisville. The city's coroner was paid handsomely to lie on the death certificate. The article didn't mention what had happened to the prostitute, but no doubt she was paid handsomely to keep quiet.

"That's interesting." I returned the newsprint to Casey. "But I'm suspicious about the discrepancy between the two newspapers. It's not unusual for this to happen. As you know, newspapers are so politically biased it's nearly impossible to know what's true and what's fiction."

Casey sighed, frustrated and clearly upset that I was challenging him. "Yes, we understand that. Those two conflicting stories are examples of how we can't believe anything that's printed about our *illustrious* neighbors. I also discovered that Uncle Fred had a large interest in the Louisville paper. Its editor, Fred Watterson, was in debt to Uncle Fred, so we suspect the heart attack story is false, made up to protect Uncle Fred's reputation and the newspaper's financial backing. The story about the baby is true. This got me to thinking that the family probably lied about what happened to Louis. If they're willing to support a false story about Uncle Fred, I'm convinced they influenced the Wilmington papers to print a false story about Louis' demise. *And* I wasn't allowed to write anything about Louis' death. Drummond, we both know that with enough money editors and coroners can be bought off."

"And prostitutes," I said with the wink of an eye. Adelia and Mr. Baer chuckled.

"Yes, Drummond," Casey said. "The woman wanted money for her baby and apparently got it, and got away with murder."

"To convince me that Louis' fatal wound wasn't self-inflicted, you'll have to provide a valid reason *why* the family wanted Louis dead?"

"All in good time," Casey said. "I'm not done setting the stage. Now, the five Wilmington papers all stated that Louis du Pont shot himself in the head inside the library at the Wilmington Club on the afternoon of December 2. He had apparently been distraught, but no newspaper ever gave a reason for his melancholy."

"He was in love with Bessie Gardner and wanted to marry her, but she married Alfred. That would be Alfred Irenee, not Uncle Fred Alfred. We do have to keep that straight, since the family likes to use the same first names over and over again."

Adelia said, "It must be difficult for someone tracing the DuPont family tree to keep it all accurate."

The Vulture continued, "Louis didn't kill himself because his brother married Bessie. The wedding took place five years ago. If Louis had been *that* distraught about it, do you really think he'd wait *five years* to put a pistol to his head?"

"It's possible." I considered suicide during the first few months after my wife died, but fortunately the feeling lessened.

Casey went on, "I'll grant you that losing Bessie to his older brother was a lingering pain. Louis saw Alfred and Bessie together at every family event. He saw them together when he visited Swamp Hall, and around town and at the mills. He saw them together when they attended plays and concerts at the Opera House. Louis felt betrayed by both of them. Bessie led him on. She let him believe she was interested in marrying him. Then along came Alfred. Perhaps Louis couldn't stand it any longer, but I can't imagine anyone killing himself five *years* after suffering a broken heart. From what I hear, Louis had plenty of girlfriends, so he couldn't have been hurting that much."

"I ask again, why would the DuPonts want Louis dead?"

Casey glared at me, but maintained his poise. "The marriage between Alfred and Bessie is unhappy. Bessie knows she married the wrong brother. People saw Louis sneaking off with Bessie. There's talk that they were having an intimate affair and that they were about to leave town together. *That's* why Louis was killed. I suspect Alfred is the murderer, or he paid somebody to do it. I need you two to get me evidence against Alfred."

"We *two*? Detective Bern works for the city. Chief Francis won't allow her to investigate a case against the DuPonts."

"Actually," Adelia said, "I quit the police force a couple days ago. I couldn't tolerate working for Chief Francis another minute. Molly was the only one who said goodbye to me. She sends her regards, by the way."

"So you want to work with me on this?" I said, somewhat eager but also tentative. It was easier for me to handle my feelings for Adelia with her out of sight. "Are you really *convinced* that Mr. Moran is correct?"

The Vulture answered. "I'm *convinced* that Louis was murdered."

I laughed. "Just like you were convinced that Jack the Ripper had come to Wilmington and killed Miss Katie Dugan."

Casey frowned. He actually appeared remorseful for having stirred up the public's fear about the Ripper. "While I admit I got carried away with my Ripper theory, this is different. By the time you hear what Mr. Baer tells you, you'll agree with us."

I had almost forgotten about the young man, even though he sat right in front of me. "I hope you're right."

Casey took out a page of notes and read from them aloud. "According to the colored steward at the Wilmington Club, Henry Carter, Louis arrived at the club at 3:30 p.m. and spoke to Henry about mailing a letter for him and keeping it confidential. Mr. Carter agreed. Louis went upstairs to the library to compose the letter. The steward heard a gunshot around 4 p.m. Mr. Carter ran to the library and found Louis slumped over at a writing desk, blood coming from behind

Louis's right ear, a one-sentence letter under Louis' left hand and a .32 caliber revolver at Louis' feet. Now instead of calling the police, Mr. Carter telephoned the club physician, Dr. James Avery Draper. Dr. Draper rushed over to the club and pronounced Louis dead. The police were *never* involved. Isn't that odd, Drummond?"

I was sarcastic. "Not when it involves our *illustrious neighbors.*"

"Well, the newspapers stated that Louis was found *on the floor* with the gun at his feet, no mention of the letter, which must've been discreetly removed before Dr. Draper arrived and probably burned. My source states that the letter was addressed to R.A.B.B.I.E. and that Louis had composed only, *I will not be able to...* Why would someone kill himself mid-sentence? And if it was a suicide note, why remove it from the scene? Its existence would only bolster the case for suicide. Also, when Louis arrived at the club he first met with Willard Hall Porter, a fellow club member."

"Yes, I know Mr. Porter. He's secretary at the Delaware Historical Society. Not to mention President of the Delaware Society for the Prevention of Cruelty to Children and the attorney for the Delaware Society for the Prevention of Cruelty to Animals. He's also Delaware's commissioner to the World's Fair in Chicago that's going on right now. To me, his word is impeccable."

"Yes. Louis told Mr. Porter that he couldn't help at the club's upcoming dance because he was going out of town and wouldn't be back for a while. Now, I ask you, Drummond, does someone plan a trip when they're about to commit suicide? Do they pull the trigger before they finish writing a letter?"

I wondered how Casey had acquired this information because he wasn't allowed in the Wilmington Club. Perhaps Mr. Baer was a member. I scrutinized the young man for a moment and wondered about Kyle's ethics. Given Casey's love for scandal, the reporter could easily fall prey to any con artist feeding him information he wanted to hear. "No," I said, "a person doesn't usually plan a trip if they're about to kill themselves, but Louis may have just said that to divert attention. It seems you've done a lot of research and you're doing a lot of speculating. How did you get testimonies from Mr. Carter and Mr. Porter?" I looked at Kyle Baer. "You've been sitting quietly all this time, sir. Are you the source from inside the Wilmington Club?"

CHAPTER 66

Kyle Baer looked up and pulled on his cuffs. "I am. I spoke to Mr. Porter and Henry Carter. Like you said, Mr. Porter's word is impeccable. Henry Carter is trustworthy. He claims he arrived on the scene right after he heard the gunshot. He saw Louis seated at the writing desk, not lying on the floor. He saw the letter addressed to R.A.B.B.I.E., but it disappeared sometime before Dr. Draper arrived. Henry swears the letter ended in mid-sentence as Mr. Moran described."

I asked, "Do you know who Rabbie is? That's a rather odd name."

"No, I never heard Louis speak it. However, it was quite common for him and me to use a sobriquet when we wrote to our Yale classmates. We especially used this tactic when we wanted to communicate something discreet or scandalous."

"Did Louis have a nickname?"

"The Count."

"What?" I said, frozen in place.

Adelia had a grin like the Cheshire cat. Seven months after the Katie Dugan case was closed, I now had a valid reason to reopen it, and reopen it I would, city officials be damned. Then if I find out that Louis du Pont had been Katie's lover, father of her baby, and her killer, and murdered by his family to keep his guilt from becoming public, then hallelujah.

"Did anyone in the Du Pont family call Louis by this nickname?" I asked.

"Not to my knowledge," Kyle replied. "It was only spoken at Yale."

"Why was he was called the Count?"

Kyle revealed a wry smile. "A lady admirer at Yale said Louis looked like a royal count. And he did, too. Louis had a very sophisticated presence, tall, dark and handsome. He was quite popular with both men and women. He had a good life and such a bright future. He was loved by many and admired by many more. Such elegant people don't kill themselves."

Kyle released some genuine feelings, but he quickly suppressed his pain, regained his composure and discreetly dabbed his eyes with a handkerchief. For his sake, everyone in the room pretended not to see his tears. I felt sorry for the young man. Kyle belonged to a social class where everything, even using the bathroom, was dictated by a set of unwritten rules that governed behavior and eliminated emotions. No wonder some wealthy gentlemen and debutantes went insane.

"When did Louis graduate from Yale?"

"In '91, although he was supposed to graduate in '89. He then attended law school at Harvard."

"Which he quit," I stated. Then remembering the young man at the Miller bar, had Louis been truly morose because he was chastised by his family or had he been mourning Miss Dugan? Was he trying to drown his guilt in alcohol?

Kyle again tugged on his cuffs. "So you heard about that? Well, to put it simply, Louis had no desire to be a lawyer. He felt it would be a charade."

"Why did Louis take longer than expected to graduate from Yale?"

"He loved college life too much and didn't want to leave. You have to understand that here in Delaware Louis was under tremendous pressure to join the family business, either as a lawyer or company executive, something he did *not* want to do. At Yale, many miles away, he was free to be himself. He loved literature and actually saw himself as a poet. He wrote for the student newspaper. He was a star athlete on the baseball and football teams. He had it all at Yale, but was miserable when he came home."

"That sounds like a good reason for suicide."

"No, Louis was only twenty-four years old and had so much to live for. And he was shot behind the right ear. I'm no expert, but from what I've heard most suicides by pistol are done through the mouth or against the temple." Kyle formed a gun with his forefinger and thumb and demonstrated the placement of the barrel behind his right ear. "It would be difficult but possible that he could've pulled the trigger from this angle, but why would he do that when it's so much easier to put the barrel to your temple or in your mouth? From where he was shot, it's more plausible that somebody came up behind him."

"Casey, I assume you went to Dr. Miles. Did he confirm suicide?"

Casey shook his head. "Dr. Miles wasn't allowed to conduct an autopsy. Louis' body was quickly removed from the coroner's office, taken to the Gaut Funeral Home and prepared for burial."

"Really?" I said, intrigued.

Casey said, "That too is suspicious. Louis was buried fast, with no real funeral, no further questions asked by a physician or the coroner. Louis' headstone only has his name, year of birth and death, nothing else. No 'beloved brother' or 'devoted son,' or anything like that, which you *do* find on other DuPont gravestones."

"Yes," I then asked Kyle, "you're certain Louis' gunshot wound was behind his right ear?"

Kyle nodded. "So says Mr. Carter and Dr. Draper."

Kyle and Casey's testimony did leave an impression on me. "Do you have a theory about who might've wanted Louis dead and why?"

Casey said, "I already told you. His brother Alfred was jealous of the continued attention Louis paid to Bessie, and he was afraid they were leaving town together."

I looked at Kyle. "What's *your* theory?"

The young man shrugged. "I don't know. Mr. Moran may be correct. I only knew Louis during our time at Yale or at the Wilmington Club. I didn't see him every day. There were long stretches of time when I didn't see him at all and he wouldn't explain the reason for his absence. He could be very mysterious and aloof when he wanted to be, but never despondent. It just doesn't make sense that he'd kill himself."

"That's hardly proof of murder."

"If Louis and Bessie had run off together," Casey said, "it would've been quite the scandal, something his family would've done everything in their power to prevent. And let's be frank, in a family of that stature, you do what you're told. If you don't, it's the poor house, or in Louis' case, death. They handle everything in the family. They shouldn't be above the law and allowed to get away with murder."

"Mr. Baer, were you at the Wilmington Club at the time of Louis' death?"

"I was not. I left for Richmond on the first of December to spend Christmas with relatives."

"Did you come home when you received news of Louis' death?"

"No, my Uncle John lives in the past. By the time I received news of Louis' death in a telegram from a mutual friend, Louis was already buried. I couldn't accept the ruling of suicide. So when I came home I went to see Mr. Moran because of his reputation for, let's say, stirring the pot. He started the investigation. Then after he read the out of town newspapers and we conducted our interviews, we then went to Detective Bern. She unfortunately couldn't help us for political reasons. So Mr. Moran and I feel we've gone as far as we can. We feel we need someone with more experience and expertise in the art of criminal investigation, and someone who doesn't care about the political implications."

"Do you know if there were other people inside the Wilmington Club at the time Louis died?"

"According to Mr. Carter," Kyle said, "he believes there were a couple gentlemen at the bar on the second floor, but he doesn't remember who they were. It was a Friday afternoon so most of the members were still at work."

"You seem awfully young to be a member at the Wilmington Club."

He nodded. "That's true, sir. I'm not a full member. I'm a legacy recruit because my father is a member. I'm currently a law clerk in Philadelphia. Once I pass the bar exam and become a full-fledged attorney, I can attain full membership with all rights and privileges. Louis of course had full membership because of his family connections."

"No doubt. My concern is that Louis has been buried and forgotten. The Du Pont family is above reproach. The second they find out that I'm looking into Louis' death, they'll use every recourse they have to stop me. And even if the impossible happens and we prove Alfred ordered Louis killed, it'll be a hollow victory. Alfred will never be arrested. All we'll have is our report and whatever Casey is allowed to print, if anything."

Casey sighed. "Yes, I agree we may never see the guilty person swing from the gallows, but at the moment, just give me something. We can at least ensure that history records it like that Cincinnati newspaper published the truth about Uncle Fred. So what's your first step?"

"Normally," I said, "when a murder has been committed, I'd examine the body and the place where the death occurred, but that's not possible. I can't interview anybody at the club because I'm not a member and won't be allowed inside. And as soon as they recognize me, they'll become mute. I don't know where to start."

"I can get you access to see the library," Kyle said. "If we go early in the morning, say tomorrow morning, chances are nobody will be around to recognize you. And you need to see the library."

"That was a rather ominous statement."

"Please, Drummond," Casey said. "You can start by questioning Dr. Draper."

"He won't talk to me, and I don't have any recourse to force him or anyone to help us."

"You can ask harmless and round-about questions. Put people at ease. Then tell them you're just looking into Louis' death for a client of yours. We're not trying to accuse anyone of anything. And you can conduct your investigation without the general public knowing about it because I won't put it in my paper. I realize this case has to be handled delicately, so this is no time for me to interfere."

I almost fainted. "Are you ill? I can't believe you're going to step back and leave us alone. That's a first!"

The reporter grinned. "I'll leave you alone. Of course, once your investigation is over and you present evidence against Alfred, I get full and exclusive rights to the story."

"Of course. I'll look into this, along with Detective Bern, but I'm afraid we'll run into one brick wall after another and in every direction we take."

"You might surprise yourself."

Kyle and I then negotiated a price for our investigative work and he agreed to come to my house in the morning so that he could escort me to the Wilmington Club. With that settled, the meeting ended. I escorted Casey and Kyle to the door. Adelia stayed behind.

"Thank you for letting me work on this with you," she said. "I know Mr. Moran and Mr. Baer have their suspicions about Louis and Bessie running off together, but just so I understand the situation, we're going to investigate Louis' death hoping to uncover any possible relationship he might've had with Miss Dugan and whether or not he killed her. Am I right?"

"You are." The chance to redeem myself and bring justice to the Dugan family ignited my passion, and the fact that Adelia was in full agreement about our course of action, and back working with me, only inspired me more. "I can't imagine *two* people in this small city sharing such a unique moniker as the Count. And I suspect Louis was the gentleman from Connecticut that Katie took to that meeting of the Raven Society because Yale is in Connecticut. And it's possible that Louis was killed because his letter to Rabbie wasn't going to be a suicide note but a confession to murder."

CHAPTER 67

"Louis couldn't normally be seen with the 18-year-old daughter of a barber," I said to Adelia while standing behind my desk. "He obviously used a false name when he accompanied Miss Dugan to the meeting of the Raven Society. Mr. Stout certainly would've remembered the gentleman's name if he had said DuPont. And it would've made for a memorable evening, not just another discussion about the *Pit and the Pendulum*. Our wealthy citizens have been known to give out false names when they're among the common people. There was a member of the Canby family who loved to play whist. He went by the name Hagar so that he could join a whist club among the mill workers."

Adelia paced my office, the heels of her boots tapping the wooden floor. "If Louis was involved with Miss Dugan, then Chief lied to us. It wasn't the Catholic Church that stopped our investigation, it was the DuPonts. That old man in the red brougham must've been a DuPont. But you didn't recognize him?"

"I never saw his face," I said. "But I can't imagine a DuPont would take the time to watch us. He'd send a lackey."

"Maybe they sent a *lackey*, as you put it, on the previous sightings, but when it came time to finally intervene and speak to the Chief personally, a DuPont handled it."

I nodded. "Agreed. And if the DuPonts are involved, it means they know Louis was intimate with Katie and was the father of her baby, and they must suspect he killed her. But how can we prove they know? How can we prove Louis killed her? And even if we can prove it, they'll be nothing we can do about it. They're above the law."

"All we can do is to try. How do you suppose Louis and Katie met?"

"That's a good question. There must've been some event where their social circles overlapped."

"How about the theatre?"

"That's possible. Louis was fond of the arts and Miss Dugan was seen attending plays. They could've crossed paths at the Opera House."

"So what's our plan of attack? How can we prove Louis fathered Katie's baby, murdered her, and was then killed by his brother to keep him from confessing? Or maybe he did kill himself because he was consumed with guilt?"

"Well, we can't examine Louis' body, so let's begin with the location of his death. I'm not a member of the Wilmington Club, but as you overheard, Kyle will take me there tomorrow morning. I am acquainted, however, with the club's President, Colonel William LaMotte. He's a board member at the historical society and I served under him at Petersburg. He'll give me an interview. We may or may not learn anything, but it's a start. I'll telephone him and set up a meeting."

"Before you pick up the phone..."

I waited for Adelia to say more, but no words came. Instead, she approached. She was cautious at first. Her eyes showed fear, yet not enough fright that she'd stop whatever was her objective. Normally, when I was unsure of a person's intent, a warning went off in my policeman's brain and I'd stand ready to defend myself. I'd been on investigations where I'd suffered bodily injury. Those had been hard lessons to learn. Yet Adelia's approach didn't appear threatening.

When she stopped, Adelia stood right in front of me, closer than she'd ever been, but not close enough that our clothing touched. Her hair smelled of jasmine. She looked up. Each eye had a pool of water that soon overflowed and sent a small stream down each cheek. She tentatively wrapped her arms around my waist, testing her boundaries until she realized I wasn't stopping her. Then she squeezed me. She stood on her toes, tilted her head back and presented her lips.

CHAPTER 68

After *seven months*, and with me already reconciled to the fact that Adelia wasn't interested in any romantic entanglements, she decided I was worthy of her affections. My first reaction was anger. How dare she treat me like this! Why did she say no seven months ago and now without any provocation on my part her body was saying yes? I thought she wanted freedom and independence. I thought she wanted to prove to all mankind that a woman could survive on her own. What had changed?

Adelia's lips were poised for my decision. I put my temper aside and touched her lips with mine, gentle and unsure at first. Then as I tasted Adelia's warmth and desire, I pressed harder, embracing her, squeezing her and feeling her respond with greater ferocity. My heartbeat pounded, my body temperature rose, and I experienced such a mix of emotions that they spilled over into pleasurable sighs. I released all the suppressed feelings I kept sealed since I met this incredible woman. Yes, I might get hurt again, but I was willing to take the chance. Sorry Jane.

When Adelia and I finally separated, she was breathing hard and staring at me with an intense hunger in her eyes that tempted me to shatter all social conventions and throw her to the floor and see what lay beneath all those layers of clothing. And in that brief moment it even seemed like she'd let me. Yet as the seconds passed, I realized that the cold wooden floor of my office wasn't the place for such a discovery. Adelia deserved better.

My breathing relaxed. "Thank you," was all I said.

"*Jag älskar dig.*"

I smiled and whispered, "Did you suddenly forget how to speak English?"

She giggled. "No. I was just saying that I'm in love with you."

I had to sit down. For the second time in my life a woman revealed her deepest feelings for me, and I knew it wasn't something to take lightly. A woman's heart was not easily won, but I needed answers. "I wanted to hear you say that months ago. What changed? Why now?"

"I guess the time apart made me realize my true feelings for you, David, but I can be *so* stubborn." She sounded stressed and paced my office again. "You have to understand, I want to prove to all segments of society that women can achieve anything they want without depending on a man. We can do more than just get married and raise a family. And I want to prove that we're more than just emotions, that we have intelligence and valuable opinions." She walked over and loosely held my hand. "I fought my feelings for you every day. I thought, no Adelia, if you give in you'll be like every other woman. Then when I came through that door today and saw you for the first time in months I couldn't avoid the truth any longer. I couldn't deny myself what was there all along." She leaned in and kissed me. "But this doesn't mean I'm going to *act* like every other woman. You're *not* my master. I *don't* have to obey you, or believe everything you say. I'm still going to have a voice. I'm still going to challenge you when I think you're wrong. I'm still supporting the women's suffrage movement."

I grinned. "I wouldn't have it any other way."

CHAPTER 69

Colonel William LaMotte was home and willing to meet. Adelia and I left my office and walked north on Market Street, joining other pedestrians. Adelia didn't say much. She didn't have to. Adelia's smiles and the way her eyes pulled me in was all the evidence I needed to indicate a bright future. It also felt good to have my old investigative partner at my side and continuing our investigation into the murder of Katie Dugan. This time, despite the enormous odds against us, I felt a resolution was possible. An arrest and conviction was highly doubtful, but perhaps Adelia and I could find the proof Casey wanted so that he could write his article and stir up trouble among the elite.

The two of us strolled past the Clayton House, and then approached City Hall. I had yet to enter the building since I quit my job and it felt odd every time I saw my former second home. I had spent so many years inside that brick structure, toiling away the hours for the citizens of Wilmington, trying to give them a sense of law and order. Did they appreciate my work? Had I made a difference?

Adelia and I greeted Joey as he sold the *Every Evening*. He was pleased to see us together again, but we only told him that I hired Adelia for my agency and that we were busy on a case. Joey informed us that Molly was looking for another job. We asked Joey to wish Molly well for us, and then we continued our walk.

Colonel LaMotte's residence was a simple row home across the street from the Grand Opera House. The billboard next to the theatre's entrance advertised concert dates for John Philip Sousa and his band.

"We'll have to go before he leaves town," I said.

"I'd like that."

Colonel LaMotte took a while to answer his front door. When he did, I was taken aback by his appearance. It had been almost a year since I last saw him, and in that time nature had taken its toll. The old soldier sported a gray Van Dyke beard and bushy eyebrows, and what hair he had remaining on his scalp had gone completely white. Instead of his usual immaculate suit, he wore a long gray robe and slippers and leaned heavily on a cane. Yet his hazel eyes still sparkled. "Detective Drummond, it's a pleasure to see you again. It's been too long, sir, too long."

"How are you Colonel?" I asked with a handshake, and then introduced my partner.

"I'm doing well, David," he said. He studied Adelia and bowed slightly. "It's a pleasure to make your acquaintance, Miss. I've been reading about you in the papers. I can't say I agree with your politics, but I admire your courage. Please, come into the parlor."

The colonel turned around and walked slowly through the vestibule, leaning heavily on his cane. There was something tragically sad about watching an old soldier. Given an option, he and other warriors like him would prefer to fight the good fight and die honorably on the battlefield. At least that was a quick death, not this long and slow process that robbed him of one faculty at a time until the final heartbeat.

The parlor was as I remembered it, walls of dark woods and a room filled with Chippendale-style furniture. The drapes were pulled back at the only window, letting in light that exposed the threadbare carpet and dust on a set of shelves stuffed with volumes on military and American history. A pair of crossed sabers was hung by the bookcase, arranged next to silhouettes of the colonel and his late wife. The portrait of a much younger officer in Union blue was displayed over the stone fireplace.

Colonel LaMotte ushered us to a group of armchairs near the hearth. On a table between the chairs were some volumes of the *Encyclopedia Britannica*, bound in leather, next to a copy of General Ulysses S. Grant's *Memoirs*.

I sat and pointed at the *Memoirs*. "Remember when we met the general at the Grand Opera House?"

"I do indeed," Colonel LaMotte said, sitting with some difficulty. He had to leave one leg extended. "That was quite a while ago, wasn't it?"

"About twenty years," I replied. I remembered thinking how short the general was. "It was a cold night."

"Yes. I'm sorry my maid is out right now or I'd offer some refreshments."

"I don't think that's necessary," Adelia said from her seat near me. "Is it all right if I take notes?"

The colonel's eyebrows went up and he spoke suspiciously. "So this is a formal testimony? Something I say may come back to me? Are you investigating something for a client? I was under the impression from your telephone call that this was to be a casual visit."

"Oh, it's casual," I replied, trying to be nonchalant. "We just have a few general questions about the Wilmington Club, but we prefer to have a record of the conversation rather than rely on memory."

Colonel LaMotte stared for a moment, still suspicious, but he said, "Fine, David. If I find any of your questions objectionable, I will stop the interview."

I breathed a sigh of relief. "That's agreeable." I then wanted to test the colonel's knowledge of our suspect. "Do you know anyone at the club, or among your friends, nicknamed the Count?"

The colonel looked puzzled, and then shook his head. "No, sir. I don't recognize the name. Is it someone from our days in uniform?"

"No, sir." I wondered if the colonel's mental capacities were fully functional. I sat back and was about to associate the name of the Count to Louis du Pont and get right to the actual purpose of our visit when Adelia stuck with what got us through the front door.

"I understand you're President of the Wilmington Club," she said. "Naturally, as a woman I'm curious about these all male clubs. I know Detective Drummond is familiar with you and the club, but would you please indulge me with some background information just to satisfy my curiosity. When was the Wilmington Club founded?"

I smiled and winked at Adelia. It was good strategy on her part to make Colonel LaMotte comfortable and engage him in friendly conversation before we made him uneasy about a death in the club's library.

"It was founded in 1855. I was one of its 12 founding members, along with such gentlemen as Victor du Pont, John Wales and Thomas Rodney. Our original name was the Wilmington Association and Reading Room."

Adelia wrote her notes. "What is the purpose of your club?"

Colonel LaMotte spoke as if he quoted directly from the by-laws: "To promote social intercourse among Delawareans and encourage the advancements of literature and art and the preservation of our state history and traditions." Then he laughed. "But in truth, it's a place to get away from our wives and responsibilities and indulge in spirituous liquors and tobacco."

Adelia smiled. "Can I quote you on that?"

He laughed. "Oh, good heavens no."

"How many members does the club have?"

"Ninety-eight at present."

"I assume all the members are professional men?"

"That is correct. Anyone who wants to be a member must be a gentleman of high quality with professional credentials, and recommended by three current members."

"What is your profession?"

"I'm retired after serving as Treasurer for the Farmers Mutual Fire Insurance Company. Before that I was a distinguished officer in the war."

I said, "Colonel LaMotte served four years as a lieutenant in the Fourth Delaware Infantry and was discharged as a lieutenant colonel. His siblings have had admirable military careers as well. He had a brother who became a general and another brother who is serving out west."

Colonel LaMotte glared at me. He had thoroughly enjoyed talking about himself and did not wish to discuss his siblings, especially Charles LaMotte, who had outshined him in everything except longevity. General Charles LaMotte was buried in the soldier's section of the Wilmington and Brandywine Cemetery.

"Detective Bern," the Colonel said, "did you know that I met John Wilkes Booth on the very day he shot President Lincoln?"

"Really?" Adelia said. "How did that come about?"

"I was having lunch at the Willard Hotel with a group of officers from the War Department when Mr. Booth entered the dining room. I didn't know the gentleman. He was recognized by one of the guests at my table, so we invited Mr. Booth to join us. I'm not usually partial to actors, but Mr. Booth did entertain us with some amusing theatre stories. He was a good conversationalist, and an upright gentleman, so I was stunned to hear he committed that heinous crime."

"That's quite a story. Did you tell the authorities?"

The colonel nodded. "I did. But by the time they came around, Mr. Booth was already dead."

Adelia nodded. "Where's the Wilmington Club located?"

"1006 King Street. It's a couple houses north of the Hilles School for Girls. We've been there for about eleven years."

"And it was in the library at 1006 King Street that Louis du Pont killed himself last December second."

CHAPTER 70

Colonel LaMotte turned pale and clenched his jaw. He leaned back in his chair and a wry smile appeared on his face. "Bravo. You spring a trap well, Detective Bern. I was taken in by your charm and beauty only to discover a snake." Then he glanced back and forth between the two of us. "So that's it. You're not interested in the club. Somebody hired you to look into the young man's suicide. Why? It was months ago. It's been forgotten. Why would you darken my door by reminding me of that horrible event?" He squirmed, appearing uncomfortable in his chair. "Quite frankly, I hardly knew the man. He hadn't even been a member for that long, and yet he had the audacity to take his life in *my* club."

"Which leads us to the question of why?" I said. "Why would he pick the Wilmington Club if he hadn't been a member for very long?"

Colonel LaMotte shrugged. "I don't know. I guess someone in his state of mind doesn't think clearly. His mother went insane. Maybe he suffered from the same affliction."

"Well, earlier I asked if you recognized the nickname the Count. We have reason to believe that the Count was Louis du Pont."

"Why didn't you say so instead of asking me if I had ever heard the name?" the colonel said, his voice rising. "You're not being very forthcoming with me, David."

Adelia said, "Last October Detective Drummond and I investigated the murder of Miss Katie Dugan. I'm sure you read about it in the newspapers. She was killed because she was with child and the father of the baby couldn't risk being exposed. We believe her lover was nicknamed the Count. We have confirmation from a Yale classmate that Louis du Pont went by this sobriquet. Someone of Louis' stature would certainly be scandalized if he had a baby out of wedlock. Now the DuPonts could certainly afford to pay off Miss Dugan to keep her quiet, but Louis was already in trouble with the family over his feelings for Bessie Gardner and for quitting law school. So bringing home a pregnant working-class girl would've riled his family even more. He was probably afraid to confront them. So he sought his own solution and killed Miss Dugan. Then he couldn't live with the guilt. We suspect he was going to expose the entire affair in a letter he was composing but was murdered and the letter confiscated. That's one scenario. Or Louis was so despondent about what he had done to Miss Dugan that he took his own life."

Colonel LaMotte continued to squirm in his chair. "It was suicide, Miss, not murder. I don't know anything about a letter. There's been so many rumors floating about that it's difficult to believe any of them."

"Rumors, sir, what rumors?"

"Oh, I don't know. I can't think of them right now."

My partner pushed on without referring to her notes. "I tend to agree with our client that it was murder because the bullet wound was behind Louis' right ear, a rather odd location for someone who commits suicide by gun. Also, upon entering the Wilmington Club, Louis told Mr. Porter that he couldn't help at an upcoming dance because he was going out of town. And Louis asked Mr. Carter to discreetly mail the letter he was going to write. Louis sat at a desk in the library and only wrote a sentence before he died. Louis addressed the unfinished letter to someone named R.A.B.B.I.E. We believe Rabbie is a nickname. This letter disappeared before Dr. Draper arrived to pronounce Louis dead. Not the coroner, mind you, but Dr. Draper, a fellow member of the club. The police weren't called. So it's all very suspicious. Why would Louis kill himself if he planned to leave town? Why did he ask for a letter to be discreetly mailed?"

Colonel LaMotte clenched his jaw and spoke with suppressed rage. "I'm sure I don't know."

"Do you know who Rabbie is?" Adelia asked.

Colonel LaMotte shook his head. "I assure you, I do *not* know who *Rabbie* is. And I certainly hope you're not implying that someone at my club is a murderer. If that's your purpose here, you may remove yourself from my house immediately and never come back."

"Were you at the club when this alleged suicide happened?" I asked.

"Alleged?" the colonel replied, his temper obvious in his voice. "No, sir, I was not present. Hardly anybody was."

"Which is another reason our client believes it was murder. Fewer witnesses."

"It's wild speculation, David. You have no proof."

Adelia said, "There are enough discrepancies in the story about what happened to Louis that might lead someone to believe murder is a possibility. You said there's been plenty of rumors floating around."

Colonel LaMotte, using his cane for leverage, pushed himself to his feet, which meant the meeting was over. "Who is this client of yours?"

I stood as well. "I'm sorry, that's confidential."

The colonel pointed toward the front door. "I'm tired and I've had enough of this conversation. The two of you will please leave my house."

Adelia stood and asked, "What're you afraid of?"

The colonel spoke in an offended tone. "I'll have you know, miss, that I'm not afraid of anything. However, I will not have the reputation of my club soiled by a pair of detectives and the wild imagination of whoever hired you. Now go."

"Thank you for your time," I said, extending my hand. Colonel LaMotte did not shake it. He glared at me and pointed at the door again. I remained polite. "I hope to see you again."

Adelia and I were soon back in the sunshine on Market Street.

I said, "That went better than I expected. And you're interviewing skills are much better. You were smart yet direct. Good job getting him to talk."

Adelia grinned. "Thank you. I learned from the best. Now what?"

"We're only a couple blocks from Dr. Draper's house. Let's see if he's home."

CHAPTER 71

The good doctor lived in a neoclassical mansion at 1101 Market Street, in the shadows of the New Castle County Courthouse. His wife answered the door. We stated our reason for the visit and requested a meeting with her husband. She agreed to let us in and escorted us to the sitting room, which had an abundance of one color — green. The walls and carpet were olive green. The Chippendale-style sofa, settee and arm chairs were upholstered in forest green, the same color as the drapes at a pair of windows. Green was my favorite color, but this was too much.

"Please be seated," Mrs. Draper said. "I'll go tell my husband you're here. Can I get you anything to drink?"

Adelia and I politely declined her offer and waited on the settee. Since we were alone, I took hold of Adelia's hand, kissed it and placed it back in her lap. She smiled as I had hoped, and might've said something but approaching footsteps stopped any conversation.

Dr. Draper appeared sporting a gray cotton suit over his lanky frame. He had a high forehead with black and white hair, an average nose and mouth, but a virtual scar on his chin. Introductions were made. "Is my wife bringing you something to drink?"

"No, sir," I replied, "we declined her offer."

"Very well. Please sit."

Dr. Draper sat across from us. His brown eyes scrutinized my partner with a lustful gaze. It was an expression I easily recognized in other men if not myself. The doctor's behavior, however, didn't arouse any jealousy. I was above such petty emotions, and quite accustomed to men paying attention because Jane had also been an attractive lady.

"My wife tells me you're investigating the Miss Dugan murder," Dr. Draper said. "I remember reading about that. If I'm not mistaken there was even some speculation that she had been killed by Jack the Ripper. However, I fail to understand how I can help. Do you have a medical question or a question about anatomy? I thought the case couldn't be solved."

"Well," I said, "you may not remember, but Miss Dugan was with child. She was overheard referring to her lover as the Count. We have since discovered that Louis du Pont went by this nickname and that you were summoned to the Wilmington Club to confirm his death."

Dr. Draper squinted. "Are you insinuating that Louis du Pont was involved with Miss Dugan? I think if that were true I would've heard something about it. The Wilmington Club may not have any female members, but some of those gentlemen gossip like a bunch of old hens." He laughed. "I was summoned to the club's library to confirm that Louis du Pont was indeed dead."

"Shot behind the right ear?"

"That's correct."

"While he was sitting at a writing desk and composing a letter?"

"He was on the floor when I saw him."

"Why did Mr. Carter telephone you instead of the police?"

"The police?" he smirked. "What could they do except look for an opportunity to extort money from the situation? No offense, sir, but we take care of our own problems. Mr. DuPont killed himself. His family agrees. They took charge of his body."

"But would the good Dr. Miles agree? The coroner was never allowed to examine the body. Who declared Louis' death suicide? Who wrote the death certificate?"

"I don't know. I saw Louis on the floor. I pronounced him dead. That's the extent of my involvement."

Adelia asked, "Did you know Louis du Pont well?"

"I only knew him as a member of the club. And I don't think he'd been a member that long, maybe less than a year. Any social interaction we may have had would've been casual and brief. If he was romantically involved with Miss Dugan, he never mentioned it to me."

"Did you ever hear him referred to as the Count?"

Dr. Draper shook his head. "No, miss."

"When you examined Mr. DuPont's wound," I asked, "did you see any burn marks on his skin?"

Dr. Draper hesitated, and then replied, "Of course, sir. He was shot at close range."

"That doesn't mean it was suicide. Someone could've come up behind him."

Dr. Draper appeared confused. "I thought you came here to discuss Miss Dugan's murder, not whether or not Louis du Pont killed himself."

"They're one and the same," I said. "Katie was with child and murdered for that reason. We suspect Louis was the father and that he killed her because a pregnant girlfriend complicated matters with his desire to run away with Alfred du Pont's wife. We think Louis was murdered to keep him from confessing. Had the letter that Louis was writing become public, the resulting scandal would've been enormous."

Dr. Draper looked dumbfounded. "Sir, I don't understand any of this. You're making some wild accusations based on what evidence?"

"That's confidential. Did you know Louis du Pont was involved with Bessie?"

"I knew they were acquainted prior to her marriage to Alfred. But to imply that their relationship continued after Bessie married is nothing but unfounded and scandalous lies."

"Do you know that for a fact?"

He frowned. "Well, no, but it's nearly impossible for anyone to keep secrets."

"So you never heard any rumors about Bessie and Louis?"

He sat back. "No, sir. I don't know anything about any of this. I was called to examine Louis and that's what I did. He was dead. There was nothing more to do. It was a clean entrance wound. No exit wound. I cannot tell you anything more. I wish I could, but I hardly knew the young man and knew nothing about his love affairs."

"Didn't the location of the wound cause you to question the ruling of suicide?" Adelia said. "Most suicides by gun are against the temple or in the mouth. How do you explain suicide with a wound behind the ear?"

"It's possible."

"But not probable.

"Are you protecting someone?" Adelia said.

"What do you mean?" he replied in an offended tone.

"You said you don't call the police. Your class handles its own problems. I already know this, but such a statement also implies that you, and others in your social status, protect each other as well. So even if you knew that Louis was murdered, and even if you knew the name of his killer, nobody in your circle will ever step forward with the guilty person's name. So, for the sake of argument, are you protecting someone?"

Dr. Draper stood. "I am not. I was summoned to the club to pronounce Louis dead and that's what I did. That's *all* I did, and *all* I know in regards to this matter. This meeting is over."

CHAPTER 72

With the approach of nightfall, and a clear understanding from Adelia that she'd like to pursue more than just a working relationship, I suggested dinner and the Sousa concert while we walked south on Market.

"I'd love that," she said.

Dinner was at A & L Ainscow Café, next to the Grand Opera House. The restaurant was known in the city as "the" place to go before and after a show. It also advertised itself as Wilmington's Delmonico, referring to Delmonico's in New York City, the first restaurant in the country to create a "dining experience." Prior to Delmonico's eateries were like Henkel's, small and dirty and their owners had an attitude toward their customers of "get them in, get them stuffed on fatty boiled or fried food, get them drunk and then get them out." Delmonico's created a clean and high-class environment with French-inspired food prepared to look good, taste good and be a good digestive experience at a reasonable price. Colonel Alfred Ainscow's and his nephew George must be succeeding in their efforts to model their restaurant after Delmonico's. They recently opened another café on Fourth Street.

I told Adelia I had yet to dine at Ainscow's as we entered the place. My attitude toward food was that I needed it to live. The quicker I consumed it the sooner I could get back to whatever I was doing. I didn't need dining to be "an experience." Of course, I needed to change my attitude tonight because I was trying to impress a woman and needed to consider her feelings and desires. As it turned out, Adelia's attitude was similar to mine.

"I'm sorry, David," Adelia said after we left the restaurant and walked under streetlamps, "but I was more comfortable at Henkel's."

"My thoughts exactly."

"*Ja*, this place was too fancy, and I never heard of Daube. And what did you have?"

"Beef Burgundy. I liked it. I thought you liked your meal."

"Oh, I did. I'm glad the waiter suggested it. I just felt that I couldn't act normal. We whispered the whole time. Our waiter was staring at us. The other diners were staring at us."

"No they weren't. I think you're just nervous because this was our first real dinner date together. And I know you liked the wine."

She smiled. "I did."

We entered the Grand Opera House and waited in line in the noisy lobby to buy a ticket to the show. A couple of ladies, in the company of their husbands, stared in my direction. They recognized me and appeared surprised to see me in the company of a female. Then I remembered they had presented calling cards in the hope that I'd date their daughters. Their gazes were almost resentful, snooty and not worth responding to.

With tickets in hand, Adelia and I flowed with the crowd through the middle entrance to the parquet. Adelia's eyes lit up like a child when she first saw the horseshoe-shaped auditorium, which sat 1900 on two levels of cast-iron chairs upholstered in maroon leather. A carved eagle with outstretched wings decorated the front and center of the proscenium arch over the stage, and above a massive maroon curtain that hung between a pair of imitation marble columns. Adelia was most fascinated by the frescoed ceiling, a huge painting of the mythical muses, the nine goddesses who presided over the arts. Electric lights were within the ceiling and small chandeliers that hung on the underside of the horseshoe-shaped balcony.

Our seats were roughly in the middle of the parquet. As Adelia and I got comfortable, she took hold of my hand and thanked me for escorting her to a "theatre show."

"Well, I hope you enjoy it."

A few minutes later, the house lights faded and a short, heavily bearded man in a blue military-style uniform came on stage to mild applause. He wore spectacles and appeared to be in his mid-thirties. He introduced himself as John Philip Sousa. He spoke about being the son of immigrants and that he had been the conductor for the United States Marine Band until last year, when he left to create his own band. Then the house lights dimmed and the curtain parted. On stage, I counted 36 men in Sousa's band wearing the same blue uniforms. The nearly packed house applauded again. When the ovation died, Sousa took his place as conductor. I held Adelia's hand. Then for the next 90 minutes the band played a mixture of marching and patriotic tunes that were appropriate for a Fourth of July parade, as well as classical pieces that were well orchestrated.

"Oh, I loved it," Adelia said when the lights went back on and we stood to leave the theatre. "Although the patriotic tunes about freedom would be more meaningful if women were truly free in this country."

A gentleman in the next row overheard her comment. "My dear

lady, you should have more respect for your country."

"I will," she said, "when my country has more respect for me."

Fortunately, the gentleman didn't escalate the situation by responding. I smiled. I admired Adelia's fighting spirit. She'd indeed be a challenge for any man, but I knew I was capable of meeting that challenge. More importantly, I wanted to.

CHAPTER 73

The next morning, Kyle Baer arrived at my door. We stepped into the promising spring day and walked south to Sixth Street. We came upon a matronly lady sweeping the sidewalk in front of her flower shop.

"Good day to you Detective Drummond," she said. "My, my, but you look swell. Are you getting married again?"

"Oh no, Mrs. Frost, nothing like that." I introduced Mr. Baer. "Good-day to you."

"You seem to be well recognized," Kyle said as we continued our walk.

"Yes, sir, my job has put me in contact with a lot of people over the years, from the poorest of the poor to the richest of the rich. To some I've become a friend or acquaintance, but to most, I'm just a familiar face. Let's hope I'm not recognized at the club."

"That must be interesting," Kyle said. "I'm only encouraged to meet people within my own social class. My friends and family refer to the working class as *Them*. It's *Us* and *Them*, just like there's a separation between Us and the Negros, or Us and the vulgar Irish Catholics. Everybody has a place and everybody knows their place."

"Well, I like fitting in *every* place."

It wasn't long before we walked past the New Castle County Courthouse and arrived on 1006 King Street, an unimpressive brick structure with a flat roof, large chimney, no shutters on the windows and only a single concrete step to the front door.

Kyle tried the door latch and found it unbolted. "As I hoped." He gently pushed the door open and peeked inside. "I don't see anybody."

"So anybody can just walk in? Nobody checks credentials?"

"We've never had any trouble," Kyle said as we quietly stepped into the vestibule. "People know their place. Now if we do encounter someone and they don't know you, remember our story."

The first floor had a well-furnished parlor to the left of a central hallway that ran the depth of the building, with a staircase on the right. High-back chairs and small tables were neatly arranged in the hall beneath portraits. Kyle pointed at a gilded-framed painting of a fully bearded man with a receding hairline. "That's Victor du Pont. He was the first Vice President and second President of the club. Correct me if I'm wrong, but I believe he died about four years ago." I told him he

291

was correct. "James Price was the first President. His portrait is further down the hall."

"Is there a portrait of Colonel LaMotte?"

"Also further down the hall."

We quietly made our way up the stairs. On the second floor, we discovered we weren't alone when Kyle and I arrived at the club's tavern. A man I didn't know and who I assumed was the bartender lazily read last night's edition of the *Every Evening* while seated at a round table. The wall behind the bar had shelves stuffed with various bottles of liquor.

Kyle said, "Good morning, Mr. Mees. Is anyone else here?"

The man looked up from his paper. "No, sir, Mr. Baer. Hardly a soul comes in here until the lunch hour. What're you doing here so early? Who you got there, a potential new member?"

"Yes, sir, this is Mr. Banks. I thought I'd show him around and see if he's interested in joining."

"Well, good morning to you, Mr. Banks. It's a pleasure to meet you. I look forward to serving you that first drink."

"Thank you, sir. Do you serve Diamond State?"

He frowned. "Beer? I can get it, but most of the gentlemen aren't partial to beer."

"Well, then, maybe I won't join."

We had a good laugh, and then Kyle escorted me into the library. The room had four large walnut bookcases lined with encyclopedias, histories and many other volumes. Newspapers from several cities were strewn on top of small tables with lamps and accompanied by oval-backed chairs. Two gray upholstered sofas filled the middle of the library along with a couple of tall floor lamps.

Kyle whispered. "Mr. Mees was here when Louis died. I already talked to him and he claims he doesn't know anything about what happened. He was serving Mr. Oswiler when he heard the shot. He ran to the library and found poor Louis at the writing desk."

"At the desk?"

"Yes, sir. He and Mr. Carter moved Louis to the floor so that Dr. Draper could examine him, but of course there wasn't anything the doctor could do."

"I assume the desk has been removed. Do you remember it?"

"It was a simple, flat top desk with some drawers and it was over there." He pointed at a small half-moon table and chair that resided between a pair of tall windows that overlooked the rear of the property.

"So whoever sat there definitely had their back turned to anyone coming in from the hallway. Did Mr. Mees see the letter?"

"He doesn't remember a letter, but he doesn't deny it existed either."

"And of course it's a new carpet," I said, looking at the maroon rug with gold trim that covered most of the floor.

"Oh, yes, a new carpet. The previous one had to be removed because of the blood stain."

I walked to the little table between the windows and sat in the chair. "So Louis starts his letter. His back is turned to anyone entering the library. Then it is possible that someone snuck up behind him. But then, after shooting him, they would've gone back out by the bar. Did Mr. Mees see anybody go past the bar after he heard the shot?"

"No."

"If Louis was murdered, how did the killer get out of the library?"

"I'll show you."

Kyle led me to a skinny doorway off set from the fireplace that anyone with a sizable girth would've had trouble fitting through. It led to a narrow set of circular stairs that could be taken to reach the first or third floor. We took the steps downward and soon arrived at the club's back door. We stepped outside into a courtyard populated by well-trimmed hedges and a flower garden.

"Louis' assassin enters the club just as we did," I said. "He goes upstairs unnoticed because the stairs are right by the front door, nobody checks credentials and at that time of day very few men are in the club. And those that are here aren't paying attention, or are too busy getting drunk. And Mr. Mees is too busy accommodating them. The library is empty except for Louis. The killer goes up quietly behind Louis and pulls the trigger. He drops the gun and uses the alternate set of stairs to get away safely. That would mean the killer is familiar with the building, so perhaps he's a member or he was told about the stairs. Mr. Carter arrives after he heard the shot. The bartender arrives. Louis is slumped over at the writing desk. He's then moved to the floor so Dr. Draper can examine him."

"Are you starting to believe our theory that Louis was murdered?"

I was still more interested in proving who killed Katie Dugan. If Louis had been writing his confession with the intent of killing himself, one would assume he'd finish the letter and have Mr. Carter mail it. To die in mid-sentence, and to have that letter disappear, added credence to the theory that Louis was murdered. However, without the letter, it was all speculation. "I must admit that I'm being persuaded by circumstantial evidence, but I'm not quite ready to accuse anyone yet. For your theory to have merit, the killer somehow knew Louis had entered the library. Was his killer following him? Maybe. Was his killer already here? I doubt it. His killer wouldn't want to be recognized, so he needed to make a quick entrance and a quick exit. According to Mr. Carter, the gunshot happened a half hour after Louis arrived. That's plenty of time for somebody here at the club to telephone the assassin."

Kyle's eyes widened. "A conspiracy?"

CHAPTER 74

I decided to directly confront the main player of Casey and Kyle's theory. From reading the Society Page of the *Every Evening* Alfred du Pont and his wife were home, but they were preparing to leave for Europe in a couple of weeks. I telephoned Swamp Hall and spoke to a butler who took great pride in being a buffer between the outside world and his boss. "I'd like to talk to Mr. DuPont about his brother Louis." I had no choice but to be honest. Visiting a DuPont under false pretenses would've banned me from ever visiting a family member again. "Please relay my message. It's Detective Drummond. He knows me. We've met on a few occasions. And I'm bringing Detective Bern with me."

The butler said he'd pass along the message. He was under no obligation to do so, or if he did, there was no guarantee that Mr. DuPont would respond. So Adelia and I were relieved when the telephone rang at my office and the butler invited us to Swamp Hall at 3 p.m.

Since Adelia could no longer use the city's bicycles, we took a streetcar to St. Joseph's Church and then walked downhill on Breck's Lane. Since the last time we saw the house, the estate had added a greenhouse off its left wing. Flower beds of blue Irises and bleeding hearts fronted the porch, and ivy clung to a good portion of the home's façade.

After using the brass doorknocker, Adelia and I were greeted by the same butler I had spoken to on the telephone. The formally-attired man was accompanied by a couple of white bull terriers who barked at us until the servant scolded them.

"Welcome," he said, and we stepped inside. The interior resembled a gothic castle with dark cherry paneled walls and thick timber crossbeams beneath a high ceiling. "Mr. DuPont will see you in the Billiard Room."

"I hope he's not expecting a game," I said, trying to inject some humor.

It didn't work. The stately butler remained stoic. He, along with his four-legged companions, escorted us down a dim and wide hallway past displays of family crests, lances, pikes, sabers, heavily-framed paintings of fox hunts, sculptures of female nudes and suits of armor.

The dogs' nails made clicking sounds as they walked on the slate floor.

Access to the Billiard Room was achieved after the butler pulled on a wrought iron handle attached to a three-inch-thick cedar door with iron tension hinges. I was fascinated to see four pool tables in the center of the large, medieval-style room. Most citizens considered billiards, because of the gambling that usually took place between players, as a pathway to a life of debauchery. More acceptable to Alfred's class were the tables set for backgammon and chess.

"Mr. Du Pont will be with you shortly," the butler said. "I will return with some refreshments."

Adelia and I waited with the two dogs in front of a large stone hearth. Over the mantel, a pair of crossed lances embossed in gold was displayed under a coat of arms with the motto: *Rectitudine Sto.*

My partner said, "*By uprightness I stand.*"

"What?"

She pointed at the family crest. "It's Latin. *By uprightness I stand.*"

I kissed her. "I'm impressed. I didn't know you knew Latin."

Adelia smiled, and then stooped to pet one of the terriers. The dog looked up at her with big brown eyes and wagged its tail, happily accepting her caress. "I'm glad I impress you." She then looked around. "I can't imagine having this much money."

"Well, don't let it intimidate you. Be tactful, but always be straight forward and honest. Like most of the men in his family, Mr. DuPont's a businessman first, so speak to him in a direct, no-nonsense manner."

A few minutes later, Alfred's short frame entered the room wearing a black suit with a high-collared white shirt. The dogs immediately mobbed him and he loved it, petting them vigorously while he said hello and I introduced Adelia.

"Please sit," he said in a gentle voice that had a nasal undertone, the result of his once broken nose. Then he confirmed his hearing condition. "And please speak up."

Adelia and I sat near the fireplace. Alfred did likewise, with both dogs seated to his left. He scratched the top of their heads and said, "They're such good dogs."

Adelia removed her notebook and pencil. The butler returned carrying a tray of glasses and a pitcher of lemonade. He set the tray on a small table, and then departed without a word.

"Help yourself." Alfred had a haunting stare that made me wonder if he was also going blind.

"Thank you for agreeing to see us," I said in a slightly raised voice while I poured a glass of lemonade. "I'd like to ask you some questions related to your brother Louis. I hope you don't mind talking about him."

"No," Alfred replied, leaning back. "I agreed to meet with you because I'm curious as to why you want to talk about him months after his death."

And to find out how much we know. I handed the glass of lemonade to Adelia. "We're investigating the murder of Katie Dugan. It happened last October. Perhaps you remember reading about it in the newspapers. Someone cut her throat and left her to die at Sycamore and DuPont Streets, in front of the Bush estate. During our investigation we discovered that Miss Dugan was with child and had a lover who went by the nickname the Count. We recently learned that Louis went by that name at Yale. Did you know your brother was nicknamed the Count?"

Alfred folded his hands and smiled. "No, I did not."

If Alfred was lying, which I suspected he was, he was good at it. His body never flinched and his voice remained calm and steady.

"Our Chief of Police said he also did not recognize the name. Yet soon afterwards he met with someone who owns an expensive red brougham and our investigation was shut down and the Dugan case declared unsolved. Chief said he closed the case because we, at that time, had suspected a priest and he feared retribution from the Catholic Church. However, since then we have learned Louis' nickname, and given his family name, I suspect it was actually *your* family Chief was worried about. Can you confirm that somebody in your family influenced Chief Francis to close our case?"

Alfred sat quietly for a long moment and I wondered if he had heard me. I was about to repeat my question when Alfred took a deep breath and said, "What was Miss Dugan's background?" I told him. "Then Miss Dugan was not a member of our society. Therefore, my departed brother would never have associated with such a common girl from the city."

Adelia said, "Your brother associated with prostitutes. They're not exactly members of your *society.*"

Alfred frowned. "I will not discuss that with you."

"You didn't answer my question," I said. "Did your family interfere in our case?"

"No."

"The evidence suggests that Louis murdered Miss Dugan because she was pregnant with his child yet was in love with your wife.

297

However, Louis couldn't live with the guilt of what he did. He entered the library at the Wilmington Club planning to confess his sin in a letter he addressed to someone named R.A.B.B.I.E. when somebody snuck up behind him and shot him. The official statement, of course, is that Louis killed himself. We doubt the official statement because witnesses saw the letter, but it disappeared, and the placement of the wound is not consistent with suicide."

Alfred stared blankly for a moment, again making me wonder if he heard me. He then burst out laughing. "Absurd, sir, absolutely absurd. My dear brother killed himself because he was heartsick over the fact that I married his great love, and that he failed to accomplish anything. He was prone to fits of depression, just like our mother."

Adelia sipped her lemonade and then said, "Your wedding was five years ago. Why would he wait that long to kill himself?"

"My brother and I had long talks over the past few years. It wasn't just losing Bessie that troubled him. That loss was on top of other painful events. He watched our mother become a raving lunatic and die in a Philadelphia mental institution. Our father died a month after our mother from consumption. Louis witnessed all of this and let it affect him deeply. As I said, he inherited our mother's fits of depression. Then, as a grown man, he failed to finish college on time and quit law school. It all weighed heavily on his soul."

"*You* witnessed what happened to your parents," I said. "It didn't cause you to kill yourself."

"I had to be stronger. I was responsible for my siblings."

"How are Anna, Marguerite and Maurice?" I said in an effort to keep our conversation friendly.

"They are well."

"As for Miss Dugan," I shifted back to our case, "it's very possible that she and Louis met each other at the Opera House. Both were fond of the arts. And Miss Dugan took a man said to be quite handsome and arrogant to a meeting of the Raven Society, a literary group dedicated to the works of Edgar Allan Poe and presided over by Dr. Bush at his home. We believe this gentleman was Louis, and he used an assumed name at the meeting. So it's very possible Louis fathered Miss Dugan's baby."

Alfred shook his head. "If he had, he would've paid for her silence and paid for the child's expenses."

"Your Uncle Fred chose not to do that," Adelia said.

Alfred cringed, and then his face turned red and I expected him to order us from his house. "He died of a heart attack."

I was blunt. "That's not what they're saying at Polly's bordello in Cincinnati. But if you want to stick to the heart attack story, that's fine."

Alfred stood. The dogs gathered around his feet. "Is there anything else?"

Adelia, now also standing, sensed the meeting was over and got right to point. "Excuse me, sir, did you kill your brother Louis or pay someone to do it because you were jealous of his attention to your wife, and were you afraid they were about to leave town together?"

Alfred revealed a crooked and strange smile. "I see Casey Moran and Kyle Baer have included you in their delusions."

Adelia's eyes widened and her mouth fell open. I, however, wasn't surprised because Alfred's family made it their business to know everything about everybody. They had spies all over the city.

"Personally," I said, facing Alfred, "I don't care if your brother killed himself or if you did it. I know we have no chance of prosecuting anyone in your family. However, I do want to know who killed Miss Dugan. I need to bring peace to her family. Louis died while writing a letter to someone named R.A.B.B.I.E. Do you know who Rabbie is?"

Alfred stated proudly. "*I* am Rabbie."

CHAPTER 75

Adelia and I left Swamp Hall unsure if we had just met a murderer, an accessory to murder, or a devoted brother.

"He's a liar," Adelia said. "You asked Alfred if he recognized the name the Count and he denied it. But if *he's* Rabbie, then he must've known his brother's nickname."

"I agree, but what can we do about it? We need to find something concrete that proves Louis and Katie knew each other."

We climbed Breck's Lane back to St. Joseph's Church. "Is there a portrait or photograph of Louis?"

"I'm sure there is."

"Well, Mr. Stout saw the Connecticut gentleman who accompanied Katie to the meeting of the Raven Society. If we can show Mr. Stout a picture of Louis he might recognize him as the man with Miss Dugan."

"An interesting idea provided Mr. Stout's memory is good enough to identify a man from his portrait. It's a long shot. And even if Mr. Stout says positively that Louis is the man who accompanied Katie that night, what can we do with that information? The family will deny everything."

We reached St. Joseph's Church and waited for a streetcar. I looked around, wondering if Adelia and I were being followed. After visiting Colonel LaMotte, Dr. Draper and now Alfred du Pont, the word must be out that we had reopened the Katie Dugan case. Yet I saw nothing suspicious. No red brougham, no strangers ducking out of sight. Were we on the wrong track or were the parties involved not concerned?

A half-hour later, when we stepped from our streetcar at the corner of Second and Market, Adelia pointed. "Look! There it is!"

The red brougham with its black-suited driver and black horse was parked curbside in front of 222 Market.

I rubbed my hands together with delightful anticipation. "Oh, I hope he's come to see us, whoever he is. I sincerely hope so. I have a few things to say to him."

I approached the brougham, peeked inside, and saw only red leather seats. The driver, holding the reins to his horse, looked down from his perch and scolded, "Mind your business, sir."

"This *is* my business. He's come to see *us*."

Adelia and I entered the building and hurried to the second floor. The door to my detective agency was wide open.

"Can we help you?" I said after entering. A gray-haired intruder was rummaging around my desk, apparently searching for something. He appeared to be my age, with a high receding hairline, thin eyebrows, a large nose and a bushy moustache almost as impressive as Mr. Stout's. His black suit and white cravat, although well-tailored and pressed, wasn't a modern style. The fashion was more fitting a social event during the Civil War. "Who are you? How did you get in? We locked the door."

Our unexpected guest collected his walking stick from against my desk and limped toward us. His brown eyes stared from behind a Pince-nez. "Good afternoon. Am I addressing Detective Drummond and Detective Bern?"

"Yes, sir. I ask again, who are you and how did you get in?"

The man gave me a dismissive wave as if I was a bug flying around his head. "I'm glad you're here. I was about to leave you a note." He straightened his back as best he could, a task that caused him to wince in pain. "I am Dr. Alexis du Pont. I have been informed that you two are looking into the suicide of Louis du Pont for Casey Moran. I'm here to tell you that you're wasting your time. Mr. Moran is mistaken in his belief that Louis was murdered. My family is satisfied with the verdict of suicide. The case is closed."

So this was the elusive Dr. DuPont, the patriarch of the clan that I had heard about but never met. I shut the door behind us and smiled. "Yes, sir. Everyone's been telling us it was suicide and that we're wasting our time."

"Then why haven't you been listening?"

"Why does Alfred feel it's necessary for you to pay us a personal visit? I'm sure you know we recently left him at Swamp Hall. And you were seen, or at least your coach was, following us during our investigation into the murder of Katie Dugan. The very fact that you're here tells me that Louis *is* guilty of getting Miss Dugan pregnant and killing her, and that Louis was killed to prevent him from confessing and running off with Bessie."

Dr. DuPont waved his hand again. "Nonsense, sir, utter nonsense. I'm here to tell you there will be no further inquiries into this matter."

"Is this how you shut down our investigation into the murder of Katie Dugan? Did you threaten Chief Francis? Are you threatening us now?"

There was no question I had no leverage against the wealthiest and most politically-connected family in the state. What a DuPont wanted, a DuPont got. But I had to fight for moral reasons, for the Dugan family, and for the sake of my own integrity.

"What happened to Miss Dugan was unfortunate," he said. "When you and Detective Bern were seen asking questions in Henry Clay Village, we decided it was time to step in and end the investigation."

"Why? What're you hiding? What're you afraid of, that we'd learn the truth about Louis? Louis was about to run off with his brother's wife. Louis killed Miss Dugan because she was with child? Well, quite frankly, I don't care if Louis was about to run off with Bessie. Do you hear me? I *don't* care if Louis was killed or if Louis committed suicide. What I want to know is who killed Miss Dugan. I need to give her family something to ease their grief."

"Louis was mistaken in his affections for Bessie. As for Miss Dugan, Louis wouldn't associate with such a common girl. He had his pick of daughters among the elite families across the east coast."

"We've already heard that too. However, Louis was a popular figure at brothels, so I'd say he associated with *common* girls quite often. And the fact that you're here proves he *was* with Miss Dugan. You wouldn't be here otherwise."

Dr. DuPont frowned and released a deep sigh. "Nevertheless, our family is satisfied that Louis committed suicide. As for Miss Dugan, Chief Francis ruled the case unsolved. You should accept it. There's nothing you can do to change that."

Adelia said, "Miss Dugan was found by Dr. Bush's home. Did you know Dr. Bush?"

"Dr. Bush and I, as fellow physicians, consulted each other often and were good friends."

"What's your background, if I may ask?"

He straightened his back. "If you must know, I was educated at the University of Penn School of Medicine. I have my own practice, but since being thrown from a horse, I've had to cut down on my activities."

"Oh, I'm sorry to hear that. When did that happen?"

"A few years ago in Louisville."

"Louisville?" I said. "Like Uncle Fred."

"There is a branch of the family in Louisville. It's common knowledge."

Adelia said, "We're you familiar with the Raven Society?"

"Yes. Dr. Bush enjoyed reading Edgar Allan Poe. He formed the literary club about five years ago as a social group to discuss the author's works. He also allowed members to write their own stories and read them. I was part of the group in the beginning, as were many others, but how many times can you discuss *The Fall of the House of Usher* before you become bored? Toward the end of Dr. Bush's life, he mentioned to me a dissatisfaction he had with the remaining members of the group. He thought the meetings had become more of a lovers' rendezvous and a place for petty jealousies. That's why he disbanded the group."

"Who were the lovers and who had the petty jealousies?" I said.

Dr. DuPont winked. "Why ask a question to which you already know the answer?"

"Do we know the answer?" I said. "We can speculate on the answer, that's all. Since you admit you were a member of the Raven Society, did you meet Miss Dugan?"

"I did not. As I said, I was a member in the beginning, but only for about a year." He limped closer to me and looked me in the eye. "In all sincerity, I do not know if Louis fathered Miss Dugan's baby or if he killed her. And so what if he did? Let the dead bury the dead."

"Let the dead bury the dead? Is that some sort of code that Louis *is* guilty of killing Miss Dugan?"

Dr. DuPont pounded his walking stick two times against the floor. "I am *not* implying anything. It's best for everybody concerned that we leave this entire situation alone. Miss Dugan's parents have suffered enough. The public turned against the young woman once her condition was revealed in the newspapers. Her parents were too ashamed to come out of their house. Do you think telling her parents who you suspect killed their daughter will change anything? And how will you tell them? The Dugans don't want to talk to you after you told them Father Milford was guilty. And you told them this without an ounce of proof. You used your speculation to justify following the priest all over the city. He left Wilmington because of you. And in regards to Louis and Miss Dugan, it's just *more* speculation. Do you think the Dugans will believe you *now*? No, sir. You have no proof of anything, and trust me, you won't find any. Whatever you say now will only bring the entire painful ordeal back to the front page of the newspapers and shame the Dugans all over again. Leave it alone. Take my advice and leave it alone."

CHAPTER 76

It was dusk when I walked Adelia home. We said nothing during the two block stroll and she seemed to sense my need for silence. I was seething, and trying to figure out a way to still investigate Miss Dugan's murder. There had to be something I could do. Where could I find solid evidence against Louis du Pont? I could try the portrait idea, but I had little faith in Mr. Stout's memory. And even if he recognized Louis, what could I do?

"Alfred," Adelia said as we arrived at the door to her building.

"What?"

"Louis talked a lot with his brother, and must've told him. He's the only person who knows the truth. Unfortunately, he's not going to tell us, and we have no means to force him. Maybe Dr. DuPont is right. We should just let the dead bury the dead."

I kissed her. "I don't want to give up."

"I know you don't. Why don't we sleep on it? Maybe in the morning we'll have an idea on how to proceed."

I didn't expect anything to be different come morning, but it was a good way to end the day and kiss Adelia good night. However, I wasn't ready to head home yet. I wanted to be alone to evaluate the situation, to relax my temper, and to scold myself. I lit a cigar and strolled up Market Street as the streetlamps came on. Of course, I wasn't really alone. There was a gathering of citizens in front of the Clayton House. I reached City Hall. Joey was gone, having sold out his issues of the *Every Evening*, but a couple of men loitered on the Hall's front steps.

The very fact that a member of the DuPont family was watching our investigation and then used their power to get our case declared unsolved meant Louis was involved. What other explanation was there? I had never been more frustrated in my life. I had the truth. I could taste it. I could smell it. Yet I couldn't do a damn thing.

I continued on, full of angry energy that would keep me awake all night. *Wait. What was that?*

I had seen something out the corner of my eye when I passed the Grand Opera House. Under lights, a new broadside had been hung next to the one for John Philip Sousa. It advertised the theater's final show of the season before the house closed for the hot summer months. WELCOME THE RETURN OF ALEXANDER FUSCO PERFORMING HIS DRAMATIC READING OF EDGAR ALLAN POE'S *THE RAVEN*, MAY 26-30 AT 8 O'CLOCK. GET YOUR TICKETS NOW! THE SHOWS ARE BOUND TO SELL-OUT.

I had to investigate. I discarded the butt of my cigar and approached the ticket booth and spoke to a young lady. "I need to see Mr. Williamson. Tell him it's Detective Drummond."

A short while later I was escorted into Mr. Williamson's well-lit office. We shook hands and he spoke to me from his desk chair. "What can I do for you, Detective Drummond?"

"What can you tell me about the actor Alexander Fusco? I see by the broadside that he's in a show that starts tomorrow?"

"Oh, yes, sir. Is he under investigation for some reason?"

"Oh, no, nothing as serious as that. I just have some questions about his background because I know I've heard the name before. I just can't remember."

"Mr. Fusco is a popular performer, one of our regular tours. His favorite productions are his one-man shows inspired by literature."

"Has he performed other works by Poe, besides 'The Raven?"

"Oh, yes, sir. Poe is his favorite author. He usually does a Poe story or poem each spring season. He did a dramatic reading of *The Cask of Amontillado* last year."

My heartbeat raced. "Now I remember. He was here in the fall too, performing in a dramatic play."

Mr. Williamson didn't remember, so he opened a ledger book on his desk. "Yes. He starred in a production of *Lost Paradise* last October 15 through 17." He flipped through more pages. "He's been performing here about twice a season for the past six years."

My mind did some quick calculations. Katie Dugan and Richard Riley attended the Sacred Heart Fair October 18 and 19 and Katie was murdered on the 19th. "What do you know about Mr. Fusco personally?"

"He was studying to become a professor of literature before he took to the stage. Seems like a strange transition. He lives in Philadelphia. He's not married. He's about 40 years old and I suspect he drinks." Then he whispered. "I think he's a little odd, too. He seems to become whoever he's portraying. Do you know what I mean? When he plays Poe, he's Poe, even off stage. Maybe that's true of all actors, but it seems odd to me"

I shrugged. "Do you know if Mr. Fusco is in town yet?"

"Yes, he arrived today. I just spoke to him a few hours ago. He bought a ticket to tonight's Sousa concert. He's staying at the Clayton. I can point him out to you when he arrives for the show."

I was too anxious to wait. "No, thank you. I'll try and catch him at the hotel."

CHAPTER 77

I debated whether or not I should have Adelia join me, but I felt there was no time to lose. So under the glow of streetlamps, I hurried the three blocks to the Clayton House and obtained the actor's room number from a desk clerk who knew and trusted me. I also borrowed a small notebook and pencil because I'd decided my best strategy to get Alexander Fusco to talk would be to impersonate a journalist. Actors were notorious egotists and the prospect of free publicity in a newspaper article would be too good to refuse.

I climbed the stairs to the third floor and knocked on door number 303.

A male voice yelled from inside the room. "Who is it?"

"Bill Graves of the *Gazette,*" I shouted through the door. "Mr. Fusco, may I have a few minutes of your time for an interview?"

The door opened fast. A short man in a wrinkled black suit who resembled the portrait of Mr. Poe in Albert Stout's bedroom greeted me with a wry smile. "Congratulations, Mr. Graves, you've done some good journalistic work to find me. Mr. Williamson must've told you I was in town and somebody at the front desk gave you my room number. Is that what happened, sir?"

"Yes, sir. It's an honor and a pleasure to meet you. I greatly admired your performance in *Lost Paradise.* When I heard you were back in town, I just had to get an interview for the *Gazette.* So please forgive Mr. Williamson. Like you, he needs publicity to sell tickets and make a living. And I do confess to a selfish motive. My article about you should benefit me as well. I just started with the paper and need to make a good impression."

Mr. Fusco laughed. "Bravo, sir." He stepped aside to let me enter his room and then he closed the door behind us. Two lamps illuminated a room that was fancier than my house. However, what caught my attention was a vase of red tulips on a table. "I don't have a lot of time, Mr. Graves. I'm about to leave for the theater to attend Mr. Sousa's final concert before I replace him on stage tomorrow."

I pointed around the room at Mr. Fusco's fine accommodations and joked, "The acting profession must pay better than I thought." He laughed. I retrieved the notebook and pencil from my vest pocket. "I just need to ask you a few questions."

I requested biographical information to put the actor at ease and he told me what I already knew. I played the part and wrote it down. Mr. Fusco added, "My dear Italian mother wasn't too happy with my decision to end my studies and become a performer."

"Is your mother still living?"

He put a hand over his heart. "Oh, a tragic story, sir. My dear mother was murdered by a transient soon after I left college. He was never found, so never punished for his crime."

"I'm sorry. What first drew you to the acting profession?"

"Oh, I saw the great E.L. Davenport at the Chestnut Hill Theatre in Philadelphia when I was a boy, so it was something I always wanted to try. I believe the title of the play was *A Way to Pay Off Old Debts*, a comedy. He came on stage and just had a commanding presence. The other actors played off of him. I remember thinking what a great power it must be to provoke emotion in people. I envied that power. I wanted to be like him. But to make my mother happy, I trained to be a professor of literature. About a year from completing my studies, I walked away from the classroom and never went back. I just couldn't do it anymore. I had to do what *I* wanted to do."

"Your one man show is a dramatic reading of *The Raven* by Edgar Allan Poe. Is he your favorite author?"

Alexander spoke in a reverent tone. "As you can tell by my appearance, sir, I am most fond of Mr. Edgar Allan Poe. Even off stage, I enjoy dressing as the man, and very much enjoy reciting his words. You should attend one of my performances. They always sell out, but I can get you backstage."

"Did you know this city has a literary society dedicated to Mr. Poe's writings?"

"You mean they *did* have a literary society. Dr. Bush was President of the Raven Society. He died last year."

"That's right, sir. Did you attend any of their meetings?"

"I was their invited guest on a few occasions, and thoroughly enjoyed my time spent with them. I did some dramatic readings. We even acted out some of the stories. It was so much fun."

"Which member of the Raven Society invited you?"

Alexander took a moment to remember. "I believe his name was Mr. Stout."

"And he in turn introduced you to Father Milford, Dr. Bush, Miss Nellie Neub and Miss Katie Dugan."

"I believe that was their names. You're obviously very familiar with the group if you can remember their names so accurately. Of course, there were other members of the group, but toward the end, just those few you mentioned were left."

I pointed at the vase of flowers. "Are you partial to tulips?"

"I am indeed, sir."

"Are they your favorite?" I asked, writing notes. "Do you have a particular favorite?"

"I love flowers in general. They have such beauty and brighten any room. If I had to pick one that is my favorite, I'd say Baby's Breath. They were my mother's favorite."

I took a deep breath to calm my heartbeat. "So when Baby's Breath is in bloom, you'd have some in your room just as you do the tulips now?"

"Correct, sir. I insist the hotel provide me with fresh flowers. So if Baby's Breaths are available, I definitely want some in my room. I make the same request of the theatre too. I *insist* on having flowers in my dressing room."

A chill ran up my spine. I could be standing face to face with Miss Dugan's murderer. I had to get him to confess. Without it, all I had was more speculation.

"You admitted to meeting a young lady named Katie Dugan. She was a member of the Raven Society. What can you tell me about her?"

Alexander reacted as if he had seen a ghost. He looked around the room as if searching for the specter. He stammered. "What did you say your name was again?"

"Bill Graves of the *Gazette.*"

"What was the name you mentioned?"

"Miss Katie Dugan. She was a member of the Raven Society. She attended plays at the Grand Opera House. She was just eighteen, black hair. She enjoyed being scared by Poe's stories. Do you recall the young lady?"

Alexander continued to look around the room as if he expected someone to jump out from behind the furniture. "Why would you ask me about a specific person in the group? I thought this interview was about me."

"You keep answering my questions with more questions. The young lady I'm asking you about was murdered last October 19. Would you know anything about that?"

Alexander's forehead broke out in a sweat. "That's awful, sir." He grabbed a frock coat that rested over a chair. "Now, if you'll excuse me, I do need to leave for the theatre."

I blocked the doorway. "*Lost Paradise* ended on October 17. Where were you on October 19? Did you stay in Wilmington for a couple of days after your show ended?"

He wiped his sweaty forehead with his coat. "I don't remember. That was months ago. Who are you, really? You sound like a copper. Now get out of my way. I have to go."

"You're not going anywhere until I get some answers. Did you stay in Wilmington after your October show ended?"

Alexander pushed against my chest, but I held my ground. "Get out of my way, please. I need to leave for the theatre. I've never been late for a performance."

I got in his face. "Did you kill Miss Dugan?"

Alexander shoved me aside and threw his coat over my head. I was in the dark and lost my balance momentarily, but kept my composure. I tossed off the actor's coat, chased him and grabbed him as he turned the doorknob. We wrestled. The little man had some unexpected strength. I attempted to get some leverage against his waist to bring him down, but I slipped on the loose carpet and went down on all fours. It gave Mr. Fusco the opportunity to put his hands together and club me with both fists against the back of my head.

Dazed, I staggered to my feet as the actor opened the door and ran into the hall. I followed, but the whole third floor was spinning. I went down to one knee. Three gentlemen watched and waited at the elevator. Alexander stopped. He seemed intent on using the elevator, but since it wasn't yet available, he appeared confused about what to do next. This delay in his escape gave me time to recover.

The actor took the stairs. I ran after him. For some reason, instead of heading downstairs to escape the hotel, he fled upward beyond the fourth floor and then beyond the fifth. He flung open a steel door and we ended up on the roof, caught in a strong breeze and with only the moon and stars for illumination.

"Don't come any closer." Alexander yelled, heading toward the Fifth Street side of the hotel.

I put my hands on my knees and yelled, "Why did you run? What're you afraid of? Did you kill Miss Dugan?"

Alexander held up two fists and clenched his jaw. Veins bulged on his neck. His eyes looked ready to pop from his skull. He screamed. "*Whore*! She was nothing but a god-damn whore! I saw it. She loved every man except *me*! She sinned with that stupid priest. She probably sinned with Mr. Stout. She sinned with some gentleman from Connecticut. I asked her to my hotel room and she said *no*. She'd rather be with those other men, any man except *me*." He took a couple of steps back, coming closer to the edge of the building while releasing a demented laugh. "I deserved some of her fruitful vine."

I stepped toward him. "Why did you kill her? If she didn't love you, you could've walked away. You meet a lot of people through your profession. You could've found someone else. It didn't have to happen."

"She deserved it. She was a damn *whore*. Just like my mother. Don't you understand? She deserved to die. My mother deserved to die. It was my duty to cleanse the world of such sinful women."

"Then why didn't you take credit for it? Don't actors want to take credit for their work? You didn't. You tried to frame Mr. Riley."

"Yeah, I wasn't about to give up my profession and go to prison. Not for the likes of her. I saw them at the fair. I watched them. I followed them. Then I overheard them talk about attending the fair again the next day. Well, that was enough for me. I was tired of her saying no to me. I stole the razor. They didn't know that I got a shave from Mr. Riley when I stayed in town. Then I followed them to the fair. I planned to kill her at the fair when I got my chance. But to my surprise she left Mr. Riley. I followed her. I wanted to see what she was up to. Do you know the damn whore then spent time on a park bench with Father Milford. How dare she do that. A priest! She was more sinful and evil than I had ever imagined. And if that wasn't bad enough, she walked in the dark to Dr. Bush's house and had a tryst with that gentleman from Connecticut, right in the dead man's house. The damn *whore*."

I stepped closer to him. "What happened to the man from Connecticut? Do you know his name?"

"Ha! The coward ran. I surprised them when they came out the back door. He screamed like a little girl and ran. Katie ran too, but I caught her."

"Please come off the roof, Mr. Fusco. I know some good lawyers. You'll get a fair trial. You might even avoid the gallows."

"Hell, no, sir! I'm not going to prison. I'm not going to any asylum. That's where my mother wanted to send me. I should get a medal for what I did. I helped purify the human race and send two sinners to hell where they belong."

I took another step closer. "Please come with me, Mr. Fusco."

"Stay away!"he said, putting a hand up. "I won't go with you. I can't go with you. Don't you understand? You give me no choice but to make this my farewell performance." He took a couple steps backwards and stood on the edge of the building.

"Please, sir, don't do this."

Alexander spread his arms wide and shouted to the heavens, "The scariest monsters are the ones that lurk within our souls." He leaned back until gravity took hold of him and he disappeared from sight. His body landed on the sidewalk with a thud. A lady screamed.

CHAPTER 78

"And that's what happened," I told Chief Francis the next morning in his office with Adelia seated next to me. Molly was present and recorded my statement.

"Do we know who typed the rendezvous note?" Adelia asked.

"I suspect it was Louis. When Kirk went for his second dime, he said the man acted like he didn't know what he was talking about. The first man must've been Louis and the second was Father Milford. It was dark, and both men had to conceal their faces. I think Miss Dugan meeting Father Milford at the Tenth Street Park became a routine that started after the Raven Society disbanded, and when the weather cooperated. Remember one of the reasons Dr. Bush disbanded the literary group was because he was tired of the flirting and petty jealousies. Miss Dugan was no doubt the cause. She not only liked to be scared. She liked the attention she got from men. As for Louis, I believe he fathered Miss Dugan's baby, but they must've quarreled about the pregnancy. She wanted to keep the baby. He abandons her. Yet he later slipped her a note that Miss Dugan interpreted as reconciliation. She still meets Father Milford at the park. Then leaves to meet Louis and is seen by the butcher, Mr. Beeson. She must've had a key to Dr. Bush's house. It wasn't found on Katie, but that's of little importance. Since the old man's death, his house became the perfect rendezvous for her and Louis to secretively meet. I'm not sure it was a coincidence or not that it was the third Wednesday of the month when Miss Dugan was killed, which was when the Raven Society held its meetings. It doesn't really matter." Adelia nodded. "I need to apologize to the Dugan family and tell them who really murdered their daughter. Then I'll make an announcement to the press identifying Alexander Fusco as Miss Dugan's killer and that he was motivated by jealousy."

Chief Francis moaned from his chair, "Do we know for certain that this gentleman from Connecticut was Louis du Pont? If we don't know 100 percent who he was, please leave mention of him out of the newspapers. We can't guess. We don't want any trouble from his family. And we don't know who truly fathered Miss Dugan's baby."

"I'm right. I know I am." Unfortunately, the more I thought about it the more I had to agree with Chief Francis. "The only thing we know for certain is that Alexander Fusco killed Miss Dugan."

"Yes" Adelia said, "we can only say who killed her, but should we?"

I took a deep breath and released it slowly. "What do you mean?"

Chief Francis answered for her. "We have another option. We could declare Mr. Fusco's death a suicide for reasons unknown and let the dead bury the dead. That way the entire episode isn't back in the newspapers and the Dugans won't have to relive their shame. After all, you're accusing Miss Dugan of having multiple lovers. The public won't be kind."

"Let the dead bury the dead," I said. "Where have I heard that before? No, sir. No, Adelia. James and Emily Dugan have a right to know who killed their daughter. I think once the murderer is revealed, and that's *all* that's revealed, the family should get sympathy."

Chief Francis leaned back in his chair. "Fair enough, but I agree with Detective Bern. The case was declared unsolved. Let's leave it that way, as far as the press is concerned. You can tell Mr. and Mrs. Dugan in confidence who killed their daughter, but when it comes to Casey and his friends, the coroner will rule Alexander Fusco's death a suicide. We don't have to tell the press any more than that."

Perhaps Chief Francis and Adelia had a point. I remembered how upset the Dugans had been when I read them the coroner's report and the anguish on Mr. Dugan's face when he asked that the pregnancy be kept private. Seven months after her murder, Wilmington has moved on. They were more concerned about the financial crisis that gripped the nation, and its affects locally. Lizzie Borden's trial was scheduled to begin on June 5, and people couldn't wait to read about it. The World's Fair in Chicago continued, and photographs of a new amusement called a Ferris Wheel was the talk of the town. Why not let the dead bury the dead? Hadn't the Dugan family suffered enough?

"All right." Part of me wasn't happy with the decision, but it seemed the best option under the circumstances. "I'll tell the Dugans in private. The public will not be informed."

Chief Francis stroked his beard. "An excellent decision, the best possible solution. You know, you two make a great team and you did an excellent job. I think I speak for Molly and myself when I say you've been sorely missed. I haven't been able to find competent replacements. Would you two have any interest in rejoining the Wilmington Police Department?"

I looked at Adelia and smiled. She smiled back at me. We simultaneously burst out laughing.

"Does that mean yes or no?"

CHAPTER 79

It meant yes. Adelia and I rejoined the police department and became a husband and wife detective team that worked together for another fifteen years. Now that my body sat confined to a chair and I barely moved without Adelia's assistance, I felt compelled to set the record straight about our first and most famous case.

Yes, I have no evidence that would satisfy a court of law, but because of Dr. DuPont's involvement, I accuse Louis du Pont of fathering Miss Dugan's baby. I accuse Louis of cowardice for running away and leaving Katie to die instead of fighting off Mr. Fusco. And to the public, Alexander Fusco murdered Katie Dugan.

Let this book set the record straight. Let this book be my legacy, penned in my 76th year, and probably my last one on earth.

CPSIA information can be obtained
at www.ICGtesting.com
Printed in the USA
BVHW03s2235090418
512943BV00002B/36/P